A TASTE FOR SCANDAL

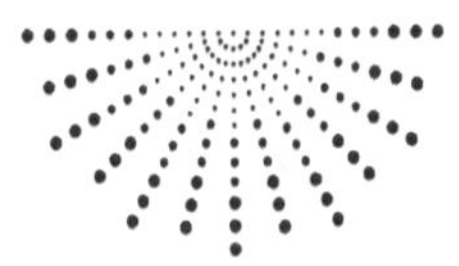

BRENDA HIATT

dolphin star
PRESS

A TASTE FOR SCANDAL
Seven Saints Hunt Club, Book 3

Copyright 2019 by Brenda Hiatt
Cover art by Dar Albert

This is a work of fiction. Though some actual historical places, persons and events are depicted in this work, the primary characters and their stories are fictional. Any resemblance between those characters and actual persons, living or dead, are purely coincidental.

Dolphin Star Press

ISBN: 978-1-947205-23-9

ALSO BY BRENDA HIATT

The Hiatt Regency Classics

Gabriella

The Cygnet

Lord Dearborn's Destiny

Daring Deception

Christmas Promises (a novella)

Christmas Bride

Azalea

Americana Dreaming

Azalea

Ship of Dreams

Bridge Over Time

The Saint of Seven Dials

Scandalous Virtue

Rogue's Honor

Noble Deceptions

Innocent Passions

Saintly Sins

Gallant Scoundrel

The Seven Saints Hunt Club

Tessa's Touch

The Runaway Heiress

A Taste for Scandal

CHAPTER ONE

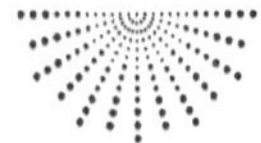

"At last!" Violet Turpin leaned forward eagerly as the carriage rounded the last curve in the road and Ivy Lodge came into view.

After a deadly dull January and February, she could scarcely wait for the adventures awaiting her. She planned to make the most of her week or so here in the Shires, before continuing on to London, where she hoped for even more excitement.

"So this be where Master Grant spends so much of his time, is it, Miss?" her maid Brigid asked.

"Yes, my brother has always been mad for fox hunting. I've always loved his stories about it, but will enjoy even more experiencing the sport for myself." While in Melton Mowbray, she was determined to join at least one hunt...somehow.

Brigid regarded her dubiously. "Think you Master Grant will allow that, Miss? Lady Rumble won't like it, that's certain."

Violet grimaced. "What Mama doesn't know won't hurt her."

She had tried more than once to inveigle her way into the small, local hunt back home in Lincolnshire, but her mother always got wind in time to forbid it. Grant, she hoped, would be less prudish. Particularly as his recent marriage had already mellowed him somewhat when last she saw him.

Still, he would likely need some persuasion. Like their mother, he often tended to assume the worst when it came to Violet.

True, eloping with a fortune hunter last autumn had been one of her more foolish starts, but as it had resulted in Grant's marriage to Dina, she hoped he no longer held it against her. The whole matter had been successfully hushed up, after all.

Dina, in Gretna Green herself, had opened Violet's eyes to Mr. Plunkett's true nature in time to prevent their marriage. When Grant arrived the next morning, he'd been so grateful for Dina's intervention, he'd agreed to her surprising request that he marry her on the spot—the only way she could safeguard her fortune from her gamester brother. Lady Rumble had put about the story that it was actually Grant and Dina who had eloped, and that Violet had gone along as chaperone. Thus far, no one outside the family seemed to be any the wiser.

"I wonder if Grant and Dina will have arrived yet?" Violet wondered aloud as the coach pulled to a halt before the picturesque manor house that served as headquarters for the Seven Saints Hunt Club.

As if in answer to her question, the front door opened and her brother and his wife emerged, waving.

Violet had the carriage door open before the coachman could jump down from the box. Hurrying up the wide steps, she delightedly hugged her diminutive sister-in-law.

"It's wonderful to see you again, Dina! I must say, your time alone with this hulking brother of mine seems to have agreed with you. You are positively glowing."

Chuckling, Grant smiled lovingly down at his wife. "She is, isn't she? I, ah, trust Mother and Father were well when you left them?"

"Perfectly," Violet replied, hugging him in turn. "When did you two arrive?"

"Barely half an hour since," Dina replied. "Come in and warm yourself while we, er, catch up on news."

Violet obligingly linked arms with her and they turned toward the house. "We can also start planning for our time in London. I am determined you will have as much fun there as I plan to, Dina. Indeed, it will be *so* much more enjoyable with you as my chaperone instead of stuffy old Aunt Philomena. We shall go to the theatre and attend balls, routs and all manner of entertainments together."

Her brother cleared his throat, giving Dina a significant look, which Violet instantly interpreted.

"Oh, do not worry, Grant, I'll not lead her into anything improper. I know the main point of my Season is to finally make my debut and to secure a good match, though I warn you I intend to hold out for romance. If a title comes with it, so much the better."

Just then, a tall man cantered past. Violet instantly recognized the broad shoulders, dark hair and chiseled profile of Lord Rushford—the man who had embodied her ideal of a romantic hero since her very first sight of him as a girl of twelve.

Alas, the earl had made clear while briefly visiting Plumrose over Yuletide that he did not regard her in a similar light. Perhaps she could change his mind on that point during her time in the Shires? If not, well, all of London still awaited her, to include—

"Oh!" She turned back toward the carriage, where her trunks were being unstrapped. "Brigid, I believe I left my book on the seat. Will you fetch it, please?"

The girl obliged and Violet took it from her before accompanying Grant and Dina into the parlor, which boasted a blazing fire.

"It's my latest favorite," Violet said, displaying the book to them.

"*The Saint of Seven Dials: The Man and the Legend*," Dina read aloud. "Is it new?"

Violet nodded. "Yes, published just last autumn. A friend gave it to me for Twelfth Night and I daresay I've read it through six times by now. I had little else to do, wet and cold as the weather has been. After learning so much about him, I very much hope to somehow meet the Saint while in London so I may assist him in his endeavors. Can you think of anything more exciting...or romantic?"

Grant shook his head. "You really are incorrigible, Vi. I hope you'll not be too disappointed when—"

He broke off as Lady Killerby entered the parlor. According to

Grant, she'd taken up residence here last autumn after her son's riding injury, since installing herself as a sort of matriarch of the hunt club.

"Welcome back to Ivy Lodge, my dear," she greeted Violet. "Lady Rumble wrote that you should arrive in time for dinner, but 'tis such a long drive I thought it unlikely. Yet here you are!"

"I left at daybreak, so eager was I to see Grant and Dina again," Violet told the dowager, a good friend of her mother's. "Especially as I *expected* to see them more than a month ago—though newlyweds that they are, I really can't blame them for wanting some extra time alone at Ashcombe."

Ashcombe was Dina's estate in Staffordshire. She and Grant had taken up residence there just after Christmas, when Dina's brother left England to escape his debts and the law. Since then, they'd been making some much-needed improvements there.

"Mother was disappointed when you did not return to Plumrose for the rest of the Yuletide season," she told them. "She quickly cheered up, however, when I pointed out to her that the more time you two spent alone at Ashcombe, the sooner she would likely see grand-children."

Grant and Dina exchanged a startled look, at which Violet laughed.

"No, no. You needn't fear I'll pester you on the topic as she has. If I did, you might change your mind about coming to Town, which would leave me to suffer another Season with Aunt Philomena as chaperone."

"Er, Violet—" Dina began, but Lady Killerby interrupted her.

"You ladies will wish to change before dinner, I imagine," she told them. "I'm just going up to do so myself. I've put you in the same room as before, as it still won't do for Miss Turpin to sleep alone in a bachelor establishment such as this."

Violet regarded her in amusement. "My reputation can surely be at no risk with you also under this roof, my lady, but I'll not argue. Come, Dina, we can talk as we change."

As they mounted the stairs, Dina sent a questioning look over her shoulder at Grant, who gave her a small nod. No doubt they had hoped to share a bedchamber this time, Violet realized. Perhaps she could ask Lady Killerby to let her sleep in her room instead of with Dina?

When Grant paused by the door of the chamber she was to share with Dina, Violet turned to her sister-in-law to suggest that, but Dina forestalled her by speaking first.

"Violet, there is something you need to know."

Her worried expression immediately sparked an answering worry in Violet. Opening the chamber door, she ushered her sister-in-law and brother inside.

"What is it?" she asked them. "Is something wrong?"

"Not…wrong, precisely," Dina replied, her color deepening. "Indeed, we are both quite delighted with the news."

Violet frowned for a moment, then gave a sudden gasp. "News? Do you mean that you and Grant—? That you—?"

Dina nodded, a smile now playing about her lips. "Yes, we learned just a few days since that we are expecting a child, most likely in October. You are the first to hear, for we feared if we wrote to your mother she would tell you before we could—and I very much wished to tell you myself."

"Oh, Dina!" Violet threw her arms around her sister-in-law. "I am beyond delighted for you both! Of course, Mama will be in absolute ecstasies when she hears. As am I!"

"You…are not disappointed?"

"Disappointed? Beside myself with joy, more like! You will find me the most doting auntie that ever was," she declared. "Why, even Mama will be hard pressed to outdo me. How lucky that we shall have this time in London before the baby comes, for the shops there will have vastly more to choose from than those in Alford or Litchfield."

Dina sent an uncertain glance her husband's way. "I appreciate the sentiment, Violet, but you go on too fast. Your brother feels—"

"Oh, pooh. Grant need not accompany us if he would rather not. Indeed, we shall do better on our own, for gentlemen never enjoy shopping so much as we ladies do. You will not mind if we leave you behind while we comb through the stores, will you, Grant?" she asked, grinning. "I promise not to overspend on myself or Dina, but when it comes to the baby, I may not be able to control myself."

His response effectively erased her grin. "You may shop to your heart's content and buy whatever you wish for yourself and the babe. Dina, however, will not be spending the Season in Town."

"Will not—? Whatever do you mean?" Violet sent an alarmed glance at Dina, who merely shrugged and smiled apologetically.

"Just what I said," her brother affirmed. "We have talked it over and agree that she will do better to spend these next months in the clean air of Staffordshire, her home, than in the fogs and dirt of London. That will be far healthier for her and for the babe."

Violet stared at him, aghast. "But...what of my Season? Must I spend it in Staffordshire as well?"

"Nothing quite so heinous as that. We'll spend a week here, as planned. Then, once we have Dina settled at Ashcombe, I shall take you to Aunt Philomena's myself. I'll not be staying, however."

"But who will escort me to all of the evening functions?" Violet demanded. "You know full well that Aunt Philomena refuses to be out past nine o'clock, which is just when most parties and performances begin. How am I to make any useful social connections whatever, given her absurdly early schedule?"

"She loves to boast of firing off her other nieces in style," Grant reminded her, "so she will no doubt wish to do the same for you. I shall impress upon her the far greater likelihood of your making a match if she takes you about to balls and such. Whether she heeds my advice or not, you'd best adhere to her rules if you don't want your Season cut short again."

Violet blinked back tears as all her hopes and dreams for the coming Season came crashing down about her ears. Determined not to spoil Grant and Dina's happiness over their lovely news, however, she strove to conceal her disappointment. Taking a deep breath, she lifted her chin and forced a smile.

"I shall do my best," she said. "Though I can't deny I'll miss having you both with me in Town, I truly am happy for you. But now, we'd best begin changing if we are not to be late for dinner."

Grant left them and Dina's and Violet's maids were summoned to help them dress. When they were on the point of leaving the chamber to go downstairs, Violet turned impulsively to Dina.

"If I am to suffer Aunt Philomena's chaperonage for another Season, I am more determined than ever to enjoy my time in the Shires. Will you help to convince Grant to let me ride in the hunts here? 'Tis something I've always longed to do."

"I'll do my best, as you've taken our news so well." Dina gave her a quick hug. "He certainly can't deny you're an excellent horsewoman. Far better than I am."

Violet thanked her for the compliment, though riding was likely the only physical skill in which she surpassed her tiny sister-in-law. Dina was amazingly adept at such unorthodox pursuits as swimming, fencing and even boxing.

Returning Dina's hug and again expressing her joy about the coming child, Violet accompanied her down to the parlor, where several gentlemen rose to greet them.

"Give you good evening, Mrs. Turpin, Miss Turpin." Sir Charles Storm, a handsome young man with light brown hair rakishly disordered, swept them a collective bow. "I see your journeys have not impaired your beauty a whit—indeed, rather the reverse."

Refusing to dwell on her diminished prospects, Violet dipped him a smiling curtsey. She knew better than to take his flattery seriously, however, for Sir Charles had made it perfectly clear at Christmas that he was by no means hanging out for a wife.

"Indeed," echoed Lord Uppingwood, another member of the Seven Saints Hunt Club—and another inveterate flirt. "Miss Turpin, I declare, you are a very vision of spring. A most welcome relief from the gray February weather we've had of late."

Violet glanced down at her pink-and-green sprigged cambric gown. "I confess, I do prefer cheerful colors to the bland shades so many ladies seem to favor."

"No wonder, as they become you so well," exclaimed little Lord Killerby, stepping forward with a bow. "I noted it when I was at Plumrose last month. It's a shame Society tries to limit debutantes to insipid white whether they look well in it or not. Though you, of course, would be enchanting in anything."

She murmured her thanks, reflecting that it was a shame she felt no particular attraction to the viscount, as he seemed less averse to matrimony than most of the others. Indeed, he had been most solicitous when he and his mother were last at Plumrose. They and Lord Rushford had escorted her home after Violet's near-kidnapping on Boxing Day—but while the Killerbys then remained at Plumrose through the first week of January, Lord Rushford had stayed but a day.

Alas, though she knew such externals should not matter, Violet could not quite overlook the fact that Lord Killerby was no taller than herself, in addition to being somewhat plump.

Lord Rushford entered the room just then, as if to heighten the contrast between the two men. "Ah, Mrs. Turpin, welcome. I am delighted to see you again. You as well, Miss Turpin." He gave them each a perfunctory bow, then went to sit near the fire, where he shook open a newspaper and began to read.

Her pride again pricked by his clear indifference, Violet turned away to direct a brilliant smile at Mr. Littleton. He instantly came forward to greet her, with a much more satisfactory outpouring of admiration.

Dinner was a lively affair, between the animated discussion of the day's hunt and the lively banter directed toward Violet and Dina. Though Lord Rushford still held himself somewhat aloof, Violet found it easier to ignore while surrounded by so many agreeable—and undeniably handsome—gentlemen.

Perhaps she focused rather too closely on the earl's words as he described that morning's running of the Quorn to Grant, but it *was*, after all, a topic that greatly interested her. When Lord Uppingwood asked Violet about her day's journey, she attempted to draw Lord Rushford into the conversation.

"Though rather chilly, the drive was quite uneventful," Violet replied. "In truth, I wish I could have ridden alongside as Lord Rushford did much of the way when he escorted me to Plumrose two months since. I'd have enjoyed it far more, I'm certain."

As she'd hoped, that drew the elusive earl's attention. "It would be a long way for a lady to ride, Miss Turpin," he said gravely, though with a trace of amusement in his gray eyes.

Lifting her chin, she met his gaze directly. "I can ride as far and as fast as any man, I assure you, my lord."

"Oh, come, Violet," said Grant, overhearing. "What is the farthest you've ever ridden at a stretch?"

She was vexed to see that Lord Rushford also seemed skeptical. "Fifteen miles, I suppose," she replied, "but only because I've never had opportunity to go farther. I should like such a chance, however. Think you the weather will be fine enough for the Cottesmore to ride tomorrow?"

"I certainly hope so," Grant replied. "I mean to fit as many hunts in as possible before we leave for London."

"Yes, with so little of the season left, I imagine you all wish to make the most of what remains." Violet directed her comment at Lord Rushford, hoping to keep him engaged.

All he said, however, was, "Always," before turning his attention entirely to his dinner.

Disgruntled, Violet did the same, wondering when Lord Rushford had grown so stodgy. He had not been so when visiting Plumrose with Grant when she was a girl. Then, he had often indulged her with exciting stories of Oxford and of fox hunting, sparking her own enthusiasm for the sport with his tales. Perhaps inheriting a title had induced him to trade fun for responsibility. A pity, if so.

Setting down his glass, Sir Charles leaned forward. "Did I hear you discussing the hunt, Miss Turpin? Thor mentioned you were an enthusiast."

Thor was the nickname all the Seven Saints gave her brother, no doubt due to his imposing size—and perhaps the fact that he would one day be Lord Rumble.

"I am indeed," she replied, "though I've not yet had opportunity to truly participate. Do convince my brother to allow me to ride in the Cottesmore tomorrow, for I am quite longing to do so."

"Don't be ridiculous," snapped Grant from his place at the table. "Ladies don't ride to the hunt, as I've told you numerous times." He shot a warning glance at Sir Charles.

He apparently did not notice. "Unless one counts Lady Anthony, of course," he said cheerfully. Grant's grimace told Violet this was precisely what he'd hoped to prevent his friend from saying.

"Lady Anthony?" she repeated, her interest quickening. "Then another woman *does* ride to the local hunts?"

"She does indeed," Sir Charles enthusiastically exclaimed. "She—" Belatedly noticing Grant's frown, he broke off. "Er, but as to you doing the same, Miss Turpin, I suppose that must be up to Thor, here."

Grant snorted. "What Anthony allows his wife to do is his own business. You, however, are currently my responsibility, so—"

"Would you forbid Dina riding if she asked?" she challenged him.

"She won't ask," he said curtly, clearly signaling that he wished the topic dropped. Unfortunately, Dina did not contradict him.

Violet was not so easily dissuaded, however. Turning a shoulder to her brother, she smiled sweetly across at Sir Charles. "Do tell me more of this Lady Anthony, for I find myself quite fascinated."

"Can't believe Thor never told you about her. She first joined the hunt this past autumn, when she was still Miss Seaton, and she astounded us all. Never knew a female could ride like that. Why, I'd give my left hand for a seat like hers. That is—" He broke off, flustered. "Er, no one tell Anthony I put it that way, eh? Didn't mean—"

"Do stifle it, Stormy," Grant advised him. Then, to Violet, "I never mentioned her to you because I knew you would immediately demand to do the same. I'll grant Lady Anthony acquits herself amazingly well, but she is an anomaly. Riding to the hounds is dangerous. Mother would never forgive me if I allowed you to attempt it."

Nettled by his praise of Lady Anthony on top of his refusal, Violet glared at her brother. "I'm quite competent on horseback myself, you know."

Sir Charles appeared alarmed at realizing he had helped precipitate the argument. "That may be, Miss Turpin, but fox hunting is nothing like riding along country lanes. There are hedges, fences, rabbit holes. Can't blame your brother a bit for not wanting to risk your pretty neck."

Violet coughed delicately. "My dear brother seems to have forgotten how much experience I have riding over rough terrain—something we used to do together in the past, and at which I frequently bested him." Then, to Grant, "I appreciate your desire to protect my neck, but you know full well I ride as well as many gentlemen who hunt, so would be at very little risk. May I at least come along to observe tomorrow's hunt?"

Grant regarded her suspiciously for a moment, then shrugged. "I suppose that is safe enough, so long as you are adequately chaperoned."

"No worries there." Sir Charles was clearly pleased to see the sticky matter settled. "Lady Killerby generally drives out with Sir George Seaton and will surely not object to Miss Turpin joining them."

At Lady Killerby's assent, Violet's spirits rose. Once on the hunting field, she could surely find a way to prove she was worthy of joining the hunt after all, despite her brother's disapproval. Maybe one of the other gentlemen could be persuaded to petition the Master of the Hunt on her behalf if Grant would not.

"How perfectly lovely." She flashed a brilliant smile at Sir Charles to allay her brother's concerns before turning the conversation to less controversial topics.

Ryan Dean, Earl of Rushford—better known to his intimates as Rush—breathed a silent sigh of relief when the ladies finally removed to the parlor at the close of the meal. Not because he was particularly fond of the port or cigars being handed round, but because of the totally inappropriate attraction he felt for Miss Violet Turpin.

When he'd arrived at Plumrose just before Christmas, he'd been thoroughly blindsided by his first encounter with Miss Turpin in nearly six years. No longer was she the gawky, tomboyish girl he remembered, mad for riding and stories of the hunt. Quite the contrary. The intervening years had miraculously transformed her into a remarkably pretty young lady, with clouds of dark curls in place of her former braids. She had also filled out, rather too satisfactorily.

His sudden awareness of Violet Turpin as a desirable woman had been as alarming as it was unexpected. That awareness was the reason he'd kept his visit to Plumrose brief, despite his original intention of staying through the entire Yuletide season. He'd had less than a day's respite, however, for Thor had shown up with her at Ivy Lodge late on Boxing Day, after foiling a kidnapping attempt by Dina Turpin's dastardly brother.

Once that was all sorted and Silas Moore banished to America, Rush had reluctantly acceded to Thor's request to assist in escorting his sister back to Plumrose. However, as she'd pointed out over dinner, he'd ridden alongside the carriage much of the way—and had left Plumrose the day after arriving.

He'd hoped that two months away from Miss Turpin's uncomfortably intoxicating influence would quash any errant feelings in that direction, but he unfortunately found himself as attracted as ever.

A throat-clearing from Thor interrupted his reverie. He turned to see his friend rise to his feet, glass in hand.

"As my sister miraculously managed to hold her tongue during dinner, I should like to take this opportunity to share with you, my closest friends, the news that Dina and I are expecting a child."

A chorus of congratulations broke out, some getting up to pummel Thor on the back and pump his hand.

"Well done, old chap, well done," Rush exclaimed, joining the celebration. "No wonder she seemed to have an extra sparkle in those green eyes of hers."

Over Christmas he'd enjoyed tweaking Thor with pretended admiration for his wife, as his friend had been pretending indifference toward her at the time. Clearly, that was no longer the case.

Thor accepted everyone's felicitations amid several more toasts, but once most of the men left the dining room to make their way back to the parlor, he turned more serious.

"I did not say so earlier, but in light of this news, I feel it would be unwise to expose Dina to the rigors of a London Season, especially as it would be her first visit to Town," he told Rush, who had lingered behind with him. "I've decided to let our aunt play chaperone to my sister again, instead."

Rush raised an eyebrow. "That did not turn out particularly well last year, as I recall. Didn't your aunt pack her off back home after only a fortnight after your sister created a scandal or two?"

Thor nodded. "In addition to being rather nearsighted, my Aunt Philomena is not the most quick-witted of women. I fear she may not be fully equal to the task, given Violet's, er, less than compliant nature. It would therefore ease my mind greatly if I knew you were about to keep an eye on her. After all, you and Killer were able to keep her out of trouble on her journey back to Plumrose two months since."

"It was but one day's drive," Rush reminded him. "After that, your mother was able to take over the task. Would *she* not be a better choice to go to London, if your aunt is not up to the job?"

Thor gave a small snort. "Of course, if I thought she could be persuaded. Mother refuses to leave my father, however, and he—"

"Not to worry, Thor." Killer, overhearing his name, had come back into the dining room. "I'll be honored to do my part toward safeguarding Miss Turpin's reputation while in London. Particularly as Rush may find the assignment tricky, what with him being betrothed and all."

Rush glared at the smaller man. "Never should have told you about that. You know it's not for public consumption until either her father or his consent arrives from India, and that likely won't be for months."

"What's this?" Thor exclaimed. "Never tell me you got yourself engaged with nary a word to any of us?"

"Except me," Killer said proudly.

Frowning him down, Rush turned back to Thor. "He called shortly after I made the offer and I unwisely confided in him. There are no firm plans yet, however, given her father's absence."

"That explains why it wasn't in the papers," Thor allowed. "Still, you could have let a few of us in on the secret. Tell me about her. Who is she? How did you come to offer for her?"

"You knew my mother passed away early last year?" Rush asked. Thor nodded. "Not till she was gone did I realize what a large role she played in managing both the estate and her extensive charitable concerns. Champion of women's rights that she was, she left her jointure to the next Countess of Rushford, whoever she might be. Given that the charities, in particular, are dependent upon that money, both my man of business and my steward urged me to find a wife as quickly as possible."

Thor's brows rose. "And who was it you found?"

"A Miss Mary Simpson, daughter to Sir Clarence Simpson, a respectably wealthy baronet. Impeccable lineage, and his lands run along one of my smaller estates. She also seemed the least presuming of the debutantes I encountered in London, most of whom were blatantly hanging out for a title. I've no doubt she'll make a creditable Lady Rushford when the time comes."

"I…see." Thor glanced at Killer, who shrugged, before turning back to Rush. "Do you…like her?"

Rush lifted a shoulder. "I scarcely know her yet. She's pretty enough, however, with a quiet, unassuming manner. Were her father not currently overseeing his India holdings, we'd likely be married already. At least this way we'll have time to get acquainted before the knot is tied."

"I suppose the delay is all to the good, then." Thor still looked somewhat dubious—no doubt because he was lucky enough to enjoy a love match, albeit after a somewhat rocky start. "Of course I can't ask you to dance attendance on Vi under the circumstances."

"I'll do it," Killer stoutly declared. "The more challenging the task, the greater the honor."

The smaller man's enthusiasm did not appear to relieve his large friend as much as he no doubt intended. Not that Rush could blame Thor for that, given Killer's penchant for taking on challenges beyond his scope. Miss Turpin, he suspected, would pose an even greater one than the horse that caused Killer's injury last autumn, for she had a definite penchant for leaping before looking.

A quality Rush told himself he did not find alluring in the least. Just as well that forming an attachment there was out of the question, given his engagement to Miss Simpson.

CHAPTER TWO

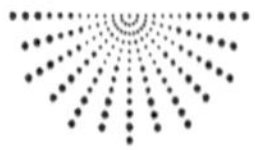

WHEN THE GENTLEMEN JOINED THE LADIES IN THE PARLOR, IT WAS CLEAR that Grant had shared his and Dina's news with them. Several of them immediately came forward to congratulate her while Lady Killerby looked on in bemusement.

"Well, this is news, indeed! Did you know of this, Miss Turpin?"

"Not until an hour before dinner," Violet confessed. "Is it not grand?"

Dina smiled apologetically at the older lady. "I am sorry not to have told you myself, Lady Killerby. I was not certain whether my husband wished it known outside the family as yet, but it seems he was unable to keep the news to himself."

Grant entered then, accompanied by Lord Rushford and Lord Killerby. "Aye, I'd thought to write to Mother before telling anyone else, but…" He shrugged.

"And now, Mrs. Turpin, what would you like with your tea?" Sir Charles asked. "Ivy Lodge's kitchens are at your disposal. Biscuits? Pastries? A rice pudding, perhaps?"

As he spoke, Mr. Littleton seized pillows from the divan to tuck around Dina while Lord Uppingwood fetched her a footstool.

"No more coddling, please," she protested. "'Tis bad enough to be treated as though I am made of glass merely due to my lack of inches. I absolutely refuse to be regarded as an invalid for the better part of a year. Women have been having babies since time out of mind without the sort of pampering that seems to be in vogue these days."

Thor smiled down at her, the love in his eyes bringing a slight lump to Violet's throat. "I insist you allow me an occasional bit of pampering, my dear, though I promise not to treat you like an invalid."

"Very well," Dina agreed, "so long as it really is occasional."

Despite her words, less than an hour later Dina concealed a yawn with her hand. "Will any of you be offended if I turn in for the night? I find myself unusually tired this evening."

"And no wonder." Lady Killerby smiled understandingly. "Traveling always fags me to death, even without the added excuse you have just now. Run along, do, and get yourself a good night's sleep. You can let me know in the morning whether you feel like riding out in my phaeton to follow the Cottesmore."

With an apologetic glance, Dina bade them all good night but Grant instantly moved to her side.

"You should have told me you were fatigued, my dear. I'll help you up the stairs and ring for your maid."

Dina laughed. "Don't be absurd. I can manage the stairs perfectly well on my own—though if you wish to come along, I'll not gainsay you."

That drew a general chuckle as the couple left the room. Given the way Dina's cheeks had pinkened, Violet thought it best to wait a bit before going up herself. She therefore joined Lord Killerby, Lady Killerby and Lord Uppington in a game of whist to pass the time.

After two hands, Lady Killerby also declared herself ready for bed and Violet had perforce to accompany her upstairs. Cautiously entering the bedchamber, she was relieved to find Dina already asleep.

When Brigid appeared a few moments later, giggling about something, Violet put a finger to her lips and nodded toward the bed.

"What is so funny?" she whispered to the maid.

"You'll not believe it, Miss," Brigid whispered back, "but Thomas, Lord Uppingwood's valet that is, mistook me for Mrs. Turpin there just now," she replied, her eyes dancing. "Gave him quite a start, I did, when I went to the kitchen to get a warming pan for your bed."

Violet gave a tiny snort of laughter herself. "I presume you set him straight?"

"Oh, he realized soon as he noticed what I'm wearing, but his face was a right picture for a moment there." Still chuckling, she began helping Violet out of her frock.

"I suppose his mistake was understandable, as you and Dina both have red hair and are roughly of a height," Violet conceded.

Beyond those basic features, the two women didn't look much alike at all. Brigid was much plumper than Dina, with brown eyes instead of green. The maid also sported a generous sprinkling of freckles across her nose and cheeks, unlike Dina. Amusing as the valet's error was, it seemed unlikely to occur again.

"That will do, Brigid," Violet said when the maid stifled a yawn. "I can brush my own hair tonight. We've both had a long day. Get you to your bed and I'll get into mine."

As Violet was not particularly tired, she moved the small oil lamp to her bedside table and pulled out her book about the Saint of Seven Dials to read herself to sleep. Opening to the place she'd marked, she was soon engrossed yet again in his daring exploits on behalf of the poor.

A master of disguise, the Saint moves at will throughout all levels of Society, from the poorest slums to servants' halls to the glittering ballrooms of the very pinnacle of London's nobility…

When her eyes finally grew heavy, she tucked the book under her pillow. Turning down the lamp, she rolled over to dream of thrilling midnight chases along London's streets.

The next morning Violet waited until Dina had dressed and gone down to breakfast before ringing for her abigail.

"No, no," Violet told Brigid when she pulled out a lilac morning gown. "Have some toast and tea brought up, then get out my habit. There is a hunt today, you know."

"Oh, did Master Grant agree to let you join it after all, Miss?" asked Brigid in surprise.

Violet merely smiled.

The gentlemen would breakfast early, she knew, as the hunt was to gather at Cottesmore House before nine. Watching from her second story window, she waited until the last one had ridden off before venturing downstairs herself.

"Good morning, sleepyhead," Dina greeted her as she passed the dining room. "Lady Killerby and I wondered whether you would rise in time to join us."

"Yes, we'll need to leave in half an hour if we are to catch the start of the hunt, for we must fetch Sir George on the way," Lady Killerby said. "Not to worry, however, there is sufficient room in my phaeton for four."

"Oh, I needn't crowd you in the phaeton," Violet told her. "I should much prefer to ride alongside. 'Twill be far more comfortable for all of us that way."

Dina regarded her with faint suspicion but Lady Killerby merely shrugged. "As you wish. We will be near enough to provide propriety. No doubt you will have a better view of the hunt on horseback, though I must say that Sir George and I always find it vastly entertaining from the phaeton."

Violet thanked her, let Dina know she'd already had a tray in her room, then continued on to the stables. There she found Farrell, her brother's groom, just leading out Grant's best hunter.

"Morning, Miss Turpin," he greeted her in obvious surprise. "If you were looking for your brother, you just missed him. He left not ten minutes ago on his hack. And I'd best hurry myself if I'm to get Othello to Cottesmore House before they begin the hunt."

"First, Farrell, would you please saddle Ares for me?" she asked, naming Grant's second-best hunter. "My sidesaddle should be to hand, as I had it sent down to the stables when I arrived."

"Ares? To what purpose, Miss?"

Turning away from the groom's suspicious gaze, she laughed. "Oh, did Grant not tell you? I am also to ride in the Cottesmore today."

Rush gazed around in approval at the crowd gathered in front of Cottesmore House. The recent dry spell, unusual for late February, combined with how little remained of the hunting season, had brought out a near-record number of sportsmen.

As always, the sights, sounds and smells of the hounds and horses created a pleasurable sense of anticipation. Gad, but he loved fox hunting! During the seven-odd months until November first, when he could again ride to the hounds, he might as well be only half alive.

All too soon he would leave Melton Mowbray to attend to estate matters at Rushford Abbey in Northamptonshire, then head to London to renew his acquaintance with Miss Simpson. He rather dreaded the latter, for he had never cared much for Town life, where riding was limited to tame canters in the park.

Still, he really should use this interim while awaiting her father's consent to get to know his bride-to-be. With any luck, he would discover that he and Miss Simpson had more interests in common than had been apparent on the surface.

"Quite a turnout, eh?" remarked Stormy from just behind him. "Always the way toward the end of the season."

"Aye, and glad I am that I can enjoy at least a few more hunts before it's over," Thor exclaimed from Rush's other side. "Not that I truly regret these last weeks at Ashcombe with Dina, or the progress we've made there."

Sir Charles laughed. "Progress indeed, I'd say! You and your pretty bride clearly put your time to good use."

"Still," Thor continued as though he hadn't heard, "I missed the hunt more than I expected. I did join the Hoar Cross thrice, but it can't compare with the hunts near Melton. This—" He waved an expansive arm at the assemblage waiting to start— "is the real thing."

"I feel the same about the Pytchley," Rush agreed, grinning. "Not bad, as the smaller hunts go, but it's but a poor substitute for—"

He broke off, for Thor was staring past his shoulder, an expression of outrage on his face.

"That hoyden! I thought I made my position perfectly clear to her." Rapping out an oath, Thor wheeled his horse about and cantered off.

Turning, Rush saw the cause of the outburst: Miss Turpin, resplendent in a sky-blue habit, mounted on Thor's second-best hunter.

Inappropriate as her presence here was, Rush could not help admiring her pluck as well as her appearance. With her riot of dark curls pulled back from her heart-shaped face and a small top hat perched above at a jaunty angle, she presented a fetching vision. He also noted that she sat her oversized steed remarkably well, as she trotted alongside the low-slung pink and green phaeton containing Lady Killerby, Sir George Seaton, and Thor's wife.

"What the devil are you doing on horseback?" Thor demanded, intercepting his sister at the edge of the gathering. "And who said you could ride Ares? He's barely broken to sidesaddle."

"He's been no trouble whatever. Not surprising, as I'm the one who first put a sidesaddle on him," she retorted. "Come, Grant, don't fuss. As I'm already here, I may as well join you."

Her unrepentant rejoinder served as a timely reminder that beneath Miss Turpin's alluring exterior she was still Thor's scapegrace little sister. Indeed, judging by the stubborn set of her jaw, his massive friend might well need assistance. He urged his mount forward.

"Only members are permitted to ride with the Cottesmore," Thor was sternly reminding her. "Even if that were not the case, a young lady like yourself has no business—"

At that inopportune moment, Lord and Lady Anthony came cantering up to join the forming hunt.

Miss Turpin gestured toward them with a triumphant grin. "What of Lady Anthony, then? I presume the Master has given *her* permission to hunt the Cottesmore. Why not me, as well?"

"She is a special case. Her father is a well-respected squire and longtime sportsman hereabouts. He personally petitioned for her to join the local hunts at the very start of the season."

Lord and Lady Anthony joined them then, neatly reining in their mounts.

"Miss Turpin, I presume?" asked Lord Anthony cheerily. "Thor did not tell us you would be joining the hunt today as well."

His wife directed a charming smile Miss Turpin's way. "I confess I shall quite appreciate having another woman in the hunt, for I sometimes feel a bit like a side show attraction."

Miss Turpin returned Lady Anthony's smile with a brilliant one of her own. Surely it was the crisp winter air and not the sudden flash of that smile that caught Rush's breath in his throat.

"Yes, we were just discussing what a shame it would be if I were not allowed to ride," Miss Turpin replied. "Is it too late to petition the Master of the Hunt on my behalf, do you think?"

Thor scowled. "This late in the season? Of course it is. Even if I were willing, which I'm not, I doubt Lord Lonsdale would agree. Get you back to Lady Killerby's phaeton. And have a care with Ares as you dismount. It's been over a year since you last rode him."

"You cannot honestly think that I am unequal to the hunt, Grant. You know better than anyone that I can handle myself on a horse." Miss Turpin's eyes now held a challenging gleam. "Or must I prove myself yet again?"

When his only answer was a scowl, she continued.

"Very well, I propose a wager. I will race you to that tree." She pointed at a hoary old oak two fields away. "If I win, you must petition Lord Lonsdale on my behalf. If I lose, I will surrender Ares, ride meekly along with Dina and Lady Killerby, and say not another word about joining the hunt."

Her eyes sparkled with mirth but Rush noticed a tightening in the muscles around Thor's mouth. He surmised that this was not the first time she had challenged her brother to a race—nor did Thor look fully confident he could best her.

Rush smiled in spite of himself. Though far too headstrong and impetuous for her own—or anyone's—good, there was no denying the girl had spirit. Nor was it like Thor to be so stodgy. A side-effect of marriage, perhaps?

"I must admit that would be well worth watching," Rush declared on sudden impulse, even as Thor opened his mouth to refuse. "In fact, I'll petition Lonsdale myself, Miss Turpin, if you can beat this lout."

Thor turned to him in shock but Stormy let out a whoop of approval and Lord and Lady Anthony both laughed. He was further rewarded by a look of surprised gratitude from Miss Turpin. How had he never noticed before that her eyes were of such a deep blue they were nearly violet? Was that why she was so named? He quickly looked away.

He knew it was irresponsible of him to encourage this start of hers, but he'd sensed last night how disappointed she was that Thor and his wife would not be overseeing her London Season after all. This seemed a relatively harmless compensation for that. He was also admittedly curious to discover whether Miss Turpin was as accomplished a horse-woman as she—and Thor, previously—had claimed.

Though he glared daggers at both Rush and his sister, Thor offered no further protests. "Bring me Othello, then," he fairly growled to his groom, dismounting from his covert hack. Then, to his sister, "That will put paid to your foolish pretensions, Vi, for you know full well Othello is faster than Ares. Nor am I out of practice riding him. You can still back out if you don't wish to embarrass yourself."

"Not a chance, my dear brother. 'Tis settled." She neatly circled her mount to bring him alongside Othello as Thor mounted. Both pointed their horses' noses toward the designated oak tree, on the far side of a small stream spanned by a narrow wooden bridge.

As he had so unwisely promoted this contest, Rush felt obliged to see it properly executed. "On your marks, then," he called out. "Get set... go!"

Thor and Miss Turpin set heels to their mounts and were off. Both fairly flew toward their goal, churning the hard earth under their horses' hooves as they galloped through the slanting wintry sunlight.

Despite the disadvantage of the sidesaddle, Miss Turpin kept pace with her brother and the formidable Othello, leaning low over the neck of her mount. She moved remarkably well—better than most men in the hunt, truth be told. And on a horse she hadn't ridden in a year? Impressive.

As they neared the bridge, two thirds of the way to the tree, Thor's mount began to pull ahead. The bridge would require a slight detour from the straightest path to the tree and was too narrow to allow both horses to cross at once. Thor had clearly realized he only needed to reach the bridge first, not the tree, and therefore spurred his mount to an extra burst of speed.

Rush experienced a distinct pang of disappointment as the gap between Miss Turpin and her brother lengthened. It seemed a shame for her to lose, given her excellent seat and fiery determination.

But then he realized she had not slowed, only veered away from the bridge into a direct line toward the tree. Surely she did not mean to leap the stream?

As Othello's hooves thundered over the bridge, Ares gathered and leapt. He cleared the stream with hardly a break in stride, his rider moving effortlessly with him. The small crowd that had gathered to watch the contest gasped in unison, then burst into cheers and laughter as Miss Turpin, having avoided the detour required by the bridge, reached the tree a full length ahead of her brother.

When the two came trotting back, Miss Turpin was in obvious high spirits, her cheeks flushed with becoming color and her eyes glittering with triumph. Thor, on the other hand, looked decidedly glum—though resigned rather than furious, Rush was relieved to see.

Ares and Othello pranced with excitement at the unexpected exertion but both riders still had their mounts well in hand.

"Earl William and his Flat Hats will *have* to let you ride to hunt after that display, Miss Turpin," Sir Charles crowed as they drew near.

"Indeed. Well, well," came the amused voice of Lord Lonsdale himself, the little race having attracted the attention of the entire hunt by now. "I do believe we may be seeing a return to the old days, when more ladies joined their lords in the hunt. Mrs…?"

"Turpin, my lord," she replied breathlessly. "Miss Violet Turpin, Grant's sister."

"Ah." The earl flicked an amused glance Thor's way. "I've no doubt you will be a credit to the Cottesmore Hunt, Miss Turpin. We can see to the matter of your membership after today's run concludes." Still smiling, he turned his horse as the horns sounded the start of the hunt.

It was all Violet could do to suppress an unladylike squeal of triumph. She'd feared Grant might renege on the wager, as he hadn't specifically agreed to her terms, but he could hardly overrule the Master of the Hunt himself!

Ignoring the mutinous look on her brother's face, she smugly turned Ares to follow the rest of the field toward the first covert. She'd wager no *man* here could have won that race in a sidesaddle. A giggle escaped her at a sudden vision of her brother's imposing frame sitting daintily sideways on a horse.

"What's so funny?" Grant cantered up behind her on his covert hack, having switched horses again to save Othello for the hunt itself.

She smiled sweetly at him. "Just imagining you in a sidesaddle, dear brother."

"Hmph. I was only trying to spare you the disgrace of a tumble by taking the bridge myself, you know. I should have guessed you'd be fool enough to jump the stream regardless," he said sourly, before startling her with a smile. "You really are an excellent horsewoman, Vi. You did me proud. Enjoy the hunt—but do try to be careful. I'd hate to explain to Mother should you injure yourself."

Setting his heels to his hack, he rode on ahead. She couldn't deny jumping the stream in a sidesaddle had been risky—but it had been worth it. Now she could afford to be more cautious. After all, she would hate for an injury to cause her to miss yet another Season, or to bar her—and perhaps other ambitious women—from joining future hunts.

"A bloody shame, if you ask me," came a disgruntled male voice from behind her. "I'd say they're letting the hunt go to the dogs, except that those creatures belong here, unlike ladies."

"Aye!" answered another. "Can't imagine what Earl William was thinking, inviting her to join. It's bad enough letting that horse-trader woman ride, showing off her stable to command outrageous prices. If he's not careful, all the young chits in the country will be vying to do the same, ruining the sport for us all. What does a woman know of hunting?"

"Nothing at all, however well she might ride," agreed a third Flat Hat disdainfully. "Thought Lonsdale cared more for the reputation of the Cottesmore than that."

"Indeed. I wonder if we oughtn't—" The gentleman broke off abruptly, perhaps realizing that Violet was within earshot. The group cantered past her in silence, though with no effort to hide the disapproval etched into every line of their faces.

Violet's cheeks burned, first with embarrassment, then defiance. Just then, Lady Anthony drew level with her.

"Pray don't take it personally, Miss Turpin. I heard much of the same when I joined the hunt last autumn. Anthony claims it's because their pride is pricked by seeing a woman ride as well—or better—than they can."

"Thank you, Lady Anthony." Violet smiled gratefully. "If half the stories I've heard of your prowess as a horsewoman are true, I daresay he is right. Why should we care what a few dandies mired in the past think of us?"

A moment later they arrived at a small thicket that might possibly conceal a fox. The huntsman and whippers-in were already throwing the hounds to draw the covert, guiding them through the low underbrush and tangles of brambles in hopes of flushing one out.

Violet watched the process with interest. Though she'd been involved in the whelping and raising of her brother's foxhounds, she'd had few chances to see them at their work. Intent on the hounds, she was startled to hear a strangely familiar voice.

"Great Scott! Never tell me my little shrinking Violet has grown up to become the stunning creature I see before me!"

Turning, she spotted the source—a tall, lean gentleman with waving blond hair, mounted on a fine bay hunter. On catching her eye, he grinned broadly and spurred his horse forward, closing the distance between them.

"Julian? Is that you?" Childhood memories flooded her at the sight of his charming, white-toothed smile.

"You *do* remember!" Julian Bigsby's smile became even broader and fine lines formed around his cool blue eyes, warming them. "Never thought to see you again—and *here* of all places! What brings you to the Shires? I imagined you married to some duke or marquess by now." He punctuated his words with a jovial wink.

"Not yet." She returned his smile. "I'm visiting with my brother at Ivy Lodge before going to London for the Season."

His smile dimmed slightly. "Ah, yes, your brother. He and his friend Dean were rather a trial to us both once upon a time, were they not? But of course we were all much younger then."

Violet frowned, puzzled, then recalled that her brother had not approved of her friendship with Julian. There had even been some sort of altercation between the young men when they were all in Lincolnshire during a school holiday, but she'd never known what it was about. Back then, of course, Lord Rushford had still been plain Ryan Dean.

"I'd nearly forgotten that. Of course, I was but a child then, only thirteen or fourteen."

The dazzling smile returned. "Ah, but even then you showed promise of one day blossoming into a beauty—a promise you have exceeded. I find myself quite eager to know more of the woman you have become."

Violet was touched that he remembered her so fondly. Flattered by his admiration after Lord Rushford's coldness yesterday, she smiled warmly in return. "I should also like to learn more of the gentleman you are now."

He leaned toward her with a roguish wink that made her cheeks warm slightly. "Surely we need not start over from scratch? May I presume upon our childhood acquaintance to use your Christian name, or will you insist that I call you Miss Turpin, as propriety demands?"

"Oh, do let's be Violet and Julian, as before," she replied. "Miss Turpin and Mr. Bigsby seem far too formal for such old friends."

His well-shaped lips curved upward. "It will be my delight to submit to your request…Violet." He held her eyes with his own, something in their expression causing a frisson of delighted alarm in her midsection. "Perhaps we—"

He was interrupted by a cry of "Tally-ho!" signaling that a fox had broken cover.

Both sorry and a bit relieved, Violet pulled her gaze away from Julian's in time to see the reddish little creature go streaking over the hill and out of sight. The hounds were after it in an instant and more than a few gentlemen let out excited whoops as they prepared to go in chase.

"We'll talk more later," Julian hastily promised before spurring his bay forward to join the other sportsmen.

The moment the pack had a sufficient lead, the hunt began in earnest. Violet set a heel to Ares' flank and he immediately leapt in pursuit. Urging him to a full gallop, they fairly flew down the other side of the hill. The keen sense of exhilaration she always felt when galloping on horseback was further heightened by that stimulating encounter with Julian and the excitement of her first hunt.

Laughing aloud, she gave herself over to the pure joy of it—the sting of the wind on her cheeks, the crisp clear blue of the sky, and the music of the hounds. The first check came all too soon, forcing her to rein in just as she pulled even with those at the forefront—Lord and Lady Anthony, Lord Rushford and a few others.

"What an absolutely splendid morning for a ride!" she cried. Ares danced slightly beneath her as if in agreement as the huntsman and whippers-in cast the hounds about the fallow field in search of the scent while the rest of the field slowly arrived.

"Indeed!" Lady Anthony returned Violet's grin, appearing nearly as euphoric as herself.

Having now seen her in action, Violet had to concede that Lady Anthony was indeed a better rider than herself. She'd never imagined a woman—or man, for that matter—could ride so, as though she and her mount were one. Lord Rushford, Lord Anthony and Grant were also superbly skilled, but Lady Anthony was truly in a class by herself. Violet's pride at seeing a member of her own sex outperform the men nearly equaled that of besting her brother earlier.

On that thought, she turned to Lord Rushford. "I must thank you, my lord, for your assistance in convincing my brother to race me. I largely owe the pleasure of this hunt to you."

While promoting the race in front of Cottesmore house earlier, Lord Rushford had quite reminded her of the dashing young man she remembered. Perhaps he hadn't grown so stuffy as she had feared? His formal reply, however, was more in keeping with his recent demeanor.

"I must hope that earning your brother's enmity will not be the price of your pleasure. It was worth it, however, to see the look on his face when you bested him. Bravo, Miss Turpin."

"Grant has never been one to hold grudges," she assured him, smiling.

His gray eyes sparkled with more amusement than his carefully schooled features revealed. "Glad I am to hear it, for you demonstrated that you've as much right to be here as any gentleman in the field. Perhaps rather more than some." He glanced pointedly at the stragglers finally coming up, among them the very men who had denigrated her earlier.

"Thank you, my lord," she replied, warmed by his praise. "Though I could wish more of the gentlemen present felt as you do."

He held her gaze and for an instant she imagined a hint of answering warmth in his eyes, though his face remained impassive. "I generally prefer to judge people on their merits, not on their status or sex. Why should you not be allowed to take part, once you proved you could ride well enough?"

Though there was nothing the least bit romantic about his words, the warmth in her belly inexplicably increased until she was sure it reached her cheeks. She suddenly felt as awkward as that fourteen year-old girl nursing a hopeless *tendre*. Lord Rushford, by contrast, wore an air of command like a well-fitted cloak.

With an effort, she found the wherewithal to respond. "Perhaps if more men took your view, more women would be allowed to prove themselves. I've no doubt that were we permitted to follow our passions and talents as men do, it would be quite a different world—and one I should enjoy a great deal more."

His brows rose but before he could respond, the baying of the hounds called away his attention. A small sigh escaped Violet as they all set off again.

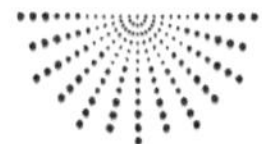

CHAPTER THREE

THE HUNT ENDED MID-AFTERNOON, WHEN THE HOUNDS LOST THE FOX'S scent and were unable to recover it despite the best efforts of the huntsman and whippers-in. Though most of the gentlemen seemed disappointed at the outcome, Violet was not. Vermin though they were generally considered, she had always thought foxes rather cute and similar enough to dogs that she could never celebrate their killing.

Lady Anthony echoed her sentiments as she and her husband joined the party returning to Ivy Lodge for refreshments.

"Anthony will have no cause to chide me for my squeamishness today," she commented, riding alongside Violet while the men engaged in laughing conversation. "More often than not, I excuse myself at the end of a hunt rather than witness the kill. It may be blasphemy to the sportsmen and farmers, but I always give private thanks when the fox escapes."

Violet smiled at the other lady, so near her own age. "I am glad to know I'm not alone in that. By the bye, Lady Anthony, I must tell you how very impressed I was by your riding today. My brother and his friends by no means exaggerated."

"Thank you. Though I never feel I can take full credit, as it is a skill I inherited from my mother, and her mother before her. You are quite an accomplished rider as well, Miss Turpin. Anthony tells me that horse is not particularly easy to handle."

Violet chuckled and patted her mount's neck. "Perhaps so, but Ares knows me quite well—or did, when Grant spent more time at home. Thank goodness he remembered how to behave under a sidesaddle." She did not add that she'd ridden longer and harder today than she had in years. No doubt her body would feel the effects tomorrow, if not sooner.

"I should never have guessed that you had not ridden him recently, for you did splendidly." Lady Anthony grinned across at her. "As I said earlier, I should love to see more ladies in the hunt."

"I hope to participate in as many as possible during my stay," Violet told her. "Especially as I fear I'll have no chance to ride at all in London."

"Why not? Riding is a perfectly acceptable pastime for a lady there, though galloping is rather frowned upon."

"So I discovered," Violet agreed with a laugh, recalling her one midnight foray last year. "However my aunt, with whom I shall be staying, keeps no riding horses, as she is no equestrienne herself. Last Season she put me off until I was, er, obliged to return home." There was no need to tell Lady Anthony why her Season had been cut short.

They then fell to discussing horses they had known over the years and riding in general. By the time they reached Ivy Lodge, they were Violet and Tessa to each other and well on their way to becoming fast friends.

Back at the house, everyone partook of the usual post-hunt repast of cold meats and ale. After seeing everyone's plates filled, Lady Killerby motioned to the other three ladies to join her off to one side.

"I've just had a splendid idea," she said. "What say you we put together a little ball for this coming Thursday?"

"A ball?" Violet glanced doubtfully around the parlor, the largest space Ivy Lodge boasted. "Here?"

Lady Killerby was undaunted. "Oh, I do not pretend it will rival any of your dear mother's entertainments at Plumrose, but if we throw open the doors between this room and the dining room, there should be room enough for two or three sets, and the pianoforte here is top notch. Thursday gives us ample time to send invitations, nor can the gentlemen beg off because of their dirt or claim to be too tired for dancing, as there will be no hunt that day."

To that they all agreed and the four ladies fell to discussing the particulars.

The Seven Saints spent an hour or two of sharing food, drink and hunting stories, after which those not staying at Ivy Lodge made to depart. Before leaving, Tessa pulled Violet aside.

"I have just had a thought," she said. "When I was briefly in Town after my marriage last autumn, Anthony arranged for me to ride a horse from his brother's stables. I am certain Lord Marcus would let you borrow him as well, for I doubt he's been ridden much since then, if at all."

Something in her hesitant, almost apologetic manner prompted Violet to ask, "Why not?"

"I fear he is rather an ill-tempered beast, and somewhat ill-favored as well. On second thought, perhaps you would rather not—"

"No," Violet quickly protested. "I have ridden more than a few horses considered ill-tempered by others. Indeed, I should quite enjoy the challenge. Do you really think Lord Marcus will not mind?"

Her spirits rose at the thought, for she had dreaded the idea of an entire spring without riding.

"His only concern is like to be your safety," Tessa assured her. "I will write to him, however, attesting that you are skilled enough to manage that horse. You would be doing the poor fellow a mercy to give him some exercise…if you are not embarrassed to be seen riding him. He *is* rather an unattractive animal."

Violet grinned. "I don't care two sticks about that. In fact, I look forward to seeing the expression on Aunt Philomena's face when he is brought round. Thank you so much, Tessa."

Lady Anthony took her leave then, but Violet anticipated more conversations with her in the coming days. All in all, it had been a wonderful day.

"Good run today," Lord Uppingwood commented when only the gentlemen remained below. "Possibly the best since the new year began."

"Aye," Sir Charles agreed. "And no matter what some sticklers in the Old Club might say, having the ladies along contributed, putting us all on our best form."

Rush sent a wary glance Thor's way, but the other man only laughed. "I believe you may be right, Stormy, for all I was opposed to allowing my sister to ride today. I noticed several taking extra pains to look good out there."

"You've forgiven me, then, for my interference this morning?" Rush asked, only half joking.

Thor shrugged. "Knowing Violet, she'd have found a way to insinuate herself into a hunt anyway. This way she at least had the blessing of the Master, so I suppose I must count myself grateful."

"Quite the handful, your sister, is she not?" quipped Roger Littleton, the youngest member of the Saints Club. "Pretty as she is, I'd not want to be the one responsible for her."

"You don't know the half of it." Thor shook his head ruefully. "Vi's been getting into scrapes since she could walk, and the older she gets, the bigger the scrapes. Er—" He paused. "Don't spread that about, eh? Wouldn't want to queer her chances of landing a decent match during the Season."

"Any chap who ends up with that whirlwind on his hands has my deepest sympathy!" Uppingwood fervently declared.

The others laughed and Rush forced himself to join in, thrusting down the surge of desire that went through him at the idea of taking Miss Turpin to wife. His appreciation for the headstrong hoyden had been more powerful than ever today. So powerful that, if it were not for his betrothal to Miss Simpson, he'd almost be tempted to take on that challenge himself.

As Thor continued to regale them with stories of the various tangles she had fallen into or, more often, created for herself over the years, a measure of reason returned. Alluring as Miss Violet Turpin was, he could scarcely conceive of a more irresponsible choice for the next Countess Rushford.

~

When Violet awoke the next morning, she was indeed sore from yesterday's exertions, but did her best to hide her stiffness from the others when she went down to breakfast. Not for the world would she give her brother the satisfaction of crowing over her about it. Still, she was just as glad that no hunts were scheduled for Sundays.

Breakfast was followed by services at St. Mary's, then a light luncheon back at Ivy Lodge. Though Violet appreciated that none of these required any sort of painful exertion on her part, there was no excitement to be found in them, either.

"Dina, what say you we visit the kennels?" she asked her sister-in-law as they rose from the table. "Given the time of year, I'll be much surprised if there is not at least one new litter of puppies there." Dina, she knew, was nearly as fond of dogs as Violet was.

"I should love that, for Foxglove will be there, as well," she said, referring to the pup Grant had given her for Christmas. "I daresay she is old enough now to leave her mother and come back with us to Ashcombe."

Grant, overhearing, decided to accompany them and short time later the three of them walked down the graveled path leading to the stables.

"I must see about leaving my little pack here when we depart," Grant commented. "As Rush is now leasing Ivy Lodge from Anthony, I suppose he's the one I should speak to about it."

"Speak to me about what?" Lord Rushford's voice from just behind them sent a little thrill up Violet's spine.

Turning, Grant grinned. "Just the man I needed to see. You won't mind me leaving Princess and the others here till summer, will you? Her pups are nearly ready to walk out with one of the local farmers, and Daisy's will be so in a month. The farmers hereabouts have more experience with foxhounds than most."

"Need you ask?" Lord Rushford replied, clapping him on the shoulder. "Of course." Then, turning a sardonic eye Violet's way, "Did I notice you limping slightly earlier, Miss Turpin? I hope you did not injure yourself in any way yesterday?"

"Not in the least," she protested brightly. "A bit of passing stiffness, perhaps, but no more. Not surprising after such a ride as we had yesterday, and that after spending all of the day before in a carriage."

"Ah, good. I should hate to think I encouraged you to overtax your abilities."

Bristling at his amused tone, Violet lifted her chin. "My abilities were by no means overtaxed, my lord, as you will see when I ride with the Quorn tomorrow."

His amusement did not abate, to her irritation. "When? Do you not mean 'if'? Or do you mean to challenge Thor here to a second race, in hopes of also convincing that Master to make an exception for you?"

"Oh, but—" She turned to her brother. "As I did so well yesterday, surely you will intercede on my behalf, Grant?"

To her dismay, he merely shrugged. "I suppose you may borrow Ares again, and if the opportunity presents I can speak to Mr. Assheton Smith, but I make no guarantees. The Quorn is easily the most traditional fox hunt in the Shires, as it's the oldest. You'd best not get your hopes up," he advised.

It was more than he'd agreed to do for her yesterday, so Violet felt sure all would be well. In her experience, there was never any call to assume the worst, when the best was yet a possibility.

They reached the kennels then, and Princess, Grant's favorite bitch, greeted both ladies enthusiastically once she'd paid first honors to her master. Her pups were nearly twelve weeks old now, but still perfectly adorable. A moment later, Violet and Dina were both kneeling in the straw, cooing over them.

"I can't believe how big they've grown." Violet caressed the largest dog pup while Dina reacquainted herself with Foxglove. "I confess, I was quite disappointed when you had them sent here from Plumrose, for I'd been visiting them almost every day."

Grant beamed at the litter. "Aye, I must begin inquiring of the likeliest farmers immediately. Farrell tells me they've been weaned for a fortnight now."

He and Lord Rushford went back to the house then, but Violet and Dina continued fussing over the pups for a bit. At Violet's suggestion, they then made friends with a few other hounds, for Grant was not the only member of the Seven Saints with aspirations of establishing his own pack.

Rush walked quickly back up the slight slope to Ivy Lodge, frowning. Really, he must get his body's instinctive response to Violet Turpin under better control before she—or worse, Thor—suspected his attraction. His friend might not bear him a grudge for the part he'd played in yesterday's impromptu race, but Rush doubted he'd forgive him trifling with his little sister.

And he could never do more than trifle, so long as he was engaged to marry Miss Simpson. With that in mind, he did his best to avoid Miss Turpin for the rest of the day.

Monday morning, Rush and Killer were the only ones in the dining room when Miss Turpin appeared for breakfast, again attired in the fetching, sky-blue habit she had worn in the Cottesmore. Rush merely nodded a greeting but Killer quickly rose to pull out a chair for her.

"Give you good morning, Miss Turpin," he greeted her. "I take it you are as eager for today's hunt as I? 'Twill only be my third since dispensing with that accursed crutch I had to use for so long."

"You seemed to do very well on Saturday," she commented charitably, for she must have noticed he was not among the better riders on the field.

"Aye, I was pleased to discover I've lost none of my skill despite being put to pasture for so long," Killer replied with a grin. "Pity Rush convinced me to sell Nimbus to him, for I feel certain I could handle him now." He shot a glance at his friend.

Rush had offered a ridiculous price for the horse in order to prevent Killer attempting to ride it again. Perhaps he should take the added precaution of having Nimbus sent up to Rushford Abbey to remove temptation completely.

"Likely you could," Miss Turpin responded sympathetically, with a quick glance at Rush. "Though if Lord Rushford has chosen not to hunt him, it is doubtless because the horse still needs more training."

"Hmph. That's exactly what Rush says," Lord Killerby grumped.

Most of the others now joined them in the dining room, to include Mrs. Turpin and Lady Killerby.

"Shall I assume from your attire that you mean to ride with the hunt again today, Miss Turpin?" asked the latter.

"That is my hope, my lady, though of course that will be up to the Master—and my brother."

Thor shrugged. "I'll not stop you hunting if Assheton Smith gives you the nod. I warn you, however, that he is not a particularly good-tempered man. Nowhere near so easygoing as Lord Lonsdale."

"Oh, but she must ride again!" Stormy exclaimed. "'Twas such a treat to see her in the Cottesmore. We will all add our voices to Thor's, Miss Turpin, should there be any difficulty."

When others spoke up in agreement, Rush remained silent, determined not to intervene this time should Assheton Smith refuse.

Which was precisely what he did, when they assembled at Quorndon Hall.

The other members of the Seven Saints made good on their promises over breakfast but their entreaties were unable to sway the Master of the Quorn. Rush suspected that certain members of the Old Club, nettled by Miss Turpin's superb performance on Saturday, had persuaded him that it would be beneath the dignity of the Quorn to allow yet another woman onto the field.

"Yes, yes, I made a special exception in Lady Anthony's case," Mr.

Assheton Smith told them testily, "and quite a lot of abuse I've taken for it since. I'm sorry, Miss Turpin. When Mr. Osbaldeston takes over Mastership of the Quorn next season, you can apply to him."

Though clearly disappointed, she gave in with good grace. "I suppose I must content myself with riding behind at a distance, as I've seen others do."

Still frowning, Mr. Assheton Smith looked to Thor. "What say you, Turpin? Are you willing to have your sister numbered among such women?"

To his sister's obvious dismay, Thor shook his head. "Sorry, Vi, it simply won't do. Mother specifically tasked me with safeguarding your reputation after, well—" He cleared his throat. "You see, the only women other than Lady Anthony who ever follow the hunts a-horse-back these days are those of, ah, easy virtue. I'd be failing in my charge if I permitted you to be mistaken for one of them."

"But—"

"I said no, Vi," he snapped. "You'll either hand Ares over to Farrell now or ride him straight back to Ivy Lodge and spend the rest of the day there."

Rush could not but share a measure of her disappointment, for he'd looked forward to seeing her riding full-out again. "Here are Lady Killerby and Sir George now," he said, hoping to console her. "You may at least follow the hunt with them."

He waved to the approaching party and Lady Killerby's driver guided the low-slung phaeton toward them.

"Give you good day, Lady Killerby. Have you room for another?" Rush inquired.

"Of course," Lady Killerby replied. "Particularly as Mrs. Turpin pleaded off at the last moment."

Thor was immediately concerned. "My wife is not ill, is she?"

"No, no, just a wee bit queasy over breakfast. Perfectly normal just now," she assured him. "I take it Mr. Assheton Smith was not to be persuaded? I feared that would be the case. Do join us, Miss Turpin."

Though Violet still looked rebellious, under Thor's stern gaze she finally nodded. "Thank you, my lady."

Just then, the horn sounded.

"Ah, they'll be starting in a moment!" Lady Killerby exclaimed. "If one of you young men will help Miss Turpin down—?"

When Rush hesitated, Killer took Miss Turpin's gloved hand in his own to swing her down from the sidesaddle. Subduing the first twinge of envy toward the smaller man he could ever remember experiencing, Rush tipped his hat to the ladies, turned his mount and went to join the others.

~

Violet fumed silently as the rest of the gentlemen trotted off to join the hunt. She'd *so* wanted to ride the Quorn. Trundling behind in the phaeton would not be the same at all.

"There! We are all quite cozy, are we not, my dear?" said Lady Killerby comfortably when Violet was ensconced in the rear seat, slightly above her hostess and Sir George. "I have an extra carriage blanket here, should you grow chilled during the chase. Henry manages remarkable speeds over rough terrain, as you may have noticed Saturday. I dare swear we will have near as good a view of the hunt as you would have on horseback, for I had this vehicle specially designed for the purpose."

"And grateful I am for that," Sir George declared. "I thought the hunt forever lost to me until the first time Lily invited me to accompany her. Not quite the same as riding to the hounds myself, of course, but there are…compensations."

The look that passed between the older couple briefly diverted Violet from her disappointment. Clearly Sir George Seaton and Lady Killerby were somewhat more to each other than "old friends." Violet suppressed a smile, for she dearly loved a good romance.

"Ah, and they're off!" Lady Killerby exclaimed as multiple horns sounded. "After them, Henry!"

With a lurch, the phaeton took off in pursuit and Violet soon discovered that Lady Killerby had not exaggerated her coachman's abilities. By the time those at the rear of the field reached the first covert, the phaeton was no more than half a furlong behind. They had ample time to catch up as the Huntsman and whippers-in cast the hounds into the covert to flush the fox.

While many of the gentlemen were occupied with changing from their covert hacks to their hunters, Julian Bigsby trotted over to the phaeton.

"What! Are you not riding today, Miss Turpin?"

Violet regretfully shook her head. "The Master would not allow it, and my brother felt it might give the wrong impression were I to follow at a distance as a few, ah, ladies have been known to do."

He snorted. "Assheton Smith has never been what I would consider forward-looking, but I'd no idea your brother had become such a stick-in-the-mud."

"He can be," Violet assured him, "particularly with regard to me." Then, belatedly remembering her manners, "Are you acquainted with Lady Killerby and Sir George Seaton?"

"Only in passing. I give you good day, my lady, Sir George." He tipped his hat politely, then turned back to Violet. "I'm minded to have a word with Assheton Smith myself. Old-fashioned he may be, but it borders on cruelty to deny the rest of us the pleasure of seeing you ride to the hounds again, Miss Turpin. I counted that a rare treat on Saturday."

She dimpled at the compliment, gazing coyly up at him through her lashes. "Flatterer. But Julian, I thought we had agreed you are to call me Violet?"

Though he shot a quick glance at the others, his dazzling smile remained in place. "I feared you might have forgotten, so dared not presume—"

"Oh, pooh. We are old friends, are we not? Which reminds me—"

Before she could finish, a hound gave cry that it had scented a fox. The whippers-in rounded up the others and a moment later the entire pack was in pursuit, baying melodiously.

"I'll seek you out again at the first check, shall I?" Julian hastily wheeled his mount around as Henry whipped up the phaeton's pair to follow the hunt.

Violet ached to be galloping along on Ares again, taking her place near the frontrunners. Instead she was forced to trail behind even the slowest riders, for there were barriers such as ditches and hedges that horses could surmount but the phaeton could not. There were gates and bridges, of course, but those took them well out of the way.

The first check did not occur for more than half an hour, by which time the phaeton had fallen a quarter of a mile behind the main pack. As Lady Killerby's coachman attempted to close the distance, Julian trotted back to meet them.

"This seems a good chance to continue our interrupted conversation," he said as they all moved forward together. "By the looks of that patch of brambles, it may take some time for the hounds to flush the fox again."

As if to confirm his words, whines and yips drifted back to them as the pack tried to penetrate a thorny tangle the much smaller fox had slipped through easily.

"Poor dogs," Violet exclaimed, imagining the scratches they must be sustaining.

"'Tis what they're bred for." Julian shrugged. "I believe you were about to tell me something when we were interrupted before?"

Violet blinked, bringing her focus back to the handsome face now regarding her intently. "Oh! Yes. I wished to ask whether you mean to attend our little ball at Ivy Lodge on Thursday? You received an invitation, did you not?"

"I did, and I thank you, my lady." He bowed to Lady Killerby from the saddle. "But I fear I'll not be able to accept as I leave for London on the morrow. This, alas, is to be my last hunt of the season. Dare I hope I shall see you there this spring, Violet?"

Though disappointed, she summoned a smile. "Indeed. In fact, I expect to arrive there within a fortnight."

"Well, that's just capital. No doubt there will be balls enough there to compensate for my missing this one. Might I engage you now for a dance at the first one we both attend, or am I too forward?"

She giggled at his absurdity. "Of course I will dance with you, Julian. As many times as you wish."

At that, Lady Killerby cleared her throat. "Now, now. You mustn't be so hasty, Miss Turpin. You cannot know what other gallants may introduce themselves to your notice before then."

"I see her ladyship means to warn me off," Julian said with a wink, "but having a few rivals will only make my pursuit of your heart a more stimulating challenge. Assuming it is yet winnable?"

Though her cheeks warmed slightly at the rapid pace of the conversation, she lifted her chin with a toss of her curls. "Winnable? Perhaps. But only by someone worthy of it."

"Then you've not set your cap at anyone yet? I am relieved, for I'd be quite heartbroken if you had. Dare I ask what sort of man you might deem worthy?" he continued in the same teasing tone.

An image of Lord Rushford arose unbidden but she quickly pushed it away.

"He would have to love me to distraction, of course," she replied lightly. "That would be the first requirement. If he can be romantic and heroic as well, so much the better. Indeed, my absolute ideal would be a man as brave, daring and selfless as the Saint of Seven Dials."

Julian blinked in surprise. "The notorious thief? Surely you do not know who he is?"

"No, though I should love to meet him. In fact, that will be my primary goal when I reach London. After reading so much about his exploits, I can easily imagine myself falling in love with that dashing scoundrel—preferably while assisting him in his noble crusade."

Lady Killerby laughed. "Come, Miss Turpin, you cannot mean that."

"Do I not?" she replied. "The Saint is both hero and rogue in one, stealing from the most undeserving members of Society right under their upturned noses and giving to those who need it most." A romantic sigh escaped her. "Yes, such a man as he could easily win my heart."

"You've a soft spot for rogues, then?" Julian leaned forward from the saddle, capturing her gaze with one so intense that Violet felt both excited and vaguely alarmed.

"Here we are, and just in time," Lady Killerby exclaimed, rather more loudly than necessary.

Pulling her gaze away from Julian's, Violet saw they'd reached the stand of brambles between two fields where the fox had taken cover. Before they could draw to a halt, the hounds flushed it out to continue the chase. Everyone, including Julian and the phaeton, immediately leapt in pursuit.

Though sorry to have her conversation with Julian interrupted, Violet was also vaguely relieved, for she'd sensed his words held more layers of meaning than she fully understood. Her attention now split between parsing their recent exchange and the ongoing hunt, she remained unusually silent for some time.

Not until the conclusion of the hunt did Violet have another opportunity to speak with Julian. As everyone made their way back toward Quorndon Hall, he again drew alongside the phaeton.

"I must return to my lodgings now to prepare for tomorrow's journey but I did not wish to leave without bidding you farewell, sweet Violet." He spoke quietly enough that Lady Killerby, chatting gaily with Sir George about the day's highlights, did not overhear. "I shall be counting the days until I see your lovely face in London."

She smiled up at him, her earlier misgivings forgotten. "I shall be staying with my aunt, Mrs. Philomena Puttercroft, in Mortimer Street. Promise you will call upon me once I arrive, for otherwise I'm like to have a deadly dull time there."

His answering smile was warm. "Of course. It will be my very great honor." He glanced over her shoulder. "Until then, my flower." Sketching a quick bow from the saddle, he touched his fingertips to his lips, winked roguishly and cantered off.

Seconds later, her brother and Lord Rushford rode up, having lingered behind with most of the others for the kill. "I hope you did not find today's hunt completely irksome?" Grant asked warily.

Lord Rushford, by contrast, did not even look at her, instead seeming focused on something in the distance.

"It could not compare to riding, of course, but Lady Killerby and Sir George were exceedingly pleasant companions," she replied graciously, with a smile for her hosts. "Indeed, I am quite grateful for their willingness to allow me to intrude on their tête-à-tête."

She had the satisfaction of seeing Lady Killerby color at her words, while Sir George noisily cleared his throat, confirming her surmise about them. Alas, that was all the satisfaction she was likely to have that day, with Julian leaving and Lord Rushford as distant as ever.

Taking leave of Lady Killerby's party, Rush and Thor cantered on ahead toward Ivy Lodge. Thor was anxious to see his wife again, to confirm that she was not truly ill.

"What do you think that bounder Bigsby was doing, talking with your sister?" Rush asked as they went, partly to distract his friend from worrying. "I didn't know they had renewed their acquaintance."

"Nor did I." Thor frowned. "I noticed him speaking to her at the start of the Cottesmore, as well. Meant to ask her about it but forgot. How long has he been riding to the local hunts? I don't recall seeing him last autumn."

Rush thought back. "Only a few weeks, I believe. I first spotted him in the Belvoir in January but as he seemed desirous of avoiding me, it's possible he arrived earlier and I missed him."

Thor chuckled. "Sounds as though our little lesson was a lasting one, then. Good."

"I hope so." But Rush had not cared for the way the man had been looking at Miss Turpin as they rode up to the phaeton. Perhaps he needed a reminder? At the very least, he would keep a close eye on Bigsby while Miss Turpin remained in the Shires.

For his friend's sake, of course.

"What say you we cut across the fields rather than taking the road?" he suggested then. "'Twill almost certainly get us to Ivy Lodge more quickly, as dry as the ground is just now."

Thor instantly agreed. The two turned their mounts to leap the low hedge bordering the road and thundered across terrain similar to what they'd already traversed during the hunt, each man busy with his own thoughts.

~

The next day saw another running of the Cottesmore, where Lord Lonsdale was perfectly agreeable to Miss Turpin participating again. As before, she acquitted herself exceedingly well.

Wednesday marked Miss Turpin's first appearance at the Belvoir, where she prevailed upon her brother to approach the Duke of Rutland and his huntsman, Goosey, on her behalf. Rush kept his distance from the discussion, but other members of the Seven Saints were not so reticent.

"On my oath, your grace, if you'd seen her in the Cottesmore you'd not hesitate to allow it," Stormy declared. Killer and Littleton chorused their agreement.

"What say you, Lord Anthony?" the duke asked, turning. "Your lady has set the standard, after all."

Anthony laughed. "Your grace cannot expect me to put any other lady on the same level as my wife? However I must say that Miss Turpin rides as well as any *other* lady I've witnessed in the saddle."

With a chuckle, the duke nodded. "Very well, then. With such champions, how can I refuse? Turpin, you may tell your sister I'll allow it."

Needless to say, Miss Turpin was ecstatic. Though careful to pay her no more attention than was wise, Rush greatly enjoyed another opportunity to watch her riding to hounds.

That he'd seen nothing of Julian Bigsby since the Quorn only added to his satisfaction. If the cad had decided trifling with Miss Turpin was not worth risking her brother's ire, Rush considered it all to the good.

CHAPTER FOUR

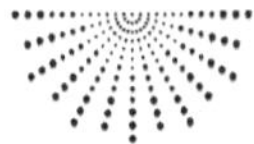

THE FOLLOWING EVENING, RUSH SURVEYED THE CROWD ASSEMBLED AT IVY Lodge with bemused detachment. He'd always felt half the point of wintering in the Shires was to escape the crush and pressures of Society. Lady Killerby had been adamant, however, that the Seven Saints must host a dance to be taken seriously as a hunt club.

He had to admit she'd made a good business of it. Ivy Lodge was filled with laughter, music and a variety of local gentry enjoying a warm escape from the February chill. Watching several couples gaily moving through the interlacing figures of a Scotch reel, their cheeks bright with exertion, he smiled despite his reservations.

"Never would have thought our little hunt club could pull off such a do," exclaimed Killer, returning from partnering Mrs. Turpin in the dance. "M'mother has really outdone herself."

Dina smiled. "Indeed she has. I am enjoying myself immensely after so many weeks devoted to nothing but estate matters. But why are you not dancing, Lord Rushford?"

"The last set had already begun when I made my way downstairs," he explained, ignoring the knowing twinkle in her green eyes. "I had some correspondence to attend to before I could see my way clear to joining the, ah, festivities."

"You are here now, however, and I see my sister-in-law heading this way. You should discover whether she is engaged for the next set."

Telling himself that he might as well get the inevitable out of the way early, just as he had with his correspondence, Rush held his ground as Miss Turpin joined them.

"I know Lady Killerby was hoping for a crush, but my goodness!" she exclaimed, fanning herself. "Perhaps it is a sign of her success to have so many people here, but I would much prefer to move through the figures without fearing I will be knocked down by someone in the next set." Her smile and sparkling eyes belied her complaint.

When she turned her animated face Rush's way, he responded with a bow. "Might I request the honor of a dance before such an unfortunate event occurs?"

"Certainly," she replied, her surprise evident. "I am bespoken to Sir Charles for the next set, but I am free for the one after that."

"I shall look forward to it, then." Perhaps he could use that dance to learn a bit more about the too-attractive Miss Turpin. Discovering more evidence of her flightiness might help to break the spell she had cast over him. He hoped so.

Soliciting Dina's hand for the set just forming, he led her to the floor.

"I must agree with Violet that I should have been quite happy had Lady Killerby been a bit less successful in filling the rooms," she confessed as they took their places. "I am glad for this chance to enjoy another dance before the crowd and heat become too oppressive."

Rush chuckled. "I shall do my best to ensure you are not trampled by any other dancers." Given Mrs. Turpin's diminutive stature, it seemed a definite risk.

Dina acquitted herself gracefully during the cotillion that followed, though she was noticeably breathless at its conclusion.

"May I fetch you a glass of something?" Rush offered.

"And risk you missing the next dance? Certainly not. In any event, here is my husband now to do that office." She turned smilingly to Thor and he circled her small waist with his arm.

Their obvious delight in each other caused Rush to feel a pang of…

not jealously, precisely, but a longing he could not define. Though he felt not the slightest inclination to attach Dina's affections himself, he could not deny a touch of envy at his friend's unmistakeable happiness in the married state. Not for the first time, he wondered if he had been too precipitate last summer in committing his future to a virtual unknown.

That unsettling line of thought was broken by Miss Turpin returning from the dance. Firmly reminding himself to use this opportunity to quash his desire for her, he extended his arm.

"Shall we?"

Her smile faltered and he realized that in his determination to resist her charms, he had spoken more formally than he had intended. Probably just as well.

Without replying, she placed gloved fingers on his arm and allowed him to lead her the five or six steps to the makeshift dance floor.

"I imagine this small gathering scarcely qualifies as a ball in your estimation, crowded though it is?" he asked as they waited for the music to begin.

After a quick, doubtful glance at him, she smiled. "You must not imagine I have extensive experience with balls, my lord. Other than our monthly assemblies in Alford, I have only attended the beginning of one, in London last year."

He recalled Thor telling him why her one London ball was cut short but before he could comment, Lady Killerby—their sole musician tonight—began a sprightly air on the pianoforte and the dancing resumed. When the figures brought Rush and Miss Turpin together again, she continued their interrupted conversation.

"What about you, Lord Rushford? Do you prefer a small, country entertainment such as this one to the grander balls found in London? I imagine you have far more experience of those than I."

He considered for a moment before replying, "Balls have never been among my favorite amusements, however large or small they may be. I would far rather exert myself on the hunting field."

"What amusements *do* you enjoy, beyond fox hunting?" she asked.

"Er…" To his secret dismay, he couldn't think of any. Odd. Surely there were numerous things he had liked to do when he was younger? "I suppose between estate business and other demands, fox hunting is the only one I've made time for lately," he finally confessed.

Her gaze now seemed almost pitying, prompting him to speak again before she could press him further on what had suddenly become an uncomfortable topic.

"What of you, Miss Turpin? What are your favorite amusements, beyond midnight gallops on purloined horses, inappropriately flamboyant gowns, and I know not what else."

"I see Grant has been carrying tales. It was just one midnight gallop," she informed him, "and scarcely anyone saw me in that scarlet gown, for Aunt Philomena whisked me out of the Trumbull's ballroom the moment I removed my cloak. I didn't even—"

She broke off as the dance again separated them. When they came back together, she continued in a slightly different vein.

"You asked about my interests, but mine are almost too many to enumerate," she said smilingly. "I enjoy all manner of socializing, in small parties or large, as well as theatrical performances and musicales, few though my opportunities have been in the country. Riding is an especial passion of mine, as you are no doubt aware by now. And lest I sound completely frivolous in comparison to someone so responsible as yourself, I also find pleasure in taking gift baskets to our poorer tenants, though I cannot call that exciting. Of course, when adventure offers in no other way, I can always find it between the covers of a book."

His brows rose. "Books?" he echoed. "You enjoy reading, then?"

"You needn't look so surprised," she admonished him. "As it happens, reading has been a pleasure of mine since I was a young girl. A pleasure I assume you do not share, Lord Rushford?"

"On the contrary, I should have listed it as one of my principal diversions beyond hunting."

The demands of the dance forced another pause, during which Rush cautioned himself that Miss Turpin's liking to read hardly negated her tendency to imprudence.

To further convince himself of that, he returned to the topic of books at first opportunity. "From what you said before, I imagine you prefer novels to more, ah, serious subjects in your reading?"

"Not always. I have lately quite enjoyed a work of nonfiction dealing with the Saint of Seven Dials. Have you read it?"

He shook his head.

"You should, as your hunt club was named in his honor. I found it quite as exciting as any novel. The more I learn of the Saint, the more I admire him. Even so, your assumption was essentially correct, for since leaving the schoolroom I have tended to seek out novels for my reading pleasure. Romantic ones, in particular." She slanted a flirtatious glance up at him.

Powerfully tempted to respond in kind, he forced himself to look away.

"Ah, I see you despise me for that," she said, misinterpreting his reaction. "May I ask if you have ever read one?"

"A romantic novel?" he asked in surprise. "No. I should say the closest I've come is the occasional romantic bit of poetry by Byron or the like."

"Ah, I thought as much. Educated as you have no doubt been in scientific methods of analysis, my lord, I am surprised that you would condemn an entire branch of literature without first studying it."

The dance required another break in conversation just then, rather to Rush's relief. He needed the time to marshal an argument against her implicit accusation of unthinking prejudice.

"Tell me, Miss Turpin," he said loftily when they next came together, "how many branches of literature did *you* sample before fixing upon romantic novels as superior to the rest?"

To his surprise, she laughed. "All, or nearly all, I should say," she replied, surprising him further. "Do you forget what a scholar my father is? Until my mother sent me away to Miss Gebhart's, he took the greater part of my education upon himself. I was only permitted to read novels when my other studies for the day were complete—perhaps why I came to think of them as pleasurable rewards. He was rather an exacting taskmaster."

Rush blinked, struggling to reconcile the idea of a studious Miss Turpin with the madcap girl he'd known and the scandal-prone woman she'd become. Fortunately, the dance ended a moment later and he was able to surrender her to her next partner.

Unfortunately for his peace of mind, it appeared the lovely Miss Turpin was not so empty-headed as he'd thought. Surely, though, a clever woman bent upon mischief was far more dangerous than a less intelligent one could be?

Not that it mattered. His tacit engagement to Miss Simpson should safeguard both his name and his heart from falling prey to such a seductive peril.

Violet was in high spirits when she took her place opposite Roger Littleton for the next set. She had quite enjoyed her conversation with Lord Rushford—and had particularly enjoyed the look of surprise on his face when he learned the extent of her education.

She was also pleased about making her first real progress in engaging the elusive Lord Rushford's interest. Not only had he asked her to dance, but he had made an actual effort to converse with her. Surely he would not have done so if he were not attracted to her?

Though she knew that many men, perhaps most men, considered women inferior in both intelligence and abilities, she'd been startled to hear such antiquated opinions from such a close friend of her brother's. She hoped she had given Lord Rushford food for thought—and perhaps the impetus to change his thinking—just now. If he danced with her again, she would attempt to build upon that start.

Lady Killerby launched into another sprightly country tune, forcing her to attend to the demands of the dance—though she could not help noticing that Lord Rushford was now partnering Miss Augusta Melks in another set.

She suddenly wondered whether his recent coolness toward herself might be *because* he was attracted? Given how leery of commitment most bachelors were, he might fear—

"—dance divinely, Miss Turpin," Mr. Littleton was saying.

Guiltily, she pulled her attention away from the other set. "Why, I thank you, sir. You are quite accomplished at the art yourself."

He preened visibly at the compliment, though privately Violet considered his dancing much inferior to her last partner's. For a man who claimed not to particularly enjoy the pursuit, Lord Rushford was remarkably skilled at it…

To avoid falling into another reverie, Violet donned a bright smile. "Pray tell me, Mr. Littleton, did you also fight in the recent wars, as so many of the Seven Saints did?"

He nodded. "Of the founding members, I believe only Lord Killerby did not—and quite bitter he is about it, too. I was not cavalry, however, so did not have the good fortune to serve under Rush, as Stormy, Anthony and your brother did. Though I saw my share of the fighting, my father was only able to purchase me a lieutenant's commission in the 45th Foot."

He went on to explain that he'd been friends with the others at Oxford prior to joining the army, as had Lord Killerby. All of them had also hunted foxes together for years.

Violet had to feign more interest than she felt, for she'd already heard most of this from Grant. She was struck, however, by the admiring way Mr. Littleton spoke of Lord Rushford and his style of command during the war. Grant often evinced that same admiration when talking about him—one reason she had fixed upon Lord Rushford as a sort of romantic ideal.

When the dance ended, Violet again glanced toward the other set in time to see Lord Rushford hastily abandoning his partner to assist a noticeably pale Dina to a nearby chair. Violet immediately excused herself to hurry over to her sister-in-law.

Grant reached his wife at the same moment Violet did. "What is it?" he anxiously asked. "Are you feeling ill?"

Dina shook her head. "Not ill, but I felt suddenly dizzy. Thankfully, Rush was near enough to catch me before I could humiliate myself completely by an undignified tumble to the floor."

Lady Killerby joined them then, having ceded the instrument to the elder Miss Melks for the next set.

"My dear! I rather feared you might be exerting yourself overmuch this evening, given your condition." She turned to the two hovering gentlemen. "One of you fetch her some lemonade and the other something to eat from the buffet in the dining room," she directed them. "Miss Turpin and I will see to Mrs. Turpin's comfort while you do so."

Both men complied with alacrity, though not without a few backward glances from Grant.

"Now, my dear, rest you quiet until you are certain you are no longer in danger of fainting. When you feel able to stand, I'll have your husband see you to your room, that you can lie down properly. An early night will be the best thing for you."

Dina gave an embarrassed laugh. "I feel so foolish, acting the weakling like this. Particularly as I have always been the very picture of health, scarcely ill a day in my life."

"I think you are doing exceedingly well under the circumstances," Lady Killerby told her comfortingly. "You will simply have to make some allowances during this time—earlier nights, a less vigorous schedule, that sort of thing. Trust me, when the babe arrives, you'll be busy enough. Conserve your energy while you can. To make certain you do, I shall tell your husband."

"Tell me what?" Grant demanded, shouldering his way through the crowd with a large glass of lemonade, looking more concerned than when he had left. "Are you truly ill after all, my love?"

Dina shook her head. "Not at all. But Lady Killerby has kindly advised me that I would do better to, ah, take things a bit easier in the coming months, difficult as it will be for me to do."

"I'm sure she's quite right. In fact, if you feel equal to walking, I'll take you upstairs right now, that we might discuss the matter rather more…thoroughly." The look he bent on Dina was enough to bring color into Violet's cheeks simply by observing it.

Appearing only the slightest bit shaky, Dina rose, now smiling.

"Shall I send up Dina's abigail?" Violet asked.

"No, dear," Lady Killerby murmured to her. "Let them have some time to themselves."

With a slightly sheepish grin, Grant took the glass from Violet and the couple made their way toward the stairs. As they went, they encountered Lord Rushford returning from the dining room with a heaped plate. Taking the plate from him, Grant spoke briefly to him before continuing up the stairs with Dina.

A set or two later, Lord Rushford asked Violet for another dance. That his thoughts also lingered on Grant and Dina and their coming addition was clear from his first words when they took their places.

"I take it you look forward to playing the doting aunt?"

"So much!" she declared. "Indeed, I shall likely do more shopping for the babe than for myself while in London. I dare swear the only person who can be more pleased is my mother."

He grinned, suddenly seeming much younger. "Ah, yes, I recall a few pointed comments she made over Christmas, when they'd scarce been married a fortnight."

They laughed together, their earlier debate forgotten as they discussed Lady Rumble's probable reaction to the news and how long she would wait before traveling to see her son and his wife. Only after the set ended did Violet recall her earlier intention to further erode Lord Rushford's antiquated prejudices. Perhaps she would have a chance tomorrow, during the running of the Quorn.

When Lady Killerby wished to retire, the two Misses Melks took turns at the pianoforte. Violet was also invited to serve that office, but as her skill on the instrument was merely passable, she demurred. After another set or two, increasingly audible rumbles of thunder induced several guests to take their leave. By midnight, only those staying at Ivy Lodge remained.

As the inmates of the house made their way upstairs, Violet tried to catch Lord Rushford's eye in hopes of again engaging him in conversation but he was sharing some jest with Sir Charles and did not even glance her way.

~

By the next morning, the ominous thunder-rumbling of the night before had fulfilled its portent with a cold, steady rain. Gazing out of his bedchamber window at the gray sheets of water sluicing past, Rush stifled a curse.

After some rather unsettling dreams, he'd hoped riding the Quorn would clear his mind. Unless the weather took a dramatic change for the better within the hour, though, the hunt would almost certainly be canceled. Over breakfast, the others expressed equal dismay at the weather.

"Knew it was too good to last," Killer said morosely. "It still seems monstrous unfair. I've had precious few hunts this season as it is."

"It's your own fault you missed so many," Uppingwood reminded him, his own disappointment no doubt making him more impolitic than usual. "If you hadn't disregarded everyone's advice about that brute of a horse—"

Miss Turpin entered the room just then, cutting short what would almost certainly have developed into an altercation. "Do you think the weather will prevent the Quorn from running today?"

"Looks pretty likely, at this point." Stormy got up to assist her. "I just hope this infernal rain stops in time for the Cottesmore tomorrow."

"So do I, for your sake. Alas, Grant has said this will be our last day at Ivy Lodge." With an audible sigh, she moved to the sideboard to fill a plate.

She looked Rush's way on returning, but he felt it wisest not to notice after conversing rather too familiarly with her the night before. When she took a seat further along the table and began to eat with a frown on her winsome face, he told himself it was for the best.

Miss Turpin's animation returned when Thor and his wife appeared a few moments later. "Ah, here you are at last. Do you think we might stay here an extra day if this rain causes the Quorn to be canceled? I should love to join the Cottesmore one more time."

"Sorry, Vi," he replied. "After her indisposition last night, I'd like to get Dina back to Ashcombe sooner rather than later. I did hope for a last hunt today, however. Think you Assheton Smith will allow his hounds to run in this rain?" he asked the others.

That returned the conversation to its original topic, predictions becoming increasingly gloomy as the rain continued unabated. Finally, just as the first few were leaving the table, a drenched footman arrived from Mr. Assheton Smith himself to regretfully inform them that the Quorn was indeed canceled for today.

With that settled, the gentlemen unhappily dispersed—some to the billiard room, others to the parlor to play at cards or to their own chambers to read or nap.

Rush decided he might as well finish the business correspondence he'd begun before last night's ball, after which he could make a visit to the stables to see how Nimbus got on. Though his groom had made fair progress with the ill-tempered gelding since his purchase, Rush felt it was time to take a hand in the horse's training himself.

"Thank you, Brigid." Violet pulled on the sturdy boots her maid had just extracted from the bottom of her trunk. "I'm sure I'll need to change into something dry for luncheon, so please have my blue cambric laid out for my return."

Leaving the chamber, she tripped downstairs and out of the front door of Ivy Lodge to hurry through the still-driving rain toward the stables. As there was no hunt to finish out her time in the Shires, she might as well visit the dog kennel again. She was eager to see whether Duchess, another of her brother's foxhounds, had whelped. On Sunday she had seemed fairly near her time.

The warm, dry stables felt like a sanctuary from the downpour when she reached it. Removing her bonnet, she shook the water off it. Then, much as a dog might, she vigorously shook out her wet hair. At a muffled oath, she wheeled around in alarm, dripping strands trailing across her face.

"Oh, dear," she exclaimed at the sight of Lord Rushford. "I had no idea you were there."

"No, I didn't imagine you doused me intentionally." He brushed the droplets she'd scattered from his coat. "Though there was a moment last evening when I suspect you'd have liked to."

She grinned. "When you ridiculed my taste in reading while professing yourself ignorant of the genre? Yes, rather."

That drew a chuckle from him. "I am forced to concede that you made a fair point. I would have little patience with someone who maligned Homer, for example, without having read him."

"I take it you have?"

"Of course." He seemed surprised she would ask. "Most of the Greek classics were required reading at school."

Violet narrowed her eyes mischievously. "Then I see you have misled me, my lord. You insisted last night you have never read works of romance, yet Homer is quite rife with it."

"Do you mean to say *you* are familiar with his works?" He raised a skeptical brow.

Her determination to further challenge his thinking instantly revived. "Surely you cannot imagine a scholar of my father's caliber neglected Homer in my curriculum? Indeed, it was dear old Homer who first kindled my interest in romantic adventures. Before I discovered more contemporary novelists and poets, Homer and Catullus were my chief pleasures among my various studies. Far more enjoyable than geography and mathematics, at any rate."

She was gratified to see dawning respect in his eyes. "Clearly your education was more thorough than I realized, Miss Turpin. I rather assumed your knowledge of Homer was limited to Keats' most recent sonnet."

"His paean to Chapman's Homer, you mean? He did wax rather lyrical on that translation, did he not? So much so, I doubt he ever read the original."

"Have you?" Lord Rushford's astonishment was obvious.

"Certainly."

"In Greek?"

She gave him a patient look. "That *is* the original, is it not? How else to peruse it untainted by some later translator's liberties?"

Slowly, he shook his head. "I owe you an apology, Miss Turpin, for I see now I've been guilty of making unwarranted assumptions about you. But tell me, what brings you to the stables in such inhospitable weather?"

Deeming it best not to dwell on her triumph, Violet submitted to the change of topic.

"I wished to see whether Duchess had whelped yet, and to visit with the other dogs, and the horses. Both hold more charm for me than billiards—not that my brother would likely allow me to play at them, anyway."

"I should rather hope not. Or am I to learn you are proficient in that as well?"

"Proficient? No. I cannot claim to be more than passable, though it is safe to say I have more skill at billiards than at the pianoforte, much to my mother's dismay."

He laughed. "I apprehend you have little patience for the accomplishments generally expected of young ladies?"

"That is putting it rather mildly," she confessed with an answering smile. "Nor were two years at Miss Gebhart's Seminary sufficient to change my mind on that score, which I doubt not was my mother's goal in sending me there. What the devil use is painting tables and netting purses anyway, if you will pardon my language? Perhaps if ladies were allowed to sell their creations, there would be some utility in such skills. But to spend hours upon hours creating indifferent works for visitors to insincerely admire seems a colossal waste of time that could be spent on more worthy pursuits."

"I…see."

Belatedly realizing that she had scandalized him, Violet turned away in mingled exasperation and embarrassment. Had she just undone all her progress in capturing his interest? Seeking a safer topic, her gaze fell upon the horse nearest them.

"This is Nimbus, is it not? The horse you bought from Lord Killerby?"

He turned to regard the animal. "It is. I recommend keeping your distance, for he is still rather an ill-tempered brute."

"Is he?" She lifted a hand toward the enormous bay gelding but quickly withdrew it when his ears swiveled backwards. She was quite familiar enough with horses to recognize that danger signal. "Yes, you are, aren't you? Poor thing. Who instilled such mistrust in you?"

"According to Miss Seaton, er, Lady Anthony, he was abused by a previous owner, though her cousin's treatment likely made him even worse. Without her intervention, I doubt he could ever have been ridden at all."

"But now he can be?" It was Violet's turn to be skeptical.

"Not by just anyone, as proven by Killer's injury. Only Lady Anthony can ride him in perfect safety, though my groom and I have now managed it a few times. It has taken considerable time and effort to win his trust, however."

To demonstrate, Lord Rushford reached up to stroke Nimbus's nose. This time the horse's ears remained forward, though he still eyed Violet warily.

"He is lucky to have found an owner willing to make that effort. Not many would, I fear."

"You are likely right, but I have always enjoyed a challenge. I believe Nimbus will eventually prove to be worth the time invested, though my fondness for horses may color my judgment somewhat."

Violet could hardly fault him for that. In fact, it revealed a side of him she had not expected—one that made him even more appealing. "Are you equally fond of dogs, Lord Rushford?" she could not resist asking.

He lifted a shoulder. "Perhaps not equally. I like them quite well, but horses have been my passion since I was a lad. It's why I went into the cavalry."

She was tempted to point out that he was fortunate to be a man, that such an option was open to him, but didn't wish to spoil their current accord. Instead, she moved toward the kennels at the rear of the stable block. "Has my brother's third bitch whelped yet, do you know?"

"Two days since. Did you not know? I'm sure he mentioned it at dinner, though now I think on it, the ladies may have already withdrawn."

At this welcome news, Violet quickened her pace. "Splendid. How many—ah, five, it appears." She peered down into the straw-lined box where the dainty brown-and-white Duchess lay nursing her brood.

"Aye, the groom said she birthed six, but one was stillborn. The remaining pups appear healthy enough, however."

"They do indeed." Violet knelt beside the box to stroke a tiny, silky back with one finger. Carefully gauging Duchess's reaction, she gently lifted the pup to examine it more closely.

"A dog, I perceive. Did Farrell say what sexes the others are?" She would not test Duchess's patience by examining them all just now.

"All dogs but one, as I recall. The stillborn pup was the only other bitch in the litter."

Nodding, she settled the still-blind creature back by his mother.

"No doubt Grant was somewhat disappointed at that ratio, for I know he hopes to add more famous bloodlines to his pack, as he did by putting the Duke of Belvoir's Rounder to Princess. He says all six pups from that mating already show great promise."

Lord Rushford knelt next to her as she continued to stroke the nursing pups. "You seem nearly as knowledgable about foxhounds as your brother, Miss Turpin."

She shrugged, disturbingly aware of his nearness. "I adore dogs and took over their care whenever my brother was from home, over my mother's objections. I also made a point of studying their blood-lines, for I should dearly love to establish a pack of my own someday."

Though she knew it was craven, she kept her focus on the puppies to avoid seeing his probable reaction to such an unorthodox statement.

"Do you know, I truly believe you could."

At the frank admiration in his voice, she looked up, startled. Instead of the disapproval she'd expected, he was gazing at her with a bemused, puzzled expression. Her earlier suspicion that he was attracted to her revived. Could it be that he held himself in check out of concern that Grant might not approve?

There was but one way to find out—and she might never have a better opportunity than this. Greatly daring, she rose up on her knees, then, when he did not immediately draw back, threw her arms around his neck and pressed her lips to his.

He froze for an instant, but then his lips softened under hers. For two, possibly three ecstatic seconds, she reveled in his kiss, before he broke away with a look of horror on his face.

"I…I beg your pardon, Miss Turpin!"

"Violet. Please." She smiled up at him, determined to show she had taken no offense. After all, she had been the one to—

"Miss Turpin," he repeated, his tone now more formal than she had yet heard it, the censure she had earlier expected now clear in his expression. "I apologize if I somehow gave you the mistaken impression that I wished to be more than your friend, for I fear that is quite impossible. I give you good day, madam."

With one swift motion he rose, then stalked out of the stables and into the rain without a single backward glance.

Violet stared after him, her cheeks burning with mingled anger and embarrassment. For one lovely moment she'd been sure she was right, but apparently her mad impulse had only provoked an equally mad response, and one he instantly regretted.

Had she completely misread his feelings, seeing only what she wished to see? It seemed so. Willfully blind to the truth, she had wantonly thrown herself at him…and he had rejected her in no uncertain terms.

How could she ever face him again?

To avoid doing so for as long as possible, she turned back to Duchess and the puppies, her eyes prickling with unshed tears of humiliation and disappointment.

CHAPTER FIVE

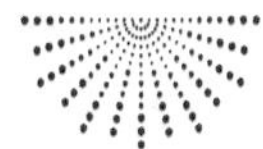

HEEDLESS OF THE CONTINUING DOWNPOUR, RUSH STRODE UP THE HILL toward Ivy Lodge, determined to put as much distance between himself and temptation as possible. Halfway there, however, he paused, recalling the stricken look on Violet's face when he pushed her away. *That* memory would likely torment him even more than the sweetness of her kiss. How could he have been so careless?

Shaking his head at his own stupidity, he resumed squelching through the mud, thinking hard. What the devil was he to do now? His unthinking response to her unexpected kiss must have revealed how much he desired her. To pretend otherwise now would invite her ridicule and scorn—or, worse, wound her even more deeply than his haughty leave-taking just now had done.

But...what choice did he have? His hasty decision last summer to offer for Miss Simpson, prudent as it had seemed at the time, now left him in a bind of his own making.

If Violet told Thor what had happened, he would feel honor-bound to offer for her even though she had been the one to initiate that kiss. He could—should—have pulled back at once. Or, far better, he should have prevented it happening at all. That he had not made him as much to blame as she.

Oddly, the thought of taking the unconventional Violet Turpin to wife, even at her brother's insistence, did not bother him nearly so much as it should. This incident only proved how headstrong and impulsive she was—in other words, a most unsuitable countess.

Unlike biddable Miss Simpson, she would never be content to live quietly at his estate in the country, raising his heirs while he pursued business and pleasure elsewhere. Surely he owed it to his family, his name and his mother's memory to marry a woman he could train up to be a model of propriety. A woman like Miss Simpson.

Of course, his engagement to Miss Simpson would not, strictly speaking, become official until her father either returned from India or sent a letter expressing his consent. Given that, if Thor should insist...

Remembering Violet's expression as he left her, however, Rush rather doubted she would mention the incident to her brother. More likely, pique or embarrassment would lead her to behave as though their kiss in the stables had never happened—in which case he would do the same.

Why that thought produced a hollow feeling in his chest, he preferred not to examine.

Though he had resolved to take his cue from her, Rush had no opportunity to do so. She did not return from the stables until after luncheon, then had a tray in her room rather than come down to dinner. Though she claimed to be too busy packing, Rush felt sure that her real reason was to avoid encountering him.

To prevent his thoughts from guiltily dwelling on her absence, Rush joined the dinner conversation about the prospects for tomorrow's hunt.

"It has scarcely rained at all since late this afternoon," Killer opined hopefully.

"True," Rush said. "It will be heavy going with the ground so wet, and the farmers won't like it, but that hasn't stopped Lonsdale in the past."

The others cheerfully agreed, everyone's spirits noticeably brighter than they had been all day. Unfortunately, rather than serve as a distraction, the discussion reminded Rush of how well Violet had ridden in her last hunt.

Shaking his thoughts free of her—again—he tried to focus on the conversation around him. He was moderately successful until he rose to accompany the others from the dining room after the traditional port and cigars—and Thor put a hand on his shoulder.

"A private word?"

Rush's heart sank. Had Miss Turpin mentioned that encounter in the stables after all? Firming his resolve to do the right thing should it become necessary, he took a deep breath and turned to face his friend. "Of course."

Oddly, Thor looked more apologetic than angry. "You'll be in London this spring?"

"In another fortnight or so, yes."

"Good. I'd like to request a…favor, once you get there."

Cautiously relieved, Rush summoned a smile. "Anything, old chap."

"I was rather hoping you'd say that," Thor responded with a grin. "I know Killer offered to keep an eye on my sister during the Season, but I'd feel much easier if you were on the job as well."

Rush's relief was abruptly replaced by a sinking sensation in his midsection. "I'll help in any way I can, of course," he promised and was rewarded by the relief now written on Thor's face.

"Thank you," he said, his gratitude evident.

Fully aware that if Thor learned of that kiss in the stables he would be within his rights to demand a far greater favor, Rush forced a smile. "No need for thanks, old chap. We are friends. You need not worry I'll shirk the responsibility. What would you like me to do, exactly?"

"If you're willing, call upon her every few days, perhaps squire her about on occasion—along with your Miss Simpson, of course. Observant as you are, I trust you beyond anyone I can think of to notice should Vi get one of her mad starts, and to step in if necessary."

Rush agreed without hesitation, thankful he had not blurted out anything about that kiss at the outset. Such a charge would entail considerable awkwardness, after what had occurred in the stables this morning—not to mention what Miss Simpson and her mother might think of it—but compared to the alternative, he was getting off remarkably easily.

"You may count on me, Thor, though I must remind you not to mention my engagement to anyone else just yet. Think how embarrassing it would be if it became common knowledge only to have Sir Clarence refuse his consent."

Though Thor laughed at such a preposterous idea, Rush could not suppress a secret wish that it might actually come to pass, thereby freeing him to pursue other...possibilities.

The next morning, Violet was in a fret to be off before any gentlemen appeared for breakfast. Once away from Ivy Lodge, there would no longer be any danger of meeting Lord Rushford's eye. At least it seemed clear from her brother's demeanor that Lord Rushford had not mentioned her indiscretion, for which she was grateful...but she still could not face seeing him again.

The night before, Violet had taken care to complete her packing down to the last detail, that there might be no delay the next morning. She had even helped with Dina's packing once her own was complete. Now, when the carriage finally left Ivy Lodge for Ashcombe, she breathed a sigh of relief.

For the next week and more, Violet was so busy that she had little time or energy to dwell on her humiliation with Lord Rushford or her dread of another Season with Aunt Philomena. Her days were filled with discussions of baby furniture and nursery decor, shopping in Litchfield for baby clothes and toys, and settling Dina's new puppy at Ashcombe.

In fact, she was having so much fun amid the joyful bustle that she felt a pang of regret when Grant finally suggested leaving for London the following day. She and Dina had grown so much closer over the past fortnight that she expected to miss her sister-in-law immensely.

When Grant and Dina said their goodbyes the next morning, all of Violet's romantic longings were reawakened. The two were so clearly in love, so loath to be separated for even a few days, that she felt a tugging at her own heartstrings.

What must it be like to feel such a strong attachment to someone? Though Lord Rushford was apparently lost to her, she still hoped to find true love while in London, Aunt Philomena notwithstanding.

"Pray do not worry, Grant," Violet said when he looked backwards out the carriage window for the third time as they drove away. "Save that one dizzy spell at Ivy Lodge and a few bouts of morning queasiness, Dina is as remarkably healthy as she has always been. I've no doubt you will find her so upon your return."

Turning from the window, he heaved a sigh. "Aye, you're likely right. Still, it goes sorely against the grain to leave her for even a week."

"A week! Surely there is no need for you to be away so long as that? It should take us but two days to reach London."

"Two very long days," he amended. "Even assuming the roads remain dry and we encounter no mishaps along the way."

Violet puckered her brow. "And then Aunt Philomena will insist you stay for at least a few days once there. Hm."

She did not particularly like to think of Dina alone in the country either, though she knew her stalwart sister-in-law would laugh at such fears. Dina was so very small and Grant so very large, she could not help wondering whether that might present complications. In fact, her brother had once voiced that very concern in response to their mother's blatant hints about grandchildren.

After a few minutes' thought, she turned to her brother. "How would this serve? If we manage more than half the distance today, I could travel the rest of the way by post tomorrow, while you hurry back to Ashcombe. That would prevent me staying alone at an inn, which I know you would never allow, and you'd only need suffer a single night away from Dina."

He regarded her in surprise, his expression suddenly hopeful. "Aye, I could be with her late tomorrow, if we push hard today." Then his face fell. "No. Mother would never let me hear the end of it if I didn't see you to Aunt P's doorstep. Tempting as your idea is, Vi, it would be most irresponsible of me."

"I imagine Mother would think it far *more* irresponsible for you to leave Dina alone at such a time," Violet insisted. "Not that she will know anything about it unless we tell her, which I swear on my honor I'll not do."

He regarded her dubiously for a long moment, then sighed. "I'll… think on it."

"Do. I'm sure you'll agree my plan is the wisest, safest course."

That he missed Dina more with each passing hour was evident. He allowed the carriage to travel until well past nightfall, before finally stopping at a coaching inn south of Northampton.

Over breakfast the next morning, he capitulated.

"I have decided you are right, Vi," he admitted. "Dina's need just now is greater than yours. However, you must *promise* not to get into any mischief between here and Aunt Philomena's."

"I'll be a very model of propriety," Violet assured him. "Pray don't worry about me, Grant, but make all haste back to Dina's side. She will be overjoyed to see you back so soon. I will explain the change of plan to Aunt Philomena when I arrive."

His relief was obvious. "Very well, though it might be best not to say precisely why Dina and I are remaining in the country. You know how Aunt P likes to gossip and I'd as lief not have our news spread all over London just yet."

"Mother will not be so reticent," Violet pointed out, "but I can simply say that you and Dina discovered more needs to be done at Ashcombe than you'd realized, which is true. That is, of course, if Aunt P allows me to say anything at all. Knowing her, she may concoct her own story before ever I get a word in."

Grant chuckled at that. "Aye, she does like to talk. Well, do what you can. I'm sending Spooner along with you for protection, by the bye. He's quite handy with a pistol, as he proved in the war."

A short time later, Violet's trunks were strapped to a bright yellow post chaise. She and her maid climbed inside while her brother's valet took a perch on the box. After giving detailed instructions to the postboy, Grant put his head in at the window.

"Well, Vi, I'm eager to be off and you've a long day ahead, so I'll say farewell. Give Aunt P my regards—if she gives you the chance."

She waved him away and he hastened to his own coach for the return journey to Ashcombe.

The knowledge that she'd acted for the best buoyed Violet's spirits for the first hour or two, as did Brigid's simple delight at again being allowed to ride inside the carriage, as she had on the way to Ivy Lodge.

"I was like to perish from the cold yesterday," the maid declared with a shiver. "I know it's not my place to complain, 'specially when most in my position have it far worse'n me, but I don't know how poor Mr. Spooner bears it. I don't believe he's ever once ridden inside."

Violet smiled. "Spooner had wartime experience, remember. He is also far more conscious of his position than you've ever been, Brigid— though that is largely my own fault. I suppose having you complete the journey to London in comfort is some compensation for what I lose by Dina's absence. I was *so* looking forward to going about with her instead of stuffy old Aunt Philomena."

Brigid clucked her tongue in ready sympathy. "Aye, you said how strict she was with you last year. Small wonder if you kicked at the traces a bit, as high spirited a lass as you are. 'Twas a shame she sent you home, for you'd've likely landed yourself a lord with another week or two in Lunnon."

"Likely so," Violet agreed with a grin, amused by her maid's blind partiality.

As the day wore on, the weather, which had started out cold but sunny, turned gray and gloomy, punctuated by an intermittent drizzle that slowed their progress. Violet's spirits gradually turned gloomy as well. She feared the dull weather was a harbinger of what a Season with Aunt P would be like, compared to the bright prospect she had envisioned a mere fortnight ago.

Rush settled back in his chair in a corner of the main room of the Guards Club, his preferred retreat when in Town. As it was past the dinner hour, few members were still about and none he knew well. That troubled him not at all, as he'd come more for relaxation than conversation, after two long days shut up in a carriage with Lord Killerby.

By prior agreement, after spending a week at Rushford Abbey, Rush had stopped at Killer's estate in Nottinghamshire and the two had traveled together to London. Killer was a nice enough fellow and an amusing companion. Still, after twenty-odd hours of talking about fox hunts past and future and their respective plans for the Season, a bit of solitude was welcome. Not having served in the military, Killer was not a member of the Guards.

He'd scarcely poured his first glass of claret when his coveted solitude was interrupted.

"Rushford? Is that you?"

Turning, he saw Lord Peter Northrup coming toward him and immediately gestured for the other man to join him at his table.

"Give you good evening, Colonel," he greeted the newcomer. "I understand from your brother that you are married since last we met?"

Lord Peter pulled up a chair. "Aye, I beat Anthony to the altar by a mere month. My parents seem quite pleased to have all five of us safely leg-shackled, not that the succession was in any danger."

The Duke of Marland, Lord Peter's father, had five sons, two of whom were well known to Rush—Anthony, of course, and Lord Peter, with whom he'd become friends during the war, though Rush was Cavalry and Northrup Infantry.

"Are you but just arrived in Town?" he asked as Rush signaled for a second glass. "I stopped in at Rushford House last night but was told you were not expected for some days yet."

Rush nodded. "I came a bit earlier than planned, due to a matter or two requiring my presence in London." One of those matters was an eagerness to see Violet Turpin again, though he'd barely acknowledged it even to himself.

"Ah. Well, I've another to put before you, now you're here. Have you seen this?" Colonel Northrup pulled out a newspaper folded back to display a particular article and laid it on the table between them.

The headline immediately caught Rush's attention: ***The Saint of Seven Dials a villain after all?*** With a startled glance at his companion, he began reading.

After an absence of more than two months, the fabled Saint of Seven Dials has resumed his activities—this time with a decidedly more sinister bent. Previously, the Saint was content to purloin valuables from the wealthiest among the ton, leaving only his famed calling card as evidence of his visits. However, two of his three recent robberies have been accompanied by a violence he previously eschewed, resulting in injuries to unfortunate staff, one serious.

"I'd never have believed it of him," Miss Agatha Chalmers told the Times. *"In the past, I rather idolized the Saint of Seven Dials, as did so many others. But he could easily have killed James, our head footman, striking him so with the fire-iron. Were it not for the card he left, I would be certain it was some other footpad who broke into my father's strongbox."*

The card Miss Chalmers mentioned was surrendered to the authorities, who are now resuming their efforts to apprehend the thief. We have been assured, however, that it bore the Saint's distinctive emblem of a numeral seven surmounted by a gold-ink halo. While it is of course possible that other, less charitably-minded scoundrels have begun copying the Saint's methods, at present these latest aggravated housebreakings are believed to be the work of one man: The Saint of Seven Dials.

"Thought it might interest you, given the name of your hunt club," Lord Peter said when Rush finished reading.

"It does indeed, though I have difficulty believing this can be the real Saint. As you might imagine, I did a fair bit of research into the Saint of Seven Dials before suggesting we name our club in his honor, nearly two years since. At the time, he'd never been known to cause anyone the least injury. In addition, he limited his depredations almost exclusively to the less, ah, sympathetic members of the nobility. Think you this might be someone else aping his style, as this article suggests? The design of his card is well known, thanks to the papers, and would be easy enough to forge."

"True, but until they catch whoever this is, everyone will assume it really is the Saint."

Rush nodded gloomily. "They will. Hm. Don't much care to have our hunt club's good name dragged through the mud by association."

"I assumed that would be the case. It's one of two reasons I sought you out on the matter."

"What's the other one?" Rush asked curiously.

Lord Peter smiled. "You were quite well known for strategy during the war, as I recall."

"As were you," Rush reminded the other man, who inclined his head modestly in acknowledgment.

Colonel Northrup's razor-sharp intellect had bordered on legendary in the Army, as had his fierceness in battle. Given what Rush knew of him, it struck him as slightly odd that the man now seemed to favor an almost dandyish style, evidenced tonight by a salmon evening jacket and pale green waistcoat. Doubtless he had his reasons.

"Between us, we can surely figure out some way to track down this imposter before he causes more harm," Lord Peter said.

Rush's brows rose. "You already have reason to believe he's an imposter, then?"

"I'm absolutely certain of it…though I'd prefer you not ask me how I know. Not before we've had a chance to talk things through a bit more."

"Of course not, Colonel," Rush replied, easily falling back into the habit of respect for a superior officer, for all he outranked a duke's fourth son on the social scale.

"No more of that, if you please, Rushford," said the other man, rather to his surprise. "I've left Army life behind and happy to do so. Here at the Guards it can be difficult to dissuade others from their reminiscences, but I'd as lief be excused from them."

"I understand," Rush replied quietly. He had painful memories of his own from the recent wars he'd prefer to forget. "If we're to work together on this mystery, pray call me Rush, as my friends do."

His companion's smile returned. "Gladly. And you must call me Peter. So, let us discuss this new, so-called Saint."

"I know only what I just read. I take it you know more?"

"A bit, though not nearly as much as I hope to." Pouring a measure of claret into his glass, Peter began filling Rush in on what he had contrived to learn over the past week.

Darkness had fallen by the time Violet's coach reached London, for rain had worsened the condition of the roads as they traveled. A yellow fog closed in as soon as they entered the sprawling city, muffling the sounds of the increasingly heavy traffic that slowed them even further.

The air thinned only slightly, when they reached Mayfair, forcing Violet to admit her brother had been right that a stay in London would not have been healthy for Dina. Finally, the hired coach pulled up before Aunt Philomena's town house.

Spooner jumped down from the box to lower the carriage steps. "This is it, Miss. Number seven Mortimer Street."

Violet stepped out of the chaise and looked up at the narrow house. "I'll have Aunt Philomena's manservant assist you with the trunks, Spooner. Wake up, Brigid, we're here."

The abigail opened her eyes and yawned. "Are we there, Miss? Goodness, I must've slept three solid hours!"

"Nearly four, I should say. Gather up whatever is in the coach while our luggage is unstrapped."

Spooner preceded her to the front door and plied the knocker. A moment later Wiggins, Aunt Philomena's elderly butler, opened to them.

"Welcome, Miss Turpin. Lady Puttercroft began to think you would not arrive before tomorrow. She is just having her nightly basin of gruel before retiring. Come up to the drawing room and I will tell her you're here."

"Thank you, Wiggins. Will you please have Robert help bring in our luggage?"

As Wiggins turned away, Aunt Philomena's voice drifted down the stairs from two floors above.

"Is that Violet's voice I hear? Are they finally come? Don't leave them standing in the hall, Wiggins, send them all up here to my rooms at once that I may speak with them."

With a tiny, rueful shrug at the butler, Violet made her way up to the second story, Brigid trailing just behind. She stopped at her aunt's open door but did not go in, thinking to continue first to her chamber to doff her traveling cloak and set Brigid to unpacking.

"Good evening, Aunt. I am sorry to be so late, but the roads—"

"Yes, well, never mind that, I'm just happy you got here before I went to my bed, as I was just about to do. I daresay I'd not have slept a wink, worrying your carriage had overturned in a ditch on some lonely stretch of road along the way. Come in, come in, do."

Violet stepped through the doorway into the chamber, where Aunt Philomena lay ensconced on a pale pink chaise longue, one foot swathed in bandages.

"And this must be the new Mrs. Turpin?" she queried before Violet could ask about her apparent injury. "Your mother wrote me that she was small and redheaded when I pressed her for a description, but she did not mention the freckles. Still, I daresay a bit of powder will cover them nicely, so no need to fret about that. Is Grant not with you?"

"No, he—" Violet began, but her aunt did not wait for her answer.

"Ah, still in the Shires hunting foxes, is he? I should have guessed it would be the case. Likely he also wished to avoid being dragged about to the shops while you and Mrs. Turpin outfit yourselves for the upcoming Season. By the bye, I mentioned to Madame Fanchot only last week that you would be coming, and your new sister-in-law as well. She remembered you well from last year but I took the liberty of informing her of your unusual coloring—" This with a nod at Brigid—

"as I knew she would wish to lay by a supply of fabrics suitable for a redheaded married lady."

Though Violet opened her mouth to disabuse Aunt Philomena of both misconceptions, she talked on, scarcely even pausing to draw breath.

"'Tis as well I spoke with her when I did, for it was but the following day that I turned my ankle tripping over that stuffed elephant's foot I used to have in the front hall. The silly thing has been banished to the attics now. Mr. Franklin proclaimed it a nasty sprain that will likely to take some time to heal. He's forbidden me to climb stairs without assistance, or to walk about unless I use a cane, which I refuse to do. 'Tis a mercy Mrs. Turpin is here to bear you company. Otherwise you would be trapped in the house as well, Violet, for I should be completely remiss in my duties if I allowed you to go about with only your maid, particularly after last year. But there! I promised myself I'd not bring that up. We will start *this* Season with a fresh slate, so to speak."

Violet's heart sank, her worst fears realized. Aunt Philomena's chaperonage would have been confining enough between her early hours and antiquated ideas about activities appropriate for young ladies. Without Dina here to play propriety, she apparently would not be allowed to leave the house at all!

"Aunt, I—" she began, determined to get the worst over at once, but Lady Puttercroft again cut her off.

"Now, where was I? Oh, yes! The very day before I suffered this infernal sprain, I accepted dear Letitia's kind invitation to spend a fortnight in Brighton taking the sea air, knowing you would have your sister-in-law here as chaperone. 'Twill be just the thing to set me up for the busy part of the Season, for I always feel better after visiting the seaside. Just now is the perfect time, too, while Town is still thin of company. I'd originally planned to leave two days hence, but now I must convince Mr. Franklin that I am fit to travel."

She directed a glare at her wrapped foot as she continued. "If he allows it, I daresay you two will scarcely miss me, what with shopping and sorting through the invitations that are bound to begin arriving once 'tis known you are here. Still, I shall endeavor to return in time for Lady Bellerby's ball a fortnight hence, for I promised to introduce you to her son. She is one of the few who generally begins her entertainments at a decent hour. If I am somehow delayed in returning home, you two must attend anyway, for she will be most disappointed otherwise."

Violet merely nodded, the beginnings of a delightfully outrageous idea darting through her brain.

"You must take advantage of this lull before the Season truly gets underway to get most of your shopping out of the way." Aunt Philomena cast a critical eye over both Violet and Brigid, still in their traveling cloaks. "Even with your outer things on, I can see you are both sadly in need of refurbishment before venturing into Society. I suggest you visit Madame Fanchot directly—tomorrow, if you feel rested enough after your journey. Your mother's last letter mentioned that this is Mrs. Turpin's first real visit to London, so I doubt she has ever seen anything the likes of that establishment. You must know, my dear, that Madame Fanchot is considered the absolute pinnacle of fashion in Town," she told Brigid. "She'll see to it that you both do credit to the Turpin name."

Brigid sucked in a breath as though to protest but Violet silenced her with a quick shake of her head—not that Aunt Philomena had hesitated anyway. Still talking away, she picked up a bell from the small table at her elbow and rang it.

"Now, I dare swear you are both fagged to death after two or three days' travel. I presume you stopped at an inn for your dinner before reaching Town? No? Then you must be famished! I'll just have Cook send trays up to your rooms, as you'll wish to get to your beds as soon as may be. She's sure to have something on hand, as I advised her earlier that you might arrive in time for a late dinner or early supper.

"Ah, Florence, there you are," she said as her abigail appeared in the doorway. "Send down to the kitchen to have two very, *very* late suppers sent up, along with a little hot negus to ward off the chill, for I observe it is still quite wintry outdoors for all it is March. Then come back to help me into my bed, for I find myself excessively fatigued.

And no wonder, for I see by the clock on the mantel that it is nearly ten, well past my usual bedtime."

Lady Puttercroft turned back to Violet and Brigid as the maid hurried off. "Mrs. Turpin, I had Mrs. Humphrey put you in the front corner bedroom, as you'll need the extra wardrobe space once your husband arrives. Violet, you are in the same room as last year, the next one along. You will no doubt want a bit of a wash before your suppers arrive, so I shall bid you both goodnight. We can chat more when we are all fresh in the morning. Now run along, both of you, and get you to your rooms!"

Thus dismissed, Violet murmured a quick good night and hurried Brigid out into the hallway, before her maid could say a word. Pulling the door closed behind her, she blessed the silence as she retreated to her room to gather her thoughts—and to plan.

CHAPTER SIX

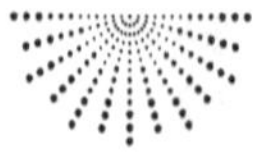

"Miss?" Brigid whispered uncertainly, following Violet into her bedchamber. "Where am I really to sleep? Surely not in that grand room next to yours? I'm feared Lady Puttercroft will be terrible put out when she kens the truth. We should have told her she made a mistake."

"She didn't exactly give us a chance," Violet pointed out, motioning Brigid to shut the door. "Besides, I've just had the most delicious idea! It's why I shook my head at you before—not that she let you say anything anyway. Help me off with my cloak while I explain."

Brigid regarded her mistress suspiciously. "Delicious idea?"

"Positively scrumptious," Violet affirmed. "Tell me, how should you like to be a lady of the quality while Aunt Philomena is away?"

"Me?" Brigid was clearly aghast. "Why, I wouldn't know how, Miss! I'd say or do something wrong the first five minutes and be found out. I've no wish to be turned out of the house or…or thrown into prison."

Violet laughed. "Oh, pooh. Pretending is not a crime, unless done for some nefarious purpose. I only wish for a bit of freedom and fun— for both of us. Aunt Philomena already believes you to be Dina, so we needn't lie, precisely. We simply won't correct her misapprehension."

"She'll figure it out in the morning, surely, when the light is better."

"I doubt it. She is quite nearsighted, you know, and too vain to wear spectacles, just as she is too vain to use a cane. The only thing apt to give you away is your accent—assuming she allows you to speak at all, which is doubtful."

Brigid still looked dubious. "Supposing she asks me a question, though? Me mum has tried and tried to get me to talk more refined like, for she says most ladies' maids do, but I can't seem to master it. She says if you was ever to turn me off, I'd never find a post near so good unless I learn proper talking."

"Turn you off! You know I'd never do that," Violet protested, for she and Brigid had practically grown up together.

Daughter to the Plumrose Cook, Brigid had progressed from under-kitchen-maid to upstairs maid and finally to Violet's personal abigail. Because of their long acquaintance, Violet allowed Brigid far more freedom than most mistresses would, often treating her more as friend than servant. It helped that the girl was an excellent keeper of secrets… and occasionally a valuable dispenser of advice. Her warnings against Mr. Plunkett had certainly been sound.

"Here, try repeating after me," she told Brigid now. "'How do you do, my lady? The weather is unusually cold for March, is it not?'"

After a moment's hesitation, Brigid said, "'Ow d'ye do, m'lidy? T'weather be…is…what was the rest?"

"No, no. You must enunciate. 'How do you do?' With an H at the start. And try not to run the words together."

"Huh…huh…hoo do yoo doo?"

Violet sighed. "I suppose we can't expect you to get it right without practice, and just now we are both fatigued. Never mind. We'd best unpack, as our suppers will be here soon."

Clearly relieved, Brigid turned to open Violet's trunk. "I knowed it wouldn't work, Miss. Once I've put your things away I'll just nip down to the kitchens and explain the mistake to the housekeeper. Like as not they have a bed for me in the attics already, and one for Mrs. Turpin's maid, too. I can tell her that one won't be needed."

"You'll do no such thing! I'm not giving up my lovely plan so easily as that. If you should be called upon to speak at breakfast, I shall tell

Aunt Philomena you have lost your voice—that you've only just got over a frightful cold and have been directed by the doctor to remain mute for the next week or two to avoid a relapse. If she indeed goes to Brighton, we need only fool her for a day or two. Which of my gowns will be easiest to take up so that you can wear it tomorrow?"

"I brung along that light blue cambric you gave me last spring. It's already hemmed and all," Brigid reluctantly admitted. "But I don't—"

"Perfect!" Violet frequently passed her cast-off gowns to Brigid or one of the other maids, but had completely forgotten that one. "It's rather out of fashion, of course, but that is no matter. Aunt Philomena will not expect Dina to have anything in the current style. Wear that until you have time to alter something else of mine."

While Brigid hung and folded the contents of Violet's trunk in the clothespress, Violet chattered excitedly about the Royal Amphitheatre and balloon ascensions and various other amusements the two of them could attend together.

She then installed Brigid in the corner room that had been designated for Dina. The meager contents of Brigid's valise looked rather lonely inside the double wardrobe, but Violet told her not to worry.

"My father has given me a generous shopping allowance, quite enough to outfit both of us in style. Tomorrow we'll visit Madame Fanchot, as my aunt suggested, and in a few days you'll be as beautifully turned out as any titled dame, mark my words."

When Jenny, Aunt Philomena's maid-of-all-work, arrived with their suppers, Violet had her set them out in Brigid's room, which boasted a larger table and an extra chair. Over the meal, Violet addressed a few more details of her daring plan.

The more she considered it, the more certain she felt that everything had worked out even better than if Dina and Grant had come with her to London. Why, with only Brigid as a companion, the possibilities were endless. She could go anywhere, do anything—to include seeking out the Saint of Seven Dials!

Nothing could be more perfect.

~

The next morning, Violet fastened Brigid into her old blue cambric and arranged her hair, a shade or two closer to orange than Dina's, into some semblance of a fashionable style. When she finished, she stepped back to survey her work.

"Very passable," she declared. "If I did not know better, I should never guess you were not a highborn lady. Just remember to pretend you cannot speak if Aunt Philomena should ask you a direct question."

Brigid still looked nervous when they returned to her sitting room a few minutes after nine o'clock—an absurdly early hour for breakfast by fashionable London standards.

"Ah, here you both are at last," Lady Puttercroft exclaimed on their entrance. "I daresay you needed the lie-in after all that traveling. Were you able to stay awake long enough to eat the supper I had Cook send up?"

Motioning the reluctant Brigid to join her, Violet seated herself at the small table. "Yes, Aunt, thank you."

"Happy I am to hear it. Her soup was particularly good, I thought, and the cold tongue."

Violet started to murmur something complimentary in agreement but her aunt hurried on into more speech.

"You will never guess what Mr. Franklin had to say when he visited me an hour since! I was ready to argue him into allowing me to travel but as soon as I brought it up, he said there should be no difficulty at all. He claimed to have informed me already that I was not obliged to remain in these rooms, or even in the house, so long as I had assistance on the stairs and used a crutch elsewhere, but I declare I cannot recall him saying any such thing."

Violet could well imagine the poor man had attempted to tell her aunt many things that she had never stopped talking long enough to hear.

"The moment he left, I penned my letter to Letitia and had Robert post it for me. But then it occurred to me, as this is Mrs. Turpin's first visit, that she might prefer that I remain long enough to get her well settled in?"

At Aunt Philomena's inquiring glance Brigid mutely shook her head. Violet opened her mouth to explain about the fictitious cold but never had the chance.

"Very kind of you, my dear, very kind indeed, and I'm sure dear Violet will have a few acquaintances she can introduce you to. Oh! That reminds me. Yesterday I had a note from Lady Simpson. She and her daughter are in Town and mean to call upon you soon. You and Miss Simpson attended Miss Gebhart's Seminary together, did you not? Such a highly regarded school for young ladies! 'Twill be nice for you to have a friend so close by, for as I recall, the Simpson house is just down the street on Cavendish Square."

"Mary is in Town?" Violet's spirits rose at the news. She and Mary Simpson had renewed their acquaintance last Season and Violet had found her every bit as sweet and unassuming as she'd been at school.

"Yes, it will ease my mind to know that Lady Simpson will be by to keep an eye on you while I am away, and to introduce you around. I daresay a morning dress or two can be delivered not many days after you visit Madame Fanchot, and then you may begin making calls yourselves. After that, invitations will begin pouring in—though, as I told Violet last year, there is no need to accept any that begin late, for I cannot stress enough the importance of a good ten hours' sleep every night. Indeed, that is what I credit for my own youthful appearance. All my acquaintances protest I look not a day over forty for all I am a full score past it."

She patted her closely-coiffed graying hair complacently.

"I told Letitia to expect me by midday tomorrow, which will mean leaving at first light. She has invited me numerous times, you know, for she is still exceedingly grateful for my assistance in finding husbands for both of her daughters during their respective Seasons. Only Hettie snagged a title, of course, but Madeline's Mr. Worthington is from a very old family and quite wealthy, so no one can say she did not do nearly as well as her sister."

While she nattered on, Violet poured out coffee for herself and Brigid.

"Your mother was quite adamant that you are not to stint on your wardrobe, for she means you to be launched in proper style this time around. Speaking of which, if you can by any means convince one of the Patronesses of Almack's to recommend you for a voucher, it would go a long way toward making everyone forget your little indiscretion with that red gown last Season."

Violet doubted anyone remembered that incident, but had no opportunity to say so before her aunt resumed.

"Madame Fanchot is growing exceedingly busy with the height of the Season approaching, but promised to make the time to lay out all her best for you. I recommend you visit her as soon as you have breakfasted, if you feel rested enough, for she is more likely to be at liberty this early in the day. I have observed that a great many members of the ton—all of her customers are members of the ton, you know—lie abed till noon. So silly that their so-called morning calls rarely occur before one o'clock in the afternoon, for by then the day is half over."

Violet knew that to point out morning calls were late because most people in upper Society entertained until the wee hours of the morning would only invite another homily about the foolishness of keeping late hours. Not that she was allowed time to speak anyway.

"Speaking of morning, or rather afternoon calls," her aunt continued, "that puts me in mind of a particularly amusing thing that happened three or four Seasons ago…"

～

"Thought I'd never get you out the door this morning," Killer complained as he and Rush bent their steps toward Mortimer Street. "Can't believe you had that much to attend to on your first day back in Town."

Rush regarded his friend with mingled amusement and annoyance. "My staff were less than prepared for my arrival last night as I'd told them to expect me next week. Then there was the pile of correspondence awaiting my attention. I've barely dealt with a tithe of it yet."

Lord Killerby shrugged. "I've a stack of letters to go through as well, but surely our promise to Thor takes precedence? I am also eager to see Miss Turpin again, for I find her high spirits quite refreshing."

"Refreshing. Yes," Rush blandly agreed.

A week of estate business had done nothing to drive Violet Turpin from his thoughts, nor had continually reminding himself of his obligation to Miss Simpson. Eager though he'd been to see Miss Turpin again, he feared doing so would only make his foolish obsession worse.

"Here we are, number seven." Killer halted before the narrow row house, similar to the others on the street. "Shall I ring the bell?"

Rush hesitated on the pavement. "Now I think on it, my first call on arriving in Town should be to Miss Simpson. Suppose word got round that I visited Miss Turpin before paying my respects there?"

Killer regarded him quizzically. "You still mean to go through with the match, then? You said not a word about it during our journey to Town."

"I made the offer, so can scarcely cry off now," Rush pointed out irritably. "Nor is there any reason I would. Miss Simpson is well enough looking and behaved, with no faults I'm aware of."

"And…you consider those qualities sufficient to justify spending a lifetime with her? I would never dream of offering for a girl I didn't hold in considerable affection."

Rush smiled, ignoring the pang his friend's words gave him. "Ah, but you were always much more of a romantic than I. You and Miss Turpin share that trait, so maybe you should consider a match there." Why that thought bothered him so, he refused to examine.

"Can't pretend I don't admire her," Killer admitted, "but once she's surrounded by other suitors, I'm not likely to fare well by comparison."

"Oh, come!" Rush chided him as they made their way toward Cavendish Square and the Simpson house. "Any woman who would refuse you merely due to a lack of inches is hardly one worth having."

Killer snorted. "Easy enough to say, for a man who tops six feet. Nay, if I'm to snag m'self a bride, as Mother keeps pestering me to do, my holdings will likely serve as a better lure than my person."

"Mind you don't fall prey to a pretty fortune hunter, then," Rush cautioned, for it was true that Killer was exceedingly wealthy—

wealthier than himself, for all Rush held the higher title. "They quite abound in London, you know."

Now his friend looked hurt. "Give me credit for more sense than that. Think you I don't know the difference between flattery and sincere interest? I've experienced more than enough of the former to spot it straight off. Easy to do when the lady spouting pretty phrases keeps casting her eyes over my head at gentlemen of superior stature, if inferior fortune."

Rush could think of no way to further reassure his friend without sounding patronizing, so remained silent until they reached the Simpson residence a few moments later. There they discovered Lady Simpson and her daughter on the point of leaving the house.

"Why, Lord Rushford!" Lady Simpson exclaimed. "How delightful to see you. We are exceedingly flattered you should come to call on your very first morning in Town, for I heard from my maid that you only returned to Town last night. Her sister is in service in Brook Street, at the house next to yours. How unlucky that my daughter and I are off to do some shopping just now. Mary, are you not pleased to see Lord Rushford?"

The diminutive blonde's assent was nearly inaudible but she curtseyed most properly, first to Rush, then to Killer, whom Rush now introduced to the ladies.

"I knew your mother fairly well some years ago, Lord Killerby," Lady Simpson said to the viscount. "Is she in London for the Season as well?"

"She spoke of coming later, perhaps in a month or so," he replied. "Meanwhile, I am honored to make your acquaintance, Lady Simpson, Miss Simpson." He bowed to each in turn. "Might we perhaps escort you to wherever it is you are going?"

Lady Simpson delightedly accepted the offer and a moment later the four of them stepped into the waiting carriage.

"I must say, this attention is most welcome, Lord Rushford," Lady Simpson remarked as the coachman whipped up the horses. "My daughter once or twice expressed doubts as to whether you meant to honor your offer, given how long it is since we have seen you. She is so modest, you see, always undervaluing her worth. This, I hope, has allayed your fears on that score, Mary?"

Miss Simpson directed an alarmed glance Rush's way before again casting her eyes downward with a small nod.

"Such a sweet, biddable girl," Lady Simpson declared with a doting smile for her daughter. "Why, I cannot count how many influential ladies of the ton—and some gentlemen, too—have told me what an exceptional wife she will make one day. Without giving specifics, as nothing can be *official* yet, I assured them that her prospects on that score are excellent." This last was said with a sidelong glance at Rush.

He cleared his throat. "Yes. Well. I can safely say that I personally have never heard even the slightest criticism of Miss Simpson. Which I'm sure speaks very highly of her."

"Indeed it does," agreed Lady Simpson. "For you must know as well as I how eager the London gossips are to create scandal out of the least thing. Any young lady wishing to keep her reputation pristine would do well to take my Mary as a pattern, as she never steps even a toe out of line. Some, I know, are not nearly so circumspect. Why, I recall one particular incident last Season—"

"Aye, those gossips love to blow even tiny missteps out of all proportion," Lord Killerby quickly put in. "Shame, really, for I hate to see a young lady's name dragged through the mud for nothing more than youthful high spirits."

Rush shot Killer a grateful glance. He'd been as alarmed as his friend that Lady Simpson might be on the point of relating one of Violet Turpin's exploits from the previous Season.

"What do you ladies go in search of today?" Rush asked, mainly to change the topic. "I confess that to my untutored eye you both already appear turned out to full advantage."

Lady Simpson preened at the compliment before detailing the various purchases they hoped to make. "Mary is also due to be fitted for three new gowns, for our invitations are already flowing in. You may rest assured that she will do full credit to her future station in life." Another significant glance at Lord Rushford accompanied her words.

However ambivalent Rush's feelings might be, it was clear Miss Simpson's mother considered their eventual marriage a *fait accompli*, of which only the date was in doubt. Had he spent more time around Lady Simpson before proposing to her daughter, he might not have— He broke off the thought, for it scarcely mattered now.

"I presume you ladies will not require our assistance while shopping?" he said when they reached Bond Street.

"I suppose not," Lady Simpson admitted with obvious reluctance. "However, I know Mary would appreciate it immensely if you could return to escort us back home."

Rush hesitated, for he still had much to do that day, but realized furthering his acquaintance with Miss Simpson should take precedence. "Of course, if you wish."

"We mean to conclude our shopping with Mary's fitting at Madame Fanchot's, so we will await you there in two hours' time, my lord." At a stern glance from her mother, Miss Simpson nodded her agreement, murmuring something that was again inaudible.

With a parting bow, Rush and Killer bade the two ladies good day and made their escape, temporary as it was to be.

"Pretty little thing, your countess-to-be," Killer commented as they walked to a nearby coffee shop.

"Aye, and I certainly could not ask for a more biddable girl. The prospect of such a mother-in-law, however…"

Killer chuckled. "No worse than my own mother, I daresay. I receive that sort of prodding about the desirability of marriage all the time, I assure you."

Rush chose not to reply. Though he could not deny a certain similarity between Lady Killerby's managing ways and Lady Simpson's, the comparison did nothing to reassure him.

Despite her urging them to depart early, a full hour passed before Aunt Philomena finally noticed the time and sent for the carriage. "The coachman should be waiting by the time you get downstairs," she said, shooing them off to shop.

Violet much preferred to walk, though she knew better than to say so to her aunt. When they stepped outdoors a few minutes later, she told the driver to return the carriage to the mews .

"After so many days' travel I am more than ready for a bit of exercise and fresh air," she told Brigid as they headed toward Bond Street. "Aren't you?"

Her maid nodded, looking around with wide eyes. "I never knowed Lunnon was so big," she whispered in awestruck tones.

"I forgot you were asleep when we arrived last night," Violet said. "All the more reason to walk, for one cannot experience London properly cooped up in a carriage."

As proof of that, Violet noticed many things along the way she had missed before—vendors on street corners selling flowers or bunches of herbs, or offering to sharpen scissors and knives. And the horses! Heavy dray horses pulling carts, smartly matched pairs drawing equally smart phaetons, prime bloods with leather-booted gentlemen on their backs—Violet loved them all. She didn't even mind the smells, scarcely noticed when riding in Aunt Philomena's stuffy coach last year.

A small urchin obligingly swept the first crossing they came to and Violet rewarded him with a penny and a smile. The delighted child gave her a gap-toothed grin in return.

"Really, things could not have fallen out more perfectly," she reflected with satisfaction as they neared their destination. "Once Aunt Philomena leaves for Brighton, we shall have the house to ourselves and all of London to enjoy as we please."

"I still don't like it, Miss." Brigid glanced nervously over her shoulder. "I overheard the housekeeper asking one of the other servants why neither of us brought our abigails. Should she mention it to Lady Puttercroft, she's bound to ask questions and then it will all come out."

Violet chuckled. "No one can mention anything to my aunt, for she never gives them a chance. Remember what she said about her physician? We need only keep up the pretense until morning and everything will be fine—though perhaps after she's gone we should bring the servants in on the scheme."

"Happen we'll have to, or I dasn't talk again the whole time we're here."

"I'm sure you'll learn to speak more properly in time, but I suggest you stay silent while we do our shopping. Madame Fanchot has the ear of every gossipmonger in Town. If word of what we are doing got around to someone like Lady Mountheath, it could wreck all."

"Who is Lady Mountheath?"

"The most spiteful gossip in all of London. She never misses a chance to destroy a reputation, given the least ammunition. It was she who spread word of my, ah, little departures from convention last year, prompting Aunt Philomena to send me away. She has two shrewish daughters who are nigh as bad as their mother and like to get worse as they age into spinsters."

Brigid looked more frightened than ever. "I do wish you'd give over trying to make me out something I'm not, Miss."

Violet sent her abigail a look both sympathetic and exasperated. "I wanted to give you a bit of fun, Brigid, but I don't wish to make you uncomfortable."

"I know, Miss, and I'm that grateful. But I'm no lady and never mean to be. Anyways, from what little I've seen of the world, I'm like to have more freedom as I am. Ladies like yourself have ever so many Society rules to follow."

"True enough," Violet agreed with a laugh. "Not that I'm particularly good at following them. If you really would prefer not to take part in this charade, you may hide in your room when we get back. I'll tell Aunt Philomena you have the headache so you need not play the role of Dina again."

To that Brigid eagerly agreed.

It occurred to Violet that she could use a similar excuse once her aunt left for Brighton. By claiming Lady Puttercroft was indisposed, she might convince some eligible gentleman to escort her about Town in her stead. One of her brother's friends, perhaps. Julian Bigsby should be in London now, as well.

Upon their entering Madame Fanchot's establishment, the famed modiste and two of her assistants came forward to greet them.

"Ah, Miss Turpin, how lovely to see you again!" the proprietress exclaimed in a distinctly French accent. "I was quite disappointed last Season that you were unable to come for your final fitting before leaving Town, but you see I remembered your size and preferences perfectly." She gestured to a table spread with shimmering satins, silks and muslins in shades somewhat brighter than most debutantes wore.

"And this must be Mrs. Turpin, the one Lady Puttercroft told me about." She turned to Brigid, who instantly looked anxious again. "What a delight she will be to dress, with such vivid auburn hair."

Violet was about to tell the modiste about the girl's fictitious cold when an interruption occurred.

"Is that Miss Turpin?" came a voice from behind her.

Violet looked around. "Lady Simpson, how nice to see you. Is Mary, er, Miss Simpson with you?"

"Aye, she is being fitted up for a few gowns." Lady Simpson gestured toward a back room. "Your aunt said you would be in Town this week. I promised her we would call when you arrived."

"Yes, she mentioned it over breakfast. Alas, she was feeling indisposed, so did not accompany me this morning."

Lady Simpson clucked her tongue sympathetically, then turned a curious glance on Brigid. "I take it this is your brother's new wife? Lady Puttercroft said she would be sharing her duty as chaperone this Season. Is this your first visit to London, Mrs. Turpin?"

With a distressed glance at Violet, Brigid mutely nodded.

"I fear my sister-in-law is somewhat indisposed as well," Violet said quickly. "That is, she recently suffered a violent cold, and has not yet recovered the use of her voice. She is otherwise feeling quite well, however—or so she assures me."

"Well, I'll not keep you from your shopping," Lady Simpson said after expressing appropriate sympathy toward Brigid. "I must see how Mary is getting on with her fitting. I know she will be delighted to see you when she is finished."

She moved off toward the back of the shop and Violet breathed a small sigh of relief at having passed the first test of her plan. As there no longer seemed a need to have expensive gowns made up for Brigid, Violet suggested Madame Fanchot begin with herself. Any extra money could go toward baby clothes.

The modiste was quick to oblige and soon Violet had the fun of sorting through the very latest patterns and fabrics. She had already selected two lengths of satin, one of calico, and a rich lilac velvet for a second riding habit when Mary Simpson finally emerged from her fitting.

The two young ladies greeted each other warmly while Lady Simpson eyed Violet's fabric choices with raised brows.

"Are not some of those rather, ah, colorful for an unmarried lady like yourself?" she inquired, fingering a magenta silk. "Or are these for Mrs. Turpin?"

The magenta would clash horribly with Brigid's hair—or Dina's, for that matter—though it would complement Violet's own coloring nicely. Alas, most would consider it inappropriate for a debutante.

"Actually—" she began, when the outer door to the shop opened and two gentlemen walked in.

Violet's breath caught in her throat on seeing Lord Rushford for the first time since their kiss at Ivy Lodge. A swirl of conflicting emotions engulfed her: embarrassment, renewed appreciation of how very handsome he was…and panic.

Both he and Lord Killerby, who was with him, were quite well acquainted with Dina. There would be no deceiving *them* about Brigid's identity! Pinning on what she hoped was a carefree smile, she frantically tried to think her way out of this pickle.

CHAPTER SEVEN

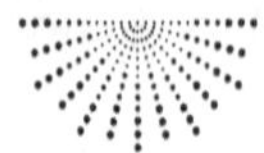

Rush stopped cold on unexpectedly encountering the girl who had dominated his dreams so much of late. Completely unprepared for the flood of sensations that assailed him, he had to fight to retain his composure when Lady Simpson turned to him with a smile.

"I must say, your timing is impeccable, my lords," she exclaimed as he and Lord Killerby entered the shop. "Mary has only just finished with her fittings and, as you see, she is renewing a previous acquaintance."

Rush was still too stunned to respond immediately. Fortunately, Killer filled the breach before his hesitation could become obvious.

"Why, Miss Turpin! We had no idea you would be here as well. What a stroke of luck. We were going to call on you later today, were we not, Rush?"

Lord Rushford finally found his voice. "Er, yes. Yes, we were. This is...a happy surprise indeed."

"Oh! I take it you both have a prior acquaintance with Miss Turpin?" Lady Simpson asked in surprise.

Miss Turpin spoke for the first time since their arrival, her voice nearly as unsteady as Rush's. "Yes, my lady. They are...both old friends of my brother's."

"Aye, we were all together in the Shires recently," Killer added. "I must say, Miss Turpin, our last hunts were not nearly so enjoyable without you."

Lady Simpson's brows rose even higher. "Never tell me you actually participated in a fox hunt, Miss Turpin?"

Rather than dissemble, she nodded. "I did indeed, my lady, more than once. I enjoyed it immensely."

"Put the rest of us to shame, she did," Killer declared. "Pity more ladies don't hunt, if you ask me."

Though Lady Simpson looked positively scandalized, her daughter gazed admiringly at Miss Turpin.

"I do wish I could have seen it. You always were the brave one, Violet, as I well remember from when we were at Miss Gebhart's together." It was the longest sentence Rush had ever heard Miss Simpson utter.

"Perhaps you can visit the Shires next autumn, Mary," Miss Turpin suggested. "I mean to go again, if my brother will allow it."

Before Miss Simpson could respond, her mother intervened. "My daughter will do no such thing. Pray do not encourage her to follow your example, Miss Turpin, for I recall all too well your lamentable tendency to disregard convention. No doubt that is why Lady Puttercroft was so happy your sister-in-law would be here to help keep an eye on you this Season."

As she spoke, she gestured toward Miss Turpin's abigail, whom Rush recalled seeing briefly at Ivy Lodge. Which made little sense.

"I, ah, yes. Well." Miss Turpin threw a decidedly flustered look toward Rush and Killer, then quickly turned away, her color rising. "Oh! I have just this moment recollected that I promised my aunt we would be back by noon, so I am afraid we must be going at once. I quite lost track of the time."

The modiste stepped forward in some concern. "But your purchases, Miss Turpin?"

"Yes, yes, you have the patterns I selected, so pray have them made up with these." She swept a hand over a shimmering pile of fabric on a nearby table. "I trust your judgment, Madame Fanchot, but should you have any questions, just send a note round and I will be happy to answer them."

"But…what of Mrs. Turpin's gowns?" The modiste looked pointedly at the maid.

Oddly, Miss Turpin made no more effort to correct Madame Fanchot's misapprehension than she had Lady Simpson's.

Rush was about to ask what the devil was going on when Violet shot him a look of mingled plea and warning that instantly aroused his suspicions.

Her next words only strengthened them. "Oh, never mind those just now. We, ah, really must get back immediately, or my aunt will be frightfully worried." With a sketchy curtsey toward them all, she ushered her maid toward the outer door.

"A moment, Miss Turpin," Rush called out.

One hand already on the door, she turned with obvious reluctance. "Yes?"

"As Lady Puttercroft is not with you, I feel I should offer you my escort back to her house. Your brother, I feel certain, would expect no less of me."

Lady Simpson frowned. "But my lord, I thought—"

Rush disarmed her with his best smile. "I'm sure Lord Killerby will be more than pleased to see you and your daughter home, my lady. It is fortunate, is it not, that there are two of us, that neither set of ladies need traverse the streets of London unaccompanied? I will call upon you once I have seen the Turpin ladies to Lady Puttercroft's."

He then turned back to Violet, who appeared to be laboring under some strong emotion. The girl was clearly up to something, and he intended to discover what.

"Shall we?" He opened the door for her and, with a look both confused and apprehensive, she swept past him with her maid.

"Have you no carriage to summon, Miss Turpin?" he asked when they had walked past several other shops.

Not meeting his eye, she shook her head. "No. I, ah, preferred to walk."

"Do you mean to say that Lady Puttercroft had no fault to find with you walking all the way to Bond Street, accompanied only by your maid? I had understood from your brother that she has a far stricter sense of propriety than to allow such a thing."

"I, ah, may not have mentioned to her that I intended to forgo the carriage. After two long days of travel, however, I very much needed to stretch my legs a bit."

"I see," he said, though he still couldn't claim he did. "Rather as you neglected to mention to Lady Simpson or the modiste that your maid is not, in fact, Mrs. Turpin? How came they to make such an error in the first place?"

Her cheeks grew noticeably pinker. "Er, well, you see… When we first arrived, Madame Fanchot jumped to the conclusion that my Brigid was Dina, because my aunt had described her and they share the same coloring."

Rush turned to regard the following maid with a critical eye and realized that much was true. The girl was also of a similarly diminutive stature, but there all resemblance ended, for their features were not at all alike.

"And you did not correct her?"

"I…I was just about to do so when Lady Simpson spotted us and made the same assumption. It occurred to me that she might not consider it quite…proper that I had walked to Bond Street with only my abigail, so I did not immediately correct her for fear she might mention it to my aunt."

"And Lady Simpson had no suspicion of the truth even after speaking with your abigail?"

Miss Turpin chewed at her lower lip before replying. "I, ah, may have implied that Dina lost her voice due to a recent cold so that Brigid's speech would not give her away," she confessed.

"So you compounded your original lapse of walking out unattended by telling Lady Simpson a falsehood. Did it not occur to you that she would discover soon enough that Mrs. Turpin is not in Town? She implied that she and your aunt are friends. I rather doubt Lady Puttercroft will be pleased to learn—"

"Oh, but you will not tell her, will you?" She looked imploringly up at him with those bewitching dark blue eyes. "We left the shop before my little fib was discovered, so there was no real harm done. If Lady Simpson should ask later, I can say that my brother and his wife went back to Ashcombe sooner than planned. No doubt my mother will be telling all the world their news soon, which would explain their sudden departure."

Thor had not been wrong that the girl bore watching—she'd been in London less than a day and was already up to mischief. He was careful not to let his amusement show, as that would only encourage her. Rush had, after all, promised to keep her out of trouble, if at all possible. Clearly the task would prove every bit as challenging as he'd feared.

When they reached the Puttercroft house a few moments later, she thanked him prettily for escorting her there. "I would invite you in, my lord, but my aunt has been rather indisposed of late. She recently turned her ankle, you see, so is unable to navigate the stairs to receive callers."

The explanation seemed plausible, but something in her manner suggested there was more to the story.

"Even so, I would feel remiss if I did not make any attempt to pay my respects to Lady Puttercroft. I'll have my name sent up and she can choose to receive me or not. That way I can leave knowing I have done my duty."

As he'd half expected, Miss Turpin seemed distressed by his insistence. She did not argue, however, and moment later they were admitted by an elderly butler, to whom Lord Rushford extended his card.

"Oh, pray do not trouble yourself, Wiggins." Miss Turpin reached for the small rectangle of parchment. "I am going upstairs to put off my cloak anyway, so I can easily take Lord Rushford's card up myself."

No doubt about it, something havey-cavey was going on. He'd give his oath Miss Turpin had no intention of telling her aunt he was here. But why? Keeping hold of his card when Miss Turpin would have taken it, he pointedly handed it to the butler instead.

"I'm sure Lady Puttercroft would prefer to have the niceties observed," he said mildly, but in a tone that brooked no disagreement.

With a bow, the butler ascended the stairs.

~

Violet's heart sank as she watched Wiggins depart. Perhaps Aunt Philomena would be too caught up in preparing for tomorrow's journey to speak with Lord Rushford?

Alas, only a moment later her aunt's carrying voice floated down from two floors above.

"How delightful! No doubt they encountered him while shopping. Pray show them all up here, Wiggins. Lord Rushford is a great friend of my nephew's, so I am certain he will take no offense if I receive him in my private sitting room rather than the parlor."

The butler returned a moment later with the dreaded summons. Violet accompanied Lord Rushford up the stairs with mounting trepidation. Surely there must be *some* way to salvage her lovely plan? She had been so close to success!

"You may wait in my chamber," she whispered to Brigid when they reached the upper landing. "No need for you to get into trouble as well." Nor did she wish to risk the girl blurting out something that might make matters even worse.

Clearly relieved, Brigid slipped into Violet's room while the others continued on. Just before reaching her aunt's rooms, Violet put a hand on Lord Rushford's sleeve. "Please, my lord, if you will just allow me to—"

But it was too late.

"Ah, Lord Rushford, welcome," Lady Puttercroft exclaimed from her chaise longue. "As you can see, I currently find it difficult to move about, so I appreciate your forbearance in attending me here." She gestured toward her foot. "Pray don't mind the clutter. My maid is in the middle of packing my things for my journey to Brighton tomorrow. No doubt my niece or Mrs. Turpin informed you of it? Where is Mrs. Turpin, by the bye?"

"Er…in her room," Violet replied with another pleading glance at Lord Rushford. His only response was a raised eyebrow, which reassured her not at all.

Her aunt, oblivious to the exchange, clicked her tongue in sympathy. "Was her first foray into the shops of London too much for her? I cannot say I am surprised, for it must seem overwhelming to someone who has spent her whole life in the country. I hope you advised her to have a lie down? She may take her luncheon on a tray if she prefers, that she can remain quiet for the rest of the day. I'll have a nice tea brought up for the rest of us."

Lord Rushford cleared his throat. "Pardon me, my lady, but did I hear you say that you mean to leave London tomorrow?"

"Aye, to visit my sister. I can scarcely chaperone dear Violet about with my foot in this state, so with Mrs. Turpin here to do that office, I thought I might as well take the sea air for a fortnight or so."

The earl turned toward Violet with an expression of disbelief. "Do you mean to tell me, Miss Turpin, that your *aunt* also believes your sister-in-law is here in Town with you?"

Trapped, Violet gave no answer beyond a tiny nod.

"Whatever do you mean, Lord Rushford?" Aunt Philomena exclaimed. "Of course Mrs. Turpin is here in Town. I met her last night and again at the breakfast table this morning. I think I can safely trust the evidence of my own eyes."

Much to Violet's chagrin, he responded, "Unless I am greatly mistaken, madam, the woman you met was Miss Turpin's abigail, whom I will admit does bear a *superficial* resemblance to Mrs. Turpin. Mr. Turpin and his wife remained in Staffordshire, to prepare for the birth of their first child later this year."

Lady Puttercroft turned to Violet in astonishment. "Is this true?" she demanded. "The young lady who traveled here with you is your maid and not Mrs. Turpin?"

Violet swallowed. "I…I fear it is so, Aunt. But on my honor, I did not set out to deceive you! When we arrived last night, you assumed that my Brigid was Dina and I, ah, merely allowed your assumption to stand. I thought—"

"I can well imagine what you thought! You thought that if I believed you to have a proper chaperone here in my place, I would depart in ignorance, leaving you to your own devices with no supervision whatsoever. Have you no shame? Your mother assured me that you had learned your lesson after I sent you home for your transgressions last Season, but I see she was wrong. Well! Now I must write to poor Letitia to tell her I will not be visiting after all. I am exceedingly disappointed in you, Violet, indeed I am."

"I am sorry, Aunt Philomena," Violet replied in a small voice. "It was wrong in me, I know." She carefully avoided Lord Rushford's eye.

"It certainly was," her aunt returned with a sniff. "Thank heaven Lord Rushford exposed your little plot before I left Town. Have you *any* idea of the scandal it would cause if it became known you were staying here all alone but for the servants? You would be quite ruined! And after I promised your mother to see you well married—though part of the blame must rest on her head for misrepresenting your improvement since last Season. Hmph."

She turned back to Lord Rushford. "I pray you will excuse me, my lord, but I must write to my sister at once to cancel my visit. Then I must decide whether to allow my niece to remain in Town, confined to the house until my ankle heals, or to send her back to her mother. I fear our tea will have to be deferred to a later date."

"Of course," he replied with a slight bow. "I am sorry to have been the bearer of such distressing news. I promise you it had not occurred to me—"

"No, no, I owe you a great debt of gratitude, my lord, for had you not stopped in, I likely would have left London on the morrow in ignorance, and there is no knowing what mischief my niece might have got into. I'm sure you understand as well as I how dangerous such a circumstance would have been!"

"I do indeed," he said with a sidelong glance at Violet. "In fact, given your current immobility and Miss Turpin's, ah, unpredictability, might I venture a suggestion?"

Lady Puttercroft regarded him uncertainly. "A suggestion?"

He inclined his head. "If you would like, I can ask Lady Simpson if she would be willing to provide a measure of supervision for Miss Turpin until you are recovered. Her daughter and Miss Turpin are already well acquainted, and from what I know of Lady Simpson, she will likely be equal to the task."

"Why, what a capital idea, my lord! If she is willing, it would be an admirable solution. I will write Lady Simpson a note now, requesting her help."

She motioned to her maid for pen, paper and a lap desk

"I will be happy to deliver it, as I mean to call there shortly," Lord Rushford offered.

"That's very kind of you, my lord. Mind you, we must make certain Lady Simpson has no inkling of what my niece attempted to do. Otherwise she'd likely refuse outright, for her ideas of propriety are quite as stringent as my own."

"I quite agree. No good can come of this incident becoming generally known."

Though mortified by their conversation, carried on as though she were not even in the room, Violet dared not intervene. Lady Simpson was like to be every bit as strict as her aunt, and sharper-eyed besides, but her chaperonage would surely be better than spending weeks here as a virtual prisoner—or being sent home.

Her aunt penned a quick note to Lady Simpson. Giving it to Lord Rushford, she bade Violet see him out while she wrote another to her sister in Brighton.

"After that, Missie, you may go to your room to think over your sins. Perhaps then you will be less inclined to make Lady Simpson regret any assistance she may be kind enough to offer."

Mutely nodding, Violet left the room with Lord Rushford, bracing herself for yet another scold. Nor did he disappoint her.

"Really, Miss Turpin, what were you thinking?" he demanded when they reached the front door. "No doubt you are vexed at me for spoiling your little game, but your aunt is quite right that it could have meant your ruin—or worse—had it succeeded."

Though she knew she had done wrong, his patronizing air made her bristle. "I told my aunt the truth that I did not originally set out to deceive her. The original mistake was hers. I would have corrected it, but she never gave me a chance. Every time I tried, she interrupted with more to say until at length the temptation to go along with her assumption became rather too great for me to resist."

"Yes, I have observed how very susceptible you are to temptation," he said dryly.

She felt her face flame, knowing he referred to her wantonly kissing him in the stables at Ivy Lodge. He made no mention of that, however.

"Witness your attempted elopement a few months since," he said instead. "If not for your sister-in-law, you would now be married to a fortune hunter."

Violet sucked in a breath. "How did you know about that? My family went to great pains to keep it quiet."

"Your brother sought my advice when he first received word you'd run off. Not to worry, I've never told another soul. The incident did, however, give me early insight into your character. I therefore felt it prudent to agree when your brother asked me to keep you out of mischief in his stead while in Town. I hardly expected to discover it necessary immediately after my arrival here, however."

"How dared Grant ask you to interfere in my life?" she demanded, brushing the rest aside. "And how dared you agree to do so? You are not my guardian, Lord Rushford. You have no right—"

"To protect you from your own folly?" he interrupted harshly. "You think I should have held my tongue upstairs and allowed you to bring probable ruin upon your head? I owe your brother a far greater debt of friendship than that. Headstrong and foolish as you are, he cares about your safety and reputation. I will therefore do my part to safeguard both, as I gave my word to do. Neither he nor Dina deserve to be embroiled in whatever scandal you are determined to create, particularly at such an important time in their lives."

Shame immediately undercut Violet's anger. "I...did not think of that."

"No, thinking ahead does not appear to be one of your strengths."

At that, her head snapped up defensively. "Do you plan your every word and deed ahead of time, my lord? How very boring that must be."

"I try to. Failing to plan during war-time held the potential for disaster, as I learned to my cost." A shadow of pain or sadness clouded his eyes, then was gone. "No doubt Lady Simpson will send word to your aunt about what she might be willing to do for you," he continued when she made no reply. "Meanwhile, do your best to stay out of trouble, won't you? Hard as I know that will be for you."

Donning his hat, his face still set in uncompromising lines, he touched the brim and departed.

Violet stood alone in the foyer for a long moment, angry and humiliated. It seemed that Lord Rushford's poor opinion of her was formed long before that foolish kiss in the stables. Today's incident had only served to lower it further. Not that she should care two straws about the opinion of someone so narrow-minded.

Mounting the stairs to her chamber to await the pronouncement of her fate, she could not understand why her heart felt so heavy.

For the second time that day, Rush turned his steps toward Cavendish Square and the Simpson house. As he walked, he struggled to place reason above emotion, which had nearly betrayed him again just now. It had been devilishly difficult to maintain his stern demeanor when Miss Turpin's pert defiance made him long to kiss her breathless instead.

Folly! he chided himself. *Arrant folly!* This latest start of hers only underscored—again—what a disastrous choice she would be for a wife.

Of course, a traitorous thought reminded him, she *did* enjoy taking gifts to her father's tenants...and she *was* extremely well-read, even compared to most men...

No. He'd made a far more eligible choice in Miss Simpson. Not to mention that if he broke that engagement only to offer for Miss Turpin, it would damage both his reputation and hers. Lady Simpson would see to that.

By the time he reached Cavendish Square, he had renewed his determination to see his prior commitment through. Still, it was with somewhat depressed spirits that he rang the bell.

"Ah, Lord Rushford," Lady Simpson smilingly greeted him. "I've just asked Lord Killerby to join us for luncheon. I felt that was the least we could do after he was so obliging as to escort us home. Won't you join us as well?"

As Lady Puttercroft's promised tea had been deferred, he readily accepted the invitation.

"I come bearing a message from Lady Puttercroft," he said then, handing Lady Simpson her letter. "She is rather hoping you might be willing to take her niece under your wing while she recovers from a sprained ankle."

Lady Simpson perused the note with raised brows. "But what of Mrs. Turpin, her nephew's wife?"

"I fear she is obliged to return to the country." Rush sent a quick, cautioning glance at Killer, lest he contradict the story. "She and her husband have happily discovered that their family is to have a new addition this year and Mr. Turpin feels she will do better away from the dirt and noise of London during these early days."

He hadn't precisely been authorized to share that, but knowing Thor's mother, it would not remain a secret for long anyway.

"Well, that is lovely news, to be sure. I cannot disagree about the unhealthfulness of London's air for a woman in her condition. What a mercy she is recovered from her cold, save for her voice. Given that, I've no objection to chaperoning the girl for a week or two."

"Then Violet will be going about with us this Season?" Miss Simpson sounded rather more animated than usual. "I should like that above all things, for she is great fun to be around."

Her mother raised an eyebrow. "Any *fun* you have with Miss Turpin will only be of the most proper sort, for I shall take this charge as seriously as her aunt would. Still, it will be no bad thing for you to have a lively companion to draw you out a bit. I shall let Lady Puttercroft know I am willing and call upon her tomorrow to discuss the details."

"Well, that's just capital," Killer exclaimed. "It is clear the young ladies already hold each other in affection. With the two of them offering twice the incentive, we must plan a few outings together, eh, Rush?"

"Undoubtedly." Rush took care to smile at Miss Simpson as he spoke, that she and her mother might credit his eagerness to the proper lady.

Lady Simpson seemed pleased by his implication that her daughter was the main attraction. Miss Simpson, however, did not notice, for her gaze had already returned to her lap.

"Excellent idea, to have Miss Turpin go about with the Simpsons," Killer commented when the two gentlemen at length left the house. "Was it yours or Lady Puttercroft's?"

"Mine," Rush confessed, "though she needed no persuasion. 'Twas the only thing I could think of that might prevent her sending Miss Turpin back to Lincolnshire and so deprive her of another Season."

"Send her back?" Killer asked in surprise. "Why would she do so?"

Rush explained the deception Miss Turpin had perpetrated upon her aunt with disturbingly near success. "Can you imagine what sort of mischief Miss Turpin would have got into had Lady Puttercroft left Town as planned?"

Killer shuddered. "It doesn't bear thinking about. Particularly as we promised Thor we'd keep her out of trouble—a greater challenge than I anticipated, it appears."

"I had fewer illusions on that head than you did," Rush assured his friend. "I suspected from the start it would be no easy task to keep her out of the scandal sheets, for she seems quite bent on landing herself there. With any luck, Lady Simpson's assistance will make our promise a bit less difficult to keep."

"Aye, it's clear she keeps her daughter on a tight rein, though it scarcely seems necessary in her case. A sweet girl, Miss Simpson. I don't wonder you fixed upon her. Meanwhile, I should say the sooner Miss Turpin can be safely married off, the better. 'Tis the only sure way to relieve both Thor and us of responsibility for her."

Rush could not disagree, though the thought of relinquishing that responsibility to another man gave him rather less comfort than it should.

CHAPTER EIGHT

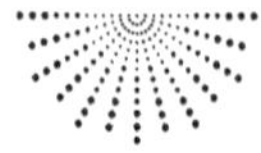

Violet found spending the rest of the day in her room tedious, once her resentment and embarrassment faded. To pass the time, she fell to rereading her favorite passages from *The Saint of Seven Dials* and fantasizing about the various ways she might help the fabled thief if she could only find him.

Her only other relief from boredom came when Brigid brought up her dinner.

"I'm sorry your plan did not work out as you'd hoped, Miss," she said, setting the tray on a small table. Though her words were sympathetic, Violet had no difficulty discerning the relief in her expression.

"No, it is I who am sorry, Brigid. I should never have insisted you attempt a role that made you so uncomfortable for the sake of my own selfish pleasure. I quite deserved what happened—though I'll not soon forgive Lord Rushford for being the instrument of my failure."

The next morning, her irritation at his lordship was somewhat appeased by her aunt's announcement over breakfast, which she was again invited to take in her chamber.

"You will be pleased to hear that Lady Simpson has offered to act as your chaperone in my stead while my ankle heals, just as Lord

Rushford suggested," Aunt Philomena said as Violet poured out the coffee. "She and her daughter mean to call upon us later this morning. I say 'us,' for it will not do for Lady Simpson to suspect I have already had reason to restrict you to your room."

"I am glad Lady Simpson agreed," Violet said, avoiding her aunt's censorious eye. "It will be pleasant to spend more time with Mary."

Her aunt sniffed. "Do not think you are being rewarded for the prank you attempted. I am taking this step for our family's sake, not yours." She continued in the same vein for the duration of the meal, concluding with, "Remember, you are to say nothing to Lady Simpson about what you attempted to do. I must hope that Lord Rushford will hold his tongue as well."

Much as it rankled to defend him, Violet felt obliged to reassure her aunt on that point. "According to my brother, Lord Rushford is a great keeper of secrets. I happen to know that the two of them got into more than a few scrapes together during their school days."

Lady Puttercroft smiled indulgently. "Yes, well, boys will be boys. Back you go to your room now, to change into whichever of your morning gowns is least outmoded. Our guests will be arriving soon."

Violet returned to her chamber grumbling over the vastly different standards applied to young men compared to young women. No one ever excused *her* bits of folly by saying "girls will be girls."

While Brigid helped her to change, Violet told her about Lady Simpson's offer.

"It might be best if you stow that blue cambric in the bottom of a trunk for the remainder of the Season. That may lessen the likelihood of Lady Simpson recognizing you as the woman she met at Madame Fanchot's yesterday."

Brigid seemed more than happy to do so. She also readily agreed to keep her hair close under her cap whenever they were in public, and particularly around the Simpson ladies. Her cheerful compliance made Violet feel even guiltier for what she'd put the poor girl through.

A short time later, Violet was summoned to join Aunt Philomena as Wiggins and her maid assisted her down one flight of stairs to the parlor. There, she settled herself in a plush armchair, her injured foot now propped on a pink velvet ottoman.

"Well! That was not so very difficult after all," she declared. "Had I attempted this yesterday, I need not have received Lord Rushford in my sitting room."

This last was delivered with such a stern look that Violet felt compelled to apologize yet again.

"I did say I was sorry, Aunt," she said meekly.

"Yes, yes, I know, and we'll not dwell further on it, so long as you adhere strictly to convention from now on. Should I hear word of any other irregularities from Lady Simpson, however—"

"You will not, Aunt Philomena, I promise you," Violet truthfully assured her. For if she *did* flout the rules again, she would make quite certain her aunt never learned of it. Nor Lord Rushford, as he'd no doubt feel obliged to carry tales again.

Her aunt frowned at Violet's attire. "I do hope Madame Fanchot can have at least one or two new dresses ready for you soon. That thing must be two or three seasons old."

Violet hoped the same, for she was quite eager to be allowed into company—and to escape her aunt's. Directing Violet to take up a piece of embroidery, Aunt Philomena progressed from one tedious topic to another until the Simpson ladies were finally announced.

"How good to see you again, Mary," Violet greeted her friend, motioning her to the chair beside hers. "I was sorry to rush off yesterday, before we'd had time to exchange more than pleasantries."

"I was sorry, too," Miss Simpson replied with a smile. "Now, however, I hope we shall see quite a lot of each other, as Mama has agreed to have you with us much of the time until your aunt is fully recovered."

Lady Simpson nodded. "I felt I could do no less for dear Lady Puttercroft, particularly as you and my Mary are such friends. She has been a bit lonely since arriving in Town, though Lord Rushford was most flatteringly attentive yesterday." She bestowed a fond look upon her daughter. "Assuming Sir Clarence's letter consenting to the match arrives within the next two months, as I expect, we will see Mary a Countess by the summer."

At her mother's words, Mary blushed deeply. "Mama, I thought we were not to make that public before hearing back from my father?"

"I agreed with Lord Rushford that it should not be put into the papers just yet," Lady Simpson allowed, "but he surely cannot mind our sharing your news with such close friends."

"I…I suppose not."

Violet felt as though an invisible hand had suddenly seized her by the throat, making speech impossible. Mary, little Mary Simpson, was *engaged* to Lord Rushford? How could that possibly be? Neither he nor her brother had said a word about such a thing while at Ivy Lodge, nor afterward!

"Next time he calls, my love, you really must exert yourself to talk more, or he may begin to believe you mute," Lady Simpson was now admonishing her daughter. "As the marriage agreements have not yet been signed, we don't wish to give him any reason to regret his offer. If you could just bring yourself to flirt with him a bit—"

She broke off at her daughter's alarmed expression.

"Well. Time enough for that, I suppose." Then, to her hostess, "I am happy to see you looking so well, Lady Puttercroft. I daresay it will not be many days before you are up and about again."

In reply, Aunt Philomena shook her head sadly. "Mr. Franklin tells me I must limit my walking for another week or two. Had I been able to go to Brighton I should not have minded, for I can take the sea air perfectly well from my sister Letitia's terrace. I had intended to spend a fortnight with her during this early part of the Season, you see. Alas, when my nephew and his wife decided to spend the spring in Staffordshire, my leaving London became quite out of the question. I am exceedingly happy for them, of course, but I was quite looking forward to seeing Brighton and my sister again. Letitia will be most disappointed, I know."

Lady Simpson clucked her tongue in sympathy.

"I cannot thank you enough for your willingness to act as chaperone to my niece during this interval," Lady Puttercroft continued.

"Otherwise she would be quite trapped in the house with me, for I could never allow her out unsupervised. Not when— Well, never mind that. 'Tis enough to say that we are both exceedingly grateful to you for your generosity."

The two older ladies then fell into conversation about the latest gossip and fashions.

Violet, finding her voice at last, turned to Mary. "Is it true what your mother says about Lord Rushford?" she asked as lightly as her lingering sense of shock allowed. "I...I had no idea you had made such a conquest."

Mary colored again. "I fear 'tis true. Lord Rushford is very obliging, but I confess that I find the thought of becoming his wife rather terrifying."

"Terrifying?" Violet was startled again. "Whatever do you find terrifying about Lord Rushford? To me, he seems quite...stodgy." She used the word as both a reminder for herself and reassurance for her friend.

"Stodgy? But he is a war hero, and so very dashing," Mary protested. "Mama persuaded me to go driving with him in his phaeton last summer and I vow I was frightened to death! I felt sure we would overturn, for it seems a most precarious vehicle."

Violet regarded her friend pityingly, though she rather envied her that experience. "Those high phaetons may look dangerous, but I assure you they are quite safe. At least in the hands of a skilled driver, as I'm sure Lord Rushford is."

"I suppose." Mary did not look convinced. "Mama of course was delighted by his offer, for she had been determined to see me wed a title."

Violet felt a sudden need to change the subject. To her relief, a footman entered just then with a message from Madame Fanchot that two of Violet's new gowns would be ready for fitting tomorrow.

"May I go, if I bring my abigail?" she asked eagerly.

Her aunt frowned. "I am afraid I do not consider your abigail alone sufficient escort for you to go to Bond Street, particularly given— That is—"

"I am to have another fitting at Madame Fanchot's myself tomorrow," Mary interrupted. "Mama, Violet may come with us, may she not?"

At Lady Simpson's ready concurrence, Lady Puttercroft could scarcely express her thanks warmly enough.

"Well, how perfect this is! I had been fretting over how my niece was to finish her shopping without Mrs. Turpin. She still needs to buy nearly everything: gloves, a new parasol... I will make a list before tomorrow."

A few minutes later the two Simpson ladies took their leave, promising to call for Violet at half past ten the next morning.

When they were gone, Aunt Philomena bade Violet go to the writing desk in the corner of the parlor to write down all the various items her aunt felt sure she would need for her Season. Tedious as the task was, Violet welcomed the distraction. The news that Mary Simpson was to marry Lord Rushford distressed her far more than it should. Had she not already abandoned all hope of winning him herself?

She tried to be happy for her friend, telling herself that they would be very well suited, given Mary's timidity and Lord Rushford's prudishness. Nor was Mary likely to mind his lordship's high-handed management of her life, used as she was to her mother doing the same. Violet was still quite vexed at his interference in her own.

Still, convincing as her internal arguments were, she could not reason away the ache in her heart at the thought of Rush marrying her friend.

Rush spent his second morning in London at Tattersall's, for he was in need of a new mount for Town. After making his selection he lingered a while, simply to be around horses a bit longer, before repairing to Rushford House to change for luncheon. Lord Peter Northrup had suggested meeting at the Guards Club again to continue the conversation begun two days earlier.

"Your note implied you had received some new information?" Rush asked when he and Peter had ordered their meals. As before, they were seated at a corner table where they were less likely to be disturbed or overheard.

"I have indeed." Lord Peter adjusted the sleeve of his lime green jacket, a striking contrast to the yellow waistcoat beneath it. "He struck again last night, broke into the Simcox house. This time a maid was able to provide a fair description, for all he wore a mask."

"And?" Rush prompted.

"She described the man as tall and thin, with blond hair. That description confirmed what I already knew—that no one who has ever been a Saint of Seven Dials is committing these burglaries."

His phrasing caught Rush's attention. "Do you mean to say that more than one man has filled that role in the past?"

After a slight hesitation, Peter nodded. "There have actually been five different Saints thus far. Something I decided you should know, if you are to help me unmask this imposter."

Rush took a moment to absorb that remarkable information. "I take it the authorities have no suspicion of this? Certainly, I've never seen anything to that effect in the papers."

Lord Peter lifted a shoulder. "I believe the, ah, Saints have taken care that they should not. It is important that the poor denizens of Seven Dials have a single hero to look up to, to give them hope. The less the authorities know of the truth the better, should a future Saint choose to take up the mantle and resume his activities on behalf of the poor."

"Then there is no current Saint?"

The other man shook his head. "The most recent one retired at the end of last year. Since then, a small group of benevolently-minded people have endeavored to provide a measure of the assistance his burglaries formerly supplied."

"You clearly know the identities of all five of the previous Saints. I, ah, don't suppose you would be willing to share that knowledge with me?"

Frowning, Lord Peter lifted a shoulder. "Their secrets are not mine to share, though I've been given permission to tell you about the two most recent. One happens to be my best friend and the other…was my wife."

"Your wife!" Rush stared. "I would never guess a woman could have—" He broke off as it occurred to him how Violet Turpin would react if she heard him utter such a statement.

Lord Peter was grinning now. "Yes, well, my wife is rather a remarkable woman. Still, I suppose it would be more accurate to say that she *pretended* to be the Saint for a fortnight or so. Her sole motive was to prevent her younger brother becoming the Saint himself by convincing him the, ah, job was already taken. She never intended to continue beyond that."

"And your friend?"

"He'd lost an arm in the war and was well on his way to drinking himself into an early grave. Taking up the Saint's cause gave him new purpose."

Rush eyed the other man speculatively. "May I surmise that his doing so was your idea?"

"It was." Lord Peter smiled crookedly. "He took a bit of convincing, but it all turned out right in the end. Since he gave it up, there's been no Saint. Perhaps there never will be, though I suppose time will tell on that score. Meanwhile, I should very much like to put this current fellow, whoever he is, out of business."

"Agreed. Dare I ask if you've conceived a plan to ensure that? His methods certainly leave much to be desired."

Peter grimaced. "Indeed. He clearly lacks the true, ah, Saintly principles, as he's not above harming others during his robberies. Nor have my sources found evidence that any of his takings have made their way to the poor. I rather hope that the clumsiness of his methods will make him easier to snare. My friend Harry had a suggestion as to the how—an obvious one, but it should serve with this fellow."

"Bait a trap and lay an ambush?" Rush guessed.

"Exactly. That ruse very nearly caught two previous Saints, though not by the authorities. Bow Street also tried it early on, but of course the original Saint was far too crafty to be caught by such means." Peter chuckled. "I don't know that any of his successors ever quite measured up to the standard he set."

Rush was now exceedingly curious to know who that first Saint was, but knew better than to ask. "I suppose our first step, then, is to decide upon the bait. Then we must contrive a way to let this false Saint hear of it, that we may catch him as he takes it."

"That is precisely what I thought we might discuss over our luncheon."

Just then a manservant approached with a tray bearing two steaming plates of beef and roast potatoes, to which the two men did ample justice while sharing ideas on how best to nab the imposter.

After completing Violet's shopping list to the accompaniment of numerous soliloquies, Lady Puttercroft ordered a light luncheon to be served in the parlor. As they ate, she continued talking about anything and everything.

"—and that piping sample Madame Fanchot sent round quite put me in mind of the trims that were in fashion some twenty years ago, when dear Sir Horace was still alive. It must have been '97, or perhaps '96…no, no, I have it, I would have been 1795, because I recall that Letitia was still expecting her second child when we had a conversation on that very thing."

Violet stifled more than one sigh as she nattered on. Thank goodness she would soon be spending most of her time elsewhere. However strict Lady Simpson might be, going about with her would be preferable to suffering her aunt's perpetual monologues.

Relief arrived sooner than expected when Wiggins came to the parlor door, a mere half hour after the dishes were cleared away. "Excuse me, my lady, but a Mr. Bigsby is below."

Violet instantly dropped her pitiful attempt at embroidery. "Julian is here? Oh, show him up, Wiggins, do."

"A *close* acquaintance of yours, I presume?" Aunt Philomena's eyebrows rose, then lowered. "Pray keep in mind that this is not the country, Miss. Here in Town, I cannot condone the use of Christian names between ladies and gentlemen who are neither related nor betrothed. Over-familiarity is well known to lead to a lack of proper respect, and a young lady must *never*—"

She broke off at Julian's entrance. Looking even more handsome than he had in the Shires, in a coat of deep green superfine and buff breeches, he bowed deeply to them both.

"I give you good afternoon, ladies. Miss Turpin, London clearly agrees with you, for you are even lovelier than I recall." Then, turning his dazzling smile on Lady Puttercroft, "And who is your pretty friend? Never say this is your aunt, for she scarcely looks old enough to be a proper chaperone."

Pinkening, Aunt Philomena tittered, her stern demeanor abruptly dissolving. "You will turn my head with such talk, young man. I am indeed Lady Puttercroft, Miss Turpin's aunt. I take it your acquaintance with my niece is one of long standing?"

"Indeed it is," he replied, bending over the gloved hand the older woman simperingly extended to him. "I first met Violet—or, I beg your pardon, Miss Turpin—when she was but a girl. I was a school chum of her brother's, you see. I'd rather hoped to presume upon such old acquaintance to invite her out for a walk."

When Aunt Philomena hesitated, he added, "You are more than welcome to accompany us, my lady, if you are concerned about propriety. And may I tell you what a very fetching shade of puce your gown is?"

Lady Puttercroft's tiny frown disappeared. "Why, thank you. It was new only a fortnight since." She smoothed her skirts complacently. "As for walking, I fear I am not equal to it just now." She nodded toward her still-bandaged foot. "I suppose there is no harm in you young people taking a brief stroll, however, so long as my niece's abigail accompanies you."

"Of course." He directed another melting smile at the older lady. "I should never dream of taking her out of your sight otherwise."

Violet jumped to her feet, eager to make her escape. "Splendid. I will run upstairs to fetch Brigid and my cloak."

On returning to the parlor, Violet found Aunt Philomena again holding forth on the subject of spring fashions—sleeves, in particular. Not surprisingly, Julian appeared as ready to leave as Violet was, rising with alacrity the instant she appeared.

"Your observations are remarkably insightful, my lady, but I know you will not wish me to keep your niece waiting. Perhaps we can renew our conversation upon my return?" With a parting bow, he escorted Violet down the front stairs and out of doors, Brigid following a few paces behind.

"I cannot thank you enough, Julian, for securing my release from the house for a bit," Violet told him as they walked. "I was like to expire from boredom."

He chuckled. "Your aunt does seem to enjoy the sound of her own voice."

"You had but the tiniest sampling just now, I assure you. She is capable of going on so for hours without ceasing. By the bye, I must compliment you on striking just the right tone with her, for she is vain enough to adore flattery."

"I have found that to be true of most women—though *you* always seem able to see through empty compliments. It is one of the many things I appreciate about you, Violet. May I still call you Violet?"

She dimpled up at him. "Of course, so long as my aunt cannot hear you. She is quite the stickler for propriety."

"Not to worry. I shall be careful to reserve any remotely improper talk for your ears alone."

The smile that accompanied his words caused a delicious quiver in her midsection. Julian, she decided, was just the tonic she needed after this morning's unsettling news about Mary and Lord Rushford.

"Did your brother and sister-in-law not accompany you to London?" he asked a moment later.

"Oh! I suppose you will not have heard. They recently learned they are expecting a child, so my brother thought Dina would do better at home in Staffordshire. Her home, I mean, for she recently took possession of her family estate. As Grant has none of his own yet, they have chosen to live there."

He smiled. "They are to be congratulated, both on the child and that they have such a place to live until your brother inherits."

"I rather hope they will remain at Ashcombe for quite a long time," she confessed. "I am exceedingly fond of my father and would much prefer his demise be delayed for many, many years."

"Of course. Though I hope whenever that melancholy time does come, you also will be well provided for. Not that I need worry, I suppose, for you are bound to have made a brilliant match long before then."

Thrusting an unwelcome vision of Lord Rushford from her mind, she laughed. "Oh, yes, no doubt! I am thankful, however, that I need not depend upon it for my future. Buried as he always is in scholarly works of the past, my father is remarkably forward-thinking about some things. He has taken steps to ensure that my livelihood will never be dependent upon some man's whims."

"Has he?" His smile broadened. "Glad I am to hear it, for I have sadly known more than one lady to settle for a less than ideal situation in order to avoid relying on her family's charity."

"Yes, it is hard to believe that in these modern times, so-called marriages of convenience are still so common an occurrence. Most young ladies would surely prefer a love match, but too many are never given that choice."

Mary Simpson, for example, whose mother was determined she marry a title regardless of her feelings. Violet shivered—and not only because of the chill breeze.

Julian noticed at once. "What a selfish brute I am, keeping you out in the cold that I may enjoy your company a bit longer. There is a cozy little coffee shop just round the next corner...unless you think it improper to accompany me there?"

The warmth in Julian's eyes made her hesitate. Surely, however, there could be nothing objectionable about them taking tea together in a respectable public establishment, with her abigail in attendance?

"I should like that very much. Thank you."

He escorted her to a nondescript cafe tucked between two more fashionable shops. "It is not much to look at," he said apologetically as he ushered her inside, "but the coffee and tea are first rate, as are the lemon biscuits."

"Oh, I adore lemon biscuits," she exclaimed, catching the door before it could close in Brigid's face. "And I happen to know they are my abigail's very favorite."

"Then it will be my honor to procure a plate for you both." The smile he sent Brigid's way raised Violet's opinion of him further.

A few minutes later they were served steaming cups of tea and a plate of biscuits that proved every bit as good as promised. While they ate and sipped, Julian told amusing stories about some of the more eccentric members of the ton and shared a tidbit or two of the latest gossip.

"I don't suppose you hear anything of the Saint of Seven Dials?" Violet asked when he paused. "I've not seen a newspaper since leaving Plumrose, nigh on three weeks ago. Indeed, the last article I read about him was before Christmas."

The look he gave her was oddly speculative. "Still enamored of that rogue, are you? Then you will no doubt be pleased to hear that he is back to his old tricks after giving the nobs a full two months' respite."

"Yes, very pleased," she agreed, her heart lifting. "I began to fear he had ceased his activities for good and disappeared from London. Now my hopes of encountering him are revived. I have read that he sometimes masquerades as a gentleman to infiltrate the wealthier households?"

"So it is rumored. Of course, there is so much speculation about his identity that many conflicting stories are in circulation. I've no doubt that is just as he prefers it."

A certain slyness in his expression prompted Violet to exclaim, "Julian! Do you know more of him than you are revealing?"

"It…would be unwise of me to admit it, if so," he replied, looking suddenly conscious.

Violet sucked in a breath. "You've guessed who he is, haven't you? Do tell me, Julian! You must know I would never betray him."

"There is no one I would rather tell, but— Great heaven, look at the time!" he interrupted himself, gesturing toward the clock on the shop's mantelpiece. "I must get you back at once if I am not to incur Lady Puttercroft's wrath and risk her forbidding you to walk out with me again."

With great reluctance, Violet rose from her chair. "I should not like that either, for this is easily the most enjoyable hour I've spent since arriving in Town."

One corner of his well-shaped mouth quirked up. "In that case, you may count on me relieving your tedium as often as your aunt will allow it."

As they made their way back, she again pressed him on the matter of the Saint of Seven Dials but he continued, though good-naturedly, to put her off until they reached the house.

Lady Puttercroft did indeed have a few tart words to say about their having been gone so long, but Julian was able to soothe her back into smiling good spirits remarkably quickly. It was with distinct regret that Violet bade him farewell.

"What a pleasant young man that is," Aunt Philomena commented when he was gone. "I would have preferred your first outing with him to be of shorter duration, but it was most gallant of him to think first of your comfort by suggesting hot tea out of the wind."

Violet wholeheartedly agreed, already impatient for her next opportunity to wheedle information about the Saint of Seven Dials from him.

"Mind, you should not appear quite so eager as you did today to walk out with Mr. Bigsby or any other gentleman," Aunt Philomena cautioned her. "You do not want to be perceived as hanging out for a husband, for nothing frightens eligible gentlemen away more quickly than an appearance of desperation. 'Tis far better to be sought than to seek."

She went on to spout more such platitudes but Violet scarcely heard a word. Instead, she was replaying in her mind every word Julian had let drop about the Saint, more and more convinced that he was her key to discovering the fabled thief's identity.

CHAPTER NINE

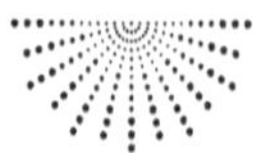

PROMPTLY AT HALF PAST TEN THE NEXT MORNING, LADY SIMPSON AND Mary called and, in as short a time as Aunt Philomena's speeches would allow, Violet left with them for Bond Street.

They stopped first at Madame Fanchot's for the two young ladies' fittings, then visited a shoemaker, a dry goods store and a milliner to supply the other items necessary to Violet's London wardrobe.

Lady Simpson bought Mary two new bonnets and a parasol as well, claiming it was none too soon for her daughter to begin thinking of herself as a countess. Nor was that the only time Lady Simpson referred to her daughter's conquest as they shopped.

Though she tried to ignore it, Violet experienced a small pinch at her heart with each mention. As Mary seemed uncomfortable hearing them as well, Violet felt justified in distracting her with amusing stories and cheeky observations about some of the people and items they encountered.

"I cannot tell you how pleased I am to spend much of the Season with you," Mary confided as they loaded their purchases into the carriage to return to Mortimer Street. "Not only are you great fun, you tend to compensate for my shyness, as you are anything but."

Violet grinned. "True enough. I shall try to keep you from hiding in corners, as you were always wont to do at school."

Mary looked both gratified and apprehensive.

As they drew up before Aunt Philomena's house, Mary suddenly said, "Mama, I have just had a thought. Why do we not invite Violet to stay with us for the next few weeks? Then Lady Puttercroft may go to visit her sister in Brighton, as she clearly wished to do, and we shall not need to fetch Violet every time we go out."

Though startled, Violet found the idea appealing. Among other things, it would spare her Aunt Philomena's inevitable reproaches if she returned late from any evening entertainments. To her relief, after a moment's consideration, Lady Simpson nodded.

"I cannot disagree that having her with us would be rather more convenient. I should also prefer to more closely supervise Miss Turpin if I am to be responsible for her reputation. I've not forgotten the whispers that circulated upon your sudden departure last Season," she informed Violet sternly. "No such starts will be tolerated from our house, I promise you."

"Of course not, my lady," Violet fervently assured her. "I realize now how wrong I was to play such pranks on my aunt last year. I would never dream of doing the same to you." Should she be tempted, she would simply have to resist—for a change.

Gathering up Violet's purchases, they went inside to put the suggestion to Lady Puttercroft. Not surprisingly, she agreed at once.

"Why, this will mean but a few days' delay of my visit to Brighton. How pleased Letitia will be! And I have been longing for a peep at my new grand-nephew, who came into this world only a few months since."

Within a few minutes everything was settled. Lady Simpson suggested Violet come to them the following afternoon, after which she could accompany them to Lady Plumfield's musicale that evening.

The moment they left, Aunt Philomena happily penned yet another letter to her sister, to advise her of this latest change in plans. Giving it to a footman to post, she turned smilingly to Violet.

"I must say, this has turned out quite splendidly! Lady Simpson has a vast circle of acquaintances she can introduce you to. She receives far more visitors than I do. Which reminds me—you had *three* gentleman callers while you were out."

"Oh?"

Lady Puttercroft nodded. "That charming Mr. Bigsby, as well as Lord Rushford and his friend Lord Killerby. All seemed quite disappointed to have missed you, though Lord Rushford expressed some satisfaction upon hearing you were with the Simpson ladies. No doubt he will be even more pleased to hear that Lady Simpson will now be able to keep you under her eye constantly.

"Speaking of Lord Rushford, was any more said today about his engagement to Miss Simpson? Really, it is quite a coup for her. After all, her father is but a baronet like my dear Sir Horace, despite his holdings in India. But then, Lady Simpson always did have...aspirations."

Violet forced a smile. "Indeed, she spoke of little else while we were out. But what can you tell me of this musicale at Lady Plumfield's tomorrow night?"

To her relief, Aunt Philomena obligingly launched into a lengthy soliloquy about the various people likely to be there and how her niece was to comport herself with each one. Dull as the litany was, Violet was grateful for the change of subject.

"With Lady Simpson on the job, think you we can consider our promise to Thor fulfilled?" Killer asked as he and Rush took luncheon together at White's.

"For the next hour or two, at least," Rush replied. "I rather doubt a single outing with Lady Simpson will cure Miss Turpin of her thirst for adventure, however."

They had called at the Simpsons' to find the ladies from home, then stopped in at Mortimer Street. There, Lady Puttercroft informed them of the ladies' shopping expedition—at great length.

Killer laughed. "No, I suppose not. Still, it's a reprieve. Where to next?"

"I'd thought to look in on Parliament," Rush replied. Though he had realized last year that he would never share his late father's zeal for the legislative process, he felt he owed it to his memory to at least make the occasional effort. "You'll come, won't you? It's as much your duty as mine, you know."

"What, waste a perfectly good day listening to old men prose on for hours when there are so many more enjoyable things to do in Town?" Killer exclaimed in horror. "M'mother insisted I attend last year and I found it deadly dull."

Rush regarded him with amusement. "You don't wish to have a say in the workings of our government?"

"A say? I'm no orator, nor have I studied up on the issues. I'll leave that to responsible chaps like yourself."

"Not really my sort of thing either," Rush confessed, "but given how prominent my father was in government, it seems rather disrespectful to ignore my obligations completely. Come, Killer, we'll put in a couple of hours, see what is being discussed, then slip away at the first break to congratulate ourselves on our virtue over a well-earned pint or two."

After a bit more urging, Killer consented, though with poor grace. "And you'll be buying those pints, for I consider myself doing you a favor by going."

"Fair enough," Rush conceded with a laugh, "though I could point out that you owe me a favor already. Had you held your tongue after I confided my intentions toward Miss Simpson to you last summer, I likely wouldn't have felt obliged to follow through so quickly with an actual offer."

"Aye, mentioning it to m'mother was a mistake, as she's an intimate of Lady Simpson's." Killer grimaced. "At the time, I merely wished to distract her from harping upon *my* need to marry—as if there is any hurry about the succession. Frightfully sorry and all that. Does this mean you are having second thoughts about Miss Simpson?"

Rush shrugged. "I came to Town last summer with the intention of finding *some* wife or other. My mother's charities currently have no one to administer them, and only my future countess can use the balance of her dowry to benefit the estate. Even the interest accrues solely to Mother's charities until I wed."

"Quite the clever manager, your mother," Killer said. "Not so dissimilar to my own in that regard, though yours never extended her management to your personal life, as mine does."

"Not while she was alive, but she's doing so rather effectively from the grave," Rush said. "The devil of it is, I primarily settled upon Miss Simpson because she did not fling herself into my path or chatter away like all the other debutantes. Based only on that, I concluded that she was the most thoughtful and responsible of the bunch. Now I've begun to wonder whether someone so used to deferring to her mother will be able to step into the breach left by mine."

Killer nodded sagely. "A valid concern, to be sure. There's no denying it's a weighty responsibility to thrust upon a girl so young and inexperienced as Miss Simpson. Were your mother still alive, she could train up your wife to the job, but as it is…"

"Yes, well, it is rather too late to think of that now. For the sake of Rushford Abbey and its dependent concerns, as well as my mother's memory, I can only hope Miss Simpson proves up to the task when the time comes."

Though looking thoughtful, Killer made no reply until they reached Westminster Palace. "You've admitted the awkwardness of keeping Miss Turpin out of trouble without making Miss Simpson or her mother suspect your motives," he abruptly said then. "Just want you to know I'm available to call upon either one when you are occupied with the other. If that might be helpful?"

"It might indeed," Rush replied gratefully. "I may well take you up on that offer. Hope you won't end up regretting it."

Grinning, Killer shrugged and accompanied Rush into the hallowed halls of Parliament, there to do their duty by crown and country however tedious it might prove.

~

The next day saw renewed preparations for Aunt Philomena's trip to Brighton. After breakfast, Violet clumsily attempted to mend a few items for her aunt while hearing about every sight and person Lady Puttercroft expected to encounter in the seaside town.

The longer her aunt droned on, the more Violet looked forward to her imminent departure, though perhaps not so much as she had before Lord Rushford spoiled her daring plan. Still, the next fortnight was sure to be far more enjoyable under Lady Simpson's roof than this one.

Except for Lord Rushford's inevitable visits there.

Those would inevitably remind her of how poor an opinion he held of herself, while at the same time forcing her to witness his courtship of Mary. No matter how prudent a match it might be, on both sides, Violet still felt a definite heaviness at heart whenever she thought of it —which was far too often.

She was chiding herself yet again for her reluctance to celebrate her friend's good fortune when Julian Bigsby was announced. Her spirits instantly buoyed, Violet set her mending aside to greet him.

"I am delighted to find you both in such excellent looks this morning," he said once the niceties had been exchanged. "May I infer that the demands of the Season have not yet proved too taxing for either of you?"

Aunt Philomena tittered. "Silly boy. I am in no condition to be tiring myself at evening entertainments as yet, and my niece does not make her first appearance on the social scene until tonight. It is well that last night's rain has ceased, both for her sake and my own, as I am to travel to Brighton on the morrow."

"To Brighton! Does Miss Turpin accompany you?" He glanced at Violet in evident surprise.

"No, I am to stay with Lady Simpson and her daughter while my aunt is away," she quickly replied, to forestall the far lengthier response Aunt Philomena would have given.

Julian beamed at her. "Glad I am to hear it, for I should hate to be deprived of your company when we've only just become reacquainted. By the bye, now the rain is past, it is quite a beautiful day. I came to beg Lady Puttercroft's indulgence to walk out with you again. Perhaps to Hyde Park?"

"Oh, I should like that above all things," Violet exclaimed. "By now I imagine the gardens are beginning to bloom. May I go, Aunt Philomena?"

"Hyde Park? Why, that must be more than a mile from here," her aunt protested in horror. "Surely you do not mean to walk so far as that?"

Careful to keep her tone reasonable, Violet insisted that a mile was not so very far. "Indeed, I frequently walk many times that in a day when I am in Lincolnshire."

"If Miss Turpin should become tired, or chilled, I will of course hire a hackney for our return," Julian promised. "You may trust me to see that she comes to no harm, my lady. By the way, is that bonnet new? 'Tis remarkably fetching."

Preening, Lady Puttercroft confessed that it was, her reservations apparently forgotten. Ten minutes, later Julian and Violet strolled toward the park with Brigid again in tow.

"You were right," Violet remarked when they had walked for some minutes. "It is much warmer today. It seems spring is arriving at last."

Julian placed a gloved hand over hers, where it rested lightly on his coat sleeve. "For me, spring arrived the moment I rediscovered you in the Shires. I daresay no flowers we see in the park will compare to the violet of your eyes."

She laughed gaily. "You are being quite absurd, Julian. I thought you knew by now that I far prefer sincerity to flattery."

"But I am sincere. Surely you do not mean to deny me the pleasure of remarking on beauty when I see it?" He playfully assumed a wounded air.

Smiling, Violet shook her head. "What will please me far more than pretty compliments is hearing more about the Saint of Seven Dials. You've discovered his identity, have you not?"

"You are the persistent one." He chuckled. "I should have known that was the real reason you wished to walk out with me again."

"Now you are the one seeking compliments. You must know it was not my only reason—though it may have contributed somewhat to my eagerness for the exercise…and your company." She slanted a flirtatious glance up at him.

In response, he pulled her arm more tightly through his with something beyond warmth in his smile. She was beginning to fear she had invited rather more than she had intended when he frowned and looked away.

"As I intimated before, it would be…unwise for me to reveal all that I know. Telling you too much might well put *you* at risk, for there is a large bounty on his head and there are some who would go to nefarious lengths to claim it."

"I will be in no danger if I never tell another soul whatever you share with me," she pointed out. "Please, Julian?"

Instead of answering, he gestured toward some crocuses blooming along the railing of a house they were passing. "Those bode well for the Park gardens, don't you think?"

Violet allowed the change of subject, but only for the moment. Before their walk concluded, she was determined to wheedle more information from him. Without Julian's assistance, she had little hope of meeting—or helping—the Saint of Seven Dials.

"Will you perchance be at Lady Plumfield's musicale tonight?" she asked, biding her time. "Lady Simpson has invited me to accompany them."

He regretfully shook his head. "I fear I was not invited. From what little I know of Lady Plumfield, I imagine she was quite selective in her guest list, limiting it to those who share her taste in music."

"Surely not," Violet protested, "for she can know nothing of mine. I was no doubt invited because my aunt enjoys that sort of thing—much more than I do. Alas, music was never one of my better subjects of study."

"We have that in common, then, for I never bothered to learn more than was required in school. I trust I will soon see you at other evening gatherings, however."

"What of Lord and Lady Jeller's ball next week? 'Twill be my first ball of the Season."

Indeed, it would be her first real ball in London, for last year she'd been hurried out of Lady Trumbull's before the dancing began. Though she did not mention that, she doubted Julian would disapprove of her little prank as Lord Rushford had.

"I had not yet responded to their invitation, but now I will certainly attend," he replied. "Would it be too bold of me to request the first dance?"

"Need you ask? You may have as many dances as you wish."

He smiled. "I doubt your chaperones would agree to that, but I should be very much obliged if you were to also reserve a waltz for me."

To that she agreed, admitting he was likely right that Lady Simpson would forbid her dancing more than twice with any one gentleman. A silly convention, but she could hardly change Society's expectations overnight.

When they entered the Park gates, she resumed her earlier line of questioning, this time taking a less direct approach.

"I must say, Julian, if you refuse to do more than drop hints about the Saint of Seven Dials, I shall begin to think you are only pretending to know his identity to impress me. Or are you simply making an educated guess?"

Though his smile showed he knew what she was about, he replied, "It is no mere guess, I assure you." Then, after a brief pause, "I see that mere hints will never content you, Violet, for you are quite the stubbornest young lady I've ever known. That was true of you even as a girl, I recall."

"Is he someone you know personally?" she asked excitedly, determined not to be put off again. "Someone in Society? Someone *I* might know?"

Shooting her a worried look, he pulled out a handkerchief to wipe his brow. "I would very much like to tell you, Violet, though I fear if I do, you will—" As he spoke, a bit of parchment fluttered to the ground, apparently from the folds of the handkerchief.

"What is that?" Before he could stop her, she pounced on the little square of paper.

Appearing alarmed, Julian reached to take it from her, but not quickly enough. With starting eyes, Violet examined her prize—a rectangle inscribed with the numeral 7, capped by a golden halo. She recognized it instantly, for it was both described and pictured in her book: the celebrated calling card of the Saint of Seven Dials.

"Julian?" Her voice shook slightly as she looked up at him, wide-eyed. Does this mean… Are you truly—?"

"Me? Of…of course not!" His expression belied his words, however, and he seemed to realize it. For a long moment he hesitated, then let out his breath in a huff. "Very well. I suppose I may as well tell you all, for you will surely ferret it out of me sooner or later. The truth is, I—"

"Ah, Miss Turpin!" came a voice from behind them.

An instant later, Lord Rushford pulled a smart high-perch phaeton even with them and doffed his hat in greeting. "Your aunt said I might find you walking in the Park."

Though his smile caused a flutter in Violet's midsection, she did not return it.

Much as she had longed for him to unbend toward her, his timing was execrable. Had he waited but another five minutes, she felt certain Julian would have confessed to her that he, himself, was the Saint of Seven Dials!

"Good morning, my lord." The chilliness of Miss Turpin's reply made Rush wonder what he had just interrupted. "My aunt was correct, as you see, though I can't think why you felt it necessary to come in search of me. Pray do not allow me to keep you from whatever else you might have planned."

Bigsby also seemed more than a little displeased by his arrival. Hm. Rather than return the man's glare, Rush broadened his smile to include him.

"My only plan was to pay my respects to you, Miss Turpin, and to see how you get on. Your aunt seemed concerned that the length of your intended walk might be too much for you, so I offered to drive you back to her house if that proved to be the case."

Bigsby stiffened. "I promised Lady Puttercroft that I would hire a hackney should Violet feel fatigued," he said, his voice brittle. "Your offer is therefore quite superfluous."

"A hackney?" Rush lifted his eyebrows incredulously. "I should say *Miss Turpin* deserves better conveyance than that." He kept his voice pleasant despite an urge to horsewhip the upstart for using her Christian name.

The other man flushed visibly at the implied rebuke. "You've no right—"

"Oh, but I have." Rush allowed a hint of steel to infuse his tone. "That right was given me by Miss Turpin's aunt as well as her brother, who expressly asked me to keep her from harm while in Town. Something I fully intend to do."

His change of manner clearly penetrated, for Bigsby hastily took a half step away from Miss Turpin. Turning a shoulder to Rush, he gave her a strained, apologetic smile.

"I fear, my dear Miss Turpin, that I have just recalled an engagement I have elsewhere, so must leave you to the more, ah, *acceptable* care of Lord Rushford. I very much hope we may continue our conversation in the near future. Give you good day." Sketching a bow, he hurried off.

Miss Turpin stared after him for a stunned moment before rounding on Rush. "That was the outside of rude, my lord! I will have you know that my aunt had no objection whatever to my walking out with Julian Bigsby, as he is an old friend. Nor can I imagine my brother would have minded, particularly as I brought my abigail along for propriety."

Rush glanced at the hovering maid. "Ah, yes. The same abigail who was willing to masquerade as Mrs. Turpin for your convenience. Pray excuse me if I consider her rather an inadequate chaperone, given your penchant for…irregularity."

"I will *not* excuse you for that," she said hotly. "Nor do I believe my brother instructed you to scare off any gentleman who shows interest, for he wishes to see me well married nearly as much as my mother does. How is that to occur if I am never allowed to converse with any gentleman but yourself?"

"Miss Turpin, you are overwrought." Perhaps unwisely, he allowed his amusement to show. "Come, let me drive you around the Park until your temper has cooled sufficiently that I can safely return you to your aunt."

She gave an indignant huff. "I will let you do no such thing. I am perfectly capable of walking back under my own power."

"*You* are, no doubt, but what of your maid?" He looked pointedly at the girl who, being a good deal plumper than her mistress, was visibly flagging.

Following his gaze, Miss Turpin bit her lip in chagrin. Refusing to admit defeat, however, she lifted her chin to face him again. "You may take my abigail back to Mortimer Street if you wish. I prefer to walk."

"Miss Turpin, you cannot think I would leave you here, more than a mile from your aunt's house, completely without escort? No gentleman would consider such a thing. I must therefore insist that both you and your maid accept my offer of a ride. Lady Puttercroft, I feel sure, would agree it is the only acceptable option, given Mr. Bigsby's unexpected departure."

"Unexpected?" she flared. "He only left because you frightened him away. I never before thought you a bully, Lord Rushford, but your actions today quite speak for themselves."

Bully? His amusement abruptly departed.

"Call it what you will," he said shortly. "Will you join me, or must we protract this argument until we attract a crowd of gossipmongers?" Several passersby had indeed paused to watch their exchange.

Though clearly longing to tell him to go to the devil and storm off, Miss Turpin looked again at her maid. Her internal struggle was evident, but compassion for the servant finally triumphed over her fit of pique. Grudgingly capitulating, she motioned her maid to allow Rush to help her into the rear seat of the phaeton. She then climbed up herself, spurning his assistance, to sit stiff as a poker beside him.

"Very well," she said just as stiffly. "You may drive us to my aunt's house, though I still maintain this entire encounter was both unnecessary and ill-timed."

"Do you think so?" Rush whipped up his pair. "I thought it remarkably well-timed, myself. It can do your reputation no good, you know, to be seen with a man like Bigsby."

She glared at him. "I cannot think why, when I find his manners far superior to yours. My aunt approves of him, as well. Perhaps you forget that I have known him since I was quite a girl. He was very kind to me then and has been equally kind since my arrival in London."

"Kind?" Rush raised a skeptical brow. "Not a word I would associate with Bigsby, though no doubt he can appear so when it serves his purpose."

"Why are you so determined to malign him?" she demanded. "You scarcely know him."

He sent a considering glance her way. "I've had little contact with him of late, 'tis true. But in my experience a man's character, once fixed, changes little as he grows older."

As a youth, Bigsby had frequently threatened and bullied smaller boys at school, something he and Thor had done their best to put a stop to. The summer Bigsby visited Lincolnshire, they had similarly discouraged his attentions toward Thor's little sister, who was no more than thirteen or fourteen at the time.

On learning he was also dallying with a farmer's daughter and more than one young serving wench in the village, they had stepped up their efforts. A minor thrashing had been sufficient to effectively convey their message.

"Lord Rushford," Miss Turpin broke into his ruminations, "if one did not know better, one might almost believe you jealous of Julian. Which would be most ungallant, as you are already betrothed to Miss Simpson."

Startled, Rush frowned. It was bad enough that Killer and his mother knew of the unofficial engagement, but apparently Lady Simpson was spreading the word as well. Not surprising, he supposed, but damned inconvenient, given his current feelings.

Keeping his eyes trained on his pair, he said, "I assure you, I have no reason whatsoever to be jealous of the likes of Bigsby, quite apart from the reason you stated. My only concern is for your welfare, and that only at the behest of your brother."

Beside him, she gave a tiny gasp and he realized he had spoken more coldly than he had intended.

"If you are at a loss for acceptable activities," he continued more gently, "why do you not go riding? Has Lady Puttercroft nothing suitable in her stables?"

"No, nothing at all. Only a pair of carriage horses scarcely fit even for that, from what I have seen."

He could not say he was surprised. "What of Lady Simpson? Your aunt said that you will be staying at her house for the next fortnight, that she may visit Brighton as she'd originally intended."

That news had both relieved and concerned him. Relieved because he could not but think Lady Simpson would do a better job of supervising Miss Turpin than her aunt had done. Witness Lady Puttercroft's approval of Bigsby. But concern because he foresaw a good bit of awkwardness given his engagement to Miss Simpson and his attraction to Miss Turpin.

"I know nothing of Lady Simpson's stables," she confessed, "but I cannot think she will have an extra riding horse for my use. While in Leicestershire, Lady Anthony mentioned writing to her brother-in-law, Lord Marcus Northrup, about the use of a particular mount, but I've no idea whether she has done so."

"I see." He knew Lord Marcus only in passing, but could approach his brother, Lord Peter, about the matter. Riding seemed more likely than anything else to distract Miss Turpin from seeking other, more objectionable, sources of amusement.

When he drew the phaeton to a halt before Lady Puttercroft's house, Miss Turpin leapt lightly to the ground, again without waiting for him to assist her.

"Politeness obliges me to thank you for conveying me here, my lord, though you did so against my wishes," she said, reaching up to help her maid.

Forestalling her, he handed the girl down himself. "Pray do not trouble yourself to speak sentiments you do not feel," he replied. "I suppose I should come in to explain the means of your return to your aunt."

"Pray do not trouble yourself, my lord," she threw back at him. "I have surely taken enough of your valuable time today. You may go about your business secure in the knowledge that you have successfully meddled in my affairs yet again."

With that, she turned and marched up the steps to the house without a backward glance. Rush waited until she and her maid were inside before chuckling to himself. She certainly had spirit, no mistake about that.

That her spirit attracted him so powerfully was damned inconvenient, however. The more time he spent in Miss Turpin's company, the less content he was with his choice of Miss Simpson. Every fresh encounter, with either lady, only confirmed how much he preferred Miss Turpin's barbed banter to the shy insipidity of his intended bride.

The fact remained, however, that as attractive as he found Miss Turpin's spirit—and person—she was hardly the proper person to take over where his mother had left off. She was far too impulsive for such a role, with a decided penchant for putting amusement over responsibility. Both that and honor dictated that his original choice would have to stand.

Meanwhile, the sooner he found a better outlet for Miss Turpin's misplaced energies, the better. Whipping up his pair, he directed them toward Lord Peter Northrup's house in Curzon Street.

CHAPTER TEN

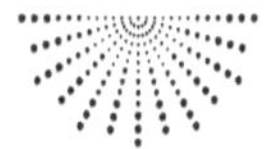

VIOLET'S TEMPER WAS STILL SIMMERING WHEN LADY SIMPSON'S CARRIAGE arrived that afternoon to transport her to Cavendish Square.

Apparently it hadn't been enough for Lord Rushford to dash her hopes of enjoying London in relative freedom. Now he'd also frustrated her dream of assisting the Saint of Seven Dials. Julian, she was sure, had been on the point of telling her everything before his lordship ran him off. Suppose he now refused to do so?

To add even more insult to injury, Lord Rushford had essentially told her outright that she was nothing to him beyond an obligation to her brother. Though she knew she should not care, that hurt most of all. If he remembered that kiss at Ivy Lodge at all, it was merely as a reminder of her flaws. She, alas, would never forget it—nor could she seem to prevent her heart from fluttering every time he was near.

Aunt Philomena, preoccupied with her own impending journey, kept her farewell uncharacteristically brief. "I shall see you again in a fortnight or so." She distractedly tucked a fan into a side pocket of her portmanteau. "With luck, you may well receive an eligible offer before then, for I've no doubt Lady Simpson will bring you along to every function they attend. Mind you be a good girl and do nothing to make her regret her kindness."

Violet promised, and was allowed to depart.

Mary greeted her eagerly on her arrival in Cavendish Square. "I am so happy that Mama agreed to my suggestion to have you stay with us. The next fortnight is sure to be far more fun now."

"I'm sure it will." Violet tried not to let her amusement show, thinking that her friend's idea of fun was likely much tamer than her own. Mary then led Violet upstairs to the room she would occupy during her stay.

"Mine is just next door, so if we are quiet, we can share confidences without Mama knowing."

"Confidences?" Violet could think of little she could truthfully tell Mary, given her own conflicted feelings. She was curious about her friend's, however. "About…your engagement, for example?"

In reply, Mary blushed. "I know I should feel extremely honored by Lord Rushford's offer, but…"

"But you still find him intimidating?"

Mary nodded. "I can't think why he ever took notice of me at all, when women of far higher rank than I, and beautiful besides, continually sought him out last Season."

"Perhaps he appreciated that you did not fling yourself at his head, as they did?"

As Violet herself had done.

"Perhaps. Goodness knows, I have never learned the art of flirtation." Not surprising, as Mary had not a coquettish bone in her body.

"Once married, that will not matter," Violet pointed out as lightly as she could manage. "Gentlemen do not expect their wives to flirt with them."

"But they do have other…expectations." Mary pinkened further.

They were now straying into territory that Violet very much preferred not to think about, but she forced herself to ask, "Is that… what worries you about marrying him?"

To her surprise, Mary shook her head. "Not nearly so much as the thought of how much responsibility I will have as his wife. Mama says that with his mother deceased, I will be expected to manage his household, something I know nothing about. I fear I shall make a botch of everything."

That, Violet had to admit, was a valid concern. Still, she felt compelled to reassure her friend. "I cannot imagine he expects you to take over his mother's responsibilities all at once. No doubt you will be given ample time to learn whatever is needful for you to know."

Though Mary looked cautiously hopeful at her words, Violet was not sorry to have their discussion cut short by the dressing bell.

Unfortunately, when she joined Mary and her mother in the drawing room half an hour later, Lord Rushford was again the first topic of conversation.

"I trust you are settling in, Miss Turpin?" Lady Simpson asked as she moved to a chair.

Violet nodded. "I thank you again for your kind invitation, my lady. My aunt wished me to convey her thanks, also."

"Pray do not mention it," Lady Simpson responded with a thin smile. "But what is this I hear about you going out driving with Lord Rushford this morning? Lady Mountheath stopped in for the express purpose of informing me about it."

Though startled, Violet answered readily enough. "It was my aunt's doing. She sent him to find me, worried that the walk back from the park might be too taxing, though of course it would not have been." Remembered anger at Lord Rushford made her flush—a flush Lady Simpson apparently misinterpreted.

"I trust you have not forgotten that he is promised to my daughter," her hostess reminded her severely.

"Of course not, my lady. As it happens, I was out walking with another gentleman when Lord Rushford insisted on fulfilling his promise to my aunt." She was about to elaborate on his rude behavior when she realized doing so might increase Mary's misgivings about him.

Fortunately, Lady Simpson seemed mollified.

"Very well. Knowing what a gossipmonger Lady Mountheath can be, I suspected there was less to the story than she implied. I am happy to learn that was indeed the case."

She rose then, to lead them into the dining room. "Perhaps you can persuade Mary to be less shy around Lord Rushford at tonight's musicale," she suggested as they went. "I begin to fear he will think she has taken him in aversion."

Violet forced a smile. "I will do everything I can to further Mary's future happiness, my lady. 'Tis the least I can do in return for your hospitality."

She chose her words carefully, for after their conversation upstairs, she was by no means convinced that Lord Rushford would make Mary happy.

Nor, truth be told, had she reconciled her own heart to the idea of their marriage, however irritating Lord Rushford might be.

Rush and Killer were among the first to arrive at the Plumfield house that evening, but discovered Lady Simpson and her two charges there before them.

"Give you good evening, ladies," Rush said, sweeping them a collective bow.

Miss Turpin merely arched an eyebrow and turned away, but Lady Simpson was all smiles.

"Ah, here you are, Lord Rushford, and in good time, too," she exclaimed. "Did I not tell you, Mary, that he would not be late?"

Miss Simpson nodded and dipped a quick curtsey, then glanced over her shoulder at the generously-proportioned apartment that had been fitted up as a music room for the evening.

"My daughter is anxious to claim a seat near the musicians," her mother explained, "for she dearly loves music. She is most proficient at it herself, you no doubt recall."

Rush blinked. "Ah, yes," he said with a somewhat belated smile. "Miss Simpson plays the harp, does she not?"

Lady Simpson nodded. "The pianoforte, as well. Her final performance last Season was particularly praised, though I believe you had already left Town by then."

"Er, perhaps so. In any event, Lord Killerby has also expressed a desire to sit in the front row, so I propose we all do so."

"The entertainment tonight will likely be first rate," said Killer as they moved toward the chairs, Miss Turpin trailing somewhat behind the others. "Lady Plumfield and m'mother were musical rivals in their younger days, you know, in both singing and the pianoforte."

Killer took a seat directly before the small dais, upon which were ranged a pianoforte, a harp and a few smaller instruments. The others followed, and Rush found himself seated between Killer and Miss Simpson, with Lady Simpson and Miss Turpin further along the row. As conversation seemed called for, he asked Miss Simpson whether she had previously heard any of the performers.

"Oh! Yes," she replied somewhat breathlessly. "All of them, I believe. Mr. Trent is quite renowned for his proficiency at the pianoforte, and Signora Bellonini may well be without equal on the harp."

"I did not know that La Bellonini was to be here tonight," Killer exclaimed from Rush's other side. "I've only had the pleasure of hearing her once, years back, before she became so celebrated. She has no doubt improved since then, though that scarcely seemed possible."

Miss Simpson's pretty face lit up with the most genuine smile Rush had ever seen on her lips. "Indeed she has, my lord. I attended two of her public performances last Season and both experiences were sublime. I very much wished to sit near her instrument tonight, something that is only possible at a private gathering such as this one."

She and Lord Killerby continued to talk about the upcoming performance while the first musicians tuned their instruments. Rush meanwhile held his tongue to avoid displaying his ignorance. He clearly needed to learn more of music, for the topic gave his bride-to-be more animation than he had ever before witnessed in her.

When the performance began, all conversation in the front row ceased. Though he could hear discreet murmuring from those seated behind them, both Killer and Miss Simpson were completely engaged in listening to the music. Rush tried to be likewise absorbed, but by the third song his attention began to wander.

In gazing about, he saw Miss Turpin's hand go to her mouth to cover a yawn. Apparently he was not the only one in the front row who might have been more comfortable toward the back of the room. With a spurt of amusement, he recalled her telling him that she was more proficient at billiards than the pianoforte.

He then recalled what had occurred shortly thereafter and hastily returned his gaze to the pair of violinists currently holding forth.

Violet stifled a yawn as one musical piece gave way to another, now by a harpist accompanied by a foppish man on the clarinet. While the performances were no doubt first rate, sitting to listen was by no means her preferred way to enjoy music. She would far rather be dancing.

Seeking any distraction that might prevent her rudely nodding off, she turned her head slightly to observe the other occupants of the first row. Lady Simpson also looked as though she were on the point of dozing, but Mary and Lord Killerby were rapt, both fully caught up in the performance. Lord Rushford, however, looked nigh as bored as she was herself.

Though not yet ready to forgive his high-handed meddling in her affairs, she could not deny that Lord Rushford was exceedingly handsome. He had also proved he could be interesting to talk to…when he was not condemning her. She looked away, telling herself that Julian surely surpassed Lord Rushford on both counts.

When the music finally concluded, the guests repaired to an adjoining room set out with a buffet and small tables to discuss the relative merits of the performances—or, for those less musically inclined, the latest gossip.

"Miss Turpin?" came a voice at Violet's shoulder as she followed the others to a table. Turning, she saw a young man whose acquaintance she had made last Season regarding her with a hopeful smile. "Dare I hope you remember me?"

"Of course, Sir Lawrence. How nice to see you again." She smiled back. Though nowhere near so handsome as Julian, or even Lord Rushford, Sir Lawrence had been flatteringly attentive last spring. "I trust you have been well?"

"Far better now I know you are in Town again. I was quite bereft when you left us so suddenly last year. Please tell me you mean to grace us for more than a mere week or two this Season?"

She could not help but smile at his eagerness. "That is certainly my intention. The family emergency that called me away was unavoidable, but it is now happily past."

As they talked, she stole a glance at Lord Rushford to see whether he was witnessing this proof that not all gentlemen held her in the contempt he did. He was occupied, however, in helping Mary to a chair, after which he immediately went to procure a plate for her.

Somewhat disgruntled, she bade Sir Lawrence a friendly adieu and went to join her party, whereupon Lord Killerby offered to supply her with refreshment.

"Rush is already getting food and drink for Lady Simpson and her daughter and likely felt three plates would be rather too much to carry back," he explained when she was unable to keep her eyes from straying toward the buffet table, where Lord Rushford had his back to her.

"Thank you, Lord Killerby. I would appreciate that very much," she said with as much grace as she could manage.

Over supper, Lord Rushford devoted his attention almost exclusively to Mary, seemingly oblivious to all the other debutantes striving to catch his eye. Not once did Violet notice him glancing *her* way—though to be fair, she did her best to avoid looking at him.

Given her scathing words on leaving him this morning, she should not be surprised if he now ignored her, but it rankled nonetheless. Not that she *wanted* him to pay attention to her—she was still too angry with him for that. She simply preferred to be the one to do any snubbing.

As they rose from the tables some time later, Lady Simpson remarked to Violet, "It is well that the weather today has been so fine. I trust it ensured your aunt a safe journey to Brighton."

Lord Rushford, overhearing, said, "Ah, yes, Lady Puttercroft told me that Miss Turpin would be residing with you for the next fortnight or so."

"Yes, 'twas my Mary's idea. Very clever of her, for this arrangement will be more comfortable for us all, in addition to allowing Lady Puttercroft to visit her sister, as she had originally planned to do."

"Very clever indeed." Lord Rushford glanced toward Violet with an enigmatic expression before turning back to Lady Simpson. "This will also allow you to better regulate Miss Turpin's activities, which is no bad thing. Though Lady Puttercroft quite properly endorses strict adherence to convention, she is perhaps not the most...observant of chaperones."

It was all Violet could do to conceal her outrage at this new betrayal by his lordship. He had wholeheartedly agreed when Aunt Philomena cautioned against mentioning Violet's earlier lapses. Why, then, should he imply that she would bear watching, before she spent a single night under Lady Simpson's roof?

"Your concern for my welfare is admirable, my lord," she told him in icy tones.

He inclined his head in acknowledgment, one brow raised in amusement. "I promised your brother no less, Miss Turpin."

The reminder did nothing to mollify her. Rather the reverse. At next opportunity, she would tell him—again—just what she thought of his interference in her affairs.

"Are you certain this is the horse your sister-in-law meant?" Rush asked doubtfully, eyeing the rangy red-and-white skewbald gelding a wary groom had just led out from Lord Marcus Northrup's stables.

Lord Marcus shrugged. "Lady Anthony's letter was quite specific. She assured me that Miss Turpin could manage him, having seen her ride to the hunt. I'll leave it to you whether to let her risk it, however. My grooms—and my wife—have made enough headway in winning his trust that he's not *quite* so bad-tempered as he was originally, but he's still skittish…and an ugly brute, besides."

Rush could not disagree with that addendum. The gelding was one of the least attractive horses he'd ever seen, with its patchy blotches, lop ears and irregular lines. Perhaps Miss Turpin would regard the animal as a project of sorts. He hoped so, for he considered it a matter of some urgency to provide her with a better pastime than seeking mischief.

"Assuming you can get a sidesaddle on him, we may as well send him 'round to Cavendish Square and see what Miss Turpin thinks," he told Lord Marcus. "If she finds him too temperamental—or ugly—to ride, I'll send him back directly and seek another mount for her."

That was agreed to, after which Rush went to collect Killer and proceeded to the Simpson house to invite the young ladies out for a ride.

Lady Simpson, as always, was delighted to see him. "I told Mary you would likely call today, my lord," she said with a triumphant smile toward her daughter as he and Killer bowed in greeting. "Have a seat, do, and I will ring for some refreshment."

Miss Simpson and Miss Turpin, who had risen to curtsey at their entrance, both kept their gazes averted—Miss Simpson no doubt from shyness, while Miss Turpin was likely still piqued about his interference with Bigsby in the park yesterday.

"Actually, my lady, we had hoped to persuade Miss Simpson and Miss Turpin to accompany us to Hyde Park, as it is remarkably fine weather for riding."

"Oh!" Lady Simpson glanced uncertainly at the two younger ladies. "I suppose that will be acceptable. Indeed, as it is Sunday, most of the fashionable world is likely to be there just now. I am not certain, however, that our stable has a mount suitable for Miss Turpin. Perhaps Lady Puttercroft's—?"

Grimacing, Miss Turpin shook her head. "I fear my aunt has only carriage horses, my lady. I…can bide here while the others go riding." There was no mistaking her disappointment. Fortunately, Rush had means to alleviate it.

"Not to worry, Miss Turpin," he said. "I encountered Lord Marcus Northrup a short while ago and he told me that his sister-in-law had suggested you have use of a particular horse she rode when she was last in Town. When I told him you were staying here, he arranged to have it sent round at once. Though perhaps I should have asked first whether your stables are able to accommodate it, Lady Simpson?"

His hostess swelled slightly with indignation. "Our stables can easily house an extra horse, my lord. I am surprised, however, that you would take it upon yourself to arrange such a favor on Miss Turpin's behalf."

"I, for one, am glad he did," Killer exclaimed before Rush could answer the implied rebuke. "Given how well Miss Turpin rides, she has surely missed it since leaving the Shires. Now she may delight everyone in Hyde Park the way she delighted those of us on the hunting field last month."

Lady Simpson sniffed. "Very well. If you will take it upon yourself to be Miss Turpin's escort, Lord Killerby, I've no objection to the girls riding out with the two of you. I will ring for some tea while they change into their habits."

During the quarter hour's conversation that followed, Lady Simpson hinted that her daughter's being seen riding with Lord Rushford would serve to publicize their engagement nearly as well as a announcement in the papers. She also made it clear she had no fault to find with Lord Killerby's outspoken admiration of Miss Turpin...so long as it was not shared by Rush.

He would need to tread carefully, he realized, if he was to avoid bringing Lady Simpson's wrath down upon Miss Turpin's head for the crime of diverting any fraction of his attention from her daughter. When the young ladies rejoined them, he was therefore effusive in his compliments on Miss Simpson's appearance.

Not until she finished blushing and stammering in reply did he turn to her companion, as though it were simply a polite afterthought. Unfortunately, seeing Miss Turpin in the same sky-blue habit she'd worn in the Cottesmore stirred up unexpectedly powerful feelings. He had to struggle to steel both voice and face to disinterestedness.

"You are quite creditably turned out as well, Miss Turpin. Shall we all repair to the mews?"

"The mews!" exclaimed Lady Simpson in surprise. "Certainly not. It would be most unseemly for the young ladies to visit there. We shall have the horses brought round to the front, as is proper."

Despite some misgivings about the ability of a stablehand to control Lord Marcus's gelding, Rush made no protest. Lady Simpson sent word to the stables, then accompanied the four younger people to the front door.

A groom already held the reins of his and Killer's mounts and a moment later two stable boys came around the corner leading two more horses—a placid little mare that was clearly Miss Simpson's, and the skewbald gelding.

Lady Simpson and her daughter both gasped at the sight of the odd-looking horse, while Killer laughed outright.

"You are jesting, Rush, are you not? Surely Lord Marcus does not mean for Miss Turpin to be seen on that monstrosity?"

Though also clearly startled, Miss Turpin moved toward the horse after only the slightest hesitation. "Lady Anthony did warn me he was not an attractive beast. I thought she might have exaggerated, but it would seem not."

"Not attractive?" Lady Simpson echoed, clearly aghast. "That is the ugliest horse I have ever beheld. I believe you would do better to bide here, Miss Turpin, than to be seen riding it in public."

Miss Turpin merely smiled, reaching one hand out to the gelding. He shied at her approach, his ears angling backward menacingly.

"It would appear Lady Anthony did not exaggerate about your temper, either," she told the horse. "I am determined we shall become friends, however, for I've no doubt we can do each other a great deal of good. Now, then." She took a small step forward.

"Careful, miss," cautioned the lad holding the skewbald's reins. "He already tried to have a bite out of me as I led him round."

That drew another gasp from the Simpson ladies. "Oh, Violet, do stay back!" Miss Simpson cried out. "He looks exceedingly dangerous."

"Miss Turpin, I must protest as well," Lady Simpson exclaimed. "Pray keep in mind that should you be injured by that beast, I will have to answer to Lady Puttercroft for allowing you to ride it."

"Nonsense," Miss Turpin assured them both. "I have handled worse, as these two gentlemen can attest. I simply need to earn his trust."

The older groom now held the horse steady while Miss Turpin stroked its neck, murmuring soothingly to it as she did so. Gradually its ears swiveled forward, though it still eyed the rest of them warily. Finally taking the reins, she nodded to the groom and he tossed her into the saddle.

Predictably, the horse shied and attempted to rear. Ignoring Miss Simpson's frightened squeak, Miss Turpin expertly pulled the gelding's head down the instant its forefeet left the ground, bringing it under control remarkably quickly.

"Well done, Miss Turpin," Killer cried.

"Indeed," Rush agreed. She might not have Lady Anthony's near-magical touch with horses, but she certainly exhibited more skill than any *other* woman he could name. More than most men, in fact. "Shall we go, then?"

Rush turned to help Miss Simpson onto her mare and discovered her groom had already done so. Ah, well.

Leaping into his own saddle, he bade Lady Simpson farewell and led the party toward Hyde Park. Both Miss Simpson and Killer, he noted, were careful to keep their own mounts well away from the skewbald gelding. More than once the spirited horse attempted to take the lead, only to be reined in by its rider. No question, she was an excellent horsewoman.

On reaching the park, Rush scanned the crowded bridle paths. "Hm. That lane leading toward the northern boundary should allow for a canter, if we are careful."

He hoped that might settle Miss Turpin's mount somewhat, since the short ride to the park had by no means done so. Unfortunately, Miss Simpson appeared absolutely terrified by his suggestion.

"Do you not canter, Miss Simpson?" he asked. When she shook her head, he strove to conceal his incredulity. "You can trot, however?"

"I...I have, my lord." She blushed scarlet. "Not...recently, however."

Rush stifled a sigh. Already the gelding was dancing sideways, clearly impatient to be moving again. It seemed cruel to limit the horse —or its rider—to the sedate walk that appeared to be all Miss Simpson could safely manage.

Killer apparently thought the same. "Suppose you and Miss Turpin go on ahead," he suggested. "Her mount is clearly spoiling to run. I can accompany Miss Simpson on a slower circuit of the park."

The diminutive blonde looked up at him gratefully. "You don't mind?"

Cheerfully, he shook his head. "Not a bit of it. Wasn't so very long ago I had to keep to that pace myself, and happy to do so, after a month and more of being unable to ride at all. Truth be told, I've far less desire than formerly to push my limits on horseback."

"Learned your lesson, did you?" Rush grinned at his friend. If so, it was all to the good, for the smaller man could easily have been killed while attempting to ride Nimbus last autumn.

Killer responded with a shrug, returning Rush's grin somewhat sheepishly. "For the present, at any rate."

"In that case, I'll take you up on your offer, for I would not mind cantering a bit. Haven't had a chance since getting to Town."

Accordingly, he and Miss Turpin set off along the least crowded path, quickly progressing from a quick trot to a hand-canter.

"That is better, is it not?" Miss Turpin said to her mount, patting its neck with a gloved hand. "I know you'd like to go even faster, but as I've already caught trouble once for galloping in the park, we must content ourselves with this. As you see, Lord Killerby was quite right," she added to Rush.

She looked so fetching—so desirable—with her dark curls streaming behind her that he had to swallow before he could reply. "That is why I made no objection to his offer."

"Even though you are promised to Mary?" She glanced sideways at him with an expression he could not decipher.

He cleared his throat. "Er...yes." What else could he say?

She startled him then by asking, "Are you certain that was a good idea? I have always believed a marriage is more apt to be happy when the couple shares at least a few interests. Given how much you enjoy horses and riding..." She trailed off.

"I'm unlikely to find a woman as horse-mad as myself, so I could scarcely make that my prime consideration when choosing a bride." Even as he spoke, he realized Miss Turpin came closer than any woman he'd met, save perhaps Lady Anthony.

"I suppose not." Did he detect regret in her tone? Her head was turned away, preventing him from reading her expression. "I imagine if someone is so much in love as to propose marriage, a lack of shared interests scarcely matters."

He started. *Love?* Surely he had done nothing to imply he was in *love* with Miss Simpson? Perhaps that simply seemed self-evident to someone who held primarily romantic views on matrimony—as Violet Turpin clearly did. There was no real reason for him to disabuse her of such an idealistic assumption, but he attempted it nonetheless.

"A man in my position must take far more than a few shared interests—or love—into account when choosing a bride," he explained. "Family background, fortune and overall suitability for the position she will hold are greater considerations." Enumerating them aloud, those criteria now struck him as not only heartless, but mercenary.

She seemed similarly struck. "Then...your *feelings* toward the lady matter not at all, so long as she meets those other requirements? To me it seems sad, almost tragic, to sacrifice both your future happiness and hers upon the altar of *suitability*. But...I suppose you know your business best."

So saying, she urged her mount a bit ahead so that they no longer rode side by side.

Just as well, he supposed, for he had no idea how to answer her charge. Especially when he felt more trapped than ever into a course he was likely to regret for the rest of his life.

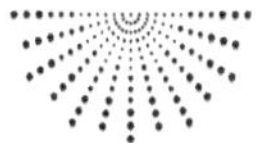

Violet was careful to stay a full length ahead of Lord Rushford for the remainder of their circuit so that he could have no further opportunity to speak with her—or to see her face. She had little doubt her feelings about his revelation were visible upon it.

Yesterday she had been guiltily relieved to learn that Mary was not in love with Lord Rushford. She had assumed that he must love her, however. How else to explain his wishing to marry her, or his attentiveness at last night's musicale?

He had exhibited none of the classic symptoms of love when around Mary, but Violet had credited that to his general air of reserve of late. Instead, by Lord Rushford's own admission, it was because his offer was motivated by purely practical concerns, in which affection played no role whatever.

Now Violet felt even more strongly than she had last night that she must intervene somehow. Lord Rushford might be within his rights to doom himself to a bleak, loveless future, but he must not be allowed to do the same to poor Mary. If this was how things really stood between them, Violet no longer had any qualms about doing whatever she could to prevent their marriage.

By the time she drew up behind Mary and Lord Killerby, who had made but little progress, Violet was once again tolerably composed. Summoning a smile, she reined her horse to a walk.

"And here we are again," she exclaimed brightly as Lord Rushford joined them. "I trust the two of you have spent your time together agreeably?"

Lord Killerby, she decided, would be a far better match for Mary. She did not seem nearly so intimidated by him, perhaps because he was so much less starchy than Lord Rushford.

"Indeed we have." He smiled across at Mary, who smiled back. "We have been discussing music, after discovering last night that we share a passion for it."

Catching Lord Rushford's eye, Lord Killerby's smile abruptly dimmed. Immediately, he fell back to allow the earl to take his place next to Mary.

"Appreciate you keeping Miss Simpson amused in my absence," Lord Rushford told his friend. "Perhaps you and Miss Turpin would like to take another circuit while we continue on?"

Violet glanced at Mary, who was no longer smiling. Instead she looked both wary and a bit tired, though she'd ridden little more than a mile since leaving the house, and all of that at a walk.

"Perhaps we should turn back," she suggested to the others. "The path is becoming rather too crowded for cantering. Nor should Mary remain on horseback for too long, as unused to riding as she is. I should hate for her to be sore tomorrow."

Though Lord Rushford frowned at her words, Mary sent her a look of thanks. No one voiced an objection, so they turned their horses to make their way back to the park gates and thence to Cavendish Square. As Violet's mount again took exception to such a slow pace, she was careful to keep him well away from Mary's horse. Lord Killerby now rode ahead with Violet, while Lord Rushford followed more slowly by Mary's side.

Observing this, as well as the byplay between them after they all returned to the Simpsons' drawing room for tea and sandwiches, Violet regretfully abandoned her new scheme to throw Mary and Lord Killerby together. Though better suited in disposition and interests, it was clear he would never attempt to advance a suit with his friend's intended bride.

Perhaps Lord and Lady Jeller's ball tomorrow night would prove a better hunting ground for Mary's love match? Violet would pay close attention to how Mary responded to each eligible gentleman there. If any appeared more likely to make Mary happy than Lord Rushford, Violet would prod her friend to creep far enough out of her shell to engage his interest.

Those plans were momentarily forgotten when Violet entered the Jellers' ballroom the next evening, in her astonishment at having apparently walked into a garden in the height of summer.

"I must say, Lady Jeller has quite outdone herself this year," Lady Simpson remarked as they progressed into the spacious ballroom, unusually large by London standards.

"Indeed!" Violet exclaimed, gazing around with wide eyes. "Where on earth did she find so many flowers at this season? Naught but crocuses were blooming in the park yesterday."

Lady Simpson smiled indulgently. "Hothouses, my dear. They are costly this early in the Season, but that makes the profusion more impressive—no doubt the precise effect Lady Jeller intended."

Whatever Lady Jeller's motives, Violet was charmed and amazed by the result. While observing the array of flowers gracing every available surface, sconce, and chandelier, she perceived several gentlemen heading their way. The first to reach them was Sir Lawrence.

"Give you good evening, Miss Turpin. Dare I hope you still have a dance free?"

Violet grinned. "As I only this moment arrived, you are the first to ask, Sir Lawrence. I shall be delighted to reserve a dance for you. Are you acquainted with Lady Simpson and her daughter?" At his negative, she performed the introduction, after which he also solicited Mary's hand for a dance.

Mary, Violet was pleased to note, managed something slightly above her usual murmur when granting it. When Sir Lawrence moved on, she complimented her friend on speaking up.

"Yes, at Mama's insistence, I am trying to make more of an effort," Mary sheepishly admitted.

"And see the effect already," said Lady Simpson, overhearing. "Lord Rushford is noticing the difference, I daresay, for he has been most attentive of late. You are promised to him for the first set, are you not?"

Her daughter nodded. "He requested it after our ride yesterday." She did not look nearly as pleased about it as her mother did.

Violet was about to point out Sir Lawrence's good points to her friend when her attention was caught by the approach of the very person she had most hoped to see tonight—Julian Bigsby. At her welcoming smile, he hurried forward.

"Miss Turpin, how nice to see you again." He swept her a bow. "Perhaps you would be so kind as to make me known to your lovely companions?" He favored both Simpson ladies with his most charming smile.

"Of course. This is Lady Simpson, at whose house I am staying while my aunt is from Town, and Miss Simpson, her daughter. Mary, my lady, this is Mr. Bigsby, whom I have known for many years. He was a school acquaintance of my brother's."

Julian's smile broadened further. "Miss Turpin has been warm in her praise of your hospitality, Lady Simpson, and has spoken most highly of you as well, Miss Simpson. I am exceedingly honored to make your acquaintance at last."

Though Violet could not recall having said anything at all to Julian about either lady, she appreciated him claiming that she had. Lady Simpson glanced approvingly at Violet and Mary, though clearly startled by his words, dimpled with pleasure.

"I thought it prudent to remind you at once of your promise to partner me in the first dance," he said to Violet. "I feared if I waited, some other gallant might drive me from your mind."

"You are as absurd as ever. Of course I have not forgotten."

He then turned a flatteringly intent look upon Mary. "Might I hope to also solicit a dance from you, Miss Simpson?"

Mary blushingly granted it, though she appeared too flustered by his blatant admiration to respond as volubly as she had to Sir Lawrence. Promising to return when the music started, he bowed over each of their hands, as well as Lady Simpson's. Then, with a glance over Violet's shoulder, he took himself off.

"Goodness, your Mr. Bigsby certainly is handsome!" Mary whispered as he moved out of earshot.

"He is not precisely *my* Mr. Bigsby, but yes, he certainly is," Violet agreed.

However, it was not Julian's looks that interested her just now, for all the questions she was dying to ask him had come crowding back. She very much hoped their dance together would allow her to get answers to some of them.

The Jeller do was already becoming something of a crush when Rush and Killer entered the florally festooned ballroom. Almost at once, they were accosted by numerous ambitious mamas eager to introduce their daughters before the dancing got underway. On finally extricating themselves from that onslaught, Rush spotted Lord Peter Northrup coming their way.

"Give you good evening, Rushford, Killerby," he greeted them. "I don't believe either of you have yet met my wife? Sarah, my love, these are two of the gentlemen with whom my brother Anthony spends his winters hunting foxes."

Lady Peter, a stunningly beautiful blonde, curtsied to them both. "I am pleased to meet you, my lords. If you are friends with Lord Anthony, I presume you are also acquainted with his wife? I quite long to see Tessa ride in a hunt one day."

"Charmed, Lady Peter," Killer replied with a bow. "And yes, you really must, for Lady Anthony is a sight to behold on horseback. As more ladies are joining the hunt of late, perhaps you can try your hand at it one day."

Smiling, she shook her head. "I fear I am no horsewoman, as my sisters-in-law will attest. Indeed, I began learning only this past year."

Rush greeted her in turn, marveling to think that this petite, very feminine lady had once been a Saint of Seven Dials. Though he could ask no questions about it in Killer's presence, he hoped at some point to hear more.

A movement of the crowd just then revealed Lady Simpson's party a short distance away—and that bounder Bigsby in conversation with them. Smoothing his instinctive frown, Rush turned back to his companions.

"Lord Peter, Lady Peter, might I make you known to Miss Turpin? She is newly in Town, the sister of another friend of ours and Lord Anthony's. At the behest of her brother, Lord Killerby and I are attempting to ease her way in Society."

Bigsby spotted their group approaching before Miss Turpin did and hastily decamped. Rush glared after the presumptuous fellow for a moment, then donned a smile as he apologized to the ladies for his lateness.

"Lady Simpson, you know Lord and Lady Peter Northrup, do you not?" he said then. "They expressed a wish to meet Miss Simpson and Miss Turpin."

After greetings were exchanged, Lord Peter said to Miss Turpin, "I understand you are acquainted with my brother Anthony and his wife?" She assented and several minutes of animated conversation followed.

When the couple moved off, Rush stepped close to Miss Turpin and murmured, "Did I not warn you against encouraging Bigsby?"

Her violet eyes widened, then narrowed. "You did, my lord. But as you gave no reason for your warning beyond vague hints, I see no reason to accede to your whims. Clearly Lord and Lady Jeller consider him acceptable enough to merit an invitation to their home, so I cannot believe most people hold him in the same low esteem you do."

"Lady Jeller is well known for her eagerness to have every event she sponsors declared a crush. She is therefore less than discriminating about the guests she invites. No doubt Bigsby took advantage of that to insinuate his way into a higher tier of Society than he merits."

"My Lord," Lady Simpson interrupted, "what are you and Miss Turpin whispering about?"

Forcing a smile, Rush turned to face her. "I was merely dispensing a bit of brotherly advice, as Miss Turpin's own brother is not here to do so."

Miss Turpin glared at him. "Yes, Lord Rushford is as eager to meddle in my affairs as ever Grant could be."

"Only at his request, I assure you," Rush snapped.

The barbed exchange appeared to reassure Lady Simpson. "Miss Turpin should be grateful that her brother has such…loyal friends." Her brittle smile encompassed Killer as well. "I perceive that the dancing is about to begin, Lord Rushford, and unless I am much mistaken, you are promised to my daughter for the first set."

"Of course. Miss Simpson, shall we take our places?"

As he and his fiancée joined a set that was forming, Rush saw Bigsby hurry over to claim Miss Turpin for the same dance. They moved to a set on the far side of the room, no doubt by design—though whose, he did not know. Likely a joint decision.

When the music began, he moved through the figures of the dance almost by rote, half his attention given to that other set instead of his own. Even from here he could tell that the cut of Bigsby's coat was more expertly tailored than the one he'd worn in the park two days since. The man was clearly trying to up his game.

Violet, meanwhile, danced as gracefully as she had at Ivy Lodge, smiling up at her partner each time they passed in a way that made Rush clench his teeth.

"Oh!" The exclamation abruptly brought his focus back to his partner. In his distraction, he had trodden on her foot.

"I beg your pardon, Miss Simpson! I have not performed this particular dance since last summer and seem to have forgotten a few moves. I will endeavor to suffer no more such lapses, or at least not to injure you if I do."

Though he was the one at fault, she seemed far more embarrassed than he, reddening and ducking her head.

Cursing his preoccupation with Miss Turpin and her partner, Rush paid close attention to his steps for the remainder of the dance. He reminded himself that he did not actually know of any *recent* indiscretions by Bigsby, despite his youthful indiscretions. It was possible, he supposed, that the man had mended his ways since their schooldays.

But he doubted it.

Violet, meanwhile, was taking every opportunity the dance offered to wheedle more information from Julian.

"When last we talked, you were on the point of telling me something important," she reminded him as they took their places. Their set was some distance from that including Mary and Lord Rushford, a circumstance for which she was grateful.

Her partner furrowed his brow. "Was I? If so, I would doubtless be wiser to deny it now."

"Oh come, Julian, you said yourself I was bound to get it out of you anyway, so you may as well tell me all. Was my guess correct? Are you…the man we were discussing?"

The start of the music prevented him answering her question, though his conscious expression was nearly answer enough. She moved through the figures impatiently until the dance brought them back together.

"Well?" she whispered. "Is it true?"

He gave her a sidelong glance that she could not read. "You always were a perceptive girl. I suppose there is little use in denying it, though this is scarcely the setting in which to discuss such matters."

Unfortunately, he was right. As crowded as the ballroom was, the couples were not far enough apart to allow for true confidences. To speak over the music was to risk being overheard by their nearest neighbors in the set.

"You *will* tell me more soon, won't you?" she pleaded before they were obliged to separate again. "If you call upon me tomorrow, perhaps Lady Simpson will allow us to walk out together, as my aunt did."

Julian merely smiled as he turned away.

"You are every bit as delightful in the dance as I imagined," he told her when they next came together, before she had a chance to speak. "I am enjoying the sight nearly as much as I enjoyed seeing you ride to the hunt last month. I recall you told me your aunt keeps no riding horses, but what of the Simpsons? I would offer to mount you myself, if it would not be considered unforgivably forward, for it seems wrong to deprive you of an activity you enjoy so much."

Violet blinked. Completely apart from the impropriety of such a suggestion, she had not thought Julian would have sufficient means for such a thing.

"I thank you, but that will not be necessary. Just this morning Lord Marcus Northrup lent me a horse for the duration of my stay in London, at the behest of his sister-in-law, Lady Anthony. I was most grateful, as you may imagine, for I have missed it dreadfully."

"I do not doubt it, for you seem formed for riding," he said as he again moved away from her.

Though she smiled at the compliment, she would much have preferred to use that brief interlude to ask more discreet questions. Alas, the dance ended without offering any further opportunity for conversation.

As Julian returned her to her party, he relieved her frustration somewhat by reminding her that she had also promised him a waltz.

"Of course," she eagerly replied. "I very much look forward to it." That, of all dances, should allow for enough private talk that she could finally learn something of his activities as the Saint—and offer to help him. She was therefore in excellent spirits when he left her...until she encountered Lord Rushford's critical eye.

"Miss Turpin, would you be willing to grant me a dance?" he asked icily.

She frowned. "I am engaged for the next with Sir Lawrence."

"Actually, I thought to request the dance following." His expression was still disapproving.

"Very well, if you like." She attempted to match his cool tone, refusing to be cowed.

He bowed stiffly and moved away. Watching him go, she reminded herself that she need not worry about losing his good opinion, as she'd never had it to begin with. It therefore mattered not how he would react if he learned of her plan to help the Saint of Seven Dials.

Not that he would, for nothing in the world could induce her to tell him. Julian's secret was quite safe with her.

Sir Lawrence came forward to claim her then, and she greeted him cheerfully. Tomorrow, she felt sure, would bring her at least one step closer to her noble goal.

Though he was careful not to let it show, Rush heralded the end of the next dance with relief. Most young ladies, in his experience, had little on their minds beyond fashions and gossip. Unfortunately, Lady Beatrice Bagford seemed shallow by even that standard.

"Do tell me whether Miss Stuckton has the right of it, Lord Rushford," she pleaded when their set concluded. "She assures me you intend to marry Miss Simpson and if she is wrong, I should take immense pleasure in telling her so."

Rush gave her a bland smile. Lady Simpson might be willing to drop hints to all and sundry, but he would honor their agreement to keep the matter private until receiving Sir Clarence's consent.

"I fear you and Miss Stuckton must learn the truth along with everyone else, Lady Beatrice, when it either appears in the papers or does not." Ignoring her pout, he sketched her a parting bow and went in search of Miss Turpin.

He saw Bigsby leading Miss Simpson to the floor as he approached. Oddly, that sight didn't bother him nearly so much as seeing him with Miss Turpin had done—no doubt because he had little fear that Miss

Simpson could be led astray. Turning his attention to her adventure-prone friend, he bowed.

"I believe the next is mine?" he said rather more stiffly than he had intended.

In return, Miss Turpin coolly inclined her head and allowed him to lead her back to the dance. When the orchestra struck up the opening strains to a waltz, however, she appeared startled, even displeased.

"Oh! I did not realize—" She broke off, frowning.

Though chagrined by her obvious dismay, Rush strove to hide it. "Do you not waltz, Miss Turpin?" he asked, despite having seen her do so at Ivy Lodge. In fact, he had requested this specific dance in hopes of speaking with her privately.

"I… Of course I do. I was merely caught by surprise, as I did not attend to the program. I, ah, did not mean to appear reluctant, Lord Rushford." She attempted to smooth over her vexation with a smile.

"Glad I am to hear it. Shall we?" Taking her gloved hand in his, he lightly placed his other hand at her waist while she tentatively set her other hand on his coat sleeve.

Facing the alluring Miss Turpin in such close proximity, he was irresistibly reminded of their encounter in the stables at Ivy Lodge. Their current posture suddenly felt rather too intimate, despite the crowd surrounding them. Rush had waltzed with dozens of ladies and had never understood why some considered the dance scandalous. Now he did.

He commenced guiding Violet about the floor to the music, hoping that might make him feel less as though he were embracing his partner.

It did not.

If anything, he was more aware than ever of her alluring form and the grace with which she moved. With an effort, he recalled his original purpose in engaging her for this dance and cleared his throat.

"Miss Turpin, as a stand-in of sorts for your brother, I feel obliged to make one more effort to warn you against over-familiarity with Bigsby. I know you had a passing acquaintance with him in your youth. However, I—and your brother—had opportunities to see him in unguarded moments at school. 'Tis that which convinced us both that he should not be trusted around any young lady of character."

Though he'd hardly expected gratitude for his advice, he was startled by the anger suddenly sparkling in her beautiful eyes.

"I'm sure you *believe* you are acting in my best interest, or at least my brother's, my lord, but you are being unreasonable in the extreme. Surely you cannot expect these vague references to whatever you knew of Julian during your school days to alter my opinion of him. People do change, you know. Did you do nothing during your youth, or during the war, that you would prefer not to be judged by now?"

Rush blinked, wondering how she guessed that. Had Thor—? No, her question was clearly rhetorical. Even so, he felt obliged to give her an honest answer.

"I admit I have done a thing or two in the past that I am not particularly proud of. In Bigsby's case, however, I am not speaking of isolated incidents, but a pattern of behavior. He had a reputation at Eton for bullying boys who were younger or smaller than himself. And in the town, he—"

He broke off, realizing how indelicate it would be to relate Bigsby's activities involving serving wenches and tradesmen's daughters.

"How long ago was that, my lord?" She was clearly not yet convinced. "Six years? Seven? How much contact have you had with Julian in recent years?"

Though his mouth tightened at her repeated use of the man's Christian name, he did not remark upon it. "By my own choice, very little, other than in passing during a few fox hunts."

"So you admit that your current poor opinion is based purely on things he did as a mere boy. As I have seen rather more of him lately than you have, you will excuse me if I rely on my own observations rather than on your recollections. I have reason to believe he has developed a far nobler side to his character than the one you recall from your school days."

Rush's brows rose in surprise. "Do you, indeed? On what evidence do you base that belief?"

To his surprise, she colored slightly and averted her eyes. "I...

cannot tell you that, but I assure you that I speak on *very* good authority."

He felt his vitals contract. He'd worried she might be developing a *tendre* for the fellow and it now seemed he was correct. The discovery caused him near-physical pain, forcing him to acknowledge that his inappropriate feelings for Violet Turpin went far deeper than he had realized.

Not that it could matter, as he'd foolishly consigned his future to Miss Simpson.

"In that case, I must hope I am mistaken about Bigsby," he said after a pause. "If I am not, however, I very much hope you will soon come to see the truth for yourself."

If she fancied herself in love with Bigsby, it was more important than ever to open her eyes to the man's true character, even as it decreased the likelihood he could do so. Did not all the poets claim that love was blind?

She shot him an uncertain look. "I am not given to self-deception, my lord. I have solid reasons for my conviction that Julian's character is much more admirable than you paint it. In the unlikely event that I *am* somehow mistaken, I will no doubt discover it in time."

"I only hope that it *is* in time," he replied fervently.

Though his earnestness clearly startled her, she made no rejoinder. Thinking it best not to press her further on the subject just now, Rush also remained silent until he returned her to Lady Simpson at the conclusion of the dance.

"I thank you for your indulgence, Miss Turpin," he said then. "I hope I have not ruined any chance of prevailing upon you to dance with me again this Season."

With a look he could not decipher, she inclined her head. "Though we seem unable to agree, my lord, I have never been one to hold a grudge. I daresay we will have many opportunities in future to argue this and other matters, whether in the dance or elsewhere."

The idea of a future spent matching wits with Violet Turpin suddenly struck Rush as remarkably appealing. Which was, of course, absurd.

Still, he owed it to Thor to somehow disabuse Miss Turpin of her misguided faith in Bigsby. No doubt the fellow had told her some story or other to convince her he was a veritable hero.

Hero? The word echoed in his head. There was but one person he knew for certain Miss Turpin regarded as such—the Saint of Seven Dials. Nor had she made any secret of that. Could Bigsby have…?

Hm.

Filing the idea away for future perusal, he reluctantly went in search of his next partner.

CHAPTER TWELVE

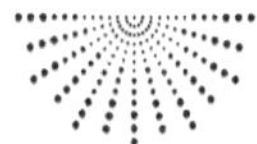

dance program, something rarely posted at country assemblies. To her
dismay, no second waltz was planned, which meant she could not
fulfill her promise to Julian—or extract more information from him. In
fact, the rest of her dances were already bespoken.

During the carriage ride back to Cavendish Square after the conclusion of the ball, she discovered another reason to regret her blunder of
waltzing with the wrong man.

"Miss Turpin, whatever do you mean by waltzing with Lord Rush-
ford this evening when Mary did not waltz with him even once?" Lady
Simpson demanded the moment they were underway. "Lady
Mountheath made a point of commenting upon it."

"I'm sorry, my lady. I, er, did not realize when I agreed to dance
with him that it would be the only waltz of the evening or, indeed, that
it was to be a waltz at all," Violet truthfully told her.

Lady Simpson was not mollified. "The dance order was posted near
the orchestra all evening. You must have seen it." She then turned on
her daughter. "And some might think *you* take your engagement no
more seriously than Lord Rushford appears to, waltzing instead with
Mr. Bigsby. Handsome though he is, you should not encourage him."

Though Mary also mumbled an apology, her mother continued to scold them both for the rest of the drive.

Adding to Violet's discomfiture was the realization that she had enjoyed her waltz with Lord Rushford, despite their argument. Or perhaps because of it? Completely apart from the way he affected her, she could not deny she enjoyed matching wits with his lordship.

Not that it mattered, as he was promised to Mary. Even if she found her friend a more suitable match, she doubted Lord Rushford would ever reciprocate Violet's lingering *tendre* for him.

No, she would be far wiser to turn her romantic inclinations toward Julian. Was not the Saint of Seven Dials the true hero of her dreams? Not only was he strikingly handsome into the bargain, Julian did not disapprove of her the way Lord Rushford did.

Having made that resolve, Violet was quite pleased the next morning when Julian called at the Simpson house before Lord Rushford did. Much as he had with Aunt Philomena, Julian did an admirable job of dividing his attention between all three ladies.

"Pray do not feel you must waste your compliments on me, Mr. Bigsby," said Lady Simpson at one point. "I am well past the age where my head can be turned by a handsome man's flattery." Her smile, however, belied her words.

Though Mary was predictably embarrassed by his expressions of admiration toward her, Violet noted that her friend did appear more comfortable with him than with Lord Rushford—at least until Julian invited the young ladies to ride out with him.

Mary immediately demurred. "I...I would rather be excused, sir, if you do not mind."

Her mother seconded her reservations. "I fear my daughter is not yet experienced with riding in Town," she told him. "I've no objection to Miss Turpin accompanying you, however, provided one of the grooms goes along. Not only for propriety, but in consideration of the uncertain temperament of Miss Turpin's mount."

Julian glanced curiously at Violet. "Spirited, is it? Having seen your performance on the hunting field, I've no doubt you manage perfectly well."

Lady Simpson sniffed. "That is what Lord Rushford and Lord Killerby claimed. She came to no harm when they all rode out on Sunday but I must still insist on sending a groom with you."

That caveat was readily agreed to, and Violet went to change into her habit. Ten minutes later, she joined Julian on the front steps.

"What a beautiful chestnut," she exclaimed on seeing his horse. "I don't know when I've seen such perfect lines or well-proportioned head. Have you had him long?"

"But a few days, actually," Julian admitted. "He didn't come cheaply, of course, but I believe he was worth every penny, for he goes as wonderfully as he looks."

The skewbald gelding was led round from the mews just then, offering a ludicrous contrast to the elegant chestnut.

"I begin to perceive Lady Simpson's reservations." Julian's brows rose in startled amusement. "Perhaps I should offer to mount you after all?"

"He may not be a pretty beast, but he went perfectly well when I rode him on Sunday," Violet replied, ignoring the latter part of his comment.

Motioning the groom to hold the skewbald steady, she allowed Julian to toss her into the saddle. They then headed for the park, the groom following on Mary's mare.

"This is perfect," Violet commented. "An even better chance to talk without being overheard than a waltz would have been last night. I didn't realize there would be but one, you see."

"Yes, you did promise it to me." He sent her a sidelong look. "I was quite eaten up with jealousy when you danced it with Rushford instead, for I've no title or rich holdings to set against his."

Her laugh was only slightly forced. "Never fear. Lord Rushford has made it perfectly plain that he has no intentions toward me whatever. In fact, he is...expected to offer for Miss Simpson." Why she did not come out and say they were already engaged, she wasn't sure. "But enough about him. I wish to hear more about *you*, Julian, and the secret you essentially admitted to me last night."

"Ah, I suspected that was why you were so eager to ride out with me today." He appeared more amused than upset. "I still maintain that it would be safest if you did not know, but as you have guessed the truth, I may as well share the sordid details."

Violet glanced over her shoulder to confirm that the groom was out of hearing—and that Lord Rushford was not about to interrupt them again.

"Please do! As you know, I have long admired the Saint from afar. I cannot express how thrilled I was to discover I actually *know* him! I liked you quite well already, of course, but now? Your cleverness—and heroism—are the stuff of legend! When I think of all you've done these two or three years past, eluding capture again and again..." Trailing off, she sighed.

"You quite flatter me! Underneath the legend you speak of, I am still the same Julian Bigsby you knew before," he replied with a self-deprecating laugh. "I must say, though, that your admiration makes me doubly glad I chose to resume my, ah, activities after a brief respite."

"No doubt the poor denizens of London's slums are grateful as well," she said warmly. "Most, I am sure, have few others they can count on when finding themselves in dire straits. What a hero you must be to them!"

He shrugged. "Perhaps so."

His modesty only impressed her further. She had always been touched by the relief and delight of her father's poorest tenants when she brought them food and medicine. How grateful must those in the slums be, given their far more desperate needs.

"Let me help you, Julian, do!" she blurted out on that thought. "I know the Saint has always worked alone, but surely there is *some* assistance I can offer?"

"Certainly not!" he exclaimed in apparent horror. "I would be the greatest cad in nature to allow such a thing. The risks—"

"I don't care about the risks," she interrupted. "My single greatest wish on coming to London was to meet and offer aid to the Saint of Seven Dials. Until last week, I thought it a mere pipe dream, but now —! Please, Julian? You *must* let me help in some way."

Though his expression was sympathetic, he shook his head. "I fear it would be far too dangerous, Violet. Even after years of experience, I have come near being caught more than once. Without someone to stand lookout—"

"Allow me to do that, then," she cried eagerly. "I do not ask to help with actual burglaries, for my inexperience there would likely increase your danger. By acting as your lookout, however, I could safeguard us both. I should also love to help in distributing your spoils to the deserving poor."

Julian smiled. "That is just like your soft heart, Violet, but the London slums are no place for a lady, believe me."

"Very well," she conceded—for the moment. "But you *will* let me keep watch the next time you act as the Saint, won't you?"

For some moments he rode in silence, clearly deep in thought, while she watched his expression for some sign he might relent. Finally, as they neared the park gates, he sighed.

"I cannot deny that having a lookout would be extremely helpful, reluctant as I am to put you in even the slightest danger."

Only a fear of spooking her horse prevented Violet from clapping her hands. "Thank you, Julian! I promise you will not regret it. When do you propose our next foray?"

He regarded her in obvious amusement. "As soon as a good opportunity presents. I am constantly on the lookout—for the sake of the poor, you know. No doubt I will hear word of something before long."

"You must tell me the moment you do," she insisted. "Meanwhile, I shall work out how best to slip out of the house without being detected. Lady Simpson is rather sharper than my Aunt Philomena, but with a bit of planning, I'm certain it can be done."

His smile was admiring. "Have I not said that you are clever? If anyone can manage such a thing, it will be you, Violet. Though if you should decide such an outing is too dangerous after all, I will completely understand."

"No chance of that," she assured him, grinning now. "Not for anything would I miss what is sure to be the adventure of a lifetime— and for a good cause besides."

~

When Rush presented himself at the Simpson house the day after the Jeller ball, he was dismayed to learn that Miss Turpin had ridden out with Bigsby only a few minutes earlier. She seemed increasingly determined to ignore his warnings about the man. He feared he knew why.

Setting aside his vexation, he summoned a cordial greeting for Miss Simpson and her mother. "I am pleased to see you both in such good looks today. Dancing late into the night has been known to overtax some ladies."

Lady Simpson gave an affected laugh. "I assure you, my daughter is made of sterner stuff than that, Lord Rushford, despite her delicate appearance. She is as well suited to the demands of a London Season as to the rigors of country life on a large estate."

She looked to her daughter for confirmation, but Miss Simpson managed only a weak, somewhat alarmed smile in response.

As before, Rush spent most of his visit attempting to draw her out, again with little success. He lingered well beyond the expected quarter hour in hopes of Miss Turpin's return, only leaving when other callers arrived. Remaining longer might seem to confirm the rumors of his engagement to Miss Simpson, something he was reluctant to do. Why that should be, when Lady Simpson clearly had no such qualms, he preferred not to examine.

On returning home, he discovered a message from Lord Peter Northrup asking him to call in Curzon Street at his convenience. Rush immediately set out, eager to share the suspicion that had occurred to him last night. Not many minutes later, he was shown into a well-appointed library.

"Good of you to come so promptly, Rushford," Lord Peter greeted him. "There's someone I'd like you to meet."

Rush turned to regard the other two people in the room—Lady Peter and a boy of fifteen or sixteen.

"My wife, of course, you met last night," Peter said. "This is her brother, William, though he prefers to be called 'Flute.' He has been of particular assistance in this current endeavor. William, Lord Rushford."

The lad bowed to Rush most properly. "Glad I am to meet you, your lordship." He spoke the words carefully, then glanced at his sister, who nodded approvingly.

"The pleasure is mine, young Flute," Rush said, receiving a grin for using the boy's preferred moniker. Then, to Peter, "What sort of assistance?"

"Information, primarily. I told you that Sarah briefly stepped into the role of the Saint of Seven Dials last year in order to prevent her brother from doing so. What I did not tell you was that Flute here acted as the Saint's primary confederate almost from the beginning of his career. He has therefore been intimately involved with the Saint's activities and is well acquainted with most of the poorer denizens of London's slums."

The boy nodded eagerly. "Aye, it were me who told the Saint when someone was in bad need of money. Then I fenced whatever he brung...brought me, so's I could pass along the blunt to them as needed it. That way no one ever knowed...knew for certain who the Saint really was."

"As you can see, my brother is still unlearning the street cant that was all he spoke for much of his life," Lady Peter said to Rush. "We are striving to improve his speech so that he can attend one of the better public schools without embarrassment."

"I should say you're doing very well indeed," Rush commended the lad. "I take it this current Saint knows nothing of how you assisted his predecessors?"

Flute shook his head. "How could he, when he's no true Saint? Certain it is, none of what he's stole so far has made its way to the poor what needs it. Keeping it for himself, I'll warrant."

"Just as we surmised," Lord Peter agreed. "William has also spoken with some of his former, ah, associates on the streets and it appears the imposter has none of the necessary contacts to easily convert his takings to cash."

"Ah," Rush said. "That would explain why he has limited most of his thefts to coin, bank notes and items generally easy to sell without arousing suspicion."

Peter smiled. "Precisely. Given that, I believe our bait should be cash. That will be more likely to tempt him than any other valuables. The difficulty will be to make sure word of it reaches only the right ears. If we cast too wide a net, we risk every thief in London attempting our target."

"As it happens, I have a suggestion on that front," Rush told him. "I have reason to suspect that a Mr. Julian Bigsby might be our man. Mind you, I've no proof whatsoever as yet, just a hunch based on a few details."

Peter appeared both surprised and slightly skeptical. "What details?"

"He is tall, thin and blond, for a start," Rush replied. "He also appears to have very recently come into a bit of money, judging by a noticeable improvement in his attire."

"Not much to go on. He could simply have had a run of good luck at the gaming tables."

"True enough," Rush conceded. "We must start somewhere, however, and from what I knew of him when we were at Eton, he's not the sort to be overly constrained by ethical considerations."

Even as he spoke, Rush wondered whether his suspicions of Bigsby were primarily motivated by the very jealousy he had denied to Miss Turpin.

Peter looked thoughtful. "What else do you know of this Bigsby? I take it he's here in London?"

"Yes, he was at the Jeller do last night, which implies he is trying to insinuate himself into higher tiers of Society than he formerly occupied. I've no idea where he lodges, however, nor who his current friends might be."

"Hm. Perhaps Flute may help us there. He is still in contact with a wide network of boys who are able to move at will throughout the dark underbelly of London. Among them, they can likely ferret out everything there is to know about this Mr. Bigsby."

Rush regarded the lad curiously. "Are you willing to do this? Will your friends be?"

"Oh, aye, m'lord," Flute replied enthusiastically. "All us boys want this false Saint caught. Giving the real Saint a bad name, he is."

"And is Lady Peter willing to have you try?" Rush looked to Peter's wife.

Though her lovely brow was furrowed, she nodded. "During my brief stint as the Saint, I gained a renewed appreciation for the straits of London's poor—and for how desperately they need a hero to look up to. For their sakes, I have agreed to allow my brother to do what he can, so long as he is careful."

"If Bigsby's our man, it's possible Flute's network of street urchins will uncover additional evidence implicating him," Peter said then. "At the least, they may discover whether anyone passed information to this false Saint that guided his earlier thefts. That could provide the perfect avenue for distributing our rumor."

Rush thought for a moment. "About that rumor. We'll want to create a narrow window of opportunity, if we're not to stake out our target for nights or weeks on end," Rush pointed out.

Peter nodded his agreement. "True, though I suspect that if we make the bait attractive enough, this fellow will take his earliest opportunity to steal it. Thus far, he's demonstrated no particular ability to control his impulses. That failing should work to our advantage."

"Hm. Think you a sum of five hundred pounds in notes would do the trick?"

"I should think so, as it's a good bit more than he's made off with in total thus far. As for location, I suggest we wait until William brings us a bit more information."

"Agreed," Rush said. He then turned to Lady Peter. "I confess, madam, that since learning you were one of the Saints of Seven Dials, I have been quite curious to hear more. I doubt not you have a few interesting stories to tell."

She and Lord Peter both laughed. "Indeed she does," Peter said. "As you know so much already, I suppose there is no harm in telling you all. Would you like to begin, my love, or shall I?"

The look that passed between them caused a twinge at Rush's heart, for it clearly spoke of their affection for each other. Alas, it was Miss Turpin's sweetly animated face that came unbidden to his mind rather than Miss Simpson's.

Fortunately, he had no time to dwell on that inconvenient observation before Lord and Lady Peter began recounting their remarkable tale.

On returning from her ride, Violet learned that both Lord Rushford and Sir Lawrence and Lord Killerby had all called at the Simpsons' in her absence. Though she expressed regret at missing them, she scarcely minded, given the success of her outing with Julian.

Before taking his leave, he was again attentively charming to both Simpson ladies but the moment he was gone, Lady Simpson turned to Violet.

"You say that you and Mr. Bigsby have been acquainted for some time. What do you know of his family?"

"His parents are dead, I believe, but an uncle of his has property in Lincolnshire," Violet replied. "We first met when he was visiting that uncle during school holidays, then renewed our acquaintance in the Shires last month, before I came to London. My aunt spoke with him at *great* length when he came to call after my arrival in Town and she found him quite unexceptionable."

Lady Simpson seemed satisfied. "He certainly is a polite young man, and quite good looking as well. Now I know a bit more about him, I've no objection to him calling here."

Violet was relieved, for she would hate to have her interactions with Julian limited, now she was so close to fulfilling her goal. He had spent the latter part of their ride regaling her with stories of his previous exploits, making her more eager than ever for their first adventure together.

During the card party she attended with the Simpson ladies, she was so distracted by thinking about it that she played very poorly. Only afterward did she recall her other goal, to find Mary a love match.

"You still seem very reserved around Lord Rushford," Violet observed to her friend when they were alone in Mary's room before changing for bed. "Is there perhaps some other gentleman you prefer over him?"

Mary glanced at her in surprise, then lowered her eyes with a little shrug. "It would not matter if I did, for Mama will never allow me to cry off."

"Even though your engagement is not yet official?" Violet asked.

Mary shook her head. "She is now quite determined that I will be a countess. Nothing short of a duke or marquess paying addresses to me is like to change her mind—not that I know any unmarried ones anyway."

"Oh, pooh," Violet scoffed. "Rank and wealth should not dictate who you choose to spend your life with. So long as a man can support you in comfort and is of good character, what matters most is that he is thoroughly in love with you—and that you love him as well."

"Does your Mr. Bigsby meet those qualifications?" Mary asked with a sly smile. "I notice that you seem to prefer his company to that of Lord Killerby or Sir Lawrence, though all three clearly admire you."

Violet grinned to show Mary she knew what she was about. "While I find Lord Killerby and Sir Lawrence perfectly agreeable, Mr. Bigsby is rather more...stimulating to converse with."

Mary looked thoughtful for a moment before asking, with surprising earnestness, "Do you believe stimulating conversation to be a good predictor of marital happiness?"

"I should think it a more likely predictor than the size of a man's estate or bank account," Violet replied. "Do not infer, however, that I have any thought of marrying Mr. Bigsby or anyone else at present. I am quite determined not to marry at all unless I am head over ears in love, and convinced that the object of my affection feels the same about me."

Mary regarded her wistfully. "I wish I could say the same. Alas, Mama has other ideas."

"Your mother will not be the one spending the rest of her life with whomever you marry," Violet pointed out. "The choice should be yours, not hers. Is not your future happiness worth fighting for?"

"You always were the bold one, Violet," said Mary admiringly. "Just now, listening to you, I almost feel as if I could. Come tomorrow, though, my resolve will waver and I will lose my courage, as I always do. Would that you were always by to embolden me."

"I promise to do what I can over the next fortnight, at least." She hoped it would be enough. Until Mary fixed her sights on someone else, she could never admit, even to herself, that Lord Rushford stimulated her far more than Julian did. Both conversationally and...in other ways.

"I am convinced that with practice you can learn to speak up for yourself," she told Mary then, "even if it occasionally means contradicting your mother. You know your own heart better than anyone. Do not fear taking a small risk now and again to safeguard it."

"I...I shall try."

Violet smiled approvingly at her friend. "That is all any of us can do."

Only two days after Lord Peter's young brother-in-law agreed to discover all he could about Julian Bigsby, Rush was invited back to Curzon Street. He again joined Lord and Lady Peter in the library, where the boy eagerly reported on all he had learned thus far.

"According to Tig, his favorite haunt is a gaming hell in Vere Street," Flute told them. "Tig also gave me a list of the blokes he seems friendly with." He glanced at Peter, who handed a slip of paper to Rush.

Glancing over it, Rush was unsurprised to note that none of Bigsby's known associates moved in the better circles of Society. "You say he's there often?"

"Aye, more nights than not," Flute replied. "Even when he goes to some Society do first, he goes there after to drink, dice and wench. Er —" He glanced at his sister. "To drink and dice, anyways."

"Good work, lad," Rush commended him. "I take it none of your compatriots heard anything directly tying Bigsby to the fellow lately pretending to be the Saint?"

The boy shrugged. "They wasn't watching him before yesterday, but they did ask around a bit. Seems he turned up in Town just a day or two before the first of these new robberies, so there's that."

"Still nothing I'd call hard evidence," Peter said, frowning. "Is there anything else?"

"Only that Tig and Stilt both heard a lad from Ickle's old gang boasting about helping the Saint of Seven Dials a week or so back. 'Course, they didn't believe him, since all of us know there's no proper Saint out there right now. Mayhap he meant this imposter though?"

Peter's eyebrows rose. "It's certainly possible. Did he say what sort of help he gave this so-called Saint?"

"No, just that the Saint paid him well for it."

"Information, perhaps," Rush guessed. "He would scarcely break into houses at random, so must have some way of choosing his targets. I should say we've nothing to lose by having Flute's friends share our rumor with that boy. If Bigsby takes the bait, we'll have all the proof we need."

"Whoever takes it, we'll be ready to catch the blackguard," Peter said. "Let's choose a location for our trap so we can craft an appropriate rumor to lure him there."

Rush was ready with a suggestion. "How about my house? That will spare us the necessity of bringing anyone else in on our scheme. I can give the servants the night off, so they'll be in no danger."

Though he did not say so, he also felt sure that Bigsby would leap at a chance to victimize him, after the way he'd humiliated the man in front of Miss Turpin.

After only a moment's consideration, Peter nodded. "I would

prefer to keep this plot to ourselves until we know whether it will bear fruit. You're certain you don't mind having your house used in this manner?"

"Not at all," Rush assured him. "After all Flute here has done for us, I'm more than willing to make this small contribution to the cause."

They then fell to discussing what false lead would prove most effective, discarding their first few ideas as either too implausible or too complicated.

"How would this serve?" Rush finally said. "Rumors are already circulating that I mean to offer for Miss Simpson. I can be seen in Threadneedle Street on Friday afternoon withdrawing several hundred pounds, in anticipation of buying a ring when the jewelers' shops open Monday morning. One of Flute's friends can claim to have overheard me saying where I mean to keep the money in the interim. With luck, word will reach Bigsby quickly enough that we can set our ambush for Saturday night."

Peter grinned. "We can add to the story that you are known to give your servants Saturday nights off. That should ensure that he won't delay his attempt till Sunday."

After fleshing out a few details, they rehearsed the story with Flute. He agreed to share their rumor with Tig and Stilt, who would then arrange to have it overheard by the bogus Saint's suspected informant. If they were correct, the boy would almost certainly pass along the news of a rich, unguarded haul to the fellow now styling himself Saint of Seven Dials.

"With luck, we'll be able to turn the imposter over to Bow Street Saturday night, whether he proves to be Bigsby or not," Peter said.

Rush nodded. Though it was perhaps unworthy, he hoped it would indeed turn out to be Bigsby. Of course, his task then would be to convince Miss Turpin that the man was merely impersonating the Saint of Seven Dials and not the real item. Otherwise, Rush doubted she would ever forgive him for conspiring to have her idol arrested.

CHAPTER THIRTEEN

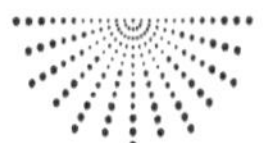

Over the next few days, Violet was alert for opportunities to remind Julian of his promise and to press him for more information. Largely due to Lord Rushford's interference, however, she found those opportunities almost nonexistent.

Though Julian called daily at the Simpson house, Lord Rushford—often accompanied by Lord Killerby—was always there before him and never left until after Julian departed. In the evening, his lordship seemed likewise determined to prevent Violet from speaking privately with Julian.

She had high hopes Thursday, when she convinced Lady Simpson to include Julian in their party for the theatre, only to have them dashed on their arrival. Lord Rushford, whose box they'd been invited to, arranged the seating so that she and Julian were too far from each other for conversation.

Friday night, however, she was finally able to grant Julian his deferred waltz during a ball at Claridge House. Resolutely ignoring the sight of Lord Rushford partnering Mary nearby, she seized the chance for a private talk.

"I begin to worry you have changed your mind about taking me on one of your adventures," Violet murmured. "Has the Saint had no recent...outings?"

Julian glanced around the crowded ballroom before answering. "No, alas, but you will be pleased to hear that he has another planned quite soon. Unless you've had second thoughts about assisting him?"

"Of course not! How can you ask? Have I not dropped hints enough these three days past?"

"You've certainly tried." Julian grinned down at her. "Though Rushford has not made it easy for you."

Though Violet had never told Julian about Lord Rushford's warnings, he'd obviously noticed the earl's efforts to keep them apart. "True, but he cannot prevent us talking now. We may not get another such opportunity, however, so you'd best tell me everything while this waltz lasts."

"Very well. Only two hours since, I received news of a rich prize that should be remarkably easy to procure. If my source was correct, the house in question will be quite empty tomorrow night, lessening the risk considerably. Perfect, in fact, for your first, ah, *outing* with the Saint."

"Tomorrow night?" Violet had scarcely dared hope her adventures would begin so soon. "I presume the owner of this prize is someone who, um, deserves the attention of the Saint? From all I have read, he generally limits his targets to those who need taking down a notch."

Julian glanced over her shoulder, a smile playing about his full lips. "Oh, this fellow is *quite* in need of that, I assure you. In fact, this should be a particularly satisfying pigeon to pluck."

"Then I have no qualms at all about helping you," she told him. "When and where shall I meet you?"

"If you can manage to slip out of the house at half past midnight, I'll meet you in the Cavendish Square mews."

She instantly agreed to do so. "We are to accompany Lord Killerby and Lord Rushford to a concert at Lady Trumbull's, but I can simply plead the headache to remain behind. As the actual concert does not begin till eleven, I doubt Lady Simpson and her daughter will be home before two, or even three."

"I will have you back well before that," he promised, smiling warmly down at her. "With luck, this will be but the first step in what I hope may be a long—and profitable—partnership."

As Saturday evening approached, Violet found it difficult to conceal her mounting excitement—which was essential if her claim of a headache was to be believed. Though hungry, she forced herself to pick at her dinner, eating little while sighing audibly.

"Is something wrong, Violet?" Mary asked concernedly after the third sigh. "Are you not well?"

Violet shook her head with mock regret. "I fear I have the most dreadful headache. It has been coming on this hour or two past. Would you mind terribly, Lady Simpson, if I stayed quietly at home tonight?"

Though her hostess was clearly surprised, she did not appear particularly displeased.

"Of course you must rest, my dear, if you are not feeling quite the thing. Mary and I will make your apologies to Lord Rushford...and Lord Killerby."

Her complacent expression told Violet she had noticed Lord Rushford's efforts to come between herself and Julian, and had credited them to entirely the wrong motive. Violet did not much care, so long as it cleared her path tonight.

Immediately after dinner, Violet went up to her room to prepare for the thrilling evening ahead. She was just pondering which shoes would be most practical should she be required to run when Brigid came in.

"Lady Simpson's abigail mentioned as how you're feeling too poorly to go out tonight, Miss. Is there anything I can get you?"

"Actually, yes," Violet replied with a grin. "I would very much like you to go down to the kitchens and get me some food, for I vow I am quite famished. If you can do so without saying it is for me, so much the better."

Brigid appeared understandably confused. "Not for you, Miss?"

Though Violet had not meant to tell Brigid of her plans, she'd never been able to keep secrets from the girl. "I am not really ill," she confessed. "I simply wished everyone to think so, that I might be free to do something else tonight—something no one else is to know about."

Brigid's confusion instantly gave way to suspicion. "Oh, Miss! What start are you about now? Not another elopement, I hope?"

"Certainly not!" Violet exclaimed. "I've quite learned my lesson *there*. Not to worry. If all goes well I will only be gone an hour or two, and with none the wiser. Believe it or not, I am going help the Saint of Seven Dials in one of his capers!"

The maid's eyes grew round. "Never say so, Miss! You've actually met him, then?"

"I have indeed. So have you, though it's probably safer if I don't tell you who he is. But there, go and fetch me something to sustain me for my adventure, won't you?"

Though still clearly alarmed, Brigid went to do her bidding and returned a short time later with meat and bread rolls wrapped in a napkin, along with a cup of strong tea. As Violet ate, the girl did her best to dissuade her from going out.

"If you're caught, you'll land in prison or worse. You might even be hanged! Please, Miss, please, can't you bide safe here instead?"

"And miss this chance to achieve my dearest wish? I should never forgive myself! If you'll just help me into my old drab day dress, you can run back off to the kitchen or wherever you like and pretend I never told you anything about it. I can easily manage the rest myself."

When Brigid still looked worried, Violet patted her shoulder. "Pray don't worry. I'm only to act as a lookout, nothing more. J— The Saint will see I come to no harm and I will be back before you know it."

With that Brigid had to be content. After buttoning Violet into the required garment she left her, though not without a last, dubious glance over her shoulder.

Realizing that Mary might peep in on her before leaving for the concert, Violet tucked her sturdy walking shoes back into the clothespress, turned down the lamp and climbed into bed, pulling the counterpane up to conceal the dress she wore. Her precaution was only just in time. Less than five minutes passed before she heard light steps in the hallway, then the sound of her door creaking open.

Violet held perfectly still with eyes closed, keeping her breathing slow and steady—with some difficulty. Though this was by no means the first time she had feigned sleep before a late night escape, never before had she looked forward to an upcoming lark as much as this one. When the door snicked shut a few moments later, she breathed a sigh of relief.

Still, she forced herself to remain quietly in bed until she was certain both Simpson ladies were safely back downstairs. Nearly half an hour crawled by before she heard Mary's door open. Her footsteps again paused briefly outside Violet's door before finally continuing toward the staircase.

Jumping up, Violet ran to the window to see the Simpsons' carriage pulling up to the door. A moment later, the two ladies were handed inside by a footman and the coach drove away.

Congratulating herself on successfully passing her first hurdle, Violet completed her preparations for her coming adventure, then attempted to read until midnight—though with frequent glances at the little clock on the mantelpiece.

Shortly after ten o'clock Saturday night, Rush opened his front door to Lord Peter's knock to discover him accompanied by his brother Lord Marcus.

"Change of plans?" he asked in surprise.

"Not at all," Peter replied. "I thought an extra person might lessen the chance of the false Saint escaping, so asked Marcus if he would assist us. He jumped at the chance."

Rush eyed the other man warily. "Then he knows? About there having been more than one—?"

"I knew long before Peter did," Lord Marcus informed him with a chuckle. "He didn't feel it was his place to tell you without talking to me first, but I happen to be one of the former Saints he told you about."

Rush blinked, then laughed. "It would appear that Saintliness quite runs in your family. I don't suppose that Anthony has also—?"

Both brothers shook their heads, grinning. "Anthony never spent enough time in London to be an effective Saint, even if he were so inclined. In fact, he knows nothing of the business at all, so it would be best if you not mention it to him."

"Of course not," Rush promised. More than ever, he longed to know who the other two Saints were. "I agree it will be easier to nab the imposter with three of us here. I've already barred some of the exits to make his escape more difficult, but he will be able to leave the same way he gets in, unless we prevent him."

Thunder rumbled in the distance as they planned their ambush of the bogus Saint. According to their rumor, the stack of notes were in a strong box in the ground floor library, which also served as Rush's office. After some discussion, it was agreed that Peter would hide in there and Lord Marcus would position himself near the front door. Rush would stake out the rear of the house, as that was the most obvious way for the thief to enter and leave unobserved.

"With those avenues of escape covered we should have him, unless he leaps from an upper window to run along the rooftops," Peter said. "From what I've learned of his prior burglaries, I seriously doubt this fellow possesses that level of dexterity."

"As do I," Rush agreed, having observed Bigsby's dancing. "What say you to a toast before we take up our positions?" He poured small measures of brandy into three tumblers and handed them round.

Raising his glass, Lord Peter said, "To an unceremonious end to the career of this false Saint of Seven Dials. Long may the true Saint's legend endure."

To that they all drank, then separated to conceal themselves as agreed...and to wait.

～

At twenty-five past twelve, Violet slipped through the scullery door to the back garden and quietly pulled it to, then cautiously made her way to the mews behind. Passing silently through the back gate, she paused to adjust the hood of her dark cloak against the falling mist and to peer down the dark alleyway. What if Julian had been prevented from—

"Violet, is that you?" came a whisper from behind her.

She started violently, then turned. "Julian? Yes, 'tis I."

A shadow detached itself from the darker shade between the stable blocks and moved through the gathering fog to join her.

"Are you certain no one saw you leaving?" he asked.

"Yes. I was perfectly quiet and encountered no one, upstairs or down, on my way out. So long as I am back before the servants wake in the morning, no one should ever know I left the house."

Julian's teeth flashed in the dimness as he smiled his approval. "Good girl. It appears you are a natural at this sort of thing."

She grinned back. "I *was* rather known for my nighttime forays at Miss Gebhart's Seminary."

"Clearly, I could not have asked for a better confederate. Shall we go?"

"Lead on, do. Are we going far?" she asked.

"Not far." He turned down the alley toward Oxford Street. "Tonight's target is in Brook Street, just past Hanover Square."

Violet swallowed, the reality of what they planned sinking in. "Whose house are we burgling? You never did say."

"Better if you don't know." He tucked her hand into the crook of his arm. "Nor will *you* be doing any burgling. You are to stay safely back as my lookout, remember?"

She nodded, not daring to argue. They walked at a leisurely pace through the light drizzle, as though out for a casual stroll, first toward Marylebone Lane, then down to Oxford Street, still busy with carriage traffic.

While waiting to cross, Violet felt her first shiver of anxiety. "Are you certain this house will be empty tonight? You will be in no real danger?"

"If my information is correct, this should be the safest caper the

Saint has ever attempted. The most rewarding, as well. Particularly if…" He trailed off.

"If what?" she prompted.

He slanted an enigmatic look down at her, a smile playing about his lips. "It occurs to me that as no one saw you leave the Simpsons' house, we could quite easily make for Scotland once I have relieved tonight's most-deserving target of a small portion of his riches. What say you, Violet? Will you?"

She caught her breath. Was Julian—the Saint of Seven Dials— proposing marriage? For an instant she was tempted. What existence could be more worthy than one as the wife, the closest possible confidante, of the hero she had so long idolized?

Before she could agree, however, reason—and her heart—intervened. She had spoken truth to Brigid that she had learned her lesson about elopements. Her last one had been a vastly uncomfortable affair, precipitated by her foolishly mistaking flattery and the promise of excitement for true love. Never again.

"I'm sorry, Julian," she replied after a moment's reflection. "Much as I admire the Saint and like you as a friend, I am by no means prepared to elope with you tonight."

He sighed regretfully. "The fault is mine, for springing such a suggestion on you without warning. I shall give you time to consider the idea, after which I will try again to persuade you."

She gave no answer and they crossed Oxford Street in silence. Traversing one long alleyway lined with stables, they then turned down another before finally stopping.

"That's the house, just there." He pointed to the rear facade of one of the elegant town houses fronting Brook Street. "Bide you here while I find a way inside. Should anyone else approach the house, hoot like an owl and I will know to hide. Mind you are not seen, however."

"Shall I draw them off after warning you?" she asked hopefully. Making bird noises from the mews scarcely counted as an adventure.

"'Tis extremely unlikely you will need to do anything at all, for I doubt I'll be disturbed. If you *should* need to warn me, you must do so from hiding. No treasure is worth risking your safety, my dear. But now the Saint of Seven Dials had best get to work." With a wink, he turned away and crept toward the back of the house.

Pulling her hood close against the increasing damp, Violet watched him anxiously, occasionally glancing up and down the alleyway for any sign of trouble. She expected Julian to pick the lock of the door leading down to the kitchens, but instead he went to a nearby window. After fiddling with it a moment, he was able to push it open. His slender build made it easy for him to squeeze between sill and sash.

With a small sigh, Violet settled in to wait in the now-steady rain, wondering again whose house this was. Suppose it belonged to someone she knew? Someone she liked?

No. The Saint was known to prey only upon the richest and most unpleasant members of Society—which explained why the Mountheaths had been robbed more than once. This house must belong to someone similarly overbearing. Had not Julian said as much last night?

Peering up and down the mews again to confirm the area was still deserted, Violet stiffened. Had that tall shadow been there the last time she looked? Though it did not move, its outlines were eerily man-like. Increasingly uneasy, she held very still and continued to watch it.

A shout from the direction of the house snatched her attention away from the ominous shadow. *Julian!* Had he been spotted?

Sudden movement caught the corner of her eye. She wheeled back around in time to see the shadow she'd been watching assume the unmistakeable shape of a tall man, cloaked and hooded.

Violet froze as he strode toward the house, then realized that her first responsibility must be to prevent Julian from being captured. On that thought, she darted from her hiding place, deliberately knocking over a metal garbage bin in passing. It clattered noisily on the cobbles behind her as she ran lightly down the alley. With any luck, the sound would both alert Julian and distract the cloaked man from investigating the commotion at the house.

As she'd hoped, she heard heavy steps behind her—closing quickly. Triumph abruptly turned to terror. She ran faster, desperately seeking a way of escape. Ducking around a corner, she slipped into an open stable, then scrambled under a stall door, startling the horse dozing there.

"Shh! Shh!" She stroked the horse's neck, trying to calm the beast before it alerted her pursuer.

Only seconds ago she'd thought it better to risk her own capture than Julian's, but now she was far less sure of that. What if this was no officer of the law? It could be a bounty hunter, or another thief who had heard about the unguarded house. What might a hardened criminal do to a woman alone, in such a place after midnight? She continued frantically petting the horse, fearing to make a sound even to soothe it.

In the alley outside the stable, she heard the heavy footfalls slow, then stop. Surely, between the fog and the rain, he could not have seen clearly which way she'd gone?

Go on, go on, go on, she prayed silently. *Don't look in here.*

For a moment, her wish seemed granted. The footsteps resumed and slowly began to recede—before the silence was shattered by a shrill whinny from the horse beside her. Instantly, a shadow loomed in the stable entrance.

"Who's there?" a deep voice demanded.

With a gasp, Violet attempted to hide behind the horse, but she was not quick enough. The stall door slammed open. Her pursuer stepped past the animal and grasped her arm with a large hand to pull her inexorably from her hiding place.

"A woman, by the size and sound of it," he muttered. The voice now struck her as oddly familiar. "Come out into the light, madam, that I may see who else the scoundrel has duped."

Though Violet pulled against him, his grip was like iron. He hauled her out into the alley, faintly illuminated by the light of a distant street lamp. There, her captor roughly pulled the hood back from her face. As he did so, his own fell away as well.

Violet's heart soared for an instant, then plummeted just as quickly on facing a furious Lord Rushford.

～

Rush stared at the girl he held, unable to believe his eyes. On realizing his quarry was female, he'd assumed it was some doxy of Bigsby's brought along to act as lookout, then to dally with afterward. Never had he thought to find Violet Turpin in such a setting.

"What are *you* doing here?" he demanded, outraged that Bigsby would put her at such risk and equally angry that she had allowed him to do so. Sudden jealousy nearly choked him at this blatant evidence that the man was far more to her than the friend she had claimed. "How did Bigsby persuade you to accompany him here? To assist him in an attempted robbery?"

"Whatever do you mean?" She gave a bad imitation of a laugh. "I... I've scarcely spoken with Mr. Bigsby for days."

He regarded her with narrowed eyes. "Not even when you waltzed together at Claridge House last night? Do you really mean to deny he brought you here?"

"Of course I deny it! Why should he do such a thing?"

"If Bigsby did not bring you here, Miss Turpin, pray tell me how you come to be in such an unlikely place at such an unlikely time of night."

Her mouth opened and closed several times. "I, ah, was unable to sleep," she said at last. "I often walk alone at night in Lincolnshire, so I thought to take a stroll. I...I find the exercise calming. I, um, may have wandered rather farther than I intended, however. When I saw these mews, I thought at first they were the ones by Cavendish Square but I, er, see now that I was mistaken."

Rush raised an eyebrow.

"Whatever your real purpose here, Miss Turpin, I must return you to Lady Simpson's house at once. It is by no means safe for a lady to be abroad in London at such an hour unescorted, not even in Mayfair. Even one so contemptuous of convention as yourself should know that."

Predictably, she bristled. "Despite whatever promise you made to my brother, you are *not* my keeper, Lord Rushford. I am no child, and I will thank you not to treat me like one."

"Then perhaps you should endeavor not to act like one," he

snapped. "You cannot have thought your actions through tonight. A frequent failing of yours, I have observed."

She gasped in outrage. "How dare you? I have most certainly—"

Her words were cut off by a flash of lightning followed almost immediately by a clap of thunder. The sound had not yet faded when the rain became a veritable downpour.

"This way." He put a hand on her shoulder to guide her back under the shelter of the nearest stable. "We'd best wait here until the storm passes."

"I will go where I please, my lord," she hissed. Shaking water from her tousled hair, she glared up at him.

Rush was suddenly struck by the similarity to their encounter in the stables at Ivy Lodge, which had haunted his dreams ever since. The rain, her wet hair, the warm, homey smell of horses…her lovely, upturned face…

Without stopping to think what he did, he pulled her to him and covered her lips with his own.

She froze in his arms for an instant. Then, before he could release her, she abruptly melted against him, eagerly returning his kiss. Her hands slid up his shoulders to draw him closer.

Rendered momentarily incapable of rational thought, he deepened the kiss, glorying in the divine sensation of her warm, pliable lips beneath his own. Surely life could offer nothing better than this? For a dozen blissful seconds they clung together, oblivious to the pouring rain, before unwelcome reason intruded. Rush reluctantly—so reluctantly!—raised his head to gaze down at Violet's stunned face.

"Miss Turpin, I—" he began huskily, not knowing precisely what to say.

She stared back, wide-eyed, but then those beautiful eyes narrowed. "Is this how you bend susceptible women to your will, my lord? I daresay it works on most of them, but I am made of sterner stuff. If you are…quite done, I will go my way, as I ought to have done at once." She attempted to pull herself from his grasp.

Though he did not release her, he now held her at arm's length instead of pressed against him. That distance, small as it was, enabled him to think more clearly.

"I cannot possibly allow you to make your own way back to Cavendish Square in the middle of the night, and in such weather, Miss Turpin—or may I call you Violet, as Bigsby does?" When she did not reply, he continued, "I really must insist that you accompany me into the house so that we may determine our best way to proceed."

She regarded him with an expression of mingled stubbornness and uncertainty, along with a trace of what he could have sworn was longing. Or perhaps he attributed his own desire to the alluring woman before him?

"House?" she finally asked. "Which house?"

"The one you were watching earlier, of course. My house."

Her shocked expression appeared genuine. "Yours?" she gasped, then visibly strove to collect herself. "I…I did not know you resided in Brook Street, my lord."

"It is fortunate for you that I do, as that gives us both a handy refuge from this deluge. Shall we?"

For a moment he feared she would again attempt to run away from him, but after a moment of obviously anguished indecision she gingerly placed her fingertips on his outstretched elbow and allowed him to lead her back the way they'd come. The formality of her action struck him as vaguely absurd after the passionate kiss they had just shared, but he did not comment on it.

Instead he attempted to focus on what he—they—were to do next.

CHAPTER FOURTEEN

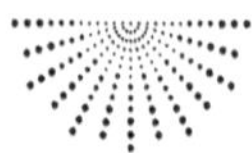

VIOLET SNEAKED A GLANCE AT LORD RUSHFORD'S PROFILE AS THEY slogged through the driving rain, still trying to recover her bearings.

That kiss had been an amazing experience—a revelation, really. A glimpse of what delights intimacy with the right man might hold. Mr. Plunkett had stolen a few quick kisses over the two days they'd spent on the road to Gretna Green, but she'd since come to consider her first *real* kiss the one she herself had stolen in the stables at Ivy Lodge. This kiss, however, had been something else entirely.

But now Lord Rushford was again treating her as though they were mere acquaintances. Clearly, that kiss had not affected him as profoundly as it had her, or he could not have released her so quickly —and she would not have felt obliged to turn so prickly, to hide her confusion.

She had heard that men put less stock in such things than women. No doubt that was particularly true for a man like Lord Rushford. A celebrated Army officer, he had doubtless shared kisses, and more, with many women over the years, both in England and abroad.

Still, he had not seemed *entirely* unaffected while they were kissing…

They reached the gate into the back gardens and she was abruptly reminded of the other stunner of the evening—that Julian had intended to rob Lord Rushford's house. Though she knew the two men held each other in dislike, she was dismayed to think something so petty could influence the noble Saint of Seven Dials in selecting a target.

"After you, madam." Lord Rushford pushed open the gate.

His cold formality made her shiver. Glancing up at him uncertainly, she preceded him into the garden.

"I presume that you feel obliged to protect Bigsby because you believe him to be the Saint of Seven Dials," he said almost conversationally as they walked toward the house. "In a moment I hope to prove that both your faith and your loyalty have been badly misplaced."

So saying, he opened the back door to reveal a long hallway. "Hello?" he called out. "Have you got him?"

In answer, more than one set of footsteps hurried toward them.

"Got him?" echoed a man familiar to Violet, though she could not instantly recall his name. "Do you mean to say that you do not?"

The other man, somewhat similar in appearance to the first, regarded her with raised eyebrows. "And who is this?"

"Miss Violet Turpin," Lord Rushford replied. "The lady to whom you lent that skewbald gelding."

"Ah, yes. Sister to one of the members of your and Anthony's fox hunting club." Then, to Violet, "Lord Marcus Northrup, ma'am. This is my brother, Lord Peter."

The man with slightly lighter hair nodded. "Yes, we met at the Jeller do a few nights since." He then turned back to Lord Rushford. "Our quarry escaped out the back, by a window. We assumed—"

"That I would capture him, as that was my post," Lord Rushford concluded. "So I should have, had I not been…detained." He slanted an unreadable look Violet's way.

Mounting anger replaced her urge to thank Lord Marcus. "Do I understand that you gentlemen laid a *trap* for the Saint of Seven Dials? How infamous! Do you not know—?"

"I'm sorry, Miss Turpin," Lord Marcus interrupted, "but we must go in pursuit at once if we're to have any chance at all of catching him. I'll leave Rushford here to explain."

So saying, the two men pelted down the hall and out the back door, leaving Violet alone with Lord Rushford.

"Well, this is awkward," he said. "I recommend you wait in the library while I find something dry for you to wear." He pointed to an open door.

"What? No! I must stop them!" She started after the two brothers, only to be barred by his lordship's outstretched arm.

"Don't be absurd. You'll never catch them on foot. Not that they are likely to find Bigsby anyway, after so long a delay."

A delay of her making—not that she was at all repentant. "I thought you a fellow admirer of the Saint of Seven Dials," she said severely. "Why else would you and the others have named your hunt club after him?"

"So I am. So are we all. That is why we are determined to stop Bigsby, who is no true Saint."

"You can't know that," she flared. "Why should you assume such a...such a thing?" She punctuated her final word with a violent sneeze.

With a muffled curse, he bundled her into the library and threw a lap rug over her shoulders. "We are both like to catch our deaths if we stand arguing in the hall while dripping wet. Sit you here by the fire while I go upstairs to change and fetch something dry for you."

Before she could utter another protest, he disappeared. For a moment she was tempted to defy him and leave the house before he returned, but by now she was shivering with cold. Pulling the rug closer, she went to the fire to warm herself. She remained standing, however, unwilling to completely submit to his high-handedness.

In five minutes he was back, now clad in loose-fitting breeches and a rough-spun shirt open at the neckline to reveal a vee of tanned skin. She was spared a temptation to stare by the necessity of catching the garment he tossed to her. It proved to be a dark woolen dress several sizes too large for her.

"Sorry," he said as she held it up. "It was my mother's. All I could find on short notice, I'm afraid. I'll leave you while you change out of your wet things."

Violet watched him go, the irrelevant thought darting through her brain that at least he did not keep fancy gowns for a mistress at his house, as she'd heard some single gentlemen did. She was reluctant to disrobe in his library, but at another violent shiver, prudence overcame modesty.

Mindful that he could return at any moment, she shrugged off her sodden cloak and with numbed fingers fumbled for the hooks of her dress. Unfortunately, it fastened down the back—the reason she'd required Brigid's help putting it on. In vain she attempted to undo the hooks herself, but could only reach the top three—not nearly enough to allow the frock to slip down over the shoulders.

Undaunted, she decided to take the deuced thing off over her head. After a few moments' struggle, however, all she managed to do was to get hopelessly entangled in wet folds of fabric that seemed to take on a strangling life of their own.

"Blast it!" she exclaimed in frustration from within the dress.

To her horror, she heard the library door open. "Miss Turpin?" came Lord Rushford's voice. "Do you require— What on earth are you doing?"

"I'm…I seem to be stuck," she admitted in a small voice. "I forgot that this dress fastens in back and when I tried to… Oh, bother!"

"Here, let me help you."

She was sure she could hear laughter behind the words—not that she blamed him, for she no doubt looked quite comical. Imagining what he must be seeing, she began giggling herself.

Giggling that abruptly stopped when she felt firm hands on her back, inexorably tugging the offending garment up and off. Though acutely embarrassed, she made no move to stop him, for it was clear she could not manage on her own.

He made short work of removing the sodden dress and an instant later nothing covered her body but a chemise and light corset. Instinctively, she brought both hands up to cover her nearly-exposed breasts. Her struggle with the dress had warmed her somewhat but now her cheeks grew positively hot. An answering flame in his eyes heated her face—her whole body—further, until he quickly averted his gaze.

The sensations she had experienced during that scorching kiss in the alleyway returned full force, making her suddenly yearn for more. Heart pounding, she took a tentative step toward him.

"My lord? Rush?"

At the nickname, her first use of it aloud, he turned back to her. The heat, she was both pleased and alarmed to see, had not left his eyes. "Miss Turpin…Violet… I—"

Suddenly she was in his arms again, being kissed as thoroughly as before. More thoroughly, for now his hands roamed up and down her thinly-clad back, leaving a trail of fire where they touched her. A small moan of pleasure escaped her, into his hungry mouth, to be echoed by a similar groan from him.

Shamelessly, Violet pressed her barely-covered breasts against the homespun of his shirt, inhaling the clean, masculine scent of him. Without the distraction of cold rain or the worry that they might be seen, she was eager to experience all the delights she could, for as long as he would provide them.

Alas, that proved not to be long at all. Mere seconds after she had mentally thrown caution to the winds, she felt the change that signaled his reason had again returned.

His hands on her back stilled, then withdrew, followed by his lips. Gently setting her away from him, he allowed his gaze to rove over her for one long moment, then turned away to noisily clear his throat.

"I…I must beg your pardon. That was inexcusable of me." His voice thrummed with something she wanted to believe was passion but feared was more likely embarrassment and regret. "To take advantage of you under such circumstances…"

Snatching up the big woolen dress, she held it before her like a shield. "I was also at fault, my lord. I…I could have stopped you had I wished to. It seems the, ah, excitement of the evening temporarily overset my capacity for good judgment, as well as yours."

She half expected him to point out that she had never demonstrated any such capacity, even while hoping he might deny that the effect was temporary. He did neither.

"Perhaps," was all he said. Then, darting a swift glance her way, he gestured toward the dress she held. "Will you…require my assistance with that, as well?"

"Thank you, no." Suddenly self-conscious, she turned her back, stepped into the outsized garment and drew it as closely about her as possible. Still feeling foolish, but far less vulnerable, she faced him again.

His lips twitched. "My mother was built on a rather larger scale than yourself, as you can see. One might say that she was a formidable woman in more ways than one."

"I understand that the late countess did a great deal of good among the poor." Violet spoke primly to hide her embarrassment.

"She did indeed. Her legacy is one that will not be soon forgotten. Now is hardly the time for reminiscences, however. We must instead discuss the future—in particular, the ramifications of this coil in which we find ourselves."

In other words, the coil *she* had created. Not that she'd known the house Julian meant to rob was Lord Rushford's. Her eyes were again drawn to that disturbing patch of bare flesh below his throat but she averted them before it could tempt her to further indiscretion.

"I, ah, suppose my best course is to take a hackney back to Cavendish Square," she forced herself to say. "I can likely slip in the same way I slipped out, before anyone notices I am missing."

"You…wish to pretend our encounter this evening never happened?"

Startled, she glanced at his face to find him frowning. "Don't you?"

As the words left her lips, she finally acknowledged what she had secretly suspected for some time: far from overcoming her youthful *tendre*, she had fallen head over ears in love with this man. Or had she loved him all along and merely pretended otherwise?

"Perhaps you are forgetting that we have already been seen together by Lord Peter and Lord Marcus Northrup," he pointed out.

"Given that, the obvious thing—the honorable thing—would be for me to marry you, and as soon as possible."

Simultaneously elated and appalled, her eyes flew wide. "Marry —!" The rigid set of his jaw effectively quenched the elation. "Surely no sacrifice so great is required," she said, swallowing her disappointment. "Particularly as you are already promised to Mary Simpson."

"No doubt she—or at least her mother—will be displeased, but I cannot help but feel that a situation such as this one takes precedence over an agreement made months ago that has yet to be formalized. Indeed, as a man of honor I see no viable alternative."

He spoke of honor, but nary a word about love—or even liking her. Lifting her chin, she sternly ordered her lips to stop trembling.

"Of course there is an alternative," she said. "The one I already suggested. I'm certain if you ask your friends to say nothing they will oblige you. Assuming I am able to sneak back into Lady Simpson's house without being missed, we may…simply go on as before."

"And if you are not?"

She bit her lip. "Even in that most unlikely event, there is no need for you to be implicated, my lord. If you can obtain a hackney for me, I will return at once. As my brother has likely told you, I have some, ah, experience at sneaking away and back undetected, so you need not worry that you will be required to sacrifice your future on my behalf."

He looked as though he wanted to argue further, but after regarding her narrowly for a long moment, he shrugged and again walked out of the room. When he returned, it was to inform her that a hackney carriage was at the curb.

Telling herself she was relieved, she threw her still-wet cloak over the ill-fitting dress and accompanied him to the front door.

"You must send me word at once if you are unsuccessful," he said as he handed her into the waiting coach. "I have already paid the shot to Cavendish Square. Good night…Violet."

"Good night…my lord." She caught herself before calling him "Rush" again. That way lay certain heartache.

With a nod, he shut her into the hackney and the driver whipped up his horse. Looking over her shoulder, Violet saw him walking toward the house without a backward glance.

Tears of disappointment pricked her eyes but she blinked them away. Surely she could not wish him to insist on marriage if he did not love her? Given her own feelings for him, she could think of nothing more painful...or humiliating. Undesirable as a loveless match might be, a match where only one partner was in love would be infinitely worse.

If she *were* caught sneaking back into the Simpson house, she was even more resolved than before to make no mention of Lord Rushford.

Rush firmly resisted the temptation to watch the hackney carrying Violet out of sight. That temptation was strong, for tonight had made crystal clear what he'd denied for the past month: regardless of how unsuitable a countess she might make, he was thoroughly in love with Violet Turpin.

He'd hoped, from the way she responded to his kisses, that she felt the same. Apparently not, judging by her reaction to his suggestion that they marry. Slowly reentering the house, he wondered what his next move should be.

He had only a few moments to contemplate his options before the two Northrup brothers returned with the news that the false Saint had indeed eluded them.

"Had too big a lead on us." Lord Marcus ruefully shook his head. "Had we but realized—"

"Yes, about that. I take it Miss Turpin is gone?" Peter asked. Rush nodded. "Then perhaps now you can explain what she was doing here and how she prevented you nabbing our imposter."

With no time to invent an alternative story, Rush simply told the truth. "Though she denied it, I believe she was acting as lookout for Bigsby. I followed her in hopes of learning who was working with him. Of course, I had no idea it was she until I caught up with her."

"Without our man, we've nothing to give the authorities," Peter pointed out. "Think you can persuade her to stand witness against Bigsby?"

Rush doubted it. "Not while she still believes him to be the true Saint. I will of course try to convince her otherwise, but..." He shrugged.

"Perhaps he left something incriminating behind that we can use?" Lord Marcus suggested.

Lacking a better idea, Rush lit every lamp and candle and they searched the library, though Peter insisted the intruder had spent only a few minutes there before fleeing. They then retraced his path of escape to the open ground floor window.

"Ah!" Peter plucked a scrap of cloth from the window frame. "It seems the fellow tore his jacket on his way out."

Rush peered at the bit of fabric. "If this can be matched to a coat of Bigsby's, we'll have something, at least."

Lord Marcus looked skeptical. "If he's at all clever, he'll dispose of it at first opportunity. Without more to go on, we don't dare break into his lodgings to search. We'd risk arrest ourselves."

"He's right," Peter regretfully admitted. "Persuading Miss Turpin to reveal what she knows is a far better option. Still, I'll hang on to this." He pocketed the scrap of torn cloth. "It may yet come in useful as evidence at some point."

The brothers then took their leave, Rush promising to do what he could to secure Violet's help.

In bed a short time later, Rush found sleeping difficult. Every time he nodded off, he was tormented by the memory of Violet Turpin's scorching kisses...and by fantasies of what might have followed had he behaved less honorably.

But that way lay madness.

The next day, as previously agreed upon, Rush and Killer called at the Simpson house to escort the young ladies for another Sunday ride in Hyde Park. Rush felt some trepidation as they were announced, wondering what sort of reception to expect. Had Violet been caught returning? If so, had she held to her promise to avoid mentioning his name, or would he be called upon to…?

Lady Simpson's greeting gave no hint that anything out of the ordinary had happened, while the two young ladies sat quietly—Violet reading and Miss Simpson doing needlework. Rush sent a quick, questioning glance at Violet while trying to quell his body's involuntarily reaction to the sight of her.

She responded with a tiny shake of her head before returning her gaze to the book she held. At this assurance that her absence had indeed gone undetected, Rush could not determine whether he felt more relief or disappointment.

"Ah, Miss Turpin," Killer exclaimed as they moved to take seats in the parlor. "I take it you are feeling quite recovered today?"

Rush blinked. How could Killer possibly know—?

Her reply clarified matters. "Yes, my headache is quite gone, my lord, thank you. I imagine it was brought on by so many late nights, after being used to country hours. A good night's sleep was enough to put me right."

She flicked another glance at Rush as she spoke and he observed that, contrary to her words, she appeared to have slept no better than he.

Lady Simpson then accosted him. "I hope, Lord Rushford, that the, ah, urgent business that prevented you attending last night's concert was successfully dispatched?" The edge in her voice signified her displeasure that he had not made his excuses personally.

"Er, yes. I would have sent word sooner, but my man of business did not contact me until I was fairly on my way out the door. As Lord Killerby arrived but a moment later, I begged him to convey how very disappointed I was to bow out on such short notice. I trust he did so?"

In fact, he had intentionally waited until the last moment to bow out of their engagement, rather than risk Miss Turpin giving Bigsby early word of his change in plans.

Lady Simpson sniffed, only partially mollified. "Yes, he was quite eloquent in your defense. I must say, both you and Miss Turpin missed an excellent performance. It was really quite stimulating."

Though Miss Turpin kept her eyes on her book, her color deepened slightly. Rush quickly looked away before his complexion could be similarly affected.

"I'm sure I would have enjoyed it exceedingly, my lady, though my taste is not equal to your daughter's or Lord Killerby's. I am striving to improve it, however."

Killer sent him an amused glance before turning back to the ladies. "I see Miss Simpson and Miss Turpin are already dressed for riding. We are fortunate to have another exceptionally fine day for it."

Though Miss Simpson looked vaguely alarmed, her mother smiled.

"Just as you are attempting to learn more of music, Lord Rushford, my daughter is striving to improve her equestrian skills. Shared interests are a good harbinger of a happy marriage, don't you think?"

Rush inclined his head in assent, though the image his wayward imagination conjured was a fetching vision of Violet flying over the countryside on horseback.

The horses were sent for and they all trooped outside. The skewbald gelding was as restive as before, but this time a groom was able to boost Miss Turpin into the saddle while she controlled the reins—a distinct improvement over the previous week.

"You and that horse appear to be getting better acquainted," Rush commented as they started off.

"I have made a point of visiting him in the stables every day, though I have ridden him but once since last Sunday." She referred, he knew, to her outing with Bigsby. "I suspect no one has attempted to befriend him since Lady Anthony left London."

Eyeing the unattractive animal, Rush could not much blame them. Still, he loved horses in general enough to appreciate Violet's compassion for this one. He liked to think he would do the same under similar circumstances.

Away from Lady Simpson's watchful eye, Rush felt somewhat less compelled to make Miss Simpson his first object of attention. She did not seem to notice, riding a little behind with Killer to discuss last night's concert.

On reaching the park, Rush again suggested that he and Miss

Turpin make a more rapid circuit or two for the sake of her mount's high spirits. The other two readily agreed.

"I take it you had no difficulties upon your return last night?" Rush said as soon as they were out of earshot.

She colored slightly. "Nothing to signify. There was one dicey moment when I heard a servant upon the stairs as I returned to my room, but I was quick enough that he did not see me. Should you wish the return of the dress I borrowed, my abigail will have it discreetly cleaned. Otherwise, she can dispose of the, ah, evidence."

"No need to return it. I must devise some method of getting your gown back to you without arousing suspicion."

"It is an old one that I never wear, now I've bought new ones. No one will notice it missing."

Rush hesitated a moment, then said, "Even though your absence was not discovered, I feel honor bound to tell you that my offer of last night stands."

The look she sent him held surprise but also, he thought, a trace of sadness. "That is very kind of you, my lord, but quite unnecessary. You must know as well as I how poorly we would suit, given our widely differing temperaments and views."

He was tempted to argue, but realized this was a perfect opportunity to speak to her about Bigsby—even though she would likely see that as yet more proof that they could never see eye to eye.

"It occurs to me that we never finished our, ah, discussion of how you came to be lurking in my mews last night."

She stiffened, as he'd known she would. That is, her head and shoulders did, though she did not allow her seat on the horse to be affected. Admirable, that.

"I can't think of anything more we need to discuss," she coolly replied. "As I told you, I was merely out for a walk and ventured beyond my reckoning."

"You persist, then, in claiming your presence behind my house had nothing to do with Bigsby? With the man you believe to be the Saint of Seven Dials?"

Though she turned slightly pale, she kept her gaze on the path ahead. "Of course not. How should it? Much as I admire the Saint of Seven Dials, I have no idea of his true identity. I find it rather amusing that you think it could be Julian Bigsby. Are you quite certain you are not jealous of him?"

Rush clenched his jaw. "Certainly not," he snapped, even while wondering again if that were the case.

Could he possibly be wrong about Bigsby? All he knew for certain was that the man who broke into his house last night was the one impersonating the Saint. Only he would have heard the rumor passed along by Flute's friends.

Violet's presence in his mews last night could scarcely have been a coincidence, however. She must have come there with *someone*, and that someone had to be the person currently styling himself Saint of Seven Dials.

"Miss Turpin—Violet," he said after another long silence between them. "I informed you last night that whoever is committing these recent thefts is not the real Saint. As one of the true Saint's admirers, I should think you would want to help us put a stop to this imposter's depredations."

"So you claimed." She cast a frowning glance his way. "But you offered not a shred of evidence. Have you any real proof that someone else is masquerading as the Saint of Seven Dials?"

Rush opened his mouth, then closed it. Lord Peter had not given him permission to share the remarkable fact that several people, not one, had worn the Saint's mask, nor the identities of any of those people. Why had he not asked last night whether he could do so?

Doubtless because he had been so distracted by what had just occurred—and by the revelation that he loved the maddening, alluring woman beside him.

"I...cannot tell you how I know, but I assure you that I do."

She raised a skeptical brow. "If you will not tell me what you know, why should I tell you anything at all? As I see it, helping you to catch the Saint of Seven Dials would be like helping the Sheriff of Nottingham capture Robin Hood!"

He tried to think of some way to convince her without betraying

Peter's confidence, but nothing occurred to him before they caught up to Miss Simpson and Killer. They appeared to have covered less than half a furlong since their departure.

Frustrated as Rush was by his failure to obtain Violet's cooperation, he doubted another circuit together would change her mind. As the park was now growing quite crowded, it might also cause talk. He therefore resigned himself to walking his horse alongside Miss Simpson while Miss Turpin began another turn about the park with Lord Killerby.

He would ask Lord Peter's permission to tell Violet at least part of the truth before broaching the subject of the false Saint to her again. But would even that be enough, if the bogus Saint was indeed Bigsby…and if her heart had already been captured by the scoundrel?

Rush feared she might choose to protect him for reasons having nothing to do with the legendary thief.

Deliciously disturbing as she found Lord Rushford's company, Violet was rather glad to leave him and his persistent questions behind for her next circuit of the park. Lord Killerby proved a far less unsettling companion.

"You and Miss Simpson have known each other for some years, have you not?" he asked as they started off—a nice, non-threatening topic.

"Yes, she and I both attended Miss Gebhart's Seminary for Young Ladies and became friends there—a friendship we renewed when I was in London last Season."

"You seem very fond of each other, though you appear to have little in common."

Violet laughed. "True, on both counts. She is far more accomplished than I, in the accepted sense, vastly surpassing me at music, drawing and needlework. Still, our personalities seem to complement each other, dissimilar as they are. I frequently urge her to be more adventurous, though to little effect thus far."

"I daresay there are few ladies of your class who can surpass you there—or on horseback," said Lord Killerby admiringly.

Struck again by how well he and Mary might suit, she turned his praise back on her friend. "To be fair, Miss Simpson has had little opportunity to practice riding. Not surprising, as it is not considered a *necessary* accomplishment for a lady. In general, her strengths are far better suited to Society than mine."

"Perhaps so, but you should not devalue your own admirable qualities, Miss Turpin."

Before she could again deflect the compliment, Violet's attention was caught by the sight of Julian riding a short distance ahead. "My lord, will you mind terribly if I leave you briefly?" she asked. "I have spotted someone I simply must speak to."

Though Lord Killerby seemed startled, he made no objection.

Urging her mount faster, she called Julian's name, whereupon he wheeled his horse around, a delighted smile breaking across his handsome face.

"Violet! Thank heaven. I prayed I might see you here today."

"I hoped the same, for I was terribly worried you had been captured." She'd found it difficult to hide her relief when Lord Rushford's questions implied he had not.

"And I dared not call at Lady Simpson's for fear *you'd* been apprehended, which obviously would have led to awkward questions. I take it you were not?"

She hesitated for a moment. "I...was not apprehended, no," she finally said, though she had indeed been caught—by Lord Rushford.

"Here, let us find a spot with a bit more privacy," he suggested, leading her down a narrower but less crowded side path. After another turning or two, they reached a small, deserted clearing, where Julian stopped and dismounted before assisting Violet to the ground.

Looping the horses' reins over a nearby shrubbery, he turned to face her, his expression now contrite. "I behaved like the greatest cad in nature last night, running off before ascertaining that you were all right."

"Not at all. It was far more important that the Saint of Seven Dials escape to continue his good work." She patted his arm reassuringly.

He frowned and bit his lip. "I suppose so, though I fear it may be some time before that occurs. That rich prize I was told about turned out to be a trap. I, ah, don't suppose you accidentally dropped word of our plans to Rushford?"

"Of course not!" she exclaimed. "I am shocked you can imagine I might do such a thing."

"Someone must have tipped him off," he replied with a shrug. "Though I had been reliably informed that the house would be empty, I arrived to discover an ambush of sorts."

"It could not have been I, as you refused to tell me whose house you intended to rob," she reminded him, still indignant.

He had the grace to look somewhat chagrined. "Yes, yes, you are right. I'm sorry. Knowing what close friends Rushford and your brother are, I thought you might take issue with it if you knew. Particularly as you have seemed more, ah, friendly toward him of late. And the way he sometimes looks at you..."

Remembering the passion of his kisses last night, Violet's insides fluttered. "I'm sure I don't know what you mean, Julian," she said primly. "Have I not told you that Lord Rushford is engaged to marry to Miss Simpson?"

"Engagements can be broken. Do you truly not care for him?"

She hesitated only an instant before replying, "Only as my brother's good friend." It was not true, but what else could she say under the circumstances?

Stepping closer, Julian caught one of her hands in both of his. "In that case, will you not reconsider your answer last night and come away with me?" he entreated with startling earnestness. "Now is the perfect time. After last night, my safest course may be to leave London for a while and I can think of no one I would rather have with me. Please say you will, Violet."

Caught off guard by that question last night, she had briefly been tempted. Now, however, she finally knew her heart. Hopeless though her love for Rush might be, she was not yet ready to choose a path of despair.

With pretended regret, she shook her head. "I'm sorry, Julian. I am no more prepared to take such a momentous step today than I was last night. But pray do not think of abandoning your work as the Saint of Seven Dials! The poor folk of London need both his help and the hope he gives them."

"If we marry, I won't need to." He spoke eagerly, gripping her hand more tightly. "Together, we can do far more good for the poor than I ever can alone. Think of the money you stand to inherit, and the noble uses to which we could put it."

His eagerness, and the mention of money, reminded her uncomfortably of Mr. Plunkett, the fortune hunter who had persuaded her to elope last autumn. Gently but firmly, she pulled her hand from his grasp.

"I'm sorry, Julian," she repeated. "It is quite impossible."

A look of frustration, even anger, flitted across his features before he schooled them into a sad smile. "You leave me heartbroken. I had begun to hope that you truly cared for me."

"I do care for you," she assured him, "but only as a friend."

She had originally thought to warn him of Lord Rushford's suspicions, but now felt oddly reluctant to do so.

"Perhaps you are right that the Saint should lie low for a while," she told him instead. "I should hate for anything to happen to you, Julian."

He reached up to touch her cheek with a gloved finger. "I am grateful for your concern, for it gives me hope. Pray send me word at once or, better, come to me yourself if you change your mind. Here is my direction." Pulling a slip of paper from his pocket, he pressed it into her palm.

"I doubt I will, Julian, but if I hear anything I think you should know, I will contrive to tell you. Now, however, I had best get back to my party before they come seeking me. It…might be best if you wait a minute or two before following."

With a nod, he boosted her into the saddle.

Trotting back to the main path, she was somewhat flummoxed at having received two proposals of marriage within an hour. Alas, she could not feel unduly flattered by either. The first had been made from a sense of duty and the second likely because of distressed circumstances.

For the first time since learning that Julian was the Saint of Seven Dials, she wondered whether his motives were truly as pure as he claimed—or if, perhaps, Lord Rushford was right about him.

CHAPTER FIFTEEN

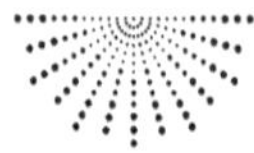

Plodding slowly along the path with Miss Simpson, Rush stifled a yawn. As always, every attempt he made to draw his fiancée into conversation fell flat. He'd begun to dread the prospect of going through life with a woman he could not talk with. One who, far from sharing his love of horses, found them positively alarming.

Then there was the inconvenient fact that he was in love with Violet Turpin…

"Ah, there you are!" he exclaimed when the others finally trotted up. "What kept you?"

Killer looked a bit awkward. "Er, Miss Turpin was, er, detained by an acquaintance."

"Oh? And who might that have been?" Rush's mind leapt instantly to a guess.

Her blush confirmed his suspicion before her words did. "Mr. Bigsby, if you must know. We only talked for a few minutes, however. Is that not true, Lord Killerby?"

"Quite true," he agreed, still appearing somewhat uncomfortable.

Rush would discover why as soon as he had opportunity. "No matter, but it is well you are back, for Miss Simpson has expressed a wish of returning home. Shall we?"

The gentlemen escorted the two young ladies back to the Simpson house, where they made their farewells. Rush waited only until he and Killer were back outside to question his friend.

"I don't suppose you know what Miss Turpin and Bigsby had to say to each other?" he asked as casually as possible.

Killer shook his head. "Didn't hear a word of it, I'm afraid. She went down a side trail with him and was gone for ten minutes or more, quite out of my sight. I had just determined it was my duty to go after her when she came back. Alone."

Rush frowned. "Alone? Did she seem distressed at all? Disheveled?"

Killer furrowed his brow in thought. "Don't think so. Why? Surely the fellow would not have attempted, er, anything he shouldn't in the middle of Hyde Park?"

"There's not much I'd put past Bigsby," Rush replied with a snort. "She clearly came to no harm, however, so I suppose there is no need to confront him about it. Are we still on for dinner at White's later?"

After he and Killer parted, Rush turned toward Curzon Street. If Violet had warned Bigsby about his suspicions, it was now more urgent than ever to convince her that he was not the true Saint of Seven Dials.

Lord Peter was alone when Rush was shown into his library. "Just the man I hoped to see," he greeted his guest. "Does this mean you were able to obtain something useful from Miss Turpin?"

"Not yet, I'm afraid," Rush admitted, moving to a chair. "I tried, but she refused to admit she knew anything about Bigsby's activities last night. She insists she was merely out for a walk when I encountered her in my mews, ridiculous as that sounds. Doubtless because she still believes Bigsby is the Saint."

Peter frowned. "Did you not tell her that you have certain knowledge that whoever is committing these thefts is not the true Saint?"

"I did, but she demanded proof—which I could not give her without your authorization, as it would expose both your wife and your brother."

"Ah. I should have thought of that. Hm. Suppose I ask Sarah to call upon Miss Turpin? I get the sense that her word might carry more weight than yours just now. Or am I wrong in thinking there was a degree of...friction between yourself and the lady in question last night?"

Though startled, Rush could scarcely deny it. "I see your reputation for perceptiveness is well deserved. There are several areas in which she and I do not see eye to eye. This matter of the Saint is merely the most recent."

"And yet you hold each other in affection? Or at least...attraction?"

Again, Rush blinked. "I, ah, cannot speak for the lady's feelings, though I fear she considers me more in the light of a nuisance than a potential suitor. I, however, have unwisely become rather...attached to her and would not like to see her hurt."

"Why 'unwisely'?" Peter asked.

"For one, I am betrothed to Miss Simpson, though no announcement will be made until either her father or his consent arrives from India. For another, Miss Turpin is as headstrong and undisciplined as any woman I have ever known. Even if I were free to woo her, I would surely do a disservice to my family name and my mother's memory to install her as Countess of Rushford."

Peter regarded him in silence for a long moment. "I see. Would it be impertinent of me to ask how you came to be engaged to Miss Simpson? Would she be heartbroken if it were broken off?"

"Does it matter? I admit I was rash to offer for a girl I scarcely knew. I realize now that I was still thinking less than rationally in the wake of my mother's passing. But whatever Miss Simpson's current feelings may be on the matter, her mother has made it more than plain that I am expected to go through with it."

"I see," Peter repeated. "And you feel Miss Simpson would make you a better countess than Miss Turpin?"

Rush raked a hand through his hair in frustration. "That's the devil of it. Now that I know her a bit better, I'd have to say no. Miss Simpson has lived her life completely under her mother's thumb and appears to have few opinions and little volition of her own."

"And Miss Turpin?" Peter prompted.

"For all of her faults, she is both intelligent and decisive," Rush admitted. "She also has a zeal for assisting the poor, much as my mother did. Thus her determination to protect the Saint of Seven Dials." He wondered why he had never before drawn that comparison.

"In that case," Peter said lightly, "I suppose we must hope everything will work out for the best for all concerned. In my experience it often does, even when present circumstances suggest otherwise."

Though he could not share the other man's optimism, Rush found his words strangely cheering. Rising, he thanked Lord Peter for his time as well as his insights.

"Say nothing of it. I will speak with Sarah upon her return, for she is as eager as we are to put this bogus Saint out of business permanently. With any luck, your Miss Turpin will give us the testimony we need after hearing the truth."

Rush was startled by a spurt of delight at hearing her called *his* Miss Turpin. Carefully concealing it from the too-perceptive Lord Peter, he bowed and took his leave before riding home deep in thought.

Violet was breakfasting with the Simpson ladies the next morning when a footman brought in a note addressed specifically to her.

"Who is that from, pray?" Lady Simpson inquired.

"I've no idea," Violet said in surprise, for neither the distinctly feminine hand nor the seal on the envelope were at all familiar.

Breaking the seal, she unfolded the small sheet of pressed paper.

My Dear Miss Turpin,

I beg you will do me the honor of accompanying me to tea today at the home of my sister-in-law, Lady Marcus Northrup. If you are amenable, I will call for you at one o'clock. Please send your reply at your earliest convenience.

Yours, etc,

Sarah, Lady Peter Northrup

Violet read the note through twice before passing it to her hostess, who was by now demanding to know its contents.

"Well! This is quite an honor," Lady Simpson declared after

perusing it. "I had no idea you were acquainted with *three* daughters-in-law to the Duke of Marland."

"I was first introduced to Lady Peter at the Jeller ball and have never met Lady Marcus," Violet admitted. "I did become fairly well acquainted with Lady Anthony while in the Shires, however."

Lady Simpson regarded her with new respect. "All are very important connections. You must write back at once to accept Lady Peter's kind invitation." She rang for paper and pen that Violet might do so without delay.

Two hours later, clad in her best new day dress, Violet found herself sharing an elegant carriage with the lovely Lady Peter for the short drive to Grosvenor Street. On their arrival, Lady Marcus greeted them both warmly.

"Thank you for indulging us on such short notice, Miss Turpin," she said. "My sister-in-law and I very much wished to talk with you today."

Though surprised by the pretty brunette's American accent, Violet did not remark upon it. "It is I who owe thanks to you and Lord Marcus for the loan of a horse while I am in London. Without it, I would likely be unable to ride at all this Season."

"You are having no difficulty managing him, then? It appears Tessa did not exaggerate when she wrote that you were nigh as good a horsewoman as herself. We must ride together one day soon. It is an exercise I also enjoy immensely, but I can rarely convince Sarah to come with me."

"I fear I am still less than confident on horseback," Lady Peter admitted. "Quinn is quite accomplished at it, however."

The two continued chatting comfortably as Lady Marcus led them up to the parlor, where an elegant tea was laid out. Violet was struck by the informal friendliness between the two, relieved to find them far less imposing than she'd feared.

"Now," said Lady Marcus as she poured out, "I imagine you are wondering why we were so eager to speak with you, so we will get to the point at once. It has to do with the Saint of Seven Dials, and the man currently styling himself as such."

Violet sucked in a startled breath. "Did…did Lord Rushford ask you to do this?" Did that mean he or Lord Peter had told them about her appearance at Rush's house two nights ago? What must they think?

"Not precisely," Lady Peter replied, taking a cup from her sister-in-law. "He asked my husband's permission to share a, ah, secret with you, in order to persuade you that this new thief is an imposter. Peter thought it might be more effective if I shared that secret myself. Quinn and I then agreed to combine forces, the better to convince you."

Now as confused as she was alarmed, Violet looked from one to the other. "A secret?"

Handing Violet her cup, Lady Marcus nodded. "What we are about to tell you could be dangerous to several people, including ourselves, should it become generally known."

Though half-fearing some sort of trick, Violet was also thoroughly intrigued. "I promise never to breathe a word of…of whatever your secret is."

"We feel sure you will not," said Lady Peter. "According to Lord Rushford, you are a great admirer of the Saint of Seven Dials."

"I am. Lately I have read quite a lot about him and enthusiastically support all he has done for the poor. 'Tis why I refused to give Lord Rushford any information that could lead to his capture."

Lady Marcus smiled. "Then you will no doubt find what we have to tell you both interesting and surprising."

"I…I will?" asked Violet uncertainly.

The two exchanged a glance. "We imagine so," said Lady Peter. "You see, contrary to all accounts currently in circulation, to include a recently-published book on the subject, there have in fact been several different Saints."

"What?" Violet gasped. Julian had never so much as hinted at such a thing! "Do you mean to say that the Saint of Seven Dials is actually a whole group of men? How can no one have suspected that?"

"Not a group, precisely," Lady Marcus clarified. "There has only ever been one Saint at a time. The original Saint, whose name I am not at liberty to disclose, operated alone for two or three years, save for a helpful street urchin or two. Upon his marriage, however, he passed the job on to another man. My husband."

Violet stared. "Lord Marcus is the Saint of Seven Dials?"

"Was," Lady Marcus corrected her. "He filled the role for most of last summer, before handing off his mask, so to speak, to a third man, who primarily used the guise of the Saint to bring a murderous traitor to justice. Once he'd done so, he also…ceased operations."

Lady Peter now took up the narrative. "After that, there was no Saint at all for many weeks. Soon the poor began to feel the pinch, lamenting the loss of their hero. My younger brother, who had worked as the original Saint's primary assistant, was preparing to take on the role himself, though he was barely sixteen. To prevent his doing so, I, ah, briefly became the Saint myself."

"You?" Violet cried, astonished. "But how—?"

"I…spent a portion of my childhood on the streets myself, you see, which equipped me rather well for the task. I only continued as the Saint for a fortnight or so, however, before Peter put a stop to it by marrying me."

Her blue eyes twinkled as she spoke, clearly enjoying Violet's reaction to the remarkable news.

"And then?" Violet asked faintly. How *very* wrong that chronicler had been!

"After I, er, retired, Peter persuaded someone else to take over, partly for that person's own good. He served as Saint most ably until the end of last year, but since then there has been no acting Saint. Most of the former ones have continued to assist the poor, however, given the pressing need."

Now Violet was confused again. "No Saint? But these recent thefts, with the Saint's card left in place of stolen valuables…?"

Both ladies shook their heads.

"He is an imposter." Lady Peter spoke with conviction. "My brother has confirmed that not a farthing of what has been stolen over the past month has made its way to the deserving poor. Whoever is committing these latest thefts is undoubtedly using the Saint's identity to avert suspicion while lining his own pockets."

"He is also besmirching the true Saints' hard-won reputation," Lady Marcus added indignantly. "Not only has this new fellow robbed some perfectly pleasant people, he has also injured more than one servant while escaping, something no *real* Saint ever did. We all fear that if he is not stopped soon, he may kill someone. His methods have been quite crude, lacking the, ah, professionalism for which the Saint was previously known."

Violet listened, aghast, as her illusions about Julian were shattered beyond repair. His lies were many. Not only had he spoken loftily about the good he was doing for the poor, he had told her tales, stretching back many months, of his supposed exploits as the Saint.

She realized now that he must have gleaned those stories from published accounts. Had she not recognized at least one from her book? At the time, she had taken that as further evidence of his veracity, when in fact it was the opposite. How could she have been so blind?

"If what you say is true, he clearly must be stopped." Violet's voice quivered with shock and indignation. "What...what do you wish me to do?"

"Help us to put an end to his activities," Lady Peter pleaded earnestly. "Lord Rushford believes you may know who the false Saint is?"

Violet swallowed. Mortified as she was that she had allowed Julian to deceive her, she could not quite bring herself to blurt out his name to these two women she scarcely knew.

"I, ah, have a suspicion, yes," she reluctantly admitted. "I should like to confirm it, however, before he is turned over to the authorities."

"Pray do not take too long over it," Lady Peter cautioned. "Once he knows we are on to him, he will very likely cut and run."

Likely true. Already, Julian had spoken of fleeing London.

"Would not that serve the purpose as well?" Violet asked. "He could then commit no further crimes in the Saint's name." And she would be spared betraying someone she had believed a friend.

Lady Marcus conceded that was true, but added, "Should he leave London, or perhaps even England, odds are he will never be caught.

On the other hand, if he were turned over to the authorities as the Saint of Seven Dials, every other person who has *legitimately* filled that role would be safe from the law."

A fair point, Violet realized. Nor did she owe Julian any particular loyalty if he had been lying to her all along. Still, she needed time to consider everything she had just learned before taking such a momentous step.

"Very well. Once I am certain my guess is correct, I will send word to you, or to Lord Rushford," she promised.

By the time Violet returned to Cavendish Square, her initial embarrassment at being fooled so easily had given way to anger over Julian's perfidy. Her inclination now was to confront him herself, but Lady Peter had likely been right. Satisfying as it might be to witness his chagrin on knowing she was on to him, it was not worth risking the *real* Saints' futures.

No, much as she dreaded doing so, she would simply have to swallow her pride and admit to Lord Rushford that he had been right from the start.

As though to test her resolve, soon after she and the Simpson ladies arrived at Lady Dunstable's ball that evening, Julian approached to request a waltz. Fearing that her sense of betrayal might tempt her to say more to him than was wise, she declined.

"I'm terribly sorry, Mr. Bigsby," she coolly replied. "I fear all of my dances for the evening are already engaged."

To her surprise, rather than argue, he merely turned to Mary and secured her hand for the waltz instead. He then bowed stiffly to them both and moved off to await the promised dance.

Lady Simpson, in conversation with Lady Mountheath a short way off, frowned after him, clearly less pleased than Mary was with his attention. Violet was debating whether to discreetly warn Mary away from Julian when Lord Rushford and Lord Killerby joined them.

"Give you good evening, ladies." Lord Killerby bowed first in Lady

Simpson's direction, then collectively to Violet and Mary. "Dare we hope that either of you still has a dance or two free?"

Violet, mindful that it would look odd if she did not dance every dance after her fib to Julian, agreed to two dances with each of them, as did Mary. She need not have been so precipitous, however. Within half an hour she was obliged to truthfully tell more than one gentleman that her dance card was full.

When the music began, Violet took to the floor with Lord Killerby, who was as pleasant and inoffensive as he had been in the park yesterday.

"Must say, I prefer Lady Dunstable's decor to the overblown profusion of Lady Jeller's last week," he commented as he led her to their set. "Flowers are all good and well, but I would rather enjoy them in a garden than a ballroom."

She absently agreed, thinking ahead to her first dance with Lord Rushford—the same waltz Mary was to dance with Julian. Should she make her confession then, before she could lose her nerve? Probably.

Unfortunately, when their waltz began an hour later, Lord Rushford made it clear he fully expected her to do exactly that.

"I'm glad to have this opportunity to speak with you," he said as they began moving among the other couples. "I observed you refusing Bigsby a dance earlier, though you clearly still had several free. I presume you now realize I have been right about him all along?"

Though she had steeled herself to set her pride aside, she could not bring herself to do so in the face of such smug assurance. "Mr. Bigsby and I had a bit of a falling out. Not that my private affairs are any of your business, my lord."

"No?" Tightening his grip on her hand, he leaned forward to look into her face. His expression now held a trace of the heat she'd seen there two nights ago. "I should like them to be, you know."

Startled and confused by his sudden change of manner, she blinked. "I... No, I cannot say that I knew that. Indeed, you told me yourself that you only concerned yourself in my affairs as a favor to my brother. Is that no longer true?"

For a long moment he did not reply. "I thought it was, when I first arrived in Town," he finally said. "I suspect now that I was merely deceiving myself."

Violet's heart beat faster. Was it possible his proposal of marriage had been prompted by more than his sense of honor?

"What...What of Miss Simpson?"

Straightening somewhat, he glanced away from her with a frown. "Yes, I suppose I still need to— That is— Never mind." His voice now became as cool as it had been warm a moment earlier. "I requested this waltz hoping you might finally admit that Bigsby has indeed been aping the Saint of Seven Dials."

Hurt and disappointed, and angry at herself for being so, Violet shook her head, not trusting her voice. She must *not* let him guess what he had come to mean to her...not unless he admitted he felt the same about her. Which it seemed he did not.

Torn between doing what she knew to be right and reluctance to expose her folly—and her heart—she remained silent for the remainder of the dance. How Lord Rushford's thoughts were occupied she did not know, but he did not appear particularly happy.

Just before parting with her, he said, "If you are unwilling to confide in me, will you tell Lady Peter what you know? The important thing is to prevent further damage by the imposter. An admirer of the true Saint should wish that as well."

"I... Yes. Perhaps I will," she replied. He bowed, his expression unreadable, and she responded with a formal curtsey, wondering why it should be so difficult to do what she knew to be right.

Rush realized even before relinquishing Violet at the end of their waltz that he had bungled things badly. He had been so heartened by her refusal to dance with Bigsby that he had overplayed his hand, allowing his smugness to show. Not surprisingly, that had kept her from admitting she was wrong, though she surely must know it now, after speaking with Lady Peter.

Then he had compounded the matter when his feelings for her led him to say more than was wise—and then drawing back the moment she again mentioned Miss Simpson. What was it about this woman that caused him to lose his vaunted capacity for planning ahead?

Necessary as it was to undo the damage, he had no opportunity to do so. His second dance with Violet allowed for no private conversation—particularly as she seemed disinclined to even make eye contact with him. Nor did Lady Simpson permit him so much as a moment apart with her as they took their leave at the close of the ball.

"What say you we invite Miss Turpin and Miss Simpson riding again tomorrow morning?" he said to Killer as they left the Dunstable house together. "Shame to waste this fine weather." It would also provide Rush the privacy he needed to apologize to Violet, and perhaps to hint at his intention to somehow break off his engagement to Miss Simpson.

Killer readily agreed, though he seemed surprised when Rush suggested calling well before noon.

The ladies were still drinking coffee in the breakfast parlor when they arrived the next day. Far from being put out, however, Lady Simpson appeared even more delighted than usual to see them.

"Ah, gentlemen, how lucky you are here so early, for it is fitting that Lord Rushford hear the happy news at once."

"News?" Rush echoed with a odd sense of foreboding.

"Aye, wonderful news, and far sooner than we expected. Not an hour since, this morning's post brought Sir Clarence's letter from India with his consent for you and my daughter to wed. Is that not famous?"

Rush's stomach plummeted. "Famous. Indeed. You...did not look to see his reply for another month or more, as I recall."

"Quite true, though apparently there can be a great deal of variation in the time it takes letters to travel from India. No doubt he was so pleased to hear of your offer that he sent his answer as expeditiously as possible. The winds were likely favorable as well."

Forcing the corners of his mouth upward a fraction, Rush darted a look at Miss Turpin, then Miss Simpson. The former was watching him fixedly, with somewhat heightened color, while the latter seemed rather paler than usual, her eyes fixed upon her lap. Neither young lady appeared any happier with this news than he was.

"I, ah, suppose congratulations are in order, then." Killer dropped abruptly into the nearest chair.

Miss Simpson's gaze flew to his face with an expression almost of panic before she again ducked her head, murmuring something unintelligible.

Rush thanked his friend mechanically. "We, ah, had hoped to invite the young ladies out riding again." He kept his tone casual with an effort, for he was now more desperate than ever to speak privately with Violet.

"Oh, but there is so much to be done!" Lady Simpson protested. "I need to send word to my husband's man of business, that he can call upon you to discuss the particulars. There is the announcement for the papers to write up, after which Mary and I must give thought to her trousseau, if we are to have everything necessary made up in time for a June wedding. Sir Clarence expects to be home by mid-May, so that will be quite perfect."

Miss Simpson suddenly spoke up, for the first time since the gentlemen's arrival. "Surely, Mama, my part in this may wait until tomorrow? Truly, I…I should rather like to go riding. To, ah, clear my thoughts before beginning all of these preparations."

Lady Simpson blinked, apparently as startled as Rush was by her daughter's sudden outspokenness.

"Very well," she said after a moment's hesitation. "I suppose an hour's delay will not signify, particularly as your father's letter is here so much earlier than I had hoped. You see, Lord Rushford? She really does wish to improve her skill on horseback."

While the young ladies changed to their habits, Rush and Killer were subjected to Lady Simpson's detailed plans for the coming weeks. To conceal his dismay, Rush turned his thoughts to what he planned to say to Violet if their ride allowed for another tête-à-tête.

All four younger people seemed noticeably more subdued than previously during their ride to the park. When Rush again suggested that he and Miss Turpin should again make a quick circuit or two while Killer and Miss Simpson followed more slowly, the others instantly agreed.

"I fear I am by no means so improved yet as to attempt a canter," Miss Simpson said apologetically.

"Of course not," Killer gallantly told her. "It would be remarkable indeed if you were. I do not mind in the least staying back with you while Rush and Miss Turpin burn off their mounts' high spirits."

Rush shot his friend a grateful glance. Though he had not told Killer about the events of Saturday night, he had clearly divined where Rush's true affections lay.

Determined not to waste this opportunity, he again launched into speech the moment they were alone. "Miss Turpin—Violet—have you given any more thought to the request I have twice made of you?"

She glanced across at him. "That I share anything I know about the Saint of Seven Dials?"

"Actually, I, ah, meant the other request." He was startled to realize he'd momentarily forgotten all about Bigsby. "That our best course, given what occurred, is to marry."

Now her color deepened perceptibly. "I...cannot claim I have not, but the arguments I put forth before still stand. If anything, the arrival of Sir Clarence's letter only strengthens them. You spoke of honor, but jilting Mary would surely be far more dishonorable than pretending our, ah, encounter never happened. Particularly as it is known to no one but we two."

"And Lords Peter and Marcus," he reminded her. "As well as their wives, I suspect, for neither is prone to keeping secrets from them."

She appeared both startled and distressed by his additions, but after a moment's silence she shook her head. "Even so, it would be worse to use Mary in that way." He thought he heard regret in her voice, however, and took heart from it.

"Then you believe your friend truly wishes for this marriage? That she is...in love with me?" Speaking that word to Violet, even in this context, sent a warmth through his vitals.

"I... Well, no. In fact, she has confessed rather the opposite to me. But a man breaking off an engagement is always seen as a more serious breach of honor than a woman doing so. While she showed unusual spirit earlier by speaking up in favor of this outing, I cannot imagine her defying her mother about something of this magnitude."

Rush pondered that for a moment. "If it is true that she has no more wish to marry me than I her, the match should certainly be broken off. I agree Miss Simpson seems unlikely to take the initiative, but perhaps between us we can convince her to do so. If we succeed, will you then consider my offer more seriously?"

Her quick intake of breath was audible even over the pounding of the horses' hooves. "I…would rather wait for that unlikely event to take place before answering such a question, my lord."

"But surely, given how many people know of our, ah, indiscretion—"

He broke off. She was right. It was unfair of him to expect a binding answer to such a conditional proposal of marriage. Anxious as he was to be secure of her, he must first settle his business with Miss Simpson.

The park was less crowded than on Sunday, allowing them to finish their circuit in far less time. He therefore suggested a second on reaching the others and was pleased when the other three were amenable.

As the discussion most important to him currently seemed at an impasse, he reverted to the other topic when they started off again.

"Are you still reluctant to help us stop the person masquerading as the Saint of Seven Dials? You must realize by now that Bigsby does not deserve your continued loyalty."

Violet pressed her lips together, her internal conflict apparent. "I… no. I feel no obligation to continue protecting Julian after my conversation yesterday with Lady Peter and Lady Marcus," she finally replied, much to his relief. "But I fear I have no real evidence beyond the stories he told me. It is entirely possible he made it all up to impress me."

"Unlikely, I should think, given that he attempted to burgle my house. It *was* he who brought you there, was it not?"

"Yes. I am sorry for committing a falsehood earlier. I believed it justified at the time, for I thought—"

"That Bigsby was really the Saint. I know."

She nodded sheepishly. "I cannot know for certain that he committed any previous burglaries, however. He told me a few tales, but— Oh!"

"What is it?"

"I have just recalled something that may indeed serve as evidence. He carries with him—or did—calling cards like those attributed to the Saint of Seven Dials. Of course, he may have destroyed them now he knows you suspect him."

Ah. "I take it you warned him about me?"

She shook her head. "I considered doing so when I spoke with him on Sunday, but…did not."

Because of Rush's warnings? Before he could ask, she continued.

"He did, however, refer to the ambush you and the others set for him and asked whether I had told you of his plans. He also talked of leaving Town, but clearly has not, as he was at last night's ball."

"Where you all but gave him the cut direct," Rush observed with remembered satisfaction. "I am pleased he will no longer be able to impose upon you, whether we can bring him to justice or not."

Coming around a curve, he again spotted Killer and Miss Simpson just ahead. Seemingly deep in conversation, they had progressed but little during this second circuit.

"Thank you for what you have told me," Rush said before they were within earshot. "The cards give us something to go on, assuming they are still in his possession."

Killer and Miss Simpson turned at their approach, Miss Simpson blushing deeply—further evidence that she was still uncomfortable in Rush's company. He grew even more determined to contrive some way out of their blasted engagement. It would surely be a relief to his fiancée, even as it freed him to court Violet Turpin properly—something he was increasingly eager to do.

CHAPTER SIXTEEN

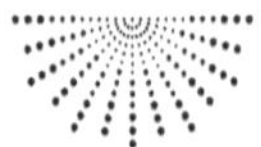

Violet went to bed early that evening, though not entirely by choice. She and the Simpson ladies had been engaged to attend a ridotto sponsored by one of the patronesses of Almack's, but over dinner Mary complained of the headache. Her mother was immediately all concern.

"In that case, you'd best go straight to bed," Lady Simpson insisted. "I have a very full day planned for us tomorrow and you will need your rest. I shall send word explaining the situation to Mrs. Cowper, that she will not think we have slighted her. We dare not risk her withdrawing your promised vouchers."

Rather than listen to her hostess's continued chatter about wedding plans, Violet went upstairs when Mary did, thinking to speak with her privately about breaking off her engagement to Lord Rushford. Alas, Mary shut herself into her room before she could ask whether anxiety about her impending marriage might have caused her headache.

Violet allowed Brigid to help her into her nightrail but felt far too agitated for sleep after the day's events—to include Lord Rushford pressing her yet again to marry him. To distract her from dwelling on that, she again pulled out her well-worn copy of *The Saint of Seven Dials: The Man and the Legend*. On this perusal, she found it quite amusing to compare the assertions of the author to what she now knew of the Saint—or Saints.

Eventually, however, her eyes grew heavy. Setting the book aside, Violet yawned and reached to turn down the lamp, only to notice a white rectangle on the carpet by the door. Puzzled, for she was certain it had not been there earlier, she rose to discover what it was.

It proved to be a sheet of letter paper, folded in half. Picking it up, Violet perused the brief message within.

My dear Violet,

I pray you will not think too ill of me when you learn that I have followed my heart rather than the expectations of my mother and Society by escaping both. Convinced as I am that Lord Rushford holds me in no more affection than I do him, I think it no great evil to free him from his obligation by marrying another. We mean to take my mother's traveling coach to delay pursuit, but I beg you to keep my departure secret until we are well on our way to Gretna Green, that our happiness may be guaranteed by lawful matrimony.

Yours, etc,

Mary Simpson

With disbelieving eyes, Violet read the note through thrice before she was able to credit its contents.

Mary, timid little Mary, had *eloped*? It seemed unthinkable, but the words she had penned admitted of little doubt. Eloped with whom, however? Mary's letter gave no clue, nor could Violet recall her speaking with overt affection of any gentleman in particular. Or…had she?

On more than one occasion Mary had commented upon how very handsome Julian Bigsby was, Violet recalled. She had also waltzed with him at every ball they had attended thus far, despite her mother's displeasure each time. Had Julian's perfidy extended even further than she'd guessed?

Violet imagined that his main goal in pretending to be the Saint of Seven Dials had been to attach both her and her fortune. Had he not quizzed her about the latter, seeming pleased when she assured him that her inheritance would come to her unencumbered?

She herself had foolishly given him the idea to begin with, rhapsodizing about her admiration for the legendary thief while they were yet in the Shires. It still mortified her to think how nearly his plan had succeeded. Had she not already been half in love with Lord Rushford, she might very well have agreed to elope with Julian.

Now that her eyes had been opened, Violet's fortune was safe from him—but what of Mary's? Or, worse, Mary herself? Violet had been the one to introduce them, secretly hoping that Julian might supplant Lord Rushford in Mary's affections. Then Violet had compounded matters by repeatedly urging her friend to be guided by her heart instead of convention or her mother's wishes—exactly what her note claimed she had done.

Foolish, foolish, foolish!

Only recently had Violet understood the hazards of elevating romance and adventure above all else, a course she had long promoted to anyone who would listen. Alas that Mary had listened to her! Those hazards were now visited upon her friend instead of herself.

Was there still time to atone for her folly by rescuing Mary from a fortune hunter she never would have met but for Violet? No matter, she clearly had a moral responsibility to try.

Spurred to action, she scrambled into the first dress she found that fastened down the front, pulled on her sturdiest boots and threw on the same cloak she had worn for Saturday night's ill-advised outing. Thrusting Julian's address and Mary's note into an inside pocket, along with every bit of cash she had on hand in case it became necessary to pursue them to the border, she quietly left her chamber.

Her first task must be to discover whether Mary and Julian had actually left London. She hoped not, as that would make her task both easier and cheaper. If they had, she would attempt to catch them up before Mary's fate was irrevocably sealed. Dina had rescued Violet from making a similar mistake in December, after all. God willing, she herself could to do the same for poor Mary.

Exactly as she had Saturday night, Violet crept down the back staircase to the kitchens. It was not so late this time, so she was forced to wait for two maids to finish arguing over whose turn it was to scrub the largest pot before she could slip unseen out of the scullery door to the gardens. As no one was waiting to escort her this time, she hurried around to the street and hailed the first hackney she saw.

"Where to, miss?" asked the driver.

She gave him Julian's direction. "Do hurry, please. My business is exceedingly urgent."

Choked as the streets were with carriage traffic, the drive took nearly half an hour. The hackney passed through progressively less genteel streets before finally stopping at what appeared to be a pawn shop, now closed and dark. Unwilling to be completely abandoned in such an unsavory-seeming neighborhood, Violet bade the driver to wait while she ascertained whether Julian—and Mary—were here.

According to the paper Julian had given her, his lodging was two floors above the shop. The front door was locked but a few minutes of anxious exploration revealed a back entrance opening onto a narrow stairway. Heart pounding, she climbed two flights of rickety steps, traversed a dim hallway, then knocked at number six.

There was no answer.

She knocked again, then again, her anxiety for Mary mounting with each passing minute. Suppose they had headed straight for Scotland from Cavendish Square? If so, she was wasting valuable time.

"Julian?" she called, her voice squeaking with worry. "Mary?"

When another minute passed with no response, she tried to force the door but without success. Fearful that the hackney driver might tire of waiting, she hurried back downstairs and was relieved to find him still there.

"Pray take me to the nearest posting inn," she breathlessly told him, blessing her foresight in bringing plenty of money. It appeared she was going to need it.

It was near midnight when a knock came on Rush's front door. As he'd already sent his butler off to bed, he hurried to open it himself and was relieved to see Lord Peter standing there.

"You got my note, then?" He opened the door wide for his visitor to enter.

"Yes, and I apologize for my lateness," Peter replied, unfastening his cloak. "Sarah and I were out so I did not see your message until we returned. You said you have new information?"

Rush led the way to his library. "Not much, but more than we had to go on before. Miss Turpin confessed to me this afternoon that Bigsby did indeed boast to her of being the Saint of Seven Dials. I should not be surprised to learn he concocted the whole scheme in order to ingratiate himself with her, for she's never made any secret of how she idolizes the Saint."

Peter moved to one of the large armchairs near the fire while Rush took the other. "Sounds like he's our man, then. Has she any proof beyond what he's told her?"

"That's the rub," Rush said. "She claims not, though he apparently flashed a calling card like the Saint's for her to see at some point, no doubt to cement his claim. If we could discover a stash of those cards on his person or at his lodging—"

"We'd at least have something to take to the authorities," Peter finished.

"Exactly. Though after our failed ambush the other night, he may well have destroyed the cards."

Peter pondered for a moment, then shrugged. "We can but hope he is not that clever. Certainly his thefts have indicated no formidable intellect. I propose we find out. Tonight, if you are willing."

"More than willing." Rush rose. "How are we to discover where he lodges?"

"Flute's young cohorts have already done that much," Peter said with a grin. "It's not in the best part of town, so we should dress down, so to speak." He glanced ruefully at his apricot coat and the chartreuse waistcoat beneath it.

"I can lend you an old cloak of mine to conceal your, ah, more noticeable attire," Rush assured him. "It will only take me a moment to change."

Hurrying upstairs to his dressing room, he quickly donned the garments he wore when working with his horses, then returned to the library. Both men pulled on nondescript cloaks, then went outside to hail a hackney. That would be less likely to arouse Bigsby's suspicions than a crested carriage.

They had the driver set them down a street or two shy of the pawnbroker's shop above which Bigsby lodged. The rest of the distance they covered on foot, hoping thus to avoid the attention of any interested passersby who might give the alarm. The shop itself was closed, of course, but in back they discovered an unlocked stairwell that led to their objective two stories above.

"Here it is. Number six," Peter whispered a few minutes later.

Rush joined him by the door. "Shall we knock, do you think?"

"I suppose that would be the polite thing to do." Accordingly, Peter rapped smartly on the door. When there was no answer after many seconds, he rapped again, then tried the handle. "Locked, of course. Fortunately, Sarah and her brother have taught me a trick or two."

Removing a thin strip of metal from his pocket, Peter fitted it into the lock and twisted it first one way, then another. Only a few seconds passed before he was rewarded by an audible click.

"Ah. There." Cautiously, he turned the handle and pushed the door open—into darkness. "Our host appears to be from home," he remarked, stepping inside the apartment.

"Careful," Rush advised him. "If he's here and hiding, he could have a weapon." Following Peter inside, he glanced around.

A narrow window admitted just enough light for him to locate a candle and tinderbox. Soon, with the assistance of a wavering flame, they were able to explore the apartment. It proved to be a squalid place that clearly hadn't been scrubbed in months, if not years. It also proved to be quite empty.

"Already scarpered, as Flute would say," Peter remarked, holding a second candle high to survey the open wardrobe and chest. Both were bare but for a few oddments, suggesting a hasty departure. "Let us see if he left anything useful behind, shall we?"

A more thorough search revealed a rumpled jacket in a corner that

Peter snatched up with a triumphant exclamation. "Aha! I do believe this may be precisely what I hoped to— Yes, I was right. Look."

Pulling a scrap of cloth from his trousers pocket, he held it against the jacket. Leaning closer, Rush saw that the scrap exactly matched a torn spot near the hem in back.

"So he did not dispose of it after attempting to rob me after all," Rush commented with satisfaction. "We likely need look no further, though I wonder..." He checked the jacket's pockets and was rewarded by finding four calling cards, all marked with a black numeral seven topped by a gold-ink halo.

"Taken together, I believe we have our proof," Peter said with a grin. "Of course, I'd have preferred to turn the man himself over to the authorities. Pity he seems to have escaped."

Rush agreed. He'd quite looked forward to having Bigsby hauled away and tried for his crimes. "We can make some inquiries. He was still in Town last night, so he may not be completely out of our reach just yet."

As they left the flat, another door in the hallway opened. "'Ere now, what's all the commotion about tonight?" an unkempt old woman demanded. "First that fancy piece bangin' on the door and shouting, and now you two. What's that pretty fellow what lives here done that everyone wants to talk to him in the middle of the night?"

Rush frowned at her. "Do you mean to say there was a woman here earlier this evening?"

"Aye, not half an hour since. High-born she looked and sounded, not the sort we often see in these parts."

"Can you describe her?"

The woman tilted her tousled gray head to one side, considering. "She wore a cloak and hood, but I seen her face clear when she turned, though she didn't see me. Pretty thing she was, with lots o' dark curls tumbling out from under the hood."

Rush froze, assailed by a sudden vision of Violet as she had appeared in the mews behind his house Saturday night—cloaked and hooded, her dark curls refusing to stay concealed.

"Did you see where she went? Did Bigsby open to her?"

"Dunno," she replied with a shrug. "Shut me door quick when she started to look my way, I did. Didn't hear much after, so I reckon he either let her in or she left. And then you lot show up and a body still can't get no sleep!"

"Our apologies, madam," Lord Peter said with a bow. "We'll take our leave now and I trust you'll be bothered no more this evening."

Rush wanted to ask the woman more questions but Peter seized his elbow and tugged him toward the stairs.

"Doubt we'll get much more out of her," he whispered as Rush relented and followed him. "But perhaps someone on the street saw something."

They hurried back down the stairwell, Peter carrying the incriminating jacket under his cloak. Once outside, Rush looked frantically about for someone, anyone, who might be able to corroborate the old woman's story and tell him where Violet had gone from here.

A scrawny urchin slouched around a nearby corner, then stopped to stare at them before beginning to back away.

"Wait!" Rush took a step forward.

Peter put a restraining hand on his shoulder. "I've a shilling for you, lad, if you can answer a question or two," he called to the boy.

The urchin paused, then moved cautiously toward them. "A shillin'? What kind o' questions? I'm no snitch."

"Not to worry," Peter assured him, holding out the promised shilling so the boy could see it. "We don't want to know who you work for or with. We're simply hoping you can tell us whether there've been any, ah, unusual visitors to this place tonight?"

"Other than the two o' you?" The lad's face split into a grin. "Aye, there was another gentry mort 'ere not long ago, a lidy. Come in a hack, she did, and had it wait for her, too."

Rush's heart began to pound. "Can you describe her? Did she leave alone or with someone else?"

"Right comely she was. Curly dark hair, gray cloak. She weren't gone more'n a few minutes before she come back and left again, off that way." He pointed. "Didn't see no one with her, but she looked to be in a terrible hurry. Heard her talkin' to someone, but it coulda been the hack driver, I s'pose."

"Thank you, my boy. You've been most helpful." Peter handed him the promised shilling.

The urchin pocketed it, tugged a lock of hair at his forehead and scurried off. Peter turned to Rush.

"Miss Turpin, you think?"

"It must have been," Rush replied. "I can't imagine why she would come here, especially knowing how Bigsby deceived her... Unless he threatened her in some way? The only way to know is to find her. Them."

He felt a horrible conviction that she had *not* left here alone, that Bigsby had used some means to persuade her to...what? Elope with him? It wouldn't be the first time she'd run off with a fortune hunter.

"I'll try to hunt down that hackney." He spoke decisively, trying to keep his sudden anguish at bay. "See if I can discover where it went. Probably hopeless, but—"

"Perhaps not." Peter laid a hand on his arm, his sympathetic expression making the weight in Rush's stomach even heavier. "Do what you can while I continue to look for clues here. Good luck, old chap."

With a terse nod, Rush strode off in the direction the boy had pointed, thinking hard.

It was possible, of course, that Violet really had left alone. Impulsive as she was, she could have come here to confront Bigsby about his deception and discovered him gone, just as they had. If so, she might already be safely back in Cavendish Square. As he could hardly call at the Simpson house at this hour to confirm that, however, he needed to rule out other, more ominous possibilities.

If his worst fears were true and Bigsby had used charm, threat or force to persuade her to elope, they could not have taken a hackney carriage to Scotland. They would need a proper coach—which meant his first stop should be the nearest place they could have hired one.

He did not know this section of London well, but vaguely recalled passing a coaching inn on the way here. Quickening his steps, he retraced their route and ten minutes later found the inn he sought. A weathered sign above the door of the small, ancient-looking thatched building proclaimed it "The Brown Dog."

Though the windows were dark, he tried the door, then pounded upon it. Long seconds passed before a harried-looking man opened to him.

"Blimey, can't a man sleep? You're the second to knock me out of me bed tonight."

Instantly seized by both hope and dread, Rush demanded, "Who were the first? Can you describe them?"

"Didn't see no 'them,' just a 'her.' Pretty lass she was, lots o' dark hair and eyes like purple vi'lets. Wanted to hire a coach on the spot and wouldn't take no for an answer. I rousted one of the post-boys and did as she asked, since she had the blunt to pay for it."

"She was alone then?" Rush asked, puzzled. "There was no man with her?"

The innkeeper shook his head. "None I saw. S'pose she could have stopped for him somewheres else. So what's it to be, then, guv? I've only got one coach left and the horses ain't my fastest, but—"

"No. Never mind." He would have a far better chance of catching them up in his own traveling coach, with his own, undoubtedly faster horses. "What color was the coach? The usual yellow?"

The man nodded, rubbing his eyes.

"Thank you," Rush said. "I apologize for disturbing your sleep. Is there a hackney stand nearby?"

"Aye, just there, two streets over." The man pointed. "G'night, then guv'nor."

Rush strode away before he could close the door.

Trusting that Lord Peter could find his own way home, Rush hurried to the hackney stand, where he offered double the usual fare for the fastest possible ride back to his house. Once there, he stopped only long enough to get a change of linen for his journey. On impulse, he also snatched up the gown Miss Turpin had left there Saturday night, now clean and dry. If he were fortunate enough to catch her, she might have need of it...after he killed Bigsby.

Adding the gown to his satchel, he headed back downstairs and out to his stables, where he caused a flurry of activity by demanding the light traveling coach and his best pair to be harnessed at once. Though he chafed at every delay, very few minutes actually passed before he was able to take the ribbons and whip up his pair, heading for the road that led north out of London.

Soon, he was barreling along the turnpike, stopping to inquire at each toll gate he passed. Unfortunately, several yellow post-chaises had come that way over the past few hours and no one was able to offer a positive identification.

Toward morning, when his pair showed signs of tiring, he stopped at a coaching inn to change horses and make more thorough inquiries. There, while paying a premium for the fastest pair the inn could boast, he learned that a young lady matching Violet Turpin's description had also changed horses there some two hours previously.

The 'ostler could not claim to have seen Bigsby, but allowed as how she must have had a gentleman with her.

"Can't see a lady like that traveling on her own, m'lord. She were in a terrible hurry, though, so I didn't ask no questions."

Rush thanked the man and continued on with the fresh pair. His presumption had clearly been correct, but whether he could catch them up in time to prevent Violet's ruin was likely to depend more on chance than anything else.

"How much longer will it take to get another pair harnessed?" Violet asked in exasperation.

Already she'd been above an hour at the posting house. At this, her second stop to change horses, she'd been glad of an opportunity to partake of a hasty breakfast and relieve herself. Now, however, she was anxious to be on her way. Based on her inquiries, Mary and Julian were more than three hours ahead of her. Not for the first time, she wished she had headed straight for Scotland rather than making that fruitless visit to Julian's lodging.

When the coach finally got underway again, she also wished she'd had the foresight to bring a change of clothes. Though she dared not stop long enough to take a room and sleep at an inn, she would certainly not be fit to be seen by the time she reached Gretna Green. That, however, was an exceedingly minor concern compared to poor Mary's fate.

Sometime in the early afternoon she fell asleep, curled into a corner of the less-than-comfortable seat, only to be awakened an hour or two later when the carriage stopped for another fresh team and postillion. Yawning, Violet stretched and stepped out of the coach to see about getting something to eat. As she had at the last two changes, she also went to inquire whether the Simpson traveling coach had been seen to pass through.

"Aye, miss, a coach such as you describe left this morning and I saw the blonde lady you mentioned as well. Right pretty little thing she was."

"This morning!" Violet exclaimed. "Are you certain?"

The man nodded. "Happen it were four or five hours ago now."

Far from catching them up, she had fallen even farther behind! At this rate, they would almost certainly be married before she could stop them. She knew of no way to travel any faster, however. Dispirited now, she thanked the man, then purchased a few meat rolls and a jug of ale from his wife, to bring along for the next stage.

She was just turning to leave with the required items when she heard a clatter out in the inn-yard.

"Here? Are you certain?" came a man's voice. A strikingly familiar man's voice.

Hurrying outside, she beheld Lord Rushford himself speaking with the 'ostler. At her appearance he turned and strode toward her.

"Thank God!" he exclaimed. "Miss Turpin, are you all right? I will take you back to London at once. Too late to avoid a scandal, I'm afraid, but—"

"What do you mean?" she asked, still stunned to see him here. "I cannot go back, not yet."

He frowned, glancing over her shoulder. "You must. However

Bigsby contrived to bring you this far, he'll take you no farther. If he tries, I'll shoot him where he stands. Where is he?"

"Nearly five hours farther along the road, from what the innkeeper just told me," she replied, more puzzled than before. "Though I see no way I can possibly catch them in time, I must try, for this is all my fault."

Now he looked as confused as she was. "Catch them?" he repeated. "Catch who?"

"Why, Julian Bigsby and Mary Simpson, of course. He has persuaded her to an elopement, which he never could have done had I not introduced them and then encouraged her to— Oh, there is no time for explanations! I must continue after them at once."

"Then…you did not elope with Bigsby yourself?"

If she had not been so worried about Mary she would have laughed. "Me? Elope with Julian? Of course not! I admit he did ask, but I refused even before I knew the truth about him. How can you think I would do such a thing now?"

"I, er, I'm sorry, Miss Turpin." He still looked somewhat dazed. "When I learned you were seen at his lodging and had hired a post chaise from a nearby inn, I assumed… But I am exceedingly happy to have been mistaken, I assure you."

Though still indignant, she realized he had drawn rather a logical conclusion based on what he knew of her earlier behavior. Not that it mattered at the moment.

"Would that I were mistaken as well, but Mary's note left little doubt. This is what she slipped under my door last night." She pulled the crumpled note from her pocket and handed it to him.

Frowning, he read it through. "Yes, she clearly intended to elope, though she doesn't say with whom. Are you sure—?"

"Who else would take advantage of her in such a way? Nor did she change her mind, for the innkeeper told me Lady Simpson's coach was here earlier today. I described it most minutely."

"What of Bigsby? Did you describe him as well?"

"To what purpose? If the coach was here, he and Mary must have been, too. Oh! Just thinking about Julian makes me so angry I could—Well. You must see that I cannot turn back now."

He regarded her thoughtfully for a moment, then shrugged. "In that case, I suppose there is nothing for it but to offer you my escort—and the use of a faster carriage. I was able to make up the two hours I was behind you on the road thus far, so we may have an outside chance of catching them before they reach the border."

She gratefully accepted his offer, though the thought of traveling so far alone with Lord Rushford made her insides flutter, even tired as she was. "How long before we can leave?"

"A few minutes, no more. I bespoke their fastest team before making my inquiries."

So saying, he led her to an elegant coach that was clearly built for both speed and comfort. Being an earl, she supposed, had some advantages. He helped her into the well-appointed interior but did not join her.

"Driving myself makes an enormous difference when time is of the essence," he explained. "Why do you not try to get a bit of sleep? You look fagged to death, if you'll pardon my saying so."

He had to be far more exhausted than she, if he had driven all the way here from London, but she was too eager to be on the road again to argue. Vowing to make him rest at the next change, she allowed him to shut her into the carriage. Vaulting onto the box, he whipped up the new pair and they continued on at a noticeably faster pace than her post-boys had driven.

Though Violet was certain anxiety for Mary would keep her awake, they had not been on the road for more than twenty minutes before she fell soundly asleep.

CHAPTER SEVENTEEN

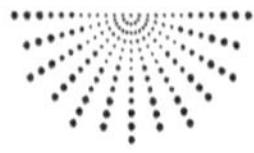

RUSH NO LONGER FELT THE SAME URGENCY DRIVING HIM NOW THAT Violet's safety was assured, but nevertheless attempted to keep the same pace, as she was clearly desperate to save her friend. Though he could not imagine Violet truly to blame for Miss Simpson's foolishness in eloping with Bigsby, he had no wish to see his fiancée fall prey to the scoundrel.

Fiancée?

Like a thunderclap, it struck him that Miss Simpson's elopement had quite effectively freed him from their betrothal. On the heels of that thought came another: this unchaperoned journey to Scotland together meant that his marriage to Violet was now more imperative than ever. His task would be to convince her of that.

By the next change of horses, Rush was finding it difficult to keep his eyes open and on the road. He sternly reminded himself that he'd endured far worse during the war, campaigning for days on end with next to no sleep. A strong cup of coffee or two would no doubt carry him through a few more hours…

Violet countermanded that idea after one look at his face when she exited the carriage. "My lord, you simply must rest. It will do neither us nor Mary any good if you land us in a ditch because you are too tired to drive properly."

"Are you suggesting we stop here for the night? We would lose any chance whatever of catching them before the border."

Though he did not add that spending a night together in a public inn would also compromise her reputation irretrievably, her blush indicated that she realized it as well.

"Of course not. But if we hire a postillion for the next stage, you can sleep inside the carriage for a few hours. We may lose a bit of ground, but not nearly so much as if you run us off the road. It is also possible they will stop for the night somewhere themselves, in which case we should catch them up before morning."

To that he agreed, for she was correct that continuing on in his current state risked an accident that might injure them both. He made inquiries while the horses were being changed and was told that a burgundy carriage carrying a couple had indeed stopped there some four hours earlier, but only long enough to change horses.

On joining Violet in the coach a short time later, he shared what he had learned. "I would never have given Bigsby credit for this degree of stamina," he commented as the postboy whipped up the horses. "He is not driving himself, however, so I must assume they are also sleeping in the coach."

"Poor Mary. I should have described to her how very uncomfortable elopements are when I encouraged her to follow her heart."

He regarded her in some amusement. "Ah, yes. I'd forgotten that this is hardly your first elopement."

"I am not eloping!" she protested. "I am merely attempting to keep my friend from doing so, which is not the same thing at all."

"Your motive may be different, but the result is the same," he pointed out. "After a days-long carriage ride to Scotland without a chaperone, your noble intentions are unlikely to stave off Society's censure."

She sucked in a quick breath. "I...did not think that far ahead. My only concern was—is—Mary. There will be time enough to fret about my own situation once she is secure."

"I envy you your ability to set your worries aside, though I suppose I should not wonder at it. You do seem to have a knack for somehow escaping the worst consequences of your various escapades. Though as I will likely be painted as the rogue who ran off with you, I cannot help giving some thought to the future."

"Nonsense! I will simply tell everyone that you did no such thing. There is no more need now for you to sacrifice your future on my behalf than there was a few nights since. Between us, I'm sure we can contrive an explanation that will let you off the hook with honor."

He leaned forward to look into her face, partially hidden in the shadows cast by the setting sun. "Suppose I do not wish to be…let off the hook?"

Her eyes flew wide. "What do you—? Do you mean to say that you —? Pray do not jest about such a thing, my lord."

"I am not jesting, Violet. As Miss Simpson's elopement has quite conveniently freed me from *that* entanglement—with honor—I find myself more than ready to enter into another, far more appealing one."

"Is…is this a proposal, my lord?"

Smiling now, he nodded. "It is. Miss Turpin—Violet—will you do me the very great honor of becoming my wife?"

Though Violet had dreamed of this moment, she could not at first believe it had truly happened. She was on the point of agreeing whole-heartedly and flinging herself into Rush's arms when she again noticed the lines of fatigue in his face. He must be delirious from exhaustion, with no idea of what he was saying.

"I…I believe you should sleep a while, my lord, before we discuss such a serious matter. Tired as you are, you cannot be in the proper frame of mind to make such a momentous decision."

He returned her gaze for a long moment, as though attempting to decipher her meaning, but then his head fell back against the squabs. "Perhaps you are right that our discussion should wait, though I assure you my offer will still stand upon waking. For now I will give you good night…my sweet."

Her heart still thrumming from the shock of his question, she watched his face as it relaxed into repose, the lines of strain gradually smoothing. Yes, there would be time enough when he woke to learn whether his offer was the product of over-fatigue or something…more. She would do well to sleep also, that she might also be in a more rational frame of mind for that discussion—not that she expected to manage it.

The day was broad when Violet awoke to discover herself again alone in the carriage. Its rapid pace told her she must have slept through their last change of horses, after which Rush had again taken the ribbons. Remembering how very tired he was, she was angry at herself for sleeping even more soundly than he.

Some two hours later the carriage again drew to a halt. Leaping down from the box, Lord Rushford opened the door.

"This should be our last change of horses before reaching the border," he told her. "According to the last toll-keeper, we are no more than an hour and a half behind them, so we *may* arrive in time to prevent a marriage. Of course, it is also entirely possible that we will not."

"We must hurry, then," she cried, renewed worry for Mary swamping all other concerns. "I should like a chance to relieve myself, however."

He smiled and helped her to the ground. "You have at least ten minutes, I should think. I will procure some breakfast for us while the team is changed out."

She went into the inn to partake of the necessary, then hastened back to the carriage.

"Are you certain you are rested enough to drive the rest of the way?" she asked in concern.

"I achieved far more on much less sleep while on the peninsula," he assured her. "If all goes well, we will reach Scotland in a few hours, at which time we can deal with whatever we discover."

Violet wondered what Rush meant to do if they arrived too late, and the knot had already been tied. He had implied he would kill

Julian had he coerced Violet herself into marriage. Would he do the same for Mary's sake? Technically, they *were* still betrothed…

"The, ah, question you asked me before you fell asleep," she tentatively began. "I, er—"

"I should not have sprung that upon you under such circumstances." He looked slightly embarrassed, the first time she could recall seeing him so. "Given both my fatigue and yours, as well as your anxiety for Miss Simpson, my timing was inexcusable."

She regarded him uncertainly. Was he expressing regret only for the timing, or for asking the question at all? "Yes, but—"

"If we're to have any hope of catching Bigsby and Miss Simpson, I fear we haven't time to discuss the matter properly just now, either. With any luck, we will have ample opportunity after reaching Scotland."

With that, he handed Violet back into the carriage and vaulted onto the box to continue their journey, leaving her to analyze every word he'd said as the countryside hurried past.

Three hours later, Rush stopped to pay the final toll before crossing the bridge that marked the Scottish border. Violet took the opportunity to lower the window and put her head out.

"What news?" she called to him.

"They passed through less than an hour since. If they bespeak a room and eat something before calling the parson, we will have them. If not—"

"We will be too late," she finished. "Do hurry!"

Shutting the window and sinking back into her seat, Violet felt selfish in the extreme for making such demands upon him to rectify a problem largely of her own making. She herself owed Mary no less, but what Lord Rushford's feelings on the matter might be, she was less certain.

Her anxiety rose to its height as they finally drew to a halt in front of the Gretna Hall Hotel. She threw open the carriage door just as Rush leapt down from the box.

"Is this where they stopped?" she breathlessly asked him.

"That is the Simpson carriage, is it not?" He pointed.

Indeed, there stood the burgundy traveling coach she had pursued for so many miles. Rush handed her down and she was hurrying forward almost before her feet touched the ground.

"Mary!" she cried out. "Are you here? Please, you must stop and listen to what I have to say before—"

She was interrupted by the appearance of Mary herself emerging from the hotel, her face radiant with happiness. Beside her, holding her hand and looking every bit as happy, was...Lord Killerby!

Rush gaped at his friend in amazement.

"Killer!? What do you here? Where is Bigsby? How—?"

He broke off as the truth hit him with blinding clarity. It was Killer, never Bigsby at all, who had eloped with Miss Simpson.

How had he not suspected before? Almost from the moment of their first meeting, she had seemed far more at ease with Killer than himself. Belatedly, he recollected their shared love of music, how comfortably they conversed when walking their horses together, the numerous times they had danced together... It made perfect sense.

The couple halted, their expressions now alarmed rather than blissful.

"Rush!" Killer exclaimed. "How did you—? That is, I never meant to— Dash it!"

At the same time, Miss Simpson—or was she already Lady Killerby?—gasped out, "Violet? How are you here, and with Lord Rushford? I asked you to delay any pursuit, not to come after me yourself! Not that it matters now."

Stepping forward, Rush's former fiancée lifted her chin to regard him squarely, something he could not recall her ever doing before. "My lord, I cannot marry you after all, for I have just become the wife of Lord Killerby. I apologize for your finding out in such a way, but I cannot be sorry, for I am persuaded this will do as much to secure your future happiness as my own."

Killer, meanwhile, eyed Rush warily. "You...you don't mean to call me out over this, do you? I'll fight you if I must, but I would far rather—"

"Oh, stop blathering and let me congratulate you," Rush interrupted. "Finding you here is a stunner, no question, but I've no doubt you will make your new bride far happier than I could have. Do you not agree, Miss Turpin?"

He turned to Violet, who still seemed to be struggling to find her voice. She gazed first at her friend, then at Killer, then back. "I...I do not know when I have ever been so surprised," she finally managed. "Mary, why did you not tell me it was Lord Killerby you meant to wed? Had you done so, I never would have...we never would have..." She glanced dazedly up at Rush.

"But I did tell you!" the new Lady Killerby exclaimed. "Did you not receive my note?"

"Of course I did. But it made no mention whatever of Lord Killerby." She pulled the much-folded piece of paper from her pocket and handed it to her friend as proof.

The former Miss Simpson read over it and gasped. "Oh, no! I was absolutely certain I had named him. But...surely you must have guessed, Violet? Who else could you possibly imagine I would elope with?"

"Bigsby," Rush answered for her. "I confess, I believed it likely as well, given what I know of the man, though when I began my pursuit I assumed it was Miss Turpin he had carried off. It appears he never had anything to do with the matter at all." He was still finding it difficult to reconcile what he had believed with the truth.

"Mr. Bigsby?" Killer's new wife repeated in apparent confusion. "I scarcely know him. Why on earth would I wish to marry *him*?"

Rush and Violet looked at each other and he was suddenly struck with the complete ridiculousness of the entire situation. She appeared similarly struck, for a small snort escaped her, then a giggle. That was enough to set him laughing as well and for a long moment neither of them could speak, they were so overcome with mirth. Perhaps it was due to exhaustion and the sudden lifting of anxiety, but he had never found anything so hilarious in his life.

When Violet was finally able to catch her breath, she turned to her friend. "I...I am sorry for believing such a thing of you, Mary, and give you both my heartiest congratulations. I feel sure you will be very happy together."

An instant later the two young ladies were laughingly hugging and crying together, while Rush and Killer looked on in bemusement. Both ladies appeared somewhat sheepish when they finally released each other, but Killer spoke before the moment could become awkward.

"I say, won't you both join us for a celebratory dinner? We thought it safest to marry straight away upon arriving. We were just coming back out to get our things from the coach when you showed up, and have yet to bespeak food or a room. We can then share our tales from beginning to end over our impromptu wedding feast."

To this everyone readily agreed. Rush and Killer carried the baggage inside, where they requested three rooms and the best meal the inn could offer, to be served two hours hence. Violet had turned to follow the newlyweds upstairs when Rush placed a gentle hand on her arm.

"A moment, if you please. If we are to relate our adventure from beginning to end, I should first like it to reach a proper conclusion. You, ah, never answered my question, if you recall."

Her lovely violet eyes met his and color overspread her cheeks. "You...you really were serious, then? It was not merely fatigue...and your sense of honor...that prompted your offer?"

Smiling down at her, he shook his head. "I won't deny the fatigue, nor the claims of honor, but I asked you to marry me because I cannot think of anyone with whom I would rather share the rest of my life. I love you, Violet, and hope in time you will learn to love me as well. Do you think you can?"

Her lips parted in surprise before curving into a most alluring smile. "No learning will be required, my lord, for I have been smitten with you since I was a girl of fourteen. Recent events have only served to strengthen that childish infatuation into something more permanent. In short, I am already quite thoroughly in love with you."

His spirits suddenly soaring, he lowered his lips to hers, right there in the main entryway of the inn. She responded eagerly, prompting him to deepen the kiss, reveling in the sweet taste of her. Reasoning that such scenes were likely no novelty here, he allowed himself to enjoy the sensations she aroused in him for some minutes before raising his head to smile tenderly down at her.

"Considering where we find ourselves, I suggest we formalize the declarations we have just made. We can then take advantage of the fine meal we are soon to enjoy to celebrate two weddings instead of one."

Her head still spinning from the most passionate kiss she had ever experienced, Violet could not immediately form a coherent reply. Even when reason finally returned, the reality seemed too good to be true. Rush, her longtime romantic ideal, not only loved her but wished to marry her on the spot!

"That…sounds like an excellent plan, my lord," she said at last. "Or may I call you Rush, as my brother does?"

"You may. In fact I infinitely prefer it. Now, if we are to make our declaration in form and have it properly recorded, I suppose we should call our host back."

When the man appeared, Rush canceled one of their two rooms and asked him to send for the parson.

"He's still here," the innkeeper told them with a grin. "Stopped in the taproom for a pint after hitching the last couple. I'll get him."

To Violet's amusement—and bemusement—the parson proved to be the same Mr. Elliot who had married Grant and Dina in December, in this very hotel. If he recognized her, however, he gave no sign. No doubt he performed so many hurried weddings he had difficulty remembering them all—and Violet had been but an onlooker then, not the bride.

The innkeeper showed them into a parlor for the formalities, where

Mr. Elliot asked whether they preferred the shorter wedding ceremony or a longer, more traditional one.

Rush turned to Violet. "What think you? The difference in fee does not signify if it matters to you."

Violet, romantic that she was, had been disappointed when Grant and Dina opted for the shortened version. Now, however, she felt rather inclined to follow their example, given how well their marriage had turned out.

"The briefer one, I think. Particularly as I should very much like a wash before dinner."

"As you wish." Rush gave her a smile that quickened her pulse before nodding to the parson.

With the innkeeper and his wife standing as witnesses, Mr. Elliot opened his register and recorded their full names, places of residence, and sworn statements that neither was already married.

"Have you both come here of your own free will and accord?" he then asked them both.

"We have," they said together. Violet felt unaccountably tempted to giggle again.

"Ryan Rowland Dean, Lord Rushford, do you take this woman to be your lawful wedded wife, forsaking all others, keeping only to her as long as you both shall live?"

"I do." He locked his gaze with Violet's. Laughter forgotten, her heart swelled within her at the tender expression in his eyes.

Turning to Violet, Mr. Elliot asked the same question.

"I do." She did not know why her voice quivered, for she felt no reluctance whatsoever to make the vow.

"Have you a ring?"

Clearly startled by the question, Rush's brows rose in consternation. "Er, no. I am afraid not."

"I have one here for purchase, if you wish." He pulled a band of what appeared to be brass from his pocket.

"I believe we will forego the ring for now," Rush told him. Then, to Violet, "I will rectify the lack immediately upon our return to London."

She grinned up at him, refusing to acknowledge the trembling in her stomach as the enormity of what they were doing sank in. "I am willing to wait," she assured him.

"In that case, Lord Rushford, please repeat after me," Mr. Elliot said. "With these vows, I thee wed; with my body, I thee worship; with all my worldly goods I thee endow; in the name of the Father, Son and Holy Ghost. Amen."

He did so. The parson then placed Violet's hand in Rush's and had her repeat, "What God has joined together, let no man put asunder."

Mr. Elliot then declared them man and wife before God and the witnesses and asked them to sign the register, which both did.

Rush paid the man's fee and…it was over. Violet could scarcely believe it. Ten minutes ago she had been plain Violet Turpin and now she was the Countess of Rushford. How could it be possible that they were truly married?

The innkeeper and his wife offered perfunctory congratulations as the parson left, but Violet scarcely heard them. Instead, she was looking at Rush, trying to divine his feelings. Was he as overwhelmed by their abruptly changed circumstances as she was?

He politely responded to the well-wishes, then turned to smile down at her. "So now we've done it. No turning back. Any regrets, Lady Rushford?"

Though her feeling of unreality increased at hearing her new name, she mutely shook her head.

"Good. Now, did you not say you wished to freshen up before dinner?"

Violet felt her face pinken, but struggled to retain her composure. "I…yes. I rather desperately need a wash, though I fear I have nothing clean to change into."

He grinned. "I took the liberty of bringing along the dress you left at my house, against the necessity of it being needed. It is clean, if rather outmoded."

"How very foresighted of you," she said, both startled and relieved. "As you are fond of pointing out, planning ahead is not exactly one of my strengths."

That elicited a chuckle from him. "It is well that it happens to be one of mine, then. I should say we are well matched. Shall we?" He extended an arm and she took it, feeling suddenly shy of him in a way she never had before.

Together, they mounted the stairs to the second story and thence to their room for the night. With a wink that made her heart accelerate, Rush turned the key in the lock. He then pushed open the door to reveal a good-sized bed with a white counterpane, as well as a dressing table already supplied with a pitcher and a ewer filled with steaming water.

"I daresay they can bring up a tub, if you fancy a proper bath," Rush said, advancing into the room. "We still have more than an hour before dinner."

Violet swallowed as it was fully borne in upon her that they would be sharing a bedchamber…as husband and wife. Widely read as she was, she had a fair understanding of what went on between married couples. Never before had she so longed to experience such things herself, however.

Greatly daring, she replied, "I confess a bath would be most welcome, after two full days and nights on the road. If you really believe there is time…" Her voice trailed off as her courage wavered.

"Should dinner be pushed back fifteen minutes, it is no great matter. I doubt Lord Killerby and his new bride will be in any particular hurry to quit their room, either."

The oblique reference made Violet's cheeks heat, but she did not draw back. "In that case, yes. I should very much appreciate a proper bath before….before dinner."

A twinkle in his gray eyes showed that he fully comprehended what she had left unsaid. "As would I. Just a moment." Poking his head into the hallway, he relayed the request to a passing maid who promised to have a tub and kettles brought up directly.

"I daresay the water's already boiling," she added with a saucy wink. "New-married couples mostly do want baths after driving here pell-mell to get themselves hitched."

She hurried off, leaving them alone again.

"We should at least remove our outer things before our bath arrives," Rush suggested, doffing his cloak.

Our bath. Violet swallowed again, thinking ahead to what that would entail.

"I, ah, yes. Luckily there is a good fire, so we, er, should not risk becoming chilled." To hide her sudden embarrassment, she turned half away from him to fumble with the fastening of her own cloak.

"Here, let me help you." Gently turning her back to face him, he undid the three buttons near her throat and the cloak fell away.

Though she was still fully dressed, Violet felt nearly as exposed as when he'd seen her in only her chemise in his library. She made a small, involuntary motion as if to snatch back her cloak and his smile deepened.

"You are one of the bravest women I've ever known, Violet. Surely you are not afraid?"

"Afraid?" Her voice came out in a squeak that did indeed sound frightened. Which was absurd. Clearing her throat, she tried again. "I don't believe I could ever be afraid of you, Rush, though I confess to some uncertainty about how to…to proceed."

He regarded her with what looked suspiciously like amusement. "I take it you did not consider such things during your previous elopements?"

"There was but one," she reminded him indignantly, but then she laughed. "I was adamant earlier that this was no elopement, yet it turned out to be one after all."

"I hope, however, it will be your last," he said, chuckling as well.

Their shared amusement did away with her embarrassment—as, perhaps, he intended?

"I believe I can safely promise you never to elope again. Believing Mary to have been taken in by Mr. Bigsby brought home to me the risks of pursuing romance and adventure to the exclusion of all else. Though I may still hope for romance—" She slanted a shy look up at him through her lashes— "I have sworn off seeking adventure."

"Ah, but not all adventures involve mad dashes across the country," he said with a wink.

Before she could ask him to elaborate, a tap came at the door, followed by two servants bearing an oversized tub and two steaming copper kettles. Behind them was the maid, bearing two more pitchers of water and a pile of drying cloths. At Rush's direction, they set out the bath and its accoutrements with practiced speed.

Once they were gone, he turned to Violet with a positively wicked smile. "Come, my dear Lady Rushford, and I will introduce you to a more domestic sort of adventure."

CHAPTER EIGHTEEN

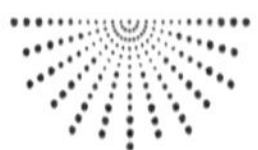

IF RUSH HAD WONDERED WHETHER VIOLET'S THIRST FOR EXCITEMENT might have led her to go well beyond what was proper with another man, her reaction now assured him she had not. He was glad, for he very much wanted to be the one to initiate her into the pleasures of the flesh.

"Come," he repeated, holding out a hand to her. "You did say you were not afraid?"

Swallowing visibly, she lifted her chin and put her hand into his. "I'm not."

"Good. I promise you I am far less dangerous than some horses you've ridden. Shall we clean ourselves up a bit? You apparently had the foresight this time to wear a dress that fastens in front, but I should still like to help you out of it."

Indeed, he could scarcely suppress his eagerness to see—to experience—what lay beneath, after his intoxicating glimpse a few nights since. When she made no protest, he pulled her closer and began undoing the hooks at her neckline. The dress parted to reveal her chemise as his fingers moved lower.

"No corset?"

"I, ah, dressed in such a hurry on discovering Mary's note, I did not call for my abigail. I also thought it unwise to tell her of my errand, with Mary's reputation at risk."

"Not to worry, I was not complaining," he assured her, continuing to unfasten her gown. "Rather the reverse. Particularly as I imagine a corset would have made your journey even more uncomfortable."

As his fingers reached her belly, he felt her trembling slightly beneath them.

"No doubt of that," she replied somewhat breathlessly. "I dispense with it as often as I can in the country, and would prefer to do so always."

"You will hear no protest from me, should you do so."

By now he had undone enough hooks that he was able to push her gown off her shoulders to slither down and form a pool of fabric around her feet. She stepped out of the garment, clad in only a thin shift, displaying a shapely calf and ankle as she did so.

"Would you feel more comfortable if I turned my back as you step into the bath?" he felt obliged to ask.

"And let you think me a coward?" She faced him bravely, though her heightened complexion betrayed her lack of composure. "You are my husband now, are you not?"

Husband. The word had never sounded so...seductive before. "I am."

With a reassuring smile, he untied the ribbons securing her chemise and a moment later it followed her dress to the floor, revealing her in all her glory.

It was now Rush's turn to swallow, his body clamoring urgently for her. Never had he desired any woman a fraction as much as this one, yet he held himself firmly in check. Not for the world would he frighten her. No, he meant to do all in his power to ensure that her first experience would be both enjoyable and memorable.

Violet dropped her gaze, embarrassed by her nakedness, only to have her attention snagged by the patch of bare chest visible above Rush's loosely-tied shirt. Unlike that night in his library, she did not look away. Instead, she reached out to tug the opening wider, that she might see more.

"You…have me at a disadvantage," she told him, though still not meeting his eye.

He chuckled in response, then pulled his shirt up and off over his head in one fluid motion, revealing the smooth, muscled planes of his chest and abdomen. Violet caught her breath. He was even more beautiful than she had imagined!

Almost of its own volition, one of her hands came up to caress the expanse, her fingers tangling in the soft curls of hair sprinkled lightly across it. Belatedly wondering if she shocked him, she finally risked a glance up at his face.

No, definitely not shocked. In fact, the heat in his admiring gaze was so intense, it instantly ignited an answering flame within her. Suddenly fearless, she moved forward to press her bare breasts against his warm chest, at the same time tilting her face up for his kiss.

He obliged her. His hands roved up and down her bare back as he deepened the kiss, increasing her eagerness. Soon, mere kisses and even caresses were not enough to content her. She wanted more.

Pulling ever-so-slightly away, she murmured, "You are not yet ready for your bath, my lord."

Another chuckle vibrated through his chest and the sensation against her breasts inflamed her further. With clumsy fingers, she began fumbling with the closure of his breeches.

"I am at least as eager as you, my love, so pray allow me," he whispered against her lips.

Deftly, he undid the buttons securing his breeches and an instant later Rush—her *husband*—stood there as naked as she. She tried not to stare, but her extensive reading had in no way prepared her for the sight. He was more magnificent than any Greek statue…and so much *larger* than she had expected. Those ancient sculptors had certainly understated the matter!

When she did not immediately move, he pulled her gently to him for another long, leisurely kiss and her momentary nervousness about what was to come evaporated. She now responded as eagerly as before, her hands sliding up his arms, then around his back as she again pressed herself tightly against him.

"Tempted as I am to postpone our baths, it would be a shame to allow the water to get cold," he murmured against her lips.

She pulled back just far enough to gaze up at him and his smile spiked her desire even higher. "You did promise me a new sort of adventure, did you not?"

"I did. We may begin it here." Leading her to the tub, he helped her step into it, then picked up one of the smaller cloths. Wetting it, he laved her back and shoulders, then slid it around to her front.

"That...feels remarkably good," she said as he massaged her breasts with the rough cloth. "Do you not mean to bathe as well?"

In answer, he stepped into the tub, facing her. "Of course. I wish to be as clean for you as you will be for me."

Greatly daring, she stooped to pick up another cloth. "Then let me help." So saying, she mimicked his motions, first rubbing the wet cloth over his back, then his chest.

When she moved lower, he sucked in a breath. "You are maddening, do you know that?"

The catch in his voice made her smile. "Am I? I do not mean to be. What do you wish me to do? Show me."

Rather than reply, he brought his own cloth lower as well, swiping its roughness over her abdomen before gliding it down to the cleft between her legs.

Violet gasped. "I...Oh!"

"Is this pleasant for you?" he whispered.

She nodded, the sensations he was producing rendering her incapable of speech. Taking her cue from him, she brought her own cloth down to circle his rampant manhood, drawing a gasp from him in turn.

"You are making it devilish hard to restrain myself," he panted.

"Then, don't." Exactly what it was her body craved she was not sure, but that he could provide it she felt certain.

Dropping the washing cloth, he massaged her cleft with his fingers instead, until she was quivering with need. Then, when she felt certain she could bear no more, he cupped her bottom, lifted her up and impaled her upon his shaft—and she exploded into ecstasy.

Over and over he lifted, then lowered her, each iteration a new summit of pleasure. Then, clasping her tightly to him, he gave a cry and pulsed into her, spending his passion as she convulsed around him.

As she descended from the heights, she felt his muscles quivering from the effort to remain upright, then realized her own were doing the same. By unspoken accord, they both crouched into the bath, her legs around his waist as his supported her.

For many minutes they clung together, joined, before he gently kissed her and fished his abandoned cloth from the water.

"Shall…we finish washing up?" Though he tried to speak lightly, the huskiness in his voice proved Rush as affected by the experience as she.

"I suppose we'd better, if we are not to be late to dinner." She attempted the same light tone, with similarly poor success.

That resulted in both of them laughing, which produced most interesting sensations indeed—so interesting that their bath was delayed for several more minutes before a second bout of passion left them both languorous enough to make use of the now-tepid water.

Violet and Rush descended to dinner some ten minutes later than planned. Just as Rush had predicted, however, they did not keep the other couple waiting, for Lord Killerby and his lady did not join them for several more minutes. Both looked even happier than before, though the moment Mary's gaze met Violet's, she blushed deeply.

"I took the liberty of ordering a bottle of the house's best wine," Rush said after greetings were exchanged. "Something appropriate for toasting your marriage…and ours."

There was an instant of stunned silence, then Lord Killerby exclaimed, "Have you really done it, then? I thought things might be tending that way, but—" He broke off, shaking his head, then stepped forward to clap Rush on the shoulder. "Well done, old chap!"

"Truly, Violet?" Mary asked in astonishment. "When we went upstairs, William—" She paused with a blush, either for using her new husband's Christian name or the mention of going upstairs— "William said he would suggest to Lord Rushford that you two should follow our example, but I thought he was jesting. I had no idea that you…that Lord Rushford…"

"Truly," Violet assured her, unable to suppress a grin. "As you were engaged to him, I did not like to confess it before, but I conceived a *tendre* for him years ago, well before I met you at Miss Gebhart's. Then, when we met again this winter…well, it is a long story and the telling can wait for another time. For tonight, let us simply rejoice that everything has fallen out so well."

Mary turned to gaze at Lord Killerby as though he were the romantic hero of her dreams, as well. "Everything has, has it not? When I think how bitterly I despaired the morning my father's letter arrived…"

"No need to dwell on that now," said Lord Killerby, taking his new bride's hand and drawing her close with a tender look. "All's well that ends well. Rush, if you will pour that excellent wine, I should like to propose a toast—to what are bound to be the two happiest marriages ever to grace England."

All four drank to that and a moment later the meal was brought in. Over the next two hours they did ample justice to the simple inn fare, for none had eaten much during their mad flights for the border. Though tired, they were all in high spirits and much laughter accompanied the tales they exchanged over the meal.

At its conclusion, Lord Killerby raised a glass for a last toast. "May the four of us enjoy many a merry gathering like this in future, as we are all such good friends. Though first, I suppose we must return to London and face the consequences of what we have done. Did you by chance leave a second note for your mother?" he asked Mary.

She shook her head. "I dared not. My hope was that Violet would delay pursuit for as long as possible, or at least persuade my mother that I would be both safe and happy with you—but clearly neither happened."

"Perhaps, had your note been a bit more explicit, it would have," Violet chided her.

"Yes, that was an oversight, to be sure," her friend admitted. "But a lucky one, as things fell out, wouldn't you say?" she added with a mischievous smile.

Violet could not disagree. Had Mary named her intended husband in her letter, Violet would have done as she asked rather than go after her…and would not now be married to Rush. And *that* she could not regret at all.

"Killer brings up a good point, however," Rush said. "You must dispatch a letter to London at once to let Lady Simpson know how things are, for by now she must be worried to death."

"I'll write to my own mother as well," Lord Killerby said. "Eager as she has been for me to marry, she'll be ecstatic—though she will no doubt ring a peal over me for not inviting her to our wedding."

Rush turned to Violet. "Your family must be also notified. I do hope your brother won't feel obliged to call me out over it."

Violet laughed. "Grant will be far too relieved at being freed from all responsibility for my behavior to bear you any ill-will. My mother will be pleased as well, though I am sure she, like Lady Killerby, would have preferred a more conventional wedding. As for my father, he will likely receive the news with his usual philosophical calm."

When a servant came to clear the dishes away, Rush requested paper, pens and ink that the requisite letters could be written and dispatched before they all retired for the night.

Ascending the stairs with her new husband shortly thereafter, Violet eagerly anticipated her next lesson in "domestic adventures."

Nor did Rush disappoint her.

After a late, leisurely breakfast the next morning, the two couples said their *au revoirs*, promising to meet again in London.

The Killerbys then departed in Lady Simpson's coach, while Rush delayed long enough to buy Violet and himself an extra change of clothes before beginning their own, more leisurely trip south. As they were in no particular hurry to reach London, they agreed to add a stop at Ashcombe, in Staffordshire, along the way.

Thor and Dina were surprised and delighted to see them, as their letter had made no mention of a visit. To Rush's relief, Violet had correctly predicted her brother's reaction to their news. Far from being angry about the elopement, he nearly fell on Rush's neck with gratitude.

"I did worry Vi might try setting her cap at you, after the way she behaved over Christmas, and at Ivy Lodge," Thor confided, once the exclamations and congratulations were over. "Much as I thought such a match would benefit *her*, however, I thought *you* too well acquainted with her madcap ways to be tempted. But instead of you persuading her to a more proper path, it appears she cajoled you onto her own improper one."

Rush returned his friend's grin. "Yes, well, I discovered that propriety has its shortcomings—though Violet and I are agreed there are to be no more elopements in our future."

"In that case, you'd best hope any daughters you have will not inherit her parents' taste for scandal," Dina said with a laugh.

Violet and Rush exchanged a startled glance, for neither had thought so far ahead as children yet, but then they joined in the laughter.

They stayed two days at Ashcombe before continuing on to London, by which time nearly a fortnight had elapsed since their departure.

"Are you certain you would not prefer to send round to Cavendish Square for your things rather than visit yourself?" he asked when the carriage drew up before his house on Brook Street. "Lady Simpson will likely forgive her daughter sooner than yourself for what has occurred, even though you were not—this time—the instigator."

"Yes, I've no doubt she considers me a veritable snake in the grass, underhandedly stealing you away from Mary. It seems craven not to face her in person, though I rather hope by now the worst of her anger will have abated."

"Discovering that Killer's fortune is greater than mine may have helped," Rush suggested.

She chuckled. "Likely so. Still, perhaps it *would* be wiser to call upon Mary and Lord Killerby to inquire about her mood before attempting to beard the dragon in her den."

Rush grinned at her apt phrasing. "An excellent idea," he agreed, opening the carriage door.

Stepping out, he handed her down and together they entered the house. As Rush had written ahead, his staff quickly assembled in the front hall, eager to be introduced to their new mistress.

"Is Lady Rushford's chamber ready?" he asked the housekeeper once congratulations had been expressed and most of the servants dispersed to their tasks.

"Aye, my lord. The next along from yours, as you requested."

"Excellent." Then, to Violet, "Before we go up, I should like to send word to Lord Peter Northrup that we are returned. I'm curious to hear whether he was able to discover anything about Bigsby's whereabouts, as he intended to do when I left him."

He dashed off a quick note to Peter, then led Violet upstairs. Unable to restrain himself, he pulled her against him for a kiss the moment they were alone in the hallway—a kiss she eagerly returned. After a few moments of delightful distraction, he finally opened the door to the room that would be hers for the remainder of their stay in London.

"It's lovely," she exclaimed, gazing around at the tasteful peach and white decor. "Was it your mother's?"

"Yes, though she never slept in it after my father passed away several years since. You may redecorate it as you please, of course, but I'm happy that you approve of it for the present."

Stepping inside, she looked pointedly at the bed before opening the door to the dressing room. That it connected to his bedchamber was evidenced by the masculine clothing on hooks and shelves.

"Indeed, I very much approve," she said, slanting a glance up at him through her lashes. "This room will be most...convenient."

Chuckling, he lowered his lips to hers for another sweet kiss. "My thoughts precisely." Then, looking over at her bed, "What say you we—?"

He was interrupted by a knock upon the front door below.

"Who that can be?" Violet exclaimed. "No one should even know we are returned yet."

"Only Lord Peter, but I can't imagine he would be calling already. Much as I chafe at the delay, I suppose we had better go down to see." After a last, quick kiss promising more delights to come, he escorted her back downstairs.

Their visitor did indeed prove to be Lord Peter, and he came bearing news of more than just Bigsby.

"Glad to see you finally chose to grace London with your presence," he jokingly greeted them upon being shown into the parlor. "Congratulations, by the way. Lord Killerby and his new bride returned three days ago and the story of your double elopement has kept the gossips happily occupied ever since."

Rush groaned. "I expected them to stop to see his mother along the way and so arrive no earlier than ourselves. On leaving Scotland, we all agreed to work out a plausible tale for public consumption once we were back in Town."

Peter grinned. "The Dowager Lady Killerby was already in London herself, got here the day after her son made off with Miss Simpson. Finding all four of you missing caused a bit of a flurry, as you may imagine, as no letters arrived for nearly a week. Now, by all accounts, Lady Killerby is delighted with the news and doing what she can to tame the gossip—though to little effect thus far, as it's far too novel a story to be easily supplanted by another."

"What of Lady Simpson?" Violet asked warily. "I dare not hope she is equally pleased by what we have done."

"Fortunately, Lord Killerby had the foresight to take his new bride to his house rather than hers on their arrival. Thus, their first meeting with the former Miss Simpson's mother was in the presence of his own. As I understand it, the elder Lady Killerby quite forcefully impressed upon Lady Simpson what a brilliant marriage her daughter had made, if to a different lord than originally expected."

He then turned ruefully to Violet. "Even so, she was apparently quite angry that you snatched Lord Rushford away from her daughter. She had your things sent back to Lady Puttercroft's. Your aunt is also returned to Town, by the bye, and taking full credit for marrying you off to an earl. None of this is what I primarily came to tell you about, however."

"Oh? Then you were able to learn something of Bigsby's movements?" Rush guessed from his satisfied countenance.

"Better than that. Young Flute and I discovered where he was hiding, waiting for a packet out of the West India docks. I went to the Runners and presented my proof that Bigsby was the Saint of Seven Dials and they wasted no time in arresting him. He now awaits trial. Handsome fellow that he is, all the ladies are demanding leniency, so I doubt he'll hang. To be honest, I suspect he is rather enjoying his new celebrity. Won't be surprised if he's able to parlay it into a rich wife after all...once he gets out of prison."

Rush and Violet both laughed.

"This neatly lets all of the *real* Saints off the hook, does it not?" she asked.

Peter nodded. "Part of my reason for turning him in. That and the substantial reward, which I and the previous Saints have agreed to use for the benefit of the deserving poor in Seven Dials. I am already taking steps to invest it profitably, that it may become a continuing trust of sorts."

"Well done," Rush said, pumping Peter's hand. "Well done, indeed. Do you not agree, my love?"

Violet, however, was frowning. "No doubt the poor will benefit from the money, but they will no longer have a Saint of Seven Dials to look to as their symbol of hope. That seems a sad loss to me. Unless..." She looked at Rush, her deep blue eyes now twinkling.

"Unless...?" he repeated, confused, but then comprehension dawned. "No. Absolutely not. I won't deny that you have managed to infect me with a degree of your, ah, lust for adventure, but not to the point that I am willing to become the next Saint myself. Especially as I have something quite different in mind."

She regarded him with mingled disappointment and curiosity. "Oh? What is that?"

"Unless you are set upon finishing out your London Season, I should very much like to take you to Rushford Abbey in a week or two. I believe you will enjoy familiarizing yourself with the estate and with the work my mother was doing to improve the lives of our tenants. In addition, I had thought to buy two or three pairs of foxhounds, that you might have the beginnings of that pack you wanted to start one day."

Violet stared at him for a long moment before flinging herself into his arms. "Oh, Rush! I cannot think of a better wedding gift you could give me."

Lord Peter cleared his throat. "I'll, ah, just show myself out, shall I? It would appear the two of you have a few…private things to discuss just now. Sarah and I will have you over in a day or two and we can talk more about the Saint business then, if you wish."

Rush scarcely noticed his departure, so distracting was the feel of Violet's body pressed against his own.

"Let us go back upstairs, shall we?" he suggested the moment the front door closed behind their visitor. "I find myself quite eager for another sweet taste…of scandal."

Keep reading for a sneak peak at the prequel to the *Saint of Seven Dials* series, ***Scandalous Virtue!***

SCANDALOUS VIRTUE (PREVIEW)

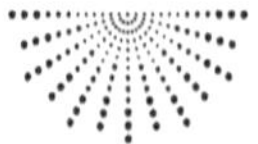

London—Late September, 1814

RAIN BEAT UPON EXPENSIVELY PANED WINDOWS while in the flickering candlelight within, the boisterous clamor hovered in volume between battlefield and bordello. John Jefferson Ashecroft, equally at home in either setting, relished the wild abandon of this latest celebration of his recent, unexpected elevation to the lofty title of Marquis of Foxhaven.

Lord Peter Northrup, fourth son of the Duke of Marland and his oldest friend, clearly did not share his enthusiasm. "Three near-orgies in three nights is a bit much, don't you think, Jack?" he whispered. "Thought you valued your grandfather's memory. This would having him rolling in his grave!"

"Mausoleum, dear boy. Nothing so crude as earth for a Foxhaven resting place! But the old fellow's gone now, so there's no one to care what I do with my good fortune—or no one whose opinion matters." Jack turned from the card table and his advisor.

"Here, Polly, lass! Bring me another pint and another kiss!" he called out to a passing maidservant.

Giggling, the girl complied, and Jack slid a hand up her skirts to sweeten his kiss. "Milor' you are a handful!" Polly informed him, wrinkling her freckled nose and winking.

Jack chuckled. "Nay, you're the handful, and a pretty one at that! What say you and I escape upstairs for half an hour? My guests will never miss me." He swept a glance about the sumptuous drawing room at the dicing, dallying throng there assembled. The marked absence of ladies—of the Quality, at any rate—gave evidence that this particular gathering lacked Society's blessing.

Then he caught Lord Peter's eye. "What? Surely you don't begrudge me a bit of revelry after the past few years of privation?"

Lord Peter snorted. "Privation? I don't recall that a light purse ever kept you from revelry in the past. Now you simply have the means to speed yourself to perdition on greased wheels."

"Ah, you have no idea how I suffered during the war," Jack informed his friend with a melodramatic sigh. "Wine, women and song were hard to come by. The sleep I lost in the search . . . ! Ask Harry over there. He has no fault to find with my present lifestyle."

"No surprise there." Lord Peter turned a judicious eye on Jack's second-oldest friend, who was enthusiastically tossing dice with his one remaining arm. The wars had left his other sleeve empty. "Harry always lived for the moment, even before his injury turned him bitter. Now he just wants company on his journey to hell."

Jack shrugged. "And perhaps I'll oblige him. He saved my life in Spain, after all."

"And you his—twice," Lord Peter reminded him. "I'd say the score's more than even."

"Polly, go ahead and take Ferny another bottle," suggested Jack, nodding toward the gesturing Lord Fernworth across the noisy room. "Perhaps by the time you return, Peter will be done with his moralizing. You're quite the spoilsport tonight, you know," he informed his friend when the wench had gone. "I can't think you accepted my invitation merely to cluck over my shortcomings like some brightly colored mother hen."

Lord Peter smoothed his gold and scarlet waistcoat. "I suppose I am acting the prig tonight. Sorry, Jack. It's just—"

A forceful throat-clearing at his elbow interrupted him. The thin, nondescript butler Jack had hired earlier that week announced, "A Mr. Havershaw, milord." The throat-clearer, just as thin as the butler but much taller, hovered behind, scowling.

He'd really have to see about a new butler, thought Jack resignedly. This Carp, or Crump, or whatever his name was, didn't seem to have a grasp of the proper procedures at all.

"Ah, yes, Mr. Havershaw," said Jack with forced cordiality while looking daggers at his oblivious butler. "I do apologize for not keeping our appointment last Wednesday. The press of business, you see—"

"Yes, I certainly do see, my lord." Mr. Havershaw scoured the room with a sour glance. "I would not have presumed to come to you, but some of these papers are quite pressing. If I could have half an hour of your time in the library?"

Jack stared at the man in disbelief. "Now?" He knew that Havershaw had enjoyed an unusually privileged position as both his grandfather's steward and lifelong friend, but this was absurd.

"If you'd be so kind, my lord. I'll not keep you long from your . . . guests."

Aware that Lord Peter, along with a growing number of the revelers, were regarding him with interest, Jack finally shrugged. "I may as well get it over, I suppose. Peter, see that no one's glass goes empty, will you? My staff leaves a bit to be desired. All right, Havershaw, the library's this way."

Havershaw headed for the hallway. "I know, my lord."

How did the man manage to make those two words sound like an insult? He was the marquis now, by God, however unprepared for the role he might be.

Once in the library, he turned to face his nemesis. "I trust you'll make this quick, Mr. Havershaw. It's most irregular for a host to abandon his guests in this manner."

He'd meant to say something far more cutting, but various childhood memories of Havershaw had crowded back. With them came an ingrained respect he was amazed could still constrain him. Other than his grandfather and, more recently, the Duke of Wellington, Jack had never cared about pleasing anyone but himself.

Lord Geoffrey, his spendthrift, gamester father and Lord Foxhaven's second son, had died when Jack was but eight. Two years later, his mother married Sir Findlay Branch, a wealthy, stuffy baronet whose apparent mission in life was to eradicate Lord Geoffrey's influences from his son.

Jack had responded with rebellion, at first subtle, then open, and finally flagrant. Before he reached eleven he was shipped off to boarding school and forbidden to return until he reformed. As a result, he spent all holidays at Fox Manor, where old Lord Foxhaven had become the only stabilizing influence in his early life. There, Mr. Havershaw had been an imposing, authoritative presence, second only to his grandfather in the boy's eyes.

"As I said, my lord, this should take but half an hour, perhaps less," said that former object of awe. Opening the satchel he carried, he pulled out a thick sheaf of papers. "There will be much more for you to go over when you finally see your way clear to visit Fox Manor, of course, but these documents are the most pressing."

Jack eyed the stack doubtfully. "I thought I'd signed all the necessary papers after Uncle Luther's funeral."

"Those to ensure your succession to the title and estates, yes. But Foxhaven encompasses a great many enterprises, some of which have been too long neglected due to your uncle's ill health."

Uncle Luther's ill health. If Jack had known when his grandfather died last spring that his uncle's health was so poorly, he might have been more prepared for the responsibilities which had descended upon him three weeks since. But no one had seen fit to tell him.

Not that he'd ever inquired.

Jack had sold out of the Army a scant six weeks after his grandfather's death—as soon as the public's enthusiasm for the war heroes began to wane, in fact—and left for Paris, where a warm welcome still awaited. He'd nearly exhausted both his funds and the goodwill of those willing to supplement them by the time he returned to England in late August. Though he wouldn't have wished poor old Luther underground, his timing had been Jack's financial salvation.

"Very well, let's get it over with. I imagine I'll feel even less like dealing with all of this in the morning." He hadn't drunk much yet, by his standards, but since his succession not a morning had come that hadn't found him cripplingly hung over. There was no particular reason to believe tomorrow would be any different.

Havershaw managed a chilly smile. "Excellent, my lord. If you would turn your attention to this? It deals with certain investments in Portugal . . ."

Forty minutes later, Jack was heartily regretting his compliance. Not that the various business matters put before him were particularly incomprehensible, or even quite as boring as he'd expected. But being dumped headfirst into Foxhaven business made him far too cognizant of the responsibilities now facing him—responsibilities he had neither the ability nor inclination to take on. Why, the very thought of Jack Ashecroft, family outcast, attempting to play the respectable nobleman was thoroughly laughable. Not that he was laughing at the moment.

He yawned.

Mr. Havershaw regarded him through narrowed eyes. "I believe that will do for this evening, my lord. There is one last thing, however, that you may wish to have now." He pulled a sealed envelope from the satchel. "A personal letter from your grandfather, to be delivered to you in the event of your uncle's death without issue."

Jack took the envelope gingerly, turning it over in his fingers several times before breaking the seal—the seal that was now his. Odd feeling, that.

The letter was but a single sheet, its brief contents scrawled in his grandfather's strong but careless hand.

My dear Jack,

If you are reading this, you have succeeded to my title and, knowing your attention to family matters, most likely unexpectedly. Rest assured that to me this event was neither unexpected, nor at all undesirable. Luther, while an estimable man, has the strength of neither character nor constitution to effectively carry Foxhaven into the future. You have. In fact, you have it in you to become the finest lord Foxhaven has known in six generations—if you can find it in you to put aside your ongoing pursuit of pleasure to tap into that inner strength I have long observed and, at whiles, attempted to nurture. It is up to you, Jack, to bring Foxhaven into its own by coming into your own. Consider it my dying request.

Ever your faithful and loving grandfather,

Julius Ashecroft, Marquis of Foxhaven

Jack sat back in his chair and read it through again, hearing his grandfather's dry, sardonically affectionate voice as he did so. He'd known Jack couldn't refuse this call to action, a call from beyond the grave from the only person he'd ever truly cared for—or who had cared for him.

Clenching the letter in one fist, Jack felt his spine stiffen with resolve. He gave a single nod. "I'll do it," he said aloud. John Jefferson Ashecroft, black sheep of the family, was going to become respectable.

"Very good, my lord," said Havershaw, just as though he knew what Jack was talking about. "He also penned an adendum." He held out a folded slip of paper.

Frowning, Jack took and opened it.

The road to hell is paved with good intentions, as your own father proved repeatedly. To assist you in your effort to reform, I have made certain financial arrangements to act as an incentive. Havershaw will acquaint you with the terms. – F.

"Terms?" Jack looked up suspiciously.

Havershaw pushed a packet of papers across to him. "The specifics are spelled out there. In brief, all monies not attached to the estates are to be held in trust until such time as the trustee determines that you have made the required transformation of character."

"The devil they are!" Jack exploded. "What utter nonsense! And just who is this trustee who will pass judgment upon me?"

"I am," replied Havershaw with a thin smile.

Nessa quietly closed the kitchen door and pulled her cloak and hood tightly about her face. Glancing up at the still-lighted windows of the narrow but imposing town house, she hoped her sister would not feel so concerned about her fictitious headache as to come to her room to check on her. If all went as planned, she'd be back inside of two hours. With luck, Prudence would never know she'd been away. Hurrying around the corner to the street, she hailed a passing hackney.

For the hundredth time she told herself she was mad to be doing this, and for the hundredth time she hushed her conscience. "King Street, St. James," she told the driver, climbing into the conveyance.

This evening was a present to herself. From the moment she'd first seen the notice in the papers about this masquerade ball, she'd been determined to attend. In London for the first real visit in her life, Nessa felt she deserved some enjoyment.

As the hackney lurched forward, she took the black feathered mask she'd bought earlier that day from the pocket of her cloak and fastened it over her eyes. No one would ever know, and she'd have a delicious memory to look back on—the first such memory in her whole sheltered lifetime. It was only fair she have this reward for leading such a virtuous existence, she reasoned.

The one thing that did cause Nessa a pang of guilt was the fact that her year of mourning still lacked nearly three weeks till completion. Not for a moment did she believe her husband would have understood, sharing, as he had, her late father's puritanical outlook on life. But she'd spent all of her four and twenty years conforming to the strictures of first the one and then the other. Now, for the first time in her life, she was free of them both—and ready to enjoy that freedom.

"This be King Street, miss," the hackney driver called back to her just then.

"Thank you," she called back. "Take me to the Upper Assembly Rooms, please. And if you could return in one hour, I'd be most grateful."

The driver assented and pulled the carriage to a halt a moment later. Nessa paid him generously, hoping thereby to ensure his return. Then, lifting her chin, she strode regally up the stairs to those same hallowed rooms that housed Almack's during the Season. Handing her cloak to one waiting lackey and her ticket to another, she swept into the ballroom.

A mere step inside the room she paused, surveying with bewildered delight this, her first masquerade. Gaily costumed revelers moved and shimmered in the candlelight of the chandeliers, dancing to the strains of a country tune or gathering in small groups to converse. Multihued dominoes vied with replicas of every historic personage imaginable.

Nessa glanced down at her own low-cut gown, smiling to think she had feared her costume too risqué. What pains she had taken to slip away from her sister and sharp-eyed abigail yesterday in order to purchase this cyprian's costume! Prudence would doubtless have a spasm if she found it hidden in the back of Nessa's wardrobe, but it was nothing compared to the plumage she saw here displayed.

"Eh there, me beauty! Might ye care to dance?" inquired a poor imitation of Henry the Eighth at her elbow.

Abruptly, she remembered her sister's objections when Nessa had first mentioned this masquerade to her, about cits and other vulgar sorts attending. In her excitement and determination to attend she'd shrugged it off, but now the evidence was before her.

"Ah, not just yet, thank you," she replied nervously, taking a step away from the man, who reeked of spirits. Somehow, she hadn't really thought about what she'd do *at* the masquerade. She'd focused all her energies on simply getting here.

The man stepped closer. "'Ere now, you're not refusing to dance with yer monarch, are ye?" he prodded with a leer. "Royal privilege and all that."

Nessa swallowed. "No, it's not that. It's only—"

"She has a prior obligation, to confess her sins," interrupted a tall, brown-robed monk. "Even Your Majesty must admit to the superior claims of the Church in such matters." The monk's accent was cultured, reassuring Nessa that this, at least, was a man of her own class.

The drunkard appeared disposed to argue, but a tilt of the monk's head and an ominous glitter of brilliant blue eyes from behind his mask dissuaded him. Muttering something about more wine, King Henry moved away.

"Thank you, sir," said Nessa, relieved. "He really was becoming most persistent."

"One can hardly blame him." The monk looked her over with a most unclerical gleam in his eye. "What do you here alone? Or is your protector busy procuring you a glass of iced champagne?"

"My—?" Nessa glanced down at her costume again and flushed. Perhaps it was a trifle *too* realistic. "No, I assure you I am here alone— but I do not intend to stay long. No more than an hour."

The monk smiled, and Nessa realized how very handsome he was, even with a mask obscuring much of his face. "Then pray, allow me to act as your escort for the brief time you mean to grace this gathering with your presence."

Nessa frowned, wondering if perhaps she had tumbled from the frying pan into the fire. "I, ah—"

"Surely you cannot feel less than safe with a man of the cloth?" he prompted. "Besides, our costumes complement each other so well."

That forced a chuckle from Nessa, making her instantly more comfortable. Surely a man with a sense of humor could not be too evil. Though why she should think that, she did not know. Neither her father nor her husband had ever shown the slightest hint of whimsy, and both had been regarded by the world as the most upright and estimable of men.

"Very well, Friar, I place myself under the protection of the Church for the present."

The tall, handsome monk took Nessa on a tour of the rooms, pointing out their shortcomings. "Makes one wonder what everyone sees in the place, doesn't it?" he asked. "But during the Season, ladies have been known to pine away or even leave Town in disgrace for being denied admittance to Almack's of a Wednesday night."

"I take it, then, that you are a regular attendee yourself, Friar?" asked Nessa, hoping to discover a bit more about him.

"Me? Hardly!" His laugh was almost a snort. "Not that I've attempted it, of course, especially since— Ah, here comes a tray of champagne! Would you care for some, milady?"

Nessa wondered what he'd been about to say. "No, thank you. Is there lemonade, perhaps?" She suspected her judgment was impaired enough this evening without adding spirits to the mix.

The monk spoke to the servant, who returned in a moment with the required beverage. With a flourish, he presented it to her. "In my present guise, I suppose I dare not request a kiss in return for such gallantry. But allow me to tell you your eyes are most haunting, even through that remarkable mask."

"You flatter me, sir." More than ever, Nessa suspected her escort's costume was decidedly at odds with the man underneath. He might be the greatest rake in all London, for aught she knew. She cast about for some way to discover his name—not that it was likely to mean anything to her, as unfamiliar as she was with London Society.

Apparently she was not alone in her curiosity. "Since you do not intend to remain for the unmasking at midnight, might I know the name of the lady I have taken under my protection?"

Though he was but mimicking her earlier words, his phrasing still caused Nessa a thrill of alarm. Surely he did not truly believe her to be as she dressed tonight, a woman of easy virtue? Considering what her life had been until now, the idea was both outrageous and highly amusing. More than ever, she knew she must guard her identity at all costs.

"You may call me Monique," she informed him. It was a name she'd always liked, and sufficiently French to fit her present role.

His well-shaped lips curved into a smile. For a fleeting moment, she wondered what it would be like to kiss those lips—then cut off such thoughts, shocked at herself. Clearly, she was taking her masquerade role far too seriously!

"Might I request this dance, Monique?" A waltz was just beginning.

"First might I know *your* name, Friar?" she asked boldly.

"In return for the dance, you may call me Brother Eligius," he said loftily, taking her hand to lead her to the floor.

Nessa hung back. "One might ask what it is you are worthy of, Brother Eligius."

"Ah, a lady who knows her Latin! Worthy of this dance, of course—and anything else you might see fit to bestow upon me," he added with a lascivious wink. She might have been alarmed were it not clear he was teasing—and if his words didn't send her thoughts down most improper channels.

She stood her ground. "I see. Perhaps I shall bestow the next dance upon you, then. This one is nearly over." That was not quite true, but she could not bring herself to admit that she had never learned to waltz. Given her parents', and later her husband's, views on the dance, she had never even dared to ask.

To her relief, the monk did not press the issue, but stood trading quips with her about both of their pseudonyms until the orchestra struck up a country dance. The dance was lively, allowing little opportunity for conversation, and by its conclusion Nessa's hour was nearly up.

The two of them had drawn many curious stares, and as they left the dance floor a lanky man dressed as a harlequin approached them.

"What a sight this is!" he exclaimed. "Have you persuaded your partner to join you in a life of virtue, J—er, Friar?" A quick motion by the monk had prevented him from uttering the monk's name, to Nessa's frustration.

"Indeed, for her I believe it won't be so much of a stretch, despite appearances," he replied, making her wonder how on earth he had guessed that. "Am I not right, milady Monique?"

"Perhaps. Perhaps not," she replied, stung that her attempt to throw off propriety had been such a failure. With sudden recklessness, she swooped up onto her tiptoes to plant a swift kiss square on the monk's mouth. Then, more shocked at her own boldness than he could possibly be, she turned quickly away.

"I really must be going, now," she said breathlessly, not meeting his eye. "I wish you success in your conversions, Brother Eligius." Before he could respond or even react, Nessa fled the scene of the most daring thing she'd ever done in her whole sheltered life.

The hackney was waiting when she stepped outdoors, and as she rode home, Nessa's brief elation ebbed. She should be pleased, she knew, that there was virtually no chance that she would ever again encounter the mysterious monk, as he'd likely identify her if she did. But somehow that reflection brought less than complete satisfaction.

Arriving back at her sister's, she again paid the driver and reentered the house as quietly as she'd left it. Her brief taste of freedom was over, with none the wiser.

~

Order the prequel to the *Saint of Seven Dials* series, **Scandalous Virtue** to continue reading!

AUTHOR'S NOTE

I know there are many, many books out there to choose from, so I want to take this opportunity to personally thank you for choosing and reading *A Taste for Scandal*. This book is the third installment in my "Seven Saints Hunt Club" series, which is obviously linked to my "Saint of Seven Dials" series. These books are set in the same "world" as my traditional Regencies and *Scandalous Virtue*, with a few of the same (fictional) peripheral characters. Though each of these books stands alone, complete in itself, some readers prefer to read them in order. With all of my Regency historicals, I thoroughly enjoyed the opportunity to stretch my wings beyond the rather strict boundaries of the traditional Regency, while still preserving the feel and accuracy of the time period.

If you enjoyed *A Taste for Scandal*, I hope you will consider leaving a review wherever you buy or talk about books to let other like-minded readers know they might enjoy it, too.

～

ABOUT THE AUTHOR

Brenda Hiatt is the New York Times and USA Today bestselling author of twenty-two novels (so far), including historical romance, traditional Regency romance, time travel romance, young adult romance, and humorous mystery. In addition to writing, Brenda is passionate about embracing life to the fullest, to include scuba diving (she has over 60 dives to her credit), Taekwondo (where she recently attained her 3rd degree black belt), hiking, traveling…and reading, of course!

Connect with Brenda at:
brendahiatt.com

www.ingramcontent.com/pod-product-compliance
Lightning Source LLC
Chambersburg PA
CBHW050828190726
48286CB00007B/2006